The Survivor

The Survivor

SYDNEY SMITH

St. Martin's Press
New York

Library of Congress Cataloging in Publication Data

Smith, Sydney.
  The survivor.

  I. Title.
PZ4.S65858Su 1979   [PR6069.M554]   823′.9′14
ISBN 0-312-77953-4   78-19422

I

Providing one regarded Special Hospital Nine from the lodge gates, at a distance of eight hundred yards, and thus framed by the oak, elm and beech-lined drive directly in front of it, one had the impression of well-bred, timeless composure.

From there one's first glimpse of Brockley Old Hall – its original nineteenth century name – was pleasing, even comforting. The façade of pale cream, patterned by its beautifully-proportioned, high, narrow windows aligned on each side of the central Corinthian pillars, was partly hidden by the trees and the shrubs of the park. The great hall seemed to gaze through its decor with dignity but without arrogance, with serenity unruffled by past turmoils or future forebodings.

As one advanced up the drive, the framework of trees thinned and one perceived, a hundred yards to the right of the main building's east wing, the weathered grey stone of the Victorian-Gothic chapel, enveloped in ivy behind a low border of yew. Then, as the last fringes of the park's foliage were dispersed by yet closer approach, the complete façade emerged and details became clear which changed the picture sadly. Though the windows of the two top floors and the end rooms at the front of the building were pale cream in colour, they were now perceptibly veiled by a faint grey lattice of iron bars. And now, at the rear and projecting beyond the east and the west sides of the main building, could be seen two-storey, red-brick extensions, some with flat roofs, others with sloping slate roofs, and tall, strictly functional chimneys.

Further behind these ugly projections were yet more grace-less blocks of red brick. With still closer approach one reached a large circular flower-bed, dividing the drive exactly opposite the wide stone steps leading to the two main doors of the pillared porch. The flower-bed, on any early autumn day, was the final touch dissolving the vision created by the view from the lodge gates. Through layers of dead leaves, a score of untrimmed bushes of dead and dying chrysanthemums contributed an air of sadness and neglect. Strategically placed on the outer perimeter of this bed a dozen or so rose bushes trailed their withered tendrils and dead brown buds that had never bloomed. At this distance the flower-bed seemed no longer out of its setting, for one now perceived that on the great building behind it, the plaster of the façade and of the cornices and pillars, as well as the paintwork, was uniformly cracked and crumbled. On the right of the great main doorway a tarnished brass plate announced, 'Visitors' Entrance. Hours Tuesdays and Thursdays 9–12: Saturdays and Sundays 9–12: 2.30–5.30'. To the left of the flower-bed a signpost indicated a wide gravelled path as the direction to 'Visitors' Parking'.

The view from the lodge gates had only been an illusion, a sort of spectre dressed in the false elegance of perspective. The reality was a wall-eyed thing of barred windows and red-brick tumours. Here on the front steps one had reached the reality of what was referred to casually as 'SP 9'.

On this particular early autumn day the enchanted mirage of unruffled serenity was banished entirely by the reality of the true preoccupations of all those – staff or patients – occupying a special hospital for the detention and treatment of the criminally insane.

A deep-throated howling, long-drawn as a dirge of despair was sweeping across the courtyard behind the main building and around the dining-hall and cookhouse blocks.

Mother Blake, the cook's wife, put her podgy hands, white with flour, to her ears and screwed up her watery blue eyes.

'It's no good, I'll never get used to it, Jim,' she told her husband. 'Are you *sure* they don't beat them up?'

Jim Blake paused, his meat chopper suspended above a sheep's carcass. 'How many times do I 'ave ter tell yer, Ma? When yer crackers yer don't need no beatin' ter yell. It's all

6

inside, see? It's the heebie-jeebies. It's all in *there*—' He tapped the side of his head with the chopper. 'Yer sees it, yer feels it, just like it's all reely 'appening. But it ain't.'

'Well, they might at least shut the windows,' sniffed Mother Blake.

Deputy Superintendent Robert Crow in his ground floor office at the back of the main building flicked the switch of his inter-phone to call the duty warden of 'A' Wing.

'Who is it this time?'

'They've had to put Frances Bright in a close supervision cell again,' came the answer. 'She tried to stab a male nurse with a piece of broken glass. Been keeping it in her mattress for weeks I'd say.'

The deputy cut in again impatiently. 'All right, the doctor'll be over with a sedative in a moment. But for Christ's sake shut the bloody windows – how many times do you have to be told? D'you want the whole pack to start up?'

He switched to another line. 'Dr Bligh? Crow here. Frances Bright again. Yes please, right away, thanks.' He sat for a moment with his eyes closed, head bent, lips pursed, an image of exasperation and fatigue. Then he picked up a red pencil and opened a foolscap folder in front of him. A black-lettered label on the cover proclaimed it as containing, 'Progress Reports on "A" Wing'.

Dr Peter Bligh, a nervous young-old intern of twenty-seven years hurried from the staff common room where he had been taking his morning coffee. He passed through the men's day room on the ground floor of 'A' Wing where there was no more than the usual brooding listlessness of half-empty minds and busy futile fingers, and the secretive murmurs of incoherent thoughts. There was perhaps a score of men in the room, sitting like statues, frozen into a fraction of time by his hurried passage. Two draughts players forgot their chequered board and stared out of the high, curtainless, barred windows, fascinated by some infinite perspective beyond the orchard outside. The letter-writers paused from their painstaking scratching on pieces of rough, lined paper. The small groups sitting side by side at the long deal tables leaned on them in silence as though listening inside their minds to a clairvoyant message. A few only marked the doctor's transit of the long room by rolling

7

their eyes shiftily upwards under their brows as he passed; a few loose lips slobbered soundlessly. One gaunt, elderly inmate lowered his week-old newspaper, bent his head to peer over steel-rimmed glasses and murmured, 'Good morning, dear doctor.'

The wailing had diminished in volume and intensity to a succession of cries ebbing away from each crescendo into a harsh series of sobs, which had the doubtful merit of identifying the origin of the distress as human.

Dr Bligh hurried on up the central stairway at the end of the day room to the women's close supervision section on the second floor, through a heavy, iron-barred gate and into a corridor off which opened eight small rooms, four on each side.

'Here, doctor,' called a voice from one of the rooms, to which the thick padded door hung outwards into the corridor.

Bligh began to unzip his black bag and his fingers felt for his injection kit. This is the fifth time this week, he told himself, and all I'm good for is to pump dope into their failures. One day it won't be just dope. It'll be something to make sure the poor bastards never scream again.

But aloud, as he dabbed gently at a speck of blood left by the needle in the woman's arm, his freckled face creased in boyish concern and his blue eyes were wide and compassionate. He said, 'There you are, Frances. Rest a little, my dear. Have a nice sleep. You know we all love you, don't you?'

In 'B' Wing the patients were passing through a period of comparative calm which had already lasted two weeks without a single notable outbreak of aggression or hysteria. For fourteen days no one had tried to go over the wall, climb up into the women's quarters on the third and fourth floors or been caught in possession of pot, heroin, purple hearts, micro-dots, whisky, rum or beer. No one had even been caught drawing obscene words or figures on the walls. Yet 'B' Wing Warden Burke and his staff still passed through moments of gloom and apprehension. For they knew, and someone unknown knew too, that a large butcher's knife was still missing.

After three weeks of panic-stricken but futile searches, Warden Burke was just beginning to favour the theory that the knife might have fallen among the kitchen refuse by accident, and been thrown into a dustbin. The attempted suicide rate among 'B' Wing's average population of around forty inmates, on the male side, was rarely more than ten a year, and not more than one out of ten attempts was successful. The attempted murder average was three or four a year, but there were never less than a good half-a-dozen cases of wounding, with weapons ranging from scalding water to heavy boots. Technically, the disappearance of any knife – but particularly a ten-inch kitchen knife – represented a grade one emergency in a community of the criminally insane.

For the first week after the knife was missed the men's 'B' Wing staff, five orderlies, three male nurses, the warden and his two assistants, had felt themselves living each minute of the day and night on the threshold of a bloody calamity. Warden Burke had failed to report the incident to the chief superintendent – in tacit agreement with his own staff, since they were all equally responsible – in the hope that the knife would be discovered before a report became inevitable. It was a gamble. At the end of two weeks it was too late to report the incident without severe admonishments. Three had now passed and the warden and his men had begun to relax, just a little. There was no nook or cranny or thread of tissue in all 'B' Wing, the carpenter's shop, the gardening sheds, the laundry, the paint-shop, the kitchens and their store-rooms, the wash-houses or even the chapel which had not been minutely scrutinized. There was no trace of the knife.

Though the majority of the 'B' Wing men seemed fairly normal for most of the time, no one of them capable of stealing such a weapon would be likely to wait three weeks without doing whatever he wanted to do with it. So the warden and his men were breathing a little more easily and the dustbin theory was beginning to seem acceptable on grounds of reason rather than hope. Now the incident was becoming simply a dark and intermittent patch of irritation at the back of Warden Burke's mind. He believed less and less that someone was hiding a knife and planning to use it. At least he hoped he believed He hoped—

Unlike the men, divided among the wings by categories, 'A' for the most dangerous or unstable, 'B' for the comparatively calm and calculable and 'C' for the outwardly quite normal, but usually with the most terrible criminal records, all three categories of the thirty-five women patients of SP9 shared the same area. Under the charge of a statuesque dame with the rank of matron and a staff of six women orderlies, ten ward-maids and six nurses, the women lived on the third floor of the front and the east wing of the building. Seven of the women were 'A' category, requiring more nursing care and surveill-ance, but less security observation apart from iron bars and locked doors; eighteen were 'B' category and seven were 'C'. Their third and fourth floor quarters, as well as being directly above the men's 'B' Wing, extended across the central front section of the building, linking 'A' and 'B' men's wings on the ground and first floors. They were the most spacious and best equipped quarters of SP9 and, theoretically, were hermetically sealed against any male intrusion from the floors below. This theory, though technically still valid, had been badly shaken in the previous month. Now, on this morning, as Frances Bright's sobs faded into the sweet oblivion of Dr Bligh's amobarbital injection, the theory of the impregnability of the women's wing was receiving another nasty jolt. Pakistani ward-maid, Probationer Nurse Mounalal Ahmed was confessing to Matron Smith that she was pregnant.

Mounalal, a fragile little thing, born twenty-two years ear-lier in Lahore, was being obliged to confirm suspicions which matron had been harbouring against her, with pleasurable anticipation, for several days. With a poise and charm which most honest Western women are unable to achieve in a lachry-mose state, Mounalal was confirming matron's direst hope. Although it was not in the least evident by her appearance, she was indeed pregnant. It was not this that upset Matron Smith, usually referred to in her absence as 'The Old Bitch', so much as the fact that Mounalal interspersed her winsome sobs with the assurance that she was not sure who was responsible. When matron asked her, in the deep-throated, expressionless mono-tone which concealed dangerously her anger and deceptively her rare moments of levity, who *could* have been responsible, Mounalal replied that she did not know who *any of them* were. This matron sternly refused to believe.

Mounalal's condition was only of importance to Matron

Smith if the responsibility for it lay with one of the patients, and less so if it were one of the staff. If it were simply some village boy, then the problem went no further than packing the girl off to her next of kin and hiring another Pakistani. But if a patient were responsible, then a serious breach of security had occurred and could be repeated unless all the details were disclosed.

In various forms sexual emotion, or lack of it, had been either the cause or the effect of most of the crimes for which the inmates of SP9 had been considered sufficiently 'insane' to be locked up in a special security hospital for an indefinite period. There was thus always the risk that sexual indulgence by any of them, man or woman, could rekindle some crazy fantasy needing blood or fire for its final consummation. In this place sex was the supreme enemy of authority; the secret ally, the divine and destructive inspiration of the insane; their permanent, though not always private, dream and despair. The staff regarded all reference to or manifestations of 'sex' among the patients with alarm, and diverted or concealed the outbreak with the sort of desperate urgency with which one might stamp out flying sparks in a hayloft.

Matron Smith's angry disbelief of Mounalal's claim that she did not even know the identity of those – in the plural – who could have been responsible was not due to moral outrage. She could hardly care less how promiscuous or amoral her girls were, so long as they kept their cavorting outside the grounds, during their once fortnightly day off. It mattered not to matron if Mounalal had submitted to the embraces of fifty anonymous aspirants in the village so long as she had not been involved, willingly or by force, with a single patient or staff member.

Her anger at what she considered the girl's stubborn stupidity was more aroused by fear than by reason. In the preceding year five ward-maids, three kitchen-maids and three women patients had become pregnant, a total of eleven unmarried women, all residing in the hospital quarters. The cases of three of the five ward-maids and two of the three kitchen-maids had presented no problem. They were simple day-off or Saturday-night-on-the-way-home casualties for which responsibility had been identified. Two others, a ward-maid and a

kitchen-maid, had paid the price of kitchen-garden assigna-
tions with male staff who owned up and were promptly dismissed. But the male elements in the other four pregnancies
were never identified.

The ward-maid took her secret back home with her to her
mother in West Wales. The three women patients, all 'C' class
and above average intelligence, had resisted blandishments
and threats, traps and interrogations by all forms of authority
at all levels.

The special board of inquiry appointed by the Home Office
reached no conclusion. The plain clothes security men of the
Prisons Investigation Branch, taciturn sleuths accustomed to
reason in terms of the ordinary criminal mind, had been
utterly at a loss in dealing with intelligent lunatics, most of
them capable of disguising their symptoms behind the reactions of well-balanced sanity at the slightest sign of danger.
Their investigations into the four unexplained pregnancies
took them weeks of measuring corridors, rooms, stairways;
timing the phases of the whole twenty-four hour routine of the
hospital in each of the wings and staff quarters in an effort to
pin down the male partner or partners on a basis of what they
described as 'material possibilities'.

A total of seventeen male patients 'confessed' to having been
responsible for the four pregnancies and this attracted long and
satisfying attention which eventually showed that that was all
they had wanted. In every case the Investigation Branch men,
to their great disappointment, were obliged to admit that the
claims to distinction of the seventeen would-be culprits were
simple fantasy. The inquiry went back to zero – and never
recovered.

Of the three pregnant inmates, one lost her baby after an
attempted suicide, the second by legal abortion and the third
by order of a magistrate, who had it sent to an orphanage at
the age of six months.

So in one year, four women, three of them criminally insane
under security detention, had managed to have, or be had by,
a man or men without anyone else knowing how, where or
when. The agonizing question for the staff, and particularly for
Matron Smith, was this: how many people were involved in
these inexplicable exploits? Four women, yes. But four men,

or three men or two men, or four women – and just one man?

It was this last possibility which gave the most anguished hours and sleepless nights to the staff, whenever they allowed themselves to dwell for long on the problem. One woman and one man on four separate occasions could be the result of four cases of exceptional carelessness on the part of the staff. Such a situation was deplorable but implied no permanent threat. But if *one* man, almost certainly a patient and therefore capable of exceptional patience and duplicity, had three times managed to have his way with women patients and once with a ward-maid, without being given away, then he was obviously not going to stop at that. And so the conviction had grown among the staff chiefs, like some horrible legend of unknown origin, that somewhere among this community of twisted satyrs there was indeed a master satyr, a creature of infinite desire and patient resolution, waiting and planning his next opportunity.

Was little Mounalal number five on the master-satyr's list and if so could she be sufficiently intimidated to give him away? This was the questioning hope which inspired Matron Smith to muster all her considerable powers of persuasion as she waited ominously, and in vain, for the little Pakistani to regain composure and explain herself coherently.

'C' Wing was a fairly modern, two-storeyed, flat-roofed building attached by a closed corridor to the rear extension of that part of 'B' Wing which was on the east end of the main building, the side nearest the chapel. On this morning the eight male 'C' Wing inmates, who were not always on the best of terms with one another due to distinctions of class and cash, were suffici-ently perturbed to be taking their morning coffee together in the private room of one of them, Robert Welles, considered to be the senior and most respected of the group – at least by the inmates, if not by the staff.

Nine years earlier as a university undergraduate, Welles had been the central figure in a sensational trial which had made front-page headlines in the national press for ten days. Then twenty years old, a brilliant Oxbridge scholar, he had mur-dered four of his fellow students over an eight month period by strangling them with piano wire. Their bodies had eventually been found, naked and weighted with stones, at the bottom of a disused and weed-grown boat-house fifteen miles from the university.

Welles, son of a wealthy and distinguished city financier, had benefited from the most dazzling legal defence money could buy. It was proved that he had latent homosexual tendencies, was impotent and his medical history showed a record of epilepsy from early childhood up to the age of fourteen. This, and the convincing manner in which he testified that he had absolutely no recollection of committing any of the murders – of which the material evidence proved him guilty beyond doubt – earned him a verdict of guilty but insane.

Legally none of the criminally insane were criminals. They were insane first, but the particular manifestations of insanity which had distinguished them from the simply 'mental' or 'lunatic' category, had been shown by police and judicial action to render them dangerous to society and its laws. Consequently they were not 'prisoners' in the criminal sense of being detained for punishment. They were 'patients' or 'inmates', guiltless judicially, but detained for unspecified periods in the hope that they could be cured, and, until then, to protect society from them.

The result was that those of them who, under a reasonable security system, needed no special nursing attention and could look after themselves without causing trouble were allowed to enjoy conditions of life and comfort which varied according to the means at the disposal of their families or guardians.

Four of the eight 'C' Wing inmates lived in their own furnished bed-sitting rooms, Welles with his own private bathroom. Whenever convenient all were allowed extra food and comforts delivered from the outside. The other four 'C' Wing men shared a dormitory, a bath-house and a large lounge of their own.

The main reason for the leadership of Welles, apart from his money and the influence of his father, was his frequent and well-informed intervention with the authorities on behalf of his fellow inmates.

In the first five years of his detention he had taken his classical English degree, with honours, by correspondence. Since then he had begun studying criminal law with reference to the insane. He knew by heart prison regulations and the history of the law's application to the criminally insane all the way up from the Criminal Lunatics Act of 1800. He was sometimes referred to by some of the more cynically minded members of the staff as 'the padded-cell lawyer', although in fact he had never been put in a padded cell in his life. All the staff, including the visiting psychiatrists, feared him and his interventions almost as much as they held in respect the quarterly visits of the Inspection Boards. No orderly, nurse, doctor, warden or even superintendent with any pretensions to ambition – or even to a reasonably peaceful life – liked having to do his job with the very letter of the law poised above him. While disliking him intensely, most of them preferred to be on the right side of Welles, who received the absolute limit of consideration from the whole staff. His only reaction was to treat them with an insolence and contempt to which, he affirmed cynically, his privileged position as a distinguished, rich and dangerous lunatic entitled him.

The subject of this morning's conference in his pleasantly arranged bed-sitting room was a new amendment to the Criminally Insane Act of 1952. According to this, criminally insane patients who were considered cured and safe for release, or at least suitable for outpatient treatment only, would first have to pass a twelve-month period living in open hostels with ordinary 'good conduct' criminals who were being prepared for probationary release from prison. Hitherto it had been the custom for pre-release mental patients to pass their final months in non-security mental homes from where they could go out to normal daily employment, passing their week-ends in their own homes. Freedom under the new system would be no less. But it would have this difference, in Robert Welles's own words to his attentive fellow 'C' men: 'Instead of being released for outpatient treatment, or to take up our normal lives again, cured of the mental illness of which we were the victims, we shall now re-emerge into the world only after twelve months association with sane, and consequently guilty, criminals ... I said *criminals*. While the law has found us either unfit to be tried, or unfit to be condemned and consequently without any criminal taint, we shall now be forced to become the associates of criminals before we can rejoin the ranks of honest citizens.' He paused for effect, stirred his coffee elegantly, sipped it and went on, 'In the eyes of the world, instead of simply being people who were once ill and are now discharged cured, we shall bear the taint of criminals released on trust.'

Welles's full, rich voice was pitched to convey righteous indignation, tempered by the restrained logic of a man of the world. His fellow patients, he noticed, seemed suitably impressed. He now had to prepare them to be indignant, where they might otherwise have been indifferent, or after official intervention, probably even grateful.

He went on: 'And now, my friends, do you know who is going to have the final word in deciding which of us – and when – shall be returned to the outside world?' Of course they did not. They sipped their coffee nervously and shook their heads.

'A little old woman who is neither a doctor nor a fully qualified psychiatrist.' Welles answered his own question with a slow deliberation intended to underline to his companions that they should feel, with him, a sense of outrage. 'She has never in her life had anything to do with mental patients. She is a state probation officer, psychiatric social assistant, with ten years' experience as a prison probationary officer and adviser – prisons only – criminals only. That is the woman they are sending here to have the last word on our fitness to join society!'

Colonel Bertrand Barthropp DSO MC OBE, Royal Army Medical Corps, retired, chief superintendent of Special Hospital Nine, rang for his secretary. With her usual noisy alacrity Rosie Fletcher swept through the baize-covered swing doors between the two offices.

'Bring me the staff list and advise Mr Slater, Mr Crow and Dr Robertson that I want to see them now.'

Rosie noted that the storm signals were out. The colonel had not looked up from the correspondence on his desk. His pipe was out. The regular puce flush of his cheeks had spread to his long grey sideboards and up to the deep pouches of his eyes.

Special Hospital Nine, until the post-war classification of mental institutions, had been generally referred to as Brockley Old Hall. For the first fifty years after the stately Georgian manor had been built in 1800 by a retired colonial governor, it had been known, after the nearby village, as just Brockley Hall. The 'old' had crept in gradually over the years and become accepted as part of the proper name about the middle of Queen Victoria's reign. The former colonial governor's descendants had bequeathed it and the twenty acres of parkland in which it stood to the state in 1881. Ten years later, after a grateful but bewildered government had added a pair of gloomy red-brick 'institutional' blocks – laundry, kitchens, boiler and store-rooms – to the back of the original building, in the central rear courtyard, the Old Hall had become the first truly progressive 'lunatic asylum' reserved especially for those judged by the law to be criminally insane.

Now the oldest, most decrepit and impractical institution of its kind, it strove to live up to its faded reputation for enlightened *avant-garde* progressiveness – long since without any justification.

Colonel Barthropp had won his Distinguished Service Order on the Northwest Frontier by pioneering a kind of sanitary system among the tribal villages of the Afghan frontier at considerable risk to his own life; his Military Cross in saving wounded on the blazing beaches of Dunkirk; and his Order of the British Empire for an anti-malarial campaign in South East Asia in the Second World War.

By some obscure reasoning, backed by a fortunate chain of acquaintances, these events had qualified him, on retirement, to serve two periods as a reasonably competent governor of open prisons. His general medical and disciplinary abilities, along with an administrative capacity of good regimental level, next earned him the offer of the post of chief superintendent of Special Hospital Nine. It happened to be on the borders of some of the best hunting country in the west Midlands, not too snob, not too expensive, but rough and rewarding.

The job of chief superintendent meant overseeing and harmonizing the work of the three main departments of the institution – administration under Deputy Superintendent Robert Crow, staff and security under Superintendent William Slater, and care and treatment of patients under the Chief Medical Superintendent Dr Ian Robertson. The total staff averaged seventy-five, of which twenty-three were women and fifty-two men. The patient strength averaged two hundred and fifty of which the women inmates usually numbered around thirty-five.

The colonel had long been aware of the frustrations of his inadequate staff and all the heart- and back-breaking shortcomings of their rambling, unfunctional quarters. This was really no place for the care or repair of deficient or broken minds.

Yet relentlessly from somewhere high in the ministerial hierarchy, remote functionaries of justice, law and health dispatched their crops of social casualties and misfits, seeming indifferent to the slender possibilities of effective salvage by Special Hospital Nine and its staff.

At the beginning, for a whole year – and he was now in his third at Brockley – the colonel had hoped to be able to leave some impact of his own personal achievement on the history of SP9. Up to the time of his retirement from the Army he had thought of practically every situation in life in terms of his own upbringing and experience – the sacred responsibilities and powers of personal leadership, the house, the school, the team, the regiment and all the rest right up to the flag. His basic old-world faith in the magic effects of a word-from-the-chap-at-the-top had even served him well as governor of his two open prisons. There, his rugged man-to-man appeals to the better sides of his charges' natures, his obviously sincere conviction that better sides existed, had often produced results which he took for granted, but which staggered some of the more disabused members of his staff. When he had eventually come into contact with sick or deficient minds, he had discovered that he was dealing with men and women who spoke another language, not quite of this world. The approaches by blithe and hearty reassurance, or deep and quiet understanding, as he interpreted them, met with one of several calculable reactions; the neurotic to the psychotic of all degrees perceived at once, consciously or otherwise, the patronizing and unsympathetic tenor of his approach. They met it with silent suspicion or loud abuse, cynicism or indifference.

After twelve months, the colonel, his pride shaken and his ideals confused, joined the local hunt and became a highly considered member of the county's social élite, the bench, the church and the landed gentry. He did not neglect his work. On the contrary, he improved it, for he confined himself to placating his staff, encouraging and co-ordinating their work, and becoming himself a bulwark between 'the Ministries' and the hospital, and above all avoiding as much as possible any contact with the patients. This morning he had bad news for what he called his 'headquarters staff', the same discouraging and irritating news which had already leaked to 'C' Wing and was the subject of Robert Welles's harangue to his morning coffee clique.

The three men he had sent for came in together; Robert Crow, deputy superintendent in charge of administration, once ranker in the regular prison service; William Slater, staff and security superintendent, dapper, brisk, efficient ex-Regular Army warrant officer, late lieutenant in the Royal Army Medical Corps; Dr Ian Robertson, a Scot of forty-nine years, psychiatrist, sociologist, chief medical superintendent, who bore up cheerfully under the burden of ten thousand problems, not one of them his own. Robertson was the true life-force of SP9.

The colonel looked up with a vague murmur, rightly interpreted by the three as a greeting and an invitation to sit down.

'My request for consideration of a staff increase on the lines we proposed is refused.' With the back of his hand the colonel scornfully pushed aside a litter of buff Ministry correspondence on his desk, and went on: 'Without any comment on the material problems, they've answered with a general statistical breakdown, which they consider shows us to be no worse off than any other special hospital – even those built for the job. For all forms of medical care, including the visiting psychiatrists, we have one qualified doctor or specialist for every thirty-two patients. For security and nursing combined, since the two must overlap all the time, we have one staff member for every seven patients. If we include kitchen, laundry and other outside staff, including the various visiting instructors, we have one staff member for every four point nine patients. The Ministry seems to think we are quite favoured. But they are simply using figures, quantities, not qualities.'

The colonel thumbed a wad of tobacco into his pipe. Dr Robertson broke the silence. 'Do they propose anything at all to help us? After all, even our staircase system was designed nearly one hundred and fifty years ago and modified well over fifty years ago. And the corridors – I still get lost in them.'

'Well, there it is,' said the colonel, 'no good arguing. They are, however, sending us a, sort of, well, reinforcement I suppose you might call her.' He fiddled among his papers and held up a folio of typewritten sheets. 'Miss Lewis,' he pronounced, 'Miss Margaret Lewis. She is appointed to SP9 as a staff psychiatric social assistant, with the particular assignment of helping the most advanced of our patients towards social rehabilitation with a view to expediting their release. It appears,' the colonel lapsed into a mumble as he ran his eyes rapidly down the foolscap pages of the memorandum from the Ministry, 'mmm mmm – yes. It appears that this lady has been a member of the prisons parole and probationary service for the past ten years, and is, here we are, and is very highly thought of for her ability to win the confidence of even the most irresponsive and recalcitrant subjects.' He looked up. 'I was quoting there. That's what they say about her at the Ministry. All this is confidential, of course. They go on to give me a few items from her official record.'

The colonel detailed the rest in his own words. It appeared this Miss – er – must remember – er Lewis, Margaret Lewis was the holder of the BEM, the British Empire Medal, for her distinguished service in prisons, as well as the Cross of Alexandra for courage, with three citations for 'meritorious action' in different dangerous circumstances.

The Cross of Alexandra had been awarded after she had crossed a prison yard alone, facing a rebellious mob of dangerous top-security prisoners, and talked the ring-leader into handing over his revolver. Two of the citations for 'meritorious action' were for 'talking down' prisoners who had escaped from their cells, one to a window ledge and the other to a roof-top, both armed and threatening to commit suicide. She had sat with one on the window ledge for three hours, and with the roof-top sitter for five hours, and persuaded both to surrender. The third citation was for having persuaded the prison drug-pedlar to reveal his sources and reform, which had qualified her for an abortive razor attack by a drug-addicted prisoner.

'Quite a formidable lady, eh?' said the colonel, looking up and turning a page.

'Splendid,' said the doctor, 'but why send her here? What is she supposed to do?'

'I've told you,' said the colonel, 'she is supposed to help our advanced patients to prepare themselves to return to normal life. Social rehabilitation or restructure, call it what you like. This she will do apparently by simply acting as the patient's friend, without any other fixed function. She will help you and your team by mixing with and getting to know, as intimately as possible, all the patients who are on the way to being considered for release.' He paused to puff his pipe reflectively. 'In a way I have the impression that she will rather seem to be, to the patients, more on their side than on ours.'

Dr Robertson, eyebrows raised, interrupted dryly, 'You may put it that way if you wish, colonel. But I must remind you that there are quite a few patients who know we are on their side too.'

The colonel was embarrassed by this slip. 'Yes, yes, doctor, I'm sorry,' he said testily, 'I did not mean to imply—' He paused, leaving the rest unsaid because he realized it was quite well understood. He had just made an implied admission that he knew most of the patients did not consider him personally to be on their side, because he was unable to communicate with them. He went on. 'Well, this lady, Miss Lewis, will have no special functions. I am asked to allow her to decide on her own programme in so far as it is compatible with the work of the medical Superintendent and his staff. Dr Robertson, you will have a veto on her activity, if you think necessary. You must discuss all that with her, yourself. Incidentally, they point out that her reports will have a decisive effect on the selection of those patients qualified to return to normal life after a probationary period in an open hostel. This brings me to the new amendment to the Act, by the way.' He explained the new system by which mental patients, before final discharge, would pass probationary periods in open hostels for criminal probationers. 'That's why the Ministry wants to make the check on our patients even more thorough beforehand, and that is part of the job of this Miss Lewis,' he explained.

'Know anything more about her, what she's like and so on?' Robert Crow asked. The colonel fumbled some more with his papers. 'Yes, here we are. Forty-eight years of age; unmarried; next of kin, a sister in Canada. She asked especially to be appointed here. Reason; she felt that after ten years in the ordinary criminal field she needed to enlarge her experience and feels capable of taking on the greater challenge of working among the criminally insane. I'm quoting again there, but it looks to me as if the Ministry is directly quoting her too.'

William Slater, junior of the hospital executives but in charge of all security, shook his head.

'Ten years of prisons is all very well. The system is pretty rigid. There's not much can go wrong and not much harm a probationary assistant, even a psychiatric one, can do. But if this old girl starts getting sloppy about some of our birds, taking liberties with security and so on, well, I can't take the responsibility. I'll tell you, sir, if half a dozen of the brighter inmates here really got together and worked things out, with the way this place is built – they could take us over. We take enough risks as it is. At practically any hour of the day there are never less than half a dozen patients with keys to let themselves through some door or other simply because I haven't enough men on duty to do the job.' He glared exasperatedly around the room. 'And now we're to have a free-lance, middle-aged spinster given the free run of the place—' He shrugged and shook his head with an air of angry resignation. 'Can't you stop this stupid appointment sir and get me half a dozen worth-while male nurses instead?'

The colonel shook his head too. 'She's reporting to me next Monday. Taking a cottage in the village. These orders come from the top. She may be a great help after all – who knows? We must give her a chance. What worries me more is what some of our advanced patients are going to do or say when they find out that, with her approval, they are going to have to pass out through the prison hostels before being completely discharged. I know a few who won't like that at all.'

Dr Robertson said nothing. He knew a few who were in the process already of expressing their disapproval. His own informant had already told him of the coffee party in Robert Welles's room. What worried the Scots doctor was: who was informing 'C' Wing of the contents of the chief superintendent's mail from the Ministry before the superintendent could even inform his own staff?

2

Colonel Barthropp was irritated with himself for feeling nervous and uncertain simply because he was about to receive a new member of staff. As he sat in his office the following Monday morning he scribbled the words 'Lewis Margaret' on his green blotting pad in an effort to remember them. Lewis was such an ordinary name. There was no sort of association to help one remember it. This elderly woman with the remarkable record of courage and persistence was evidently very highly thought of by the Ministry. She was probably quite well known to the press too. Would she throw her weight around? Would she snoop, turn the place upside down with her criticisms, her reports to the Ministries? Was she a raw-boned dame with a masculine, jack-booted mind, or a wiry old lady with a trunkful of Bibles? Could she possibly be something in between? These and even wilder speculations had been preoccupying not simply the staff, but some of the patients for almost a week now. Before she had even been seen in the place, Margaret Lewis was already a figure of legend and speculation.

The door of the Colonel's office half opened and Rosie Fletcher leaned in. 'Colonel, look out of the window, I think it's her. She parked a Mini in the car park and now she's coming to the front door.' Her excitement reduced her usually rasping voice to a harsh, excited whisper.

The whole of the central part of the main building on the ground floor had been divided by thin hollow brick and plaster walls to make offices for the superintendent and his staff. There were also four small private interview rooms for visitors. The colonel's office, the largest, was on the left of the main entrance, from which it was guarded by the match-box of an office occupied by Rosie. Through one of his windows the colonel saw a thin, compact, neat-looking woman circling the flower-bed on her way to the front steps. She carried a small folding umbrella and a large, expensive, black calf shoulder-bag. She wore a beret-style fur hat rather towards the back of her head. Her hair was dark grey and her fine, sharp face appeared to be slightly tanned.

By the time he had taken in these details she was up the steps and out of sight. The colonel was fiddling with the folder on his desk when she was announced by Rosie. He stood up awkwardly and took her hand. It was long and slim and practically lost in his own great paw, yet her grip was decisive and surprisingly strong. She was of more than medium height for a woman, slender, and she carried herself with an air of complete self-possession. As she moved back from shaking hands, half turned to seek the chair and then sat down, the colonel noted the smooth muscular control of her movements. There was nothing either maternal or masculine about her. Her clean-cut face promised humour, perception and firmness of character as well. Her eyes, dark . brown, were direct and candid. Her mouth was thin, almost hard, with dry, straight lips which at moments tended to make an infinitely small downward movement at the corners. She had made no cosmetic effort to conceal the small webs of finely-etched creases at the corners of her eyes and her mouth. The colonel's immediate reaction was that it was on the whole a likeable, reliable, friendly face, intelligent and understanding. She must have been quite handsome, or at least striking twenty years earlier. Her greying hair was pulled back from her high narrow forehead and tied into an untidy chignon on her neck. She had not prepared herself on her toilette to make an impression on anyone.

'Well, Miss—' the colonel glanced swiftly down at his blotting pad, '—Miss Lewis, that is correct, is it not? Yes. Well I'm extremely glad that the people at the Ministry have accorded us the help of someone of your qualities and experience. You know, no doubt, how badly we need help. You, I gather, have your own ideas on how you want to go about your work here. I can assure you that whatever you wish to do, we shall be delighted to help you, and of course, grateful.' He leaned back in his chair. It was clumsy, but he felt he had done his best. Maybe he had even gone a bit too far. Anyhow, now it was her move. He began filling his pipe.

Miss Lewis took an embarrassingly long time to reply. Not that she seemed in the least embarrassed herself. She acknowledged the colonel's brief discourse with a small, economical smile and a slight inclination of the head. Then she leaned forward and looked out of the window towards the drive, thoughtfully. She seemed lost in reflection, toying with the gloves in her lap. The colonel had time to feel mildly irritated by the degree of self-possession implied by this calculated delay in her reply.

'Thank you, colonel, you are too generous.' Her voice was extraordinarily young, low but distinct, compelling but friendly. 'You know that I have never dealt with mentally afflicted people before. At least only on exceptional occasions. It has never been part of my regular work. Without wishing to appear egoistic, I sincerely felt that I needed to expand my experience. Now that the policy is to deinstitutionalize mental treatment as much as possible, I felt that the consequent need for releasing more mental prisoners—' she paused, shocked by her slip and began again – 'for releasing more mental patients would give me an opportunity to help where it was particularly needed. I placed my request for transfer from prisons to special hospitals about four years ago. I have had several offers since then, but they were for work in vast, impersonal institutions where I felt I should be rather lost. When Brockley Hall was suggested and I learned of its comparative intimacy – of course its name I knew already – I was very glad of the opportunity to come here.'

'What is your plan of work precisely, Miss Lewis? The Ministry says you will deal with advanced patients, all those likely to be considered for release in the near future.'

'Frankly, colonel,' she answered spreading her hands before her, 'I have no plan of work.' The colonel decided she had remarkably fine hands. She went on, 'My mind is quite open on my work, but I think I should meet, with your permission, all the staff, get to know them, listen to them, mix with them in their work right away and then I'm sure that my presence and my work will automatically fall in with a pattern based on the customs and needs of your hospital.'

She smiled and her eyes creased deeply at the corners. The effect was pleasant, disarming. The woman had great charm, decided the colonel. 'Very well,' he said at last, feeling considerably relieved that the ordeal he had so feared had passed off so smoothly, even agreeably. 'I propose that you start officially tomorrow. Come and see me here at about twelve-thirty and I'll take you in to meet the staff at lunch. Then in the afternoon you can have a walk around the place with Staff Superintendent Slater, and then Dr Robertson will give you a general briefing on those patients likely to be of interest to you and you can decide with him how you proceed from there. I must explain that as far as treatment and medical care are concerned I am not in the picture. Dr Robertson as medical superintendent has the last word on those subjects.'

The sense of informal interview was over now. The colonel enveloped himself in a relaxing haze of tobacco and prepared to satisfy his own personal curiosity about this slightly baffling woman.

'You know, Miss Lewis,' he began rather deferentially, 'it seems odd to find someone like yourself, obviously an old hand in this, er, business, yet without the usual – how can I express it? – without the usual bureaucratic inhibitions of a government servant. How did you come to enter the service?'

She looked at him gravely for a moment and then, as though resolving her reply, dropped her eyes to her gloves again. She spoke quietly. 'My father was a member of the Indian Civil Service. I was brought up in India. My mother died when I was very young and of course I devoted my life to looking after my father. While still a child I took preliminary training as a Queen's Nurse in India. My father was a district commissioner and naturally I had a great many social services to organize among the poor people of his district. It was rather larger than England and Wales put together. When we returned to England my father retired and died two years later. As I had a great deal of experience in all kinds of social services and a

27

little in nursing, I looked for something to do in that line. With the help of a former Civil Service colleague of my father's, I qualified in social psychiatry and obtained my first job as a magistrate's court probationary officer, and, well,' she looked up smiling, 'from then on my responsibilities and experience grew, until, well – you know my record I'm sure.'

The colonel had listened enchanted to this story, an amiable surprise spreading across his face. It was not the concise simplicity of her account which touched him so much as the fact that some of his best Army years had been spent in India. This woman, as the daughter of a senior Indian Civil Servant was, after all, someone on his own social level. He puffed delightedly at his pipe. 'India,' he rumbled, 'that's splendid, my dear Miss Lewis. I love the place. At least I did. British India y'know. Peshawar, 'Pindi, Muree, marvellous names. Spent ten years there myself.'

'I went to school in Muree,' said Miss Lewis, 'the Lord Linlithgow *Lycée* for girls. In the summer my father and I usually went to Kashmir. We took a houseboat on the Shalimar Lake at Srinigar.'

'Well, well.' The colonel was very nearly moved beyond words. 'Srinigar – to Special Hospital Nine. You see what time's done to us, eh?' And then, as though this remark implied perhaps a trace of disloyalty to the present, he added rather gruffly, 'Still – we're probably a lot more useful here than ever we were in Srinigar, eh Miss Lewis? The days of houseboats on the lake of Shalimar, Pukka Sahibs and idle Memsahibs – all very well before Gandhi and his mob kicked us out, but there's no place for that now. "They are not long, the days of wine and roses" – as the poet said. Well, we've got a job to do now and it's a, well, rewarding one. We're very proud of Hospital Nine although,' he paused and changed to a gloomier tone, 'God knows, thanks to your friends at the Ministry, with the understaffing and the overcrowding we can do little more than shelter and feed our patients. Nine tenths of our work is to keep the place running and our patients safe and secure, weather-proof and nourished and as calm as possible. If the other tenth could be honestly assessed in cures, I mean people really cured and returned to normal life, even then I should be happy. Ninety per cent of our job should be curing

28

people and ten per cent running the place. But it's the other way around. Don't let me discourage you, Miss Lewis, I'm sure you know what you're in for. But I must point out one basic essential about this job. The difference between making an old lag go straight and straightening out a bent mind is, well, in fact there's no comparison at all. One is a matter of morality, largely, the other's a major psychic operation in what is a comparatively unknown field of medicine. You cannot cure a psychotic or a schizophrenic simply by appealing to the standards and values of behaviour, conscience, pride, self-respect, decency by which we live. There's a lot more to it than that. There's something quite mysterious, intangible, about sick minds. I'm sure you've had lots of time to think about your decision and I realize your psychiatric qualifications, so,' and his voice tailed away rather apologetically, 'you know what you're up against. I apologize for seeming to treat you as a complete amateur. I didn't mean that. Anyhow, you know you can count on us to give you all the help you need – to help us.'

This pretty little ending to a speech which, having started in Kashmir seemed to be getting out of hand, pleased the colonel quite as much as it seemed to do Miss Lewis.

As he finished speaking she had risen to her feet and stepped to the front of his desk. She held out her hand with a quick gesture and her voice sounded dry and a little husky.

'Colonel, I can't tell you how much comfort you have given me. I was quite petrified at the thought of this meeting. It meant so much to me. Now I know, thanks to the kind and understanding way in which you've spoken, that everything is going to work out all right. I shall be able to,' she faltered and was lost for words for a moment, 'to – render the service here for which I have prayed so hard for so long.' The sudden tension in her voice, the strained formality of her words, provoked a brief and awkward silence as the colonel, perplexed and embarrassed, took her hand, and shook it rather vaguely. The movement had the effect of arousing Margaret Lewis from her reverie. For an instant her lively brown eyes had seemed to burn black and sightless and her last words – 'so hard for so long' – had been spoken almost as in a dream.

'Well, come along my dear,' said the colonel, trying to efface the curious moment of tension by a burst of lively joviality. 'I'll show you back to your car by the side way, and look forward to seeing you tomorrow – er – Memsahib.' Miss Lewis joined in his laughter at this quaint anachronism and her voice was gay and relaxed once more.

'To think I've had to come all the way to Special Hospital Nine to be called Memsahib,' she said.

3

The Diary of Margaret Lewis

EXTRACT I

Bay Tree Cottage
Brockley Village
Staffordshire   September, 1974

This journal, despite the heading of the page, is written by
Edith Margaret Hayes, from birth to the age of fifteen years an
inmate of the Indian Railways Orphanage of Murree, India.

I know no more of the origins of my birth than the fact that
my father was an English engineer of the Indian Railways. My
mother was an Anglo-Indian and not married to my father.
He never wished to see me and within a few days of my birth
had me sent to the Railways Orphanage. My mother, I
learned many years later, died in poverty and disgrace, a
whore in Calcutta, a few months after my birth. My father
died a few years later, with neither word nor testament for me.
The orphanage was on the outskirts of the town, a little way
down the hill from the magnificent Lord Linlithgow *Lycée* for
girls. To us, at the Railways, as our red-brick institution was
called, the *Lycée* was some kind of heaven, occupied by beautiful young creatures whose fathers were district commissioners
or more, and some Indians, but no less than the daughters of
Rajahs and Princes. The glimpses we had of the *Lycée* and its

boarders, and the tales we heard tell of them as well as those we probably invented ourselves, made it for us the ultimate ideal in beauty, comfort, position, pleasure and above all, love. We had none. About one third of us at the Railways were illegitimate and more than half were the unwanted products of mixed liaisons. Happiness is relative, and as most of us had never known what it was, we could hardly be called unhappy. We were very happy at Christmas when anonymous presents arrived for general distribution, and when, rarely and only for a very few, there was a visit from a relative or the friend of a relative.

When I was fifteen I was allowed to spend four months of one summer as nurse to the children of a district commissioner and his wife, a Mr and Mrs Craig, who spent their summers in the Muree Hills. This was a heavenly experience. For the first time it brought me a small glimpse of the expansive love and comfort of people who lived in the world and not in an orphanage. When I was sixteen the Craig's obtained legal guardianship over me and I quit the Railways for good, to become the permanent nurse–companion of their three children. In fact, though I 'helped', I was treated as one of the family. Sometimes we spent the summer in the hills, but once we stayed in a vast houseboat on the Kashmir lake of Shalimar. When I was eighteen, for reasons of health Mrs Craig was obliged to return to England and her husband obtained a job in the India Office in London. My passport declared me to be 'Margaret Lewis, pseudonym Craig'. Once back in London, the children – a boy of eighteen and twin girls of seventeen – went off to college and there was nothing further for me to do, though I loved the Craigs as though they had been my parents. It was Mr Craig who at this time told me the truth about my mother and father. He had even traced my mother's family back to my great-grandparents.

My brief life with the Craigs had given me some of the characteristics and polish of someone of better class than I really was. I had acquired a good 'upper class' accent, a certain poise, good manners and I could pass anywhere as a young woman of excellent family. Except in my dark brown eyes, my Indian blood was not at all evident and my hair, inherited from my Irish grandfather, was a rich dark tawny. Yet my upbringing at the Railways had not been a complete loss. It had given me other equally useful qualities which were never effaced – the patience and humility of an institute-bred orphan and the capacity to endure thankless drudgery without malice.

I had always had a liking for nursing. I suppose too that deep in my institute-formed mind a matron, in her uniform and regal, starched headress, represented to me a sort of supreme authority – the peak of all reasonable ambition. Mrs Craig knew such a matron. She had been a sister in a large hospital in the Craig's district in India and was now matron at a great London general hospital, Matron Marion Blake. She was an imposing yet remarkably vivacious and warm character who made my nineteenth year, my first year out in the world, as a humble probationer nurse, an exhilarating experience. But at the end of that year, very suddenly and very happily, I married a young doctor, Alan Hayes. During my year at the hospital I had begun night-school classes in social psychiatry and I continued them after our marriage. We were very poor but marvellously happy and lived in a studio-flat somewhere off the Gray's Inn Road while Alan finished his time as a hospital intern.

Our baby girl was born a year after our marriage and we named her Cheryl. When Cheryl was two Alan acquired a junior partnership in a busy practice on the outskirts of Exeter and there in the next two years I was able to continue my nursing and psychiatric studies and added considerably to my qualifications. At the end of that time, when Cheryl was four, we moved again. This time Alan obtained a practice of his own, modest, and in a poor area, but giving him the independence and time for the hospital study he needed. It was in the Staffordshire mining town of Cranosely Hill. There too, in a large hospital at Essingdon Chase, I continued my own studies.

By the time Cheryl was ten I was a district visitor for the regional social assistance office. Ever since I had begun my studies as a probationer nurse under Matron Blake in London I had always worked under my maiden name, the name of my mother, with which I had been baptized in the orphanage. The orphanage curate baptized me Margaret after one of the sisters and Edith Lewis after my mother. I never knew my father's name.

A week or so before Cheryl's twelfth birthday, I decided to

give up my social work and devote more time to her. I had felt qualms for a long while about the division of my time between my daughter and my time-consuming job, although Cheryl had always been a day boarder at all her schools and in her baby days had been well looked-after in a kindergarten during my working hours. At twelve she was a little woman and I felt that she needed closer care and affection, though we had always been a united and deeply affectionate little family. We had always hoped for more children and in our disappointment we were certainly drawn closer together.

My immediate decision to stop work and give all my time to making my daughter happy, and a good woman and wife someday, was a very sudden one.

It was the time of the winter holidays. Cheryl had been out with friends all the afternoon, skating on a local pond. There were deep snowdrifts everywhere and the weather was cold and bracing. It was late in the afternoon, just before dusk, when Cheryl returned, glowing, rapturous from her afternoon on the ice. As she came into the sitting-room, skates in her hand, shaking her long, dark, wavy hair from her red woollen bonnet, her dark eyes, much darker than mine, were ablaze with the joy of living. It was then that I suddenly saw her as a woman and realized that the years when she might need me and my help the most were just beginning.

Mr Craig, when he told me the truth of my birth and parentage, had told me that my mother had only one half Indian blood.

Her maternal grandmother had been the daughter of a distinguished Kashmiri Brahmin family – one of the highest Indian castes. The Kashmiri people are also noted for being the palest, and the most beautiful, of all the Indians. My mother's mother had married an Irishman, a soldier of the Indian Army, who had abandoned her when his regiment returned to Britain. My mother consequently could easily be mistaken for a full-blooded European and I was told by Mr Craig that she had always considered herself to be European and never spoke of her Indian mother, or family. My father, the railway engineer was, I was told, a Scot. With my tawny dark hair, my light brown eyes, my unusual height for a woman, I presume I took after my father, or my maternal grandfather, or both – a

Scot and an Irishman. There were never any outwardly perceptible Indian characteristics in my appearance, though I know there certainly are in my nature.

Cheryl had reverted a little more in appearance to her Kashmiri great-grandmother. Her hair was a dark soft torrent, fine and wavy, almost black but with a touch of tawny when the light was behind it. The long, curved eyelashes were obviously not those of a Northern European. Yet with her dark, nut-brown eyes she could easily have passed as an Indian. Her teeth too were abnormally white for anyone but an Asiatic or of a Mediterranean origin. Her skin was pale without being sallow, her face long and slender, proud in repose, but intense and passionately expressive of whatever possessed her. It was something more than all that which touched me when she came home from skating on that February afternoon. It was as if one afternoon had suddenly set alight a flame of womanhood, kindling a new fire in the child whom I had thought of, until that moment, as still my baby – a school girl in her first year at grammar school. Perhaps I was a little frightened, but I felt that I had seen and understood in time, and pride and love, more than fear, were what moved me. Her photograph beside me now still gives me, whenever I look at that tender and passionate face, the same mixture of pride, love and fear, all of them – too late.

The details of the transformation of Cheryl from a child, to a woman, to a lost creature and finally to the battered remains of only her body I will recount in chronological detail, just as it happened.

In this present introduction, I want to tell you, my judges, how I managed to become appointed to Brockley and my reasons.

Four years after I gave up my job to devote more time to my child, after a series of terrifying and bewildering experiences lasting throughout her fifteenth year, she died, almost skinned alive, in a terrible ceremony carried out by a sect of drugged and mystic maniacs. In the preceding months, despite all the vigilance of the police and Alan and I, they had sapped away her physical and mental being.

A man was eventually arrested and charged with her murder. It seemed to my husband and me, as the last year of

Cheryl's life emerged, quite incredible that such things could have happened to our child while we had thought ourselves to be giving her all the loving care and protection of simple people. That of course was the trouble – we were very simple people.

The trial too was like a slow death. It was impossible not to listen, not to read, not to *know*. Yet that knowledge to us was like death or some kind of hell after death. It is hard to explain. When the knowledge of pain, the suffering of a being one loves gradually unfolds – along with the growing realization that one can never offer comfort nor forgetfulness, or hope for the awakening that comes after a nightmare – the most painful reaction, beyond sorrow and shock, is one of utter frustration. There is no one, nothing, to take in one's arms; there is no night to shield and no silence to drown the realities being hammered into one's mind. Some people can find their own escape in hysteria or unconsciousness or even crazy illusion. There was no comfort of any kind for Alan or me. I had a feverish desire to be able to pull over myself some huge black canopy of soundlessness and darkness; to escape into the comfort of a senseless void. But I could find none. I could not cry. Sleep and forgetfulness were impossible.

I had never had any particularly religious feelings. In fact my years at the Railways had soured my mind against any kind of dogmatic religion. I tried to pray. But to whom, and for what? No – there were no prayers, no tears, no escape from the clarity of mind that imposed the torture of logical, detailed imagination even of those facts which still mercifully remained in comparative obscurity. My mind seized on all of them and, like some frantic computer, worried them, dissected them, projected them in sound and colour, depth and dimension until sometimes I tried stupidly to suffocate my consciousness under a heap of pillows, cushions, blankets, behind drawn curtains and locked doors. Even Alan was no refuge. What was it that made us afraid to talk to one another about the appalling story the police, the lawyers and the newspapers relentlessly unfolded day after day? One felt sometimes that a whole sea of curiosity and unwanted commiseration lapped around the little villa where we lived, immured by the curiosity of millions of people who knew everything about us but of whom we had never heard nor wished to hear.

Alan lived like someone in a dream. Perhaps that is how I seemed to him too. Perhaps, probably in fact, he was living in the identical hell to that which enclosed me. I don't know. I never asked him, never tried to explain anything, never sought nor offered comfort. Sometimes, rarely, we lay in each other's arms, yet daring no question, no word, dry cheek against dry cheek, eyes open on darkness. We knew each other's thoughts yet were too – would the word be prudish? – to put them into words. Each knew what the other felt, yet each was afraid to put the test of appeal for help or comfort, because each knew that it would fail. That we could be comforted, even by one another, perhaps especially by one another, would imply some degree of acceptance, or attenuation, of the truth. We did not want to resign ourselves to or diminish in any way what we knew we had to accept.

We both had a good many friends when the whole thing broke. By the end – well, we may still have had some goodwill, but certainly no one was prepared any more to show it openly to us. We had not reacted in the way that made the sympathy of others rewarding to them. Our failure to meet tears of sympathy with tears of gratitude was no doubt chilling. The way in which we remained dry-eyed, refusing to plunge into a sort of communal grief, must have puzzled and hurt many of our friends and others who quite certainly suffered for us and felt rebuffed that they were unable to suffer with us. And so both of us together, and each of us individually, became increasingly lonely, and nothing healed.

From the time of the man's arrest until the final Assize Court trial six months passed and it was not until then that I really began to grasp the fact, which of course had always been perfectly obvious, that the whole of the circumstances involving Cheryl and her end were not simply isolated impersonal phenomena like an accident or an illness, but that there was a man involved, a man who had by some means of his own bewitched her and transformed her from what she was into a mindless puppet at the service of himself and the followers of his evil sect. But until the final trial and its farcical ending, those facts had been part of a whole, not capable of being considered by us in isolation from the rest, and allowed to engender other emotions beyond grief and shock. I suppose it was because we had not been able, until the final trial, to think in terms of a 'survivor' of this disaster, and then in the differing terms of what is implied by the word. First of all, someone who had been there before it all happened, and thus belonged to the time when it need not have happened or might not have happened. Then, someone who had passed through it all and emerged like a victor. Someone who had been able to commit more than simple assassination and perhaps was not even to pay for it. Someone involved and whom time would disinvolve.

It is a cruel reflection on the way the mind reasons and on the fragility of our conventions that from the moment I grasped the conception of a 'survivor' I began to suffer a fraction less because I began to offset a little of my pain by the thought of guilt, punishment, the revenge that would be exacted by society. But first came the feeling that here, in this 'survivor', was an object which above all would *explain*, and in that explanation, though it could never expiate, at least there might be revealed something to lessen the hurt even by an infinitely small degree for us, the still-living. What despicable and stupid hopes and mean consolations we cling to when we are suffering. In fact nothing he could say or reveal could in fact change the effect of what had happened – Cheryl's death and the manner in which it had been brought about. Yet there was for a while this curious movement towards hope, almost as if one walked back along a road towards the scene of a tragic motor car accident, saying, 'Here – at this point, nothing had happened; everyone was present and alive and probably happy; here – at this fraction of space, if he or she had done this or that instead of whatever they did do, then nothing would have happened. How precious is that space, that moment, that thought! A few more steps – and here it was – they died and the two cars began to disintegrate. One hundred paces more and all along here are the traces of disaster – the broken pieces, the scarred surface. And now a few more paces further on. Nothing happened here at all. There are no traces, no reflection of what ended a few yards before.'

In a few paces we have been able to traverse with our minds and even with our eyes all the little distance from nothing, to disaster, and to nothing again. We have been able to stand on the very place and say 'Oh – if only – here,' and a step further on add, 'Yes, but here—' That is a sort of parallel to the first feeling one had about the 'survivor'. He belonged to the disaster at a time before it happened, when it happened and now – after. He was going to take us back to when, and – if. Though we knew that his account would pass remorselessly on, there remained some vastly illogical desire to *know* – like playing a game in the past tense with hope.

When that fantasy was exhausted, and it finally died in the first two days of the main Assize Court trial, it was replaced by the second cruel and mean consolation. The survivor was now on trial for his life, for the death penalty was still effective in law at this time. He too was to become human refuse, a sack of interred human putrefaction. What there would be for us after that, or I should say, what there would have been left for us after that, I cannot imagine. But it did not happen. After the third day of the proceedings the defence produced expert witnesses and a huge dossier of medical evidence accompanied by a claim that damage to the central nervous system of the accused man, by drugs and abnormal practices, made him 'unfit to plead'. With eighty per cent of the evidence unheard the judge accepted the defence claim and the trial was stopped. The 'survivor' was committed to a special hospital, to be chosen by the Home Secretary, for psychiatric and other treatment, for the duration of 'Her Majesty's pleasure'.

I had seen the man, the survivor – his name is Michael Loft – altogether on three occasions, each very brief, in the early preliminary Court hearings when he had nothing to say, at the time when our own personal disaster had still not allowed our minds to separate or identify the role of any particular individual. I had looked at him with no emotion, nor even very great consciousness at that time. I remember that he appeared fairly young, perhaps twenty-two or three. He was tall, dark and stooped. Long, shaggy hair fell to his rounded shoulders from which his scraggy neck projected, supporting with seemingly infinite fatigue a great gaunt head. His face was long, his jaw massive. Heavy lids stayed lowered and unblinking over eyes sunk in wide dark cavities, almost as shadowed as the hollows of his cheeks. 'Cavernous' was the only word that came to my mind at that time and that was really all I thought of him. Any other impressions I might give now would not be true of that time but only the consciously-created after-thoughts of ten years. Life only really began to exist for me from the moment that his trial ended in what was nothing more for him than a life sentence as a sick man. But whereas his acquittal – I have never been able to think of it in other terms – caused me at first a perplexing absence of clear thought, it was the final blow to Alan. As the months had passed he had declined into an almost permanent state of stupe-faction. He ate and slept a little, he received his patients and visited the hospital as usual, but in every positive action to which his existence obliged him, he resembled a machine grad-ually running down. He was losing all momentum, and he was quite clearly destined to stop very soon. Six months after the trial he was too weak to leave his bed. A month later, with no word of complaint, with no true symptom but what his own doctor vaguely described as 'a tired heart', he simply stopped living. The only contact we had during that last month was during the long hours I would sit by his bed holding one of his still, listless hands. Sometimes it would respond to my pressure, and on his shrunken face of transparent parchment there would seem to pass the ghost of a smile. Though we never spoke beyond the most basic material needs for communica-tion, those long hours during which his hand rested in mine brought us even more perfect communion than words which could never have expressed our sorrow, and the love we had once lived as three. His renunciation of life was for me the gradual birth of fire.

All this and more we told each other without a spoken word. We just knew. He begged my forgiveness for his de-parture and I gave him my understanding of it. I had enough sadness to encompass his decision to leave, for as such I accepted it.

It is certain that those who would still have called them-selves my friends felt confirmed in their convictions of my heartlessness and insensitivity by the way in which I reacted to Alan's departure. To them it must have seemed like a supreme calamity, challenging if not survival, at least sanity. But after our hours of perfect communion I saw my attitude as fitting in perfectly with a pattern of destiny which I had accepted. Alan's eventual departure, so expected and accepted as it was, hardly ruffled my mind, and a sense of his perpetual personal presence was added to that which I had already begun to perceive of Cheryl. My daughter too had come back to me. And to these facts I now recognized and added one other which had not been so clear to me at the beginning. The survivor, by the grace of someone's God, had been left to *me*. It was when I reflected on this fact that I realized how intolerable life would have become if authority, through the law, had simply effaced him with its impersonal retribution and handed him over, with smug reluctance, to meet his maker on a full stomach and a priest's prayers.

I have always felt that death is more intimate than any other event in existence because it is the one great violation, the violation of life. It is our most intimate moment, to be shared or witnessed only by those we love or who love us. It is an innocent intimacy shared with them and with God. The violation of Cheryl's life had been carried out by some sub-human, beast-like stranger. As no one else should do, except those who loved her, he knew the last conscious cry, the last convulsive movement of her body. He was a rapist of life, and now he was to be allowed to live indefinitely, defiling in his thoughts and memory a ceremony which was the prerogative of a god. Such a privilege has no price, but at least one could demand the maximum possible payment. So it seemed to me then, and always has, that he, the violator, should in his turn lose the intimacy of death. It should belong to an ordinary human, it should be no communion with God, no perfect consummation of life. It was for me now, who bore Cheryl, to be the master of Loft's last moments, to efface like a sacrilege Cheryl's death from his lewd memory.

I have never seen my need and my duty to separate Loft from his life – preferably under the greatest possible degree of mental and physical suffering – as a matter of ordinary vengeance. I see it as a sort of spiritual–physical surgery for the restoration of the intimacy and innocence of my child. Vengeance, yes – that will be there too as a gratuitous consequence of this act. It will be fear, and then pain – as prolonged as possible.

41

By this reasoning, the product of inevitable and logical thought, only a short while after Alan's death my spirit and my body were restored to a clarity and vigour which I had never felt before in my life. I knew an exhilaration which gave me the absolute conviction that I should be able to do whatever I wished to do; that no patience, no ingenuity, no resolution could be too great for me to achieve the final act required before I too could go on and merge eternally with the waiting spirits of my two loved ones. When one has nothing more to lose, one's strength is incalculable. This force is what I was referring to when I wrote – as I knew then – that fire was born into me.

For some weeks after the natural course of my future was revealed to me I lived solely in the ecstasy of that knowledge. The survivor was to die – I was to destroy him. The practical implications of this decision became evident soon after, but though seemingly insurmountable, they gave me no special concern.

A few days after the collapse of the trial the newspapers had reported that Michael Loft had been sent to the famous asylum for the criminally insane at Brockley Old Hall. There were no special hospitals then, only Brockley and two other similiar institutions for those who were judicially and administratively categorized as 'criminally insane'. The severest cases always went to Brockley, and the name, in the public's mind, carried something sinister and terrifying. At least I knew now that there would be no problem for me to find Loft for a whole lifetime. But the real problem was how should I, a private individual, and the mother of Loft's victim, gain access to this man in a closely supervised institution for the criminally insane?

Alan died a little less than five years after I had given up my work as a regional social assistance officer. Ever since I had begun my working training as a nurse and then psychiatric social assistant in London and Exeter I had kept my maiden name. Alan and I had felt that as he was a doctor, we should maintain separate identities in our professions. By the time I had sold our small house in Staffordshire, everything except a few pieces of furniture, a year had passed since the publicity of the trial and the committal of the survivor to Brockley. In popular terms the whole affair was already veiled in people's memories by more front-page scandals and sensations which in their turn were being fast forgotten. 'The Loft case' was no longer a familiar phrase for the average individual. During the case only our family name had been used. I had suffered almost no personal publicity. I was required to be available to give evidence but was never called because Alan knew as much as I had ever known, and it was felt by both the defence and the prosecution, though for opposing reasons, that under the circumstances an anguished mother should not be displayed in court.

After I had established myself in a small flat in the south, near Southampton, I had no difficulty in obtaining work in a new area, with my previous record and references. I began as a social security worker, which involved child and family care and supervision, mostly in distressed homes. I had explained for the record that my husband had died while we were living in the north of England and I wished to register again under my previous working name of Margaret Lewis.

If anyone in that first year of my lone return to the south ever associated me with the Hayes family of the 'Loft case' they kept quiet about it, either due to uncertainty or consideration. The one important thing was that no association between the Margaret Lewis of the present and the Margaret Hayes of the past should ever arise in the official mind or the records. Much as it hurt me, I even disappeared for ever from the ken of my foster-parents – for as such I regarded the Craigs. By the end of that first year I felt quite certain that I had established a distinct breach between the two identities, and that I was really consolidating myself in the role that would eventually lead me to my objective. But how soon? My early optimism about this problem was soon discouraged. I found that I was very many technical steps down the ladder by which I could reach a post in a criminal insane asylum, unless I wanted a simple job as a ward-maid or a nurse. But with my experience and qualifications I could hardly seek a job of that kind without arousing too much curiosity and anyway I was not the type to look for or to get that sort of job. What I required were more specialized qualifications and experience in criminal prison work before I could hope to apply for a grade of work which would seem appropriate for me. So my difficulties were enormous, and made more so by the particular requirements of my ambition. I suppose I could have applied for a job under another name in some menial task at Brockley in the hope of making some swift contact which might permit me to dispatch Loft quickly with a knife or a bullet. But if my identity were to be discovered first, or my attempt to kill him failed, then I should never have another chance in my life. This I could not possibly risk. In any case, I did not see my task as some brusque, haphazard assassination. Loft, in my scheme of things, was never, is never, destined to die with the dispatch of a simple execution. I needed regular, unsuspected access to him to do my duty as it should be done. After a great deal of reflection and examination of the professional administrative possibilities leading the way I wanted to go, I decided that I should give up all hope of short cuts and time-saving. First priority should go to obtaining the confidence of the authorities and eventual access, unlimited and uncontrolled, to Loft himself. After all, I had my whole life. I was living for nothing else. Provided I finally got what I wanted, time would be unimportant. The only really vital thing in my life was to succeed in doing what I wanted with Loft. My researches showed that I should establish myself, by experience and trust, in the criminal field. My qualifications pointed towards the job of court probationary officer. Within a few weeks of making this decision I had found a very junior version of the job I required. My first step towards Brockley was made.

You who will read this will have my records at your disposal and will already know of my long, slow progress in prison probationary work, through membership of prison boards and inspection committees and so on, up to my eventual posting here, at my own request, for a job which I have more or less created myself, planting the idea in the official mind over a certain period, with constant difficulty. Only my record of prison work and the public recognition I obtained could have permitted the manipulations and red-tape cutting which I have had to employ to get the position I have at Brockley. Everything I have done for years, everything I have seemed to be, has been calculated to this end, even my outward character. Since my first decision to reach the survivor I have become not two people, but three.

The first and only true one is my real self. At heart I am retiring, shy, lacking in natural physical courage, and I know no joy I care about but that of the love between members of a family. That passionate feeling for family, the way I savoured every instant and situation of our own family life, comes most certainly from my orphanage upbringing. My true self is also not gregarious, not very gay nor sprightly, though I love children and their play. But I love unhappy people too and I am capable of feeling and sharing their unhappiness rather more than I am of talking them out of it and helping them to fight it. This true person is not ambitious and has no innate qualities for material success. Of the other two people I have become, each has drawn some of my true qualities and combined them with others which are false but necessary to my purpose.

My two 'false' personalities, 'interior' and 'exterior' are these: the false interior Margaret Lewis is the one never perceived by others. This person is a schemer, a calculator, a dissembler, always alert for information and opportunities which may be used to forward the main purpose. The interior person is quite ruthless and amoral, no lie, deception or subterfuge is excluded so long as it may benefit the objective of my life. This interior person is a sort of dynamo as well as a regulator for the 'exterior' person. But it is here that the fire inside me dwells. The 'exterior' character I have always projected, the false Margaret Lewis, is gregarious, self-possessed, capable of agressiveness in a good cause, physically courageous, with a good, rather ironic sense of humour, unsentimental but capable of well-controlled administrative compassion within the relevant regulations; a devoted servant of everything that stems from the establishment, even to the degree of directing at it from time to time a little well-considered and regretfully-expressed criticism. This apparent tendency towards a limited liberalism is considered at the more constipated levels of the establishment to be a sign of 'intellectualism', amusing and not too dangerous so long as it is not pushed too far. I decided on this very slight degree of nonconformity in my external character because, so long as it does not shock, and once a degree of eccentricity has been conceded by authority, one is given just a slight fraction of flexibility in one's actions. This has been useful several times in my relations with Ministries and with stepping over red-tape. Along with these characteristics of my public self is a certain spinsterish quality which, in keeping with my experience, has a very slight masculine tendency, an air of intransigent authority and forthright speaking, to which events oblige me from time to time. There are many other subtle adjuncts to this exterior Margaret Lewis which it is not necessary to explain, for they are all within the range and conform to the general principles of the character which I have described.

Sometimes in the bright light of my day's work, vibrant with action and authority on which very often other people's happiness and welfare depends, I wonder for an instant whether the exterior Margaret Lewis is not showing too dominating a tendency and whether there is not some danger that it may replace the real one. But in the evening and at night I am no longer alone. I feel a pulse of yearning and indescribable tenderness in the darkness and I know that my two loved people have come back from the lost ranges of the day in a calm more peaceful than peace, more comforting than words. Then I know who I am again. And I remember that I cannot fail.

I have been writing all night and I have just heard the birds signalling the first light. Yesterday I met the chief superintendent of Brockley, the colonel. That is one man whom I can write off as being of no danger to my intentions. He is honest and decent and stupid and touching and I am sorry that one day I shall be the cause of great distress to him. Yet I am relieved to realize that he is what he is. I need to try and refresh my memories of Kashmir and Muree and India generally. The bond can be infinitely useful.

One explanation is needed for this journal, which I shall try and continue to the end. One of its purposes will be to help me arrange and co-ordinate and understand my own thoughts and actions – to keep me on the track. Another will be to serve as an explanation for those – police and lawyers no doubt – who will be called on to find out why the woman known as Margaret Lewis turned out to be, at the very least, a dedicated murderess. It is not that – after it is done – I shall ever need to defend myself, or make excuses or explain to anyone. This journal will supply the information which will be all official justice will require. If anyone cares to *understand* my motivation, what I write should certainly help. It will all be there, motives and means, answered and signed, waiting for whoever comes.

Tomorrow, starting at the normal staff midday meal, I meet my fellow workers at Brockley, and I suppose at least some of the patients.

I am not afraid.

I am not in a hurry. I do not mind whether, to begin with, the survivor is among them or not.

I can still wait.

Now I know that it *will* happen.

4

Staff lunches at Brockley Old Hall were, in general, never much more than gloomy, hasty, and in a culinary sense, sordid affairs.

The best thing about the soup was the prepared packets of flavouring with which Ma Blake gave taste to the watery distillation of cabbage, potato, bones and barley. The most filling elements of the meat or fish courses were the generous dollops of lumpy mashed potatoes and the watery folios of cabbage. The pudding, whatever its apparent substance or colour, was mainly flour and suet, enriched with a pale yellow liquid alleged to be custard and small black inedible droppings named currants. Three times a week there was cheese and on the other days, the cheapest fruit in season. The menus inspired comment without conversation. Since the rest of the events in each day were already the subjects of official business, no one had much to say at meals except on occasions such as Derby Day, the Cup Final or the Boat Race.

The lunch at which Margaret Lewis was first introduced to all the staff together was memorable for an unusual liveliness, marked by a buzz of conversation and, for a reason which no one could have explained precisely, a feeling of general cheerfulness and relief. Perhaps unconsciously this reaction stemmed from the very evident good humour of the colonel.

The response to his request for staff increases may have been disappointing, but at least he appeared to have found some consolation in the appointment of Miss Lewis, the new arrival of uncertain standing. However, the matter of her status, if not of her exact functions, was quickly established by the colonel. He presented Miss Lewis to all the twenty-one members of the staff who regularly lunched together as though she were a distinguished visitor, continually called her, waggishly, 'Memsahib' and generally gave a confused impression that he and Miss Lewis were old friends from the great and stately days of the British Raj in Poona. Had she been a different sort of woman, the colonel's attitude could have established her total unpopularity with most of the senior staff and made it practically impossible for her to work effectively. But her behaviour was modest and enchanting, quite beyond reproach. As Superintendent Slater said in a stage whisper to his neighbour at the top end of the table, 'This woman's a master.' And so she was. Without either rejecting or ridiculing the colonel's overdrawn presentation of her, which would have been unkind and ill-mannered, Miss Lewis managed nevertheless to convey to all those to whom she was introduced that she had no illusions or pretensions about her vague appointment and that if she should ever prove to be of any service to SP9 it could only be through the advice and help of its truly professional staff. It was quite clear that this modesty was sincere. She had a direct and simple and rather dry way of expressing herself. She rarely spoke without at least the trace of a friendly smile. She was placed at the top table at the ends of which, lengthwise, were the two junior tables, making an inverted U. She sat between the colonel and Matron Smith. On the other side of the colonel was Dr Robertson, who soon found that the chief superintendent, particularly in his expansive mood, was an insurmountable barrier to consecutive and coherent conversation with Miss Lewis. Matron Smith, who always reacted to any new situation with instinctive hostility, quickly found that none of her usual ploys seemed to disconcert Miss Lewis in the slightest and swiftly decided that she could be more convenient as an ally than an enemy.

'I hope you will be able to spare a good deal of your time for my women,' she said. 'They see no other women than myself and the nurses, and I think they feel they have no one they can confide in outside those – doctors and psychiatrists included – who are having professional contact with them. I think you can do them a great deal of good if they can think of you simply as a woman *confidante*.'

'A sort of non-institutional ally,' suggested the colonel tactlessly.

Dr Robertson leaned forward from the other side. 'I may say this applies just as much to the men patients as to the women,' he said. 'Where you can help us most is in gaining the confidence of two distinct kinds of patients – two extremes almost. The first are those who are too confused to be able to benefit from serious analytical treatment. I mean those who are still at the stage of frightened children or animals. The others are those who in a certain sense are too composed, too sure of themselves to benefit from analytical treatment. These people, for much of the time you are with them, can almost convince you, and can certainly convince some people, that they are as normal or balanced – I don't like the words sane or insane – as anyone outside. They believe it themselves. They are arrogant, stubborn, suspicious, capable of the most incredibly subtle simulations and pretences and they often have an IQ twenty-five per cent higher than the average man or woman. I believe this is the class of patient where your work can be the most valuable – just so long as you don't let them convince you with their particular brand of "I'm-really-sane" story.'

Miss Lewis had listened fascinated, her nut-brown eyes – as always when she was deeply absorbed – growing darker, while in the heart of the pupils there sparkled a bright pin-point.

'Do they really do that?'

The doctor laughed. 'Indeed. Some of the older ones will tell you quite seriously that they are only alive today and only here because a clever lawyer saved them from hanging or from hard labour for life by convincing a judge and jury that their crime was so terrible that only a madman could have committed it.'

Miss Lewis's voice fell almost to a whisper. 'Are there any here who really are guilty because they are sane, but who escaped either hanging or life imprisonment because of a legal quibble about their mental state?'

The whisper was embarrassing and she put her hand to her throat and gave a short dry cough as though to clear a temporary irritation. Then, her voice a little stronger, she went on, 'I mean, in other words, are there any real *sane criminals* here?'

Dr Robertson had been talking in an easy conversational tone, relaxed and unrestrained, until this question. Its directness seemed to shock him. The half smile of friendly consideration which had played on his bland pink countenance dropped away like a mask. For a moment he looked down at the table, stroking his cheek with the index finger of his right hand. 'No – no,' he said, thoughtfully, 'I can't say that. Even if it were true, I don't think I should say it. All those who are here are here because a whole mass of experts, legal, criminal, medical, not to mention juries, have judged on all the evidence that they *should* be here.' Then as if he had been able to reassure himself of some doubts of his own, his voice quickened and he forced a half smile as he added, 'No, my dear Miss Lewis, have no fear, there are no sane monsters hiding among our patients. There are no guilty. You can be reassured – whatever any of them may tell you – they all need our help.' The slight tension was broken now and there was almost a trace of friendly mockery in her voice as Miss Lewis replied, 'You still frighten me a little doctor. I shall need a good deal of advice from you to prevent my being simple and naïve. I am supposed to have a way of inspiring trust among ordinary criminals, so it's normal that when trust is shown to me I am apt to believe it's sincere. If it were the gambit of some unbalanced mind I doubt if I should recognize it as such. After all, I am not a fully qualified psychiatrist and I suppose I can make some very silly mistakes among your patients. Oh, well,' and she looked from the doctor, to the colonel, to the matron, 'I can only say that I will try and pull my weight at SP9 and not be a nuisance to you, as soon as possible.'

'Of course you will, Memsahib,' boomed the colonel, and added as though he were talking about a game of polo, 'You'll soon get the hang of it.' He then plunged into some tiresome reminiscences about a duck-shoot in Gilgit twenty-five years earlier to which Miss Lewis felt obliged to listen. It was, in the colonel's mind, part of their common association from their Indian past and so was well meant. He was trying to set her at ease with mutual nostalgia.

Matron Smith, as the senior woman staff member, won priority for Margaret Lewis to pass the rest of the afternoon with her in the women's wing on the second floor of the main building.

Each of the wings, including the women's, was a self-contained security unit. All doors giving access to the outside were security doors, plain steel grilles behind the normal heavy wooden doors, which were also kept locked. Inside each wing there was complete freedom of movement except for the men's and women's close supervision cell areas. But inside the wing units there were no locked doors between day-rooms, dormitories, wash-rooms and other facilities. The thirty-five women on the whole of the third floor lived in quarters from which all evidence of institution and restraint had been removed as much as possible, though the muslin and chintz curtains of the windows failed to efface the rigid outlines of the grey iron grilles on the outside. The armchairs and settees in the main day room were bright and flowery, the main dormitory's bedspreads matched the curtains and there were some frilly dolls and round-eyed teddy bears on some of the beds. Matron occupied a combined sitting-room and office. In one corner an electric kettle stood on a small cupboard above tea-making chattels and rows of cups and saucers. There was a tall vase of tastefully arranged autumn leaves and a well polished Chippendale desk – obviously no Ministry issue – with some silver-framed family photographs and a Victorian cast-iron fireplace laid with unlit logs.

'Of course I cannot tell you in technical terms the precise mental condition of my patients,' said matron, preparing to make tea – she never drank coffee after lunch – 'but I think an explanation of the three categories may be enough for you to understand, to begin with, anyway. Of our thirty-five women, ten are category "A", that is to say they are still hysterical, depressed and sometimes dangerous. At least sixty per cent of them will never improve because they suffered brain-tissue damage either at birth or in subsequent accidents. They pass their time in separate quarters to the others. Then the "B" category women, we have eighteen. They are less violent and irresponsible but they still need fairly close nursing and security care. There is hope that most of them will recover, some entirely, others sufficiently to be sent to hostels for outpatient treatment. You'll find quite a few of the "B" girls interesting and pleasant, some quite normal for weeks on end. Then we have seven "C" class women, who are the nearest to social rehabilitation. Eventually all these will be released, some quite cured, others for indefinite outpatient treatment. Between them these seven have accounted for fifteen children killed, five adults killed and eight permanently disabled. I'll ask them in to meet you presently, one by one, and you'll see that despite this terrible record you could pass quite an agreeable afternoon taking tea with any one of them without noticing more eccentricity than you would in most normal women.'

Matron was an expert in monologue, and here she had the material for it. There was simply nothing for Miss Lewis to say as she sipped tea and listened to the case histories of the seven sisters of category 'C'.

Annie McBride was thirty-seven. At the age of twenty she had become virtually the slave-wife of a man twice her age, a sadist and a pervert. After five years she was little more than a stupefied automaton with the drooling mouth of an imbecile and glazed eyes opening like dark holes onto an empty mind. Her husband had killed himself in a final paroxysm of black mysticism and it was in the subsequent inquiries that their history was gradually uncovered. In law Annie had been an accessory to the debauch and murder of at least three small children, probably more, though their bodies were never found. That was twelve years ago. For her first seven years she had resisted all contact, with a zombie-like indifference. Five years ago, like some wintry tree in the first days of spring sun, she had suddenly begun to respond, as though a thin sap of understanding was forcing its way painfully through the sclerotic channels of her mind. Now, except for occasional periods when she retreated to a tortured world of her own, with all her external senses as though switched off, she was a pleasant, gentle woman, capable of consoling one of her fellow patients through a transient crisis of terror or fury with all the firm tenderness of a nurse or a doctor.

Martha Payne nine years earlier had brought seven children into a one-room world and went out of her mind when her husband beat her because she told him she was expecting an eighth. She cut his throat with a bread-knife while he lay in a drunken stupor and then, one by one, pushed her seven children out of the window of her tenth storey room, while the neighbours battered on the locked door and heard the screams of the children fading all the way to seven successive dreadful thuds on the backyard cement below. If Martha remembered that night now she never said or did anything to show it. She had spent her first two years alone in a padded cell between week-long bouts of tearless weeping and attempts to crack her skull against the door, the walls, the floor. She was now devoutly religious and was blessed with occasional mild hallucinations in which her children told her marvellous stories of life in heaven and their love for their mother. She never spoke of her husband.

Elspeth Blount, elementary school teacher, choir mistress of her local chapel, had all the physical attributes of a handsome and desirable woman, except her face which resembled that of an amiable bull-dog, including the whiskers and warts. Somewhere in this complex contradiction was the explanation for her sudden predilection for shoplifting. Not ordinary, general, economic shoplifting, but a specialized branch devoted entirely to children's clothing. She was undetected, on her own evidence later, for the first five years. Then she was caught with two full bags of new children's clothing, hung by a belt under her skirt. She was put on probation and ordered to undergo psychiatric treatment. A year later she was caught again and this time fined. One year later she was trapped by a store detective and this time the police searched her small house on the outskirts of Birmingham. It was stacked from the cellar to the loft so tightly with children's clothing and toys, that the kitchen, where she slept and lived, was the only room in the house it was possible to enter. The value of her loot was estimated at more than four thousand pounds, enough to stock a large shop. Lonely Elspeth Blount had never, to that point or subsequently, tried to explain or defend her shoplifting activities, which had passed completely beyond her control, to the police, the doctors, the psychiatrists or the nurses. It was a subject she would never discuss, but turned aside with a wispy, secretive smile and a fluttering touch of her hands to her wild mop of straggling grey hair. At fifty years of age her unfulfilled virgin body was still lusty, lithe and ripe and those who saw for the first time the face that went with it were shocked, even

54

revolted, by the grotesque contrast. Later, for all its gruesome features, people who came to know Elspeth Blount well found that her face could convey, in its own peculiar way, all the normal human emotions, and most of hers were gentle and attractive. She spent her time in SP9 knitting baby clothes and then hiding them. The nurses found them, unravelled them and gave her back the wool to start again. She should never have been in a hospital for the criminally insane, but the magistrates who had tried her last case had misunderstood the whispered advice of the Court Clerk and sentenced her to three years in prison instead of detention in an ordinary mental institution. It didn't matter to Elspeth. She was quite happy and she sang beautifully, and often alone, in chapel every Sunday, her bagful of knitting beside her.

The fourth of the seven 'C' sisters was May Saunders, a sturdy, simple, likeable young woman of twenty-one with a pretty freckled face framed by long, wavy copper hair. May had made off at different times with four small babies, left in their perambulators on pavements in shop doorways by their trusting mothers, in cities as far apart as Glasgow, Birmingham and London. Of these four, two had died, probably due to tenderness or else forced neglect resulting from May's efforts to escape detection. May had no grain of vice or malice in her character. She was fairly simple and in her simplicity had been tortured and bewildered by her overwhelming sense of protection and love for babies and very small children. If she had not been brought up by devout Sisters in a state-subsidized orphanage, in fear and distrust of any contact with males, if she had ever been made aware of the symbolism of the love she was taught to have for the infant Jesus, she could have been a prolific and devoted mother of broods of her own children.

But institutionalized childhood, charitable and well meaning, had simply created, with May, the inevitable end product – an easily certifiable institutionalized adult, unaware of many of the realities of the world outside the grey walls, almost as if there had existed some Ministerial injunction on state orphans tucked away under some amended sub-section, saying 'Never let them go.'

Elaine Gordon, debutante, well-educated if not so well-bred daughter of a wealthy family, had always been an eccentric and unsatisfied mystic, intelligent, highly-strung. She was a highly-regarded and well-paid interior decorator, a minor name in the gossip columns of the London press until one day she made the transfer to a page one court report as another second class celebrity in the growing constellation of pot smokers. From then on for two years very little was heard of her until she was arrested and charged with the murder by poison of a woman rival. Her trial revealed her to have become the chief witch of an important West End coven. At her 'fashionable' trial she claimed that her victim had died of a potion not intended to kill, but to turn her into a bat. She boasted of having similarly dosed a score of other individuals, men and women, who had earned her disapproval. Police inquiries during the trial revealed that she was telling the truth, although the victims had not become bats – they had at the time been thought to be subject to food poisoning and had only been saved from excruciating deaths by rapid application of stomach pumps. Elaine Gordon's lawyers changed their plea from 'not guilty' to one of 'unfit to plead' due to diminished responsibility, a theme which was not unsupported by the generous but quite emotionless use of four letter words and torrents of well-rounded abuse by Miss Gordon in giving her evidence in cross-examination. There was no doubt that drugs and her traumatic practices in the name of witchcraft, even on the twin-set and pearls level of a Mayfair W1 coven, had been enough to sever the slender threads of her grasp of reality and pitch her into a black turmoil of mind in which she was convinced of her right and powers of life and death. Nine years of SP9 had plucked most of the fantasies from her mind and restored her almost to her former level of tolerable eccentricity. She was the instructress of the weekly art classes and the women's classes in weaving and home decoration. She was the only patient allowed to use filthy language without reprimand because she did so without intent to shock or insult, but with a disarming lack of inhibition which belonged to her basically honest nature. This characteristic was not always appreciated by those who did not know or understand her – such as the members of a Parliamentary Committee being shown around SP9, to whom Dr Robertson had wished to present Elaine Gordon as one of the more successful examples of mental therapy. After matron, in the day room, had called Elaine's name vainly three or four times while the committee of MPs waited awkwardly, there had come a shrill response from the toilets in the corridor, 'I'm in here, having a pee, god dammit!' She was thirty-nine years old now, with loose, flowing black hair, a saturnine beauty and a frightening directness of manner well-served by her capacity for forthright expression. Everyone liked her and Dr Robertson had taken to remarking that the world would undoubtedly be a better place for her release from Special Hospital Nine.

Sally Price was a fragile, dainty little creature with wide, wondering eyes who at thirty-two still looked at times like a rather grave young girl of twelve. She was the daughter of an alcoholic father who had murdered her mother while Sally, then exactly twelve years old, screamed in the corner of the room. From then on she had been brought up with foster parents, a kindly elderly couple. Once past adolescence Sally from time to time reverted to the trauma which had followed the death of her mother and this had proved fatal to one of her boy friends whose usually acceptable advances had been met by a knife blade slipped between the ribs during a warm good-night embrace. After a year in a special institution Sally returned to normal life, but her affection proved fatal, in the same way, to yet another young man. This time the treatment lasted two years and Sally was then allowed to marry an understanding individual, a little older than herself and well aware of her past. In the sixth month of her pregnancy she strangled her husband while he slept. Now she showed no more than a sulky disposition towards men and was never known to have attacked anyone in SP9, where she usually appeared as one of the most normal and inoffensive of the women patients. There was no doubt in the minds of the psychiatrists that without any warning hysterics or crisis, Sally would kill again, whenever the occasion offered, and she was in SP9 for an indefinite period.

The last and eldest of the seven 'C's was Mary Ford, addressed always by staff and patients as 'Mrs Ford', never either as just 'Ford' or 'Mary'. She was fifty-six years old, the imperious widow of a banker, clinging tenaciously to the prized middle-class status to which her deceased husband's accountancy and her own desperate efforts at self-education had finally raised her, before her fall. Though Mrs Ford had, like the others, her own small bed-sitting room, its outside bars screened by frilled muslin curtains, she managed to give the impression to herself and those around her that it was in fact a semi-detached villa with all mod cons and garage for two cars in a 'nice' residential area. This was indeed the kind of place where she had lived the triumphant summit of her life until, five years after the late Mr Arthur Ford's death, she had been identified as one of the most expert and vicious anonymous letter writers in the annals of this venomous pastime. The late Mr Ford had suffered from insomnia all his life and had filled in the many dark hours of his despair recounting in detail the loves, problems and affairs of the clients who needed his aid, his patience, his understanding and above all his signature on their overdrafts.

Mr Ford was an uncomplicated man whose knowledge of his customers had never formed for him any kind of pattern of human folly or drama, nor had it given him any sense of power over their lives, beyond that which lies in the normal process of foreclosing a mortgage or fixing a reasonable level of interest. Mrs Ford had always listened with patience and seemingly no great interest to his pillowcase monologues. It was only after her husband's death that, in some way as yet unexplained, all his insomniac narratives flooded back to the consciousness of Mary Ford, not only in the minutest detail, but in a way in which Arthur Ford's simple mind had never perceived the social and financial associations of his clients – classified and co-related as though by a computer. Mary Ford added to this the pointless malice of a human mind to create an intriguing network associating facts and people in the most unpleasant ways. The lonely widow almost as though hearing the echo of her dear departed Arthur in every word she wrote – or rather, printed, with lettering cut from newspapers – embarked on a campaign of anonymous letter writing as cruel as it was subtly calculated. Though her information came from only one source, and that one out-dated, her insinuations were so devious, her muck-spreading so well devised, that no one could have suspected the hand and mind of the sorrowing widow Ford. She even went so far as to write a few letters to herself, insinuating – and it was not far from the truth – that Arthur Ford himself had connived at certain of the irregularities, moral and fiscal, which she had revealed elsewhere. She was thus able to share the commiseration reserved for the growing band of those who were compelled to defend themselves against the increasing weight of the only-too-true revelations continued in her anonymous courier.

She followed up her attacks so well that one banker, one real-estate agent and the middle-aged wife of one of her husband's friends killed themselves in the five years of her operations. How many other homes, hearts or nerves were broken by her unbelievably efficient and cruel campaigns was never known. She was eventually discovered by a combination of painstaking police deduction and the sort of carelessness which grows from over-assurance. In the beginning she had posted her letters from places as much as a whole day's train journey away from her home, to the north, south, east and west. Gradually, with the lengthening years of impunity, she shortened her journeys, but always along the same directions so that eventually the police, building up the dossier of this nameless fiend, found that on a map the postmarks eventually showed lines converging towards the pleasant residential suburb where Mrs Ford lived. From then on a series of police 'mere formality' checks, consisting of friendly chats with the widow Ford herself, were enough to provoke an outburst of hysterics which told the whole story. In fact she was only a lonely old woman trying to compensate for her own lost status and unhappiness by ruining the lives of others. She did not receive a simple criminal sentence. Thanks to a brilliant lawyer who persuaded a jury that she was crazy and more to be pitied even than her victims, as well as a sensational and vindictive press publicity, she was consigned to SP9. Dr Robertson, with the agreement of some of his outside colleagues, was engaged in preparing to have her discreetly removed to a milder form of detention. She was a lightweight for SP9.

As she finished her story of each of the seven, matron had sent for them one by one to meet Margaret Lewis. Matron Smith's sense of hygiene and discipline, and her knowledge of ward procedure were everything they should have been. Only the vital quality of warmth and natural affection for her fellow beings was missing.

As each of her patients was called in turn to meet – 'a new friend who has come to help us all' – she could not resist dropping the quasi-conspiratorial tone of her voice with which she favoured Margaret Lewis for her voice of authority used for addressing those whom she considered, if not quite as underlings, certainly as inferior individuals.

The usual easy-mannered poise of Margaret Lewis was evident during most of these brief and embarrassing confrontations. Only at one of them did she seem to be touched by a sudden and unidentifiable emotion. This was the moment when the five minute interview with May Saunders, the orphanage-bred stealer of children, was being brought to a brisk close by Matron Smith. Margaret Lewis had said very little while matron had made small-talk, asking the shy but striking-looking girl with her dark blue eyes and auburn hair about her current activities, her sewing class and a new dress she was making in the hope of being allowed to go to the patients' Christmas dance. May answered matron's barked queries softly, her slender fingers playing with a necklace of green glass beads.

'How happy are you, May?' Margaret Lewis asked suddenly. It was a strange and almost brutal question in that place, yet posed in a relaxed and friendly voice. May turned to Margaret Lewis and her colourless face, with a wide sensitive mouth, large heavy-lidded eyes, puckered in hesitant bewilderment. For a moment she looked wonderingly into the steady gaze of the older woman and then the heavy sensual lids lowered and she was absorbed in thought. She looked up again to reply and the half-smile she gave seemed a little shy. 'Happy?' She pondered the word. 'Well, I suppose I'm not particularly happy.' The word seemed to be underlined as though qualified. 'Nor particularly unhappy either, really.' She shook her head slowly and her eyes widened, 'What does it matter? Happiness doesn't seem very important. I mean, I'm not *at all* unhappy either, if that's what you wanted to know. After all, I was brought up in an institution and there's not much difference' – a quick side-glance at matron – 'well, I suppose you could say this is really even a bit better. There's always so much to do, and so many people here, and one can, in a way I mean, be useful. At least I try.'

Margaret Lewis stood up and in an impetuous movement, with one hand on the girl's shoulder, kissed her lightly on the cheek.

'Well, I'm happy,' she said smiling, 'happy to have met you and to think that we shall see a lot of each other and that you may be able to help me too.' May flushed, turned and as she left the room put one hand to her cheek as though to feel the imprint of a kiss.

Margaret Lewis sat down and matron, embarrassed, coughed and poured some more hot water into the teapot. They neither of them made any comment on the incident. But it was quite obvious, by her fussy preoccupation with the tea things, that Matron felt it was rather unusual and outside proper hospital procedure. The other 'introductions' ranged from the easy-going cordiality of Elaine Gordon, the former West End witch, who lit up a cigarette in a long ivory holder particularly to annoy matron, to the dry hostility of Mary Ford, the banker's widow. Although she was always well behaved so long as she was left to her own devices in her own room, she was the least amenable to orders from anyone except Dr Robertson – the only member of the staff whom she considered her social equal.

She despised the colonel for having retired before becoming a general and for having betrayed his class and his rank by accepting a Civil Service post in a state institution. She had managed to exude a kind of patronizing salon-charm for the benefit of Miss Lewis, who was astonished to find her the very opposite of the legendary tight-lipped and acidly disapproving anonymous letter writer. The widow was buxom, as feminine as a fat cat and almost as comely. As far as it became a banker's widow, in whatever circumstances, she permitted herself a genteel affability at the end of the encounter. 'Well, since you too are obliged to stay in this place,' she sniffed, 'call in on me for tea and a chat any time, my dear, and we can talk together on things that *really* matter. I have some charming photographs of the last holiday my poor Arthur and I spent together, in Menton, you know.' Miss Lewis half expected her to add that she was At Home on the first Tuesday of each month.

It was late when matron had finished her presentations of not entirely subdued star patients.

'It's too late for you to start with Dr Robertson now, my dear,' she announced. 'I have just one of my staff I would like you to meet. Of course you will meet the others in the normal course of your work, but this one – well – I rather need your help. She gave Miss Lewis a résumé of the story of the unsolved pregnancies, and the fifth, the new one which was as yet the stubbornly maintained secret of the Pakistani ward-maid Mounalal. She was still not noticeably pregnant except perhaps for the unconsciously protective movement of her hands across her stomach in moments of repose and a pale tightening of her forehead and around her deep-set dark eyes. Mounalal sat down after offering a thin flabby hand like a little bunch of joss-sticks, and a wan smile, to Miss Lewis.

'Mounalal,' said matron, in what was for her a tone of silky ingratiation, 'Miss Lewis is joining us as a,' she hesitated, 'well, as an adviser and friend. She is not a nurse, not a doctor, not an – an inspector – or anything like that. Perhaps she can help you. You know, my dear, don't you, that is all we want to do?'

The wispy, graceful creature in her white ward smock nodded with small conviction and it seemed Miss Lewis's turn to say something. That something came rather like an electric shock to the little Pakistani, almost as much as to matron. For Margaret Lewis, speaking in a Punjabi dialect of Urdu said, 'You are a very pretty little girl, my dear. Please do not be afraid – I am truly your friend.'

Rapidly in the same language Mounalal replied, 'What – you speak Punjabi? I'm so happy to meet you, Memsahib.'

Margaret Lewis leaned forward and took the girl's hand. She felt a pulse of relief as the long, slender fingers tightened on her own as if in instinctive trust and recognition. She answered in English. 'I used to live in your country. That is – before it was Pakistan – when it was all India. I spoke Hindi and Urdu almost better than English and when I was a little girl my – governess – was Indian and of course our bearers and the rest of the staff in the house—' She went on hastily, 'And as well very many of my father's friends, and my own schoolfriends too. So you see, we can have lots to talk about. I love your country. Perhaps you can tell me what it is like today. It is so many years since I was there. You were hardly born when I left – with my parents.'

Mounalal was about to speak when matron stood up and ended the meeting abruptly. 'It's rather late now, Miss Lewis,' she said. 'I'm so glad that you can be such a friend to Mounalal. She will be able to continue her work, if she wishes, for at least a month or so, and you will, I'm sure, be a great help to her. Thank you Mounalal, my dear, you may go.'

Turning to Margaret Lewis she smiled wryly, 'Well, there you are. There's a problem for you which I'm sure you never expected. If you can find how that girl became pregnant you will be relieving us all of a terrible load of worry. I think the language will be a compelling link between you.'

5

Dr Robertson's office-surgery was a cramped affair of camou-
flaged hardboard partitions and hollow brick and plaster walls,
situated on the first floor of the central part of the main building, adjoining the infirmary and opposite the large main surgery and laboratory shared by the rest of the medical staff for
general consultations. It contained an all-purpose adjustable
surgical examination couch in one corner, a floor-to-ceiling
glass-fronted medicine cupboard, a small hand-basin with running water, a weighing machine, a small table with scales in a
glass case, and the doctor's own desk, in front of which were
two small wooden armchairs, with rumpled and faded flat cushions over the straw seats. To move around this slightly re-
stricted area without actually knocking anything over one had
to proceed by movements combining some of the elements of a
waltz and a shimmy.

Ian Robertson at forty-nine was only impressive to anyone
to whom his pale-grey eyes behind their heavy horn-rimmed
spectacles had directed their unwavering and almost expressionless attention for several moments. Otherwise he was a
most ordinary looking individual, his pale, toneless hair thinning into streaks of grey but still with a resolutely defiant quiff
rising above his high, narrow forehead. His face was oval, rosy,
still unlined but without any noticeable characteristics. He was
of medium height, sloppily dressed, and his voice, with the
faintest perceptible trace of a Glaswegian accent, was dry and
monotonous. The matron's exposé of her seven 'C' patients

had left no time on the previous evening for any other meetings between Miss Lewis and the rest of the staff. In fact, after a long wait for Dr Robertson, there was only time for him to make an appointment with her at nine o'clock the following morning in his surgery–office.

There was no note of formality in his voice as he greeted her – gesturing helplessly at the stacks of files which shared his desk with a half-opened medical bag, parcels of pharmaceutical trade samples, correspondence and minutes from the Ministries, a telephone and avalanches of documents of all kinds sliding remorselessly out of the IN and OUT trays.

'Look at it, my dear – isn't it appalling?' His lips pursed in a half-whistle of dismay. Yet somehow he gave the impression that he was not in the least appalled. He smiled, 'Ah, well—' Leaning back in his chair he looked at Margaret Lewis for the first time as though really seeing her and she felt the cool but not unfriendly assessment of his pale eyes on her face, her hair, her clothes, her hands – all measured, weighed, evaluated in a glance so swiftly enveloping that there was not an instant to spare for hesitation or embarrassment by either of them.

'Miss Lewis – er—'

'Yes, doctor?'

'Suppose *you* start. Don't bother about formality with me. Don't think of me as chief medical superintendent. Inside, you must be bursting with questions. Now, just get on with asking them – ask and ask and ask. I'll tell you everything I can and then you tell me how you envisage starting your work. And I'll give you a friendly push in the right direction – and off you go. How about that?' She laughed with frank surprise and pleasure at the simplicity of his approach, while he sat with a solemn patience waiting for her to begin.

'First, doctor, do I need to know all the case histories of the patients with whom I shall be most concerned?'

The doctor stabbed the air with a bone paper knife picked up from his desk. 'Ha – a good question indeed. I imagine that yesterday Matron gave you her seven-part, all-technicolour drama on her "C" patients so that you shall never forget that Mary Ford is a vicious old snob; Elaine Gordon a man-mad witch, and – let's see – yes, May Saunders a child's skull-smasher, and so on. On no account think of them as people, eh? Get it fixed right away in your mind that they're all crazy, vicious and murderous, eh?' The doctor's voice kept to its level monotone. Only a flush warming his smooth pink face and the sharp, irritated flick of the paper knife on his fingers gave some clue to the anger and irony behind his words.

'Well, my answer to that one is very positively no, you do not need to know the case histories of the patients immediately. I do. My psychiatrists do, and my doctors. You need to get to know the patients first. Then, if you like, look up their case histories and see what people they once were. That way, without prejudice, you'll have formed a fair idea of what they can be made into again. In the men's "C" wing there is a comparable group to the women whom you met yesterday. But for the present don't bother about their records. Get to know them and make up your own mind about them. If you've judged them as objectively and as effectively as your experience and your perception should qualify you to do – well – their case histories won't have much effect on you. Next question?'

Much as the doctor's answer to her first question had seemed to reassure her, Miss Lewis now broached her second with a hesitation bordering on timidity.

'You remember at lunch yesterday, doctor, I asked if any of the patients here were really quite sane, only here because a lawyer saved them from criminal punishment by successfully pleading insanity?'

'Yes, I do.' The doctor's face resumed its usual owlish lack of expression. But the bone paper-knife kept on flicking in his restless fingers. Miss Lewis sensed that she was approaching something akin to danger. She had clearly seen the doctor's reaction once to this question – anger – and then an unconvincing dismissal of the problem with an assurance that it did not even exist. But for reasons of her own she was determined to pursue it. Now the doctor stood up behind his desk, seemingly deep in thought. When he pushed back his chair, there remained just the space, lengthwise, behind the desk for perhaps half a dozen short paces. The doctor waited, as though listening, rapt, then walked from one end of his desk back to the other, idly bouncing the edge of the paper-knife on the desk edge as he went. Miss Lewis ventured on. 'Doctor, I do realize that it was perhaps the wrong time and place to pose such a question yesterday, and I apologize. But, well, if now—' She was lost for a moment for the words with which she hoped to convey the regret but also the insistence with which she felt she must pursue the question. But the paper-knife clattered on the desk before she could continue, and she looked up at Ian Robertson's face ready for cold irritation or even anger, to meet instead an expression of patience, along with some minute, unidentifiable reflex of his face muscles, which managed to convey a sense of deep compassion. No storm broke. The monotone of his voice was for once lightened by a note not far removed from pleading.

'You must not ask yourself, nor me, nor anyone else that question. All those who are here, are here because they've been judged fit to be here, by the proper authorities. That's enough for us. Our job is to get them fit to be put *out* of here.' Again the paper-knife stabbed the air in pace with his slowly emphasized words and the doctor was no longer even looking at her. He might have been addressing the very back rows of a class of a hundred students as he slowly paced the short stretch between the ends of his desk.

'Who is to say if *any* man or woman who commits a crime against society is sane – and therefore guilty? Guilt should carry its own acquittal, on grounds of so-called insanity if you like, because guilt is not a normal human state, while sanity *is*.' He paused, leaned towards her, his eyes seeking hers. 'At least that's my view.' He said it almost as though issuing a challenge, and then went on, 'Crime is a reaction to pain. Pain, social pain, mental pain, anguish – whatever you like to call it – is suffered because of the inadequacy of an individual to face up to the problems, or a particular problem, of life. And so – it hurts. And he or she reacts, and sometimes becomes a criminal. Some, we say, are guilty criminals because they knew what they were doing and they knew it was wrong. Others are in such pain of reason and spirit that they don't know any more what is right or what is wrong. These are not guilty, not sentenced by the law, which itself makes the distinction between these two kinds of sufferers. Those whose pain eliminated guilt from their actions are simply detained, to be cured. The line the law and society has drawn between these two groups, the guilty and the mentally sick, is terribly fine. So fine that no single individual should ever be called upon to make the distinction. Yet, though it is fair that such a line should be drawn, it would be strange indeed, if in the drawing, some errors were not made and some people were sentenced as wicked when in fact they are ill, and some treated as sick when in fact the law should call them criminals and punish them.' He paused and stopped his patient little march, and turning towards Miss Lewis, leaned on his desk, slapping his right hand on its surface to emphasize his next slowly spoken words: 'But for god's sake don't start worrying about which of them are what, here. Take them all for what they seem to be – sick people – and help us to bloody well get them out.' His last words were too much of a plea to sound insolent or brutal. The doctor flopped into his chair and ran his fingers through the limp quiff above his forehead. He was embarrassed. He pushed his glasses higher up on his nose and, head lowered, looked at her with mock penitence and the faint ghost of a smile. It found no flicker of response in the face of the woman who had listened to his plea. She seemed, as she leaned, chin in hand, on one arm of her chair, to be far away, and her darkened eyes smouldered as if with the reflection of some monstrous shadow veiling the distant parkland beyond the grey bars of the window. Now, in a matter-of-fact tone, though with perhaps just a trace of conciliation in his voice, the doctor began speaking again.

'Eh – well – there it is, my dear. I apologize for having brought down on your head, even so briefly, my not exactly orthodox ideas on guilt and innocence – I know they don't belong here, nor in any Ministry. But sometimes they get the better of me, and off I go. Forget it. But now – more questions, please.'

She made a physical effort, a tiny shake of her head, a fluttering movement of one hand towards the desk, as though to rouse herself. Her voice sounded level and businesslike and she acknowledged the invitation with the habitual twitch at the etched corners of her mouth, a movement that her eyes confirmed to be truly a smile.

'Tell me, doctor, if you were in my place, how would you set about my job to give the best possible value to the staff and patients here?'

'Well – really—' The doctor now seemed relieved and relaxed. 'That is the question to end all questions. But I'll tell you exactly. For the immediate future, start with matron's seven "C" women, but don't bother too much with Mary Ford, we're going to get her out of here as soon as possible, anyway. Keep notes, prepare your own dossiers on all patients you meet. Equally, get to know, and I mean get to know well, the "C" Wing men as well as some of the "B". This is a bigger job because there are more of the men. At least twenty-five "C" men, I think at the moment. However there are about half a dozen who don't need much bothering about because they are already recommended and will be leaving us within the next twelve months, providing they maintain their progress. Among the "B" men, although you may find him interesting as a case, there's nothing to be done about the man called Loft. We shall certainly let him go to a lower scale security institution, but for his own sake we'll never let him out into the normal world again. They wouldn't give him a chance to live normally. He looks too much like the classic caricature of the monstrous madman, although I'm convinced he's harmless, and even – if ever we could penetrate his isolation – highly intelligent and fully aware of what goes on. Then, take a look at the weekly programmes. There is always some class or study-group under way and you will always be welcome to drop in and participate, which will give you a great chance to evaluate those in whom you may be interested. Here,' he opened a large cardboard-bound folder, 'today for example. There's a women's dressmaking class from eleven to twelve. Ten to eleven there's a mixed social competence class – the mixed classes are always well attended, you can count on that. This afternoon there's a soil conservation class in the gardening barn; a cooking class, and English literature study – oh, plenty of things going on. Rural studies, folk-dancing, mixed too, by the way. Then there are the permanent daily occupations, carpentry shop, masonry training, the piggery, that's men, poultry, that's women, market gardening and rabbit breeding, men too. In fine weather you'll find groups, men and women, sitting around in the park only too happy to chat. When you have a good idea of the – population – and those who interest you especially, I shall want you to go and visit relatives and friends to take a look at the available surroundings in which those relatives and friends, in a very qualified sense I'm afraid, neighbours as well, all conspire unconsciously to make life hell for the released inmate. It's not so much the problem of returning people to sanity that is our most difficult problem. It's a matter of finding understanding surroundings and lives for them, in which the taint of having once been mad doesn't pursue them and drive them mad again, perhaps even more so than ever. Your judgement on the release of patients will be that much more valuable if you know the surroundings waiting for them. It's simple. Just the sort of work you did in your probationary officer days.'

'I've no more questions, doctor. It seems to me the best thing to do now is just to get on with it.'

'That's it.' He stood up. 'There's just one final thing I want to say. I shall count very much on you Miss Lewis. I promise you my confidence and my confidences on whatever goes on in here. I shall respect completely – to hell with Ministries and so on – whatever you wish to tell me in confidence. All I beg of you is – never hide anything from me. Even your wildest fears, or suspicions or discoveries. Tell me. Superintendent Slater will give you a pass key and you can start finding your way around. Good luck.'

6

Dr Bligh was the junior member of the medical staff, finishing his last year as a hospital intern in a special hospital because he had believed that he might wish to qualify as a psychoanalyst. This prospect began to fade within his first days at Brockley. Since then he had felt obliged to adopt a forced jocularity and an exaggerated cynicism to cover the fact that he felt quite incapable of coping with mental affliction. It frightened him. He found it intensely painful and sad and he disbelieved that its cure could possibly approach, even remotely, an exact science. Sometimes he wondered in desperation whether six months' service in a special hospital was not the best argument he knew in favour of euthanasia. In any case he was now certain that his destiny was that of a general family doctor with a nice little suburban practice in which eighty per cent of his work would range between the normal problems of maternity and senility.

He had joined up with Miss Lewis and Administrative Superintendent Crow in a corridor, on their way to visit the patients at work in the outlying buildings behind the hall. They had chatted with a working party in the kitchen garden, with some of the women arranging a withered array of flowers in the chapel, and others feeding the hens and pottering about in the hen-houses. Now they were inspecting the piggery, with its two boars, eight sows and four litters of a round dozen each of noisy little piglets.

Dr Bligh, in spite of the noise, found pigs restful and was

inclined to linger, chatting with the two 'C' Wing and four 'B' Wing patients cleaning out the sties and preparing the swill. Miss Lewis and Robert Crow, once the good-mornings had been exchanged and the introductions made, seemed disinclined to stay. Miss Lewis had seemed quite keen to visit the piggeries and especially curious to learn that the six patients working there were without any kind of permanent surveillance. Technically they were under the control of a male nurse who was attending the market-gardening class in the gardening shed a hundred and fifty yards away. In fact he strolled over casually to see what they were doing a couple of times during the morning and then left them to their not very exacting task, which left them most of their time for chatting, smoking and listening to a transistor.

Out of their hearing Crow explained, 'None of these men are dangerous – at the moment. They belong to balanced groups, and the most tiresome thing they might be likely to do at the moment would be to try and escape. But the waste land, and the trees back there, to the wall—' he gestured towards the northern end of the park – 'is out of bounds and it's unlikely that anyone could get across without being spotted. The main wall the other side of the wood is too high for anyone to be able to climb without some kind of help. Anyway there are always too many people about at the back here during normal working hours for any attempt to escape.'

Miss Lewis had made a point of saying something polite or indicative of interest to each of the men working at the piggery, in order to identify herself, and them, but the moment the introductions were over, she seemed to lose interest.

'That sow, in there,' said Dr Bligh, nodding towards one of the sties, 'is the only one of these beasts that is ever unpleasant. She bites her husbands with malice, has a tendency to overlay her infants and occasionally charges at whoever is cleaning out her sty. She's a clear psychotic, I suppose. I wonder what her trouble is?'

Miss Lewis picked up the ironic note of his mock gravity in her reply. 'I expect she's probably the most intelligent of the lot and she has decided she doesn't like being a pig.'

Dr Bligh tut-tutted – 'Dear Miss Lewis, that sort of reasoning is treasonable talk here. You are inviting the supposition that some of our patients are only here because they're too intelligent to put up with life outside.'

'Are you certain that is never the case?'

The question was lightly put, with a note of ridicule, as though the questioner would have added her own answer if it had not seemed too obvious. But in Bligh's reply there was no reflection of the ridicule, or of the irony of a few moments earlier. 'In fact, there are several patients who believe that is why they are here. They are the ones who have worked it all out, the ones who believe that they belong to the real intellectual aristocracy of the world, free and all-powerful because they have elected not to be sane. Well—' he seemed a little taken aback by the sudden earnestness of his own words, 'you'll find out who they are. But they are the ones who make me want to get out of this place and open up a nice little suburban practice. They terrify me.'

Miss Lewis replied as though she were not quite certain how to react to this unexpectedly sharp turn in the conversation. 'You don't sound at all as though the treatment of mental disorder is quite your vocation.'

'No, it certainly is not,' said Bligh positively, 'and between you and me I feel that I'll end up here as a patient myself one day. Sometimes I wonder if I'm not one already. That's why – well – I say some rather outrageous things from time to time. I simply have to be cynical and shocking to give myself the impression that I'm letting off the pressure and delaying the moment when I pack up and take the next bus to anywhere. No, I have quite the wrong kind of mind for this sort of place. I have too much imagination. The horror these people represent – not just in terms of their own lives – but in the lives of hundreds and hundreds of other people. The unbelievable wretchedness they have sown around them. The incredible farce that we go through in the belief that we are curing them, when we even admit to ourselves that one out of three will be back again – often after having committed a fresh piece of molestation or mayhem – ruining the life of some perfectly innocent child or individual.'

The young doctor reached the end of his bout of exasperation. He leaned over the sty wall and scratched the nose of the psychotic sow, which responded with short grunts of satisfaction.

Miss Lewis let a good two minutes pass before she asked mildly, 'Well, what's the alternative – your alternative? Should they all be locked up like wild beasts and left to rot – or maybe just quietly put to sleep with an injection?'

The doctor's reply was slightly edgy. 'Yes, yes, of course you are right. We've got to try, I know. But I'm the wrong type for this kind of fight. I made a great mistake coming here. They need level-headed people like you, with faith in something or other, and courage and all that.' He turned to look her straight in the eyes. 'You know I sort of feel that you, and people like you, are wearing armour. You are impeccable and indestructible and untouchable. You believe absolutely. You defend your own faith and your own goodness with a sort of god-like assurance. It must be marvellous to be as strong as that. What makes you like you are? I mean, what is *your* armour?'

She laughed, and turned quickly away from the grave scrutiny of his solemn young face. 'I didn't know I was armour-plated,' she replied. 'You mean, I suppose, what is my faith in life?'

The doctor nodded. 'That's the sort of thing.'

'It's really quite easy. I know what I want to do, and I'm doing it. It's all a question of knowing what you want and going and getting it. Something will come along and make you tick too, one day – a girl, children or maybe a new bug that no one can identify – some mystery that will make a mission for you.'

The young man nodded again and sighed. 'Yes, I suppose you're right. A purpose in life, they call it. Everything's so simple after that.'

Robert Crow came out from his inspection of one of the sties. 'Come on, let's go,' he commanded briskly. 'Next stop the gardening and rabbit block.'

The main building of the gardening unit, or block, was a great wooden barn painted black with creosote. There was no loft, and all the way up to the roof it was divided down the middle by a board wall. Now, in the half reserved for potting and horticultural classes, about twenty patients lounged on wooden benches on three sides of their instructor, a local horti-culturist giving a demonstration of soil testing. He was evidently keen on his job and quite absorbed in his lecture, though no member of his class looked as though he might ever, of his own free will, test so much as one grain of soil. On one of the back rows of the benches a game of cards was in progress. Two or three of the class were reading books, others seemed to be dozing.

The barn, a solidly-repaired oaken relic of late Victorian days, now divided into two sections, had two adjacent entrances from the conservatory, a long lean-to, glass-panelled construction against the south wall of the barn, facing towards the back of the main hospital building. The planked roof of the barn, once tiled, was now covered with an ugly tarred-grit roof. Around the walls of the horticultural section hung the bric-à-brac of gardening and along some of the beams of the roof were nailed rows of what looked like rabbit pelts, turned inside-out and stuffed with straw. The male nurse in charge of the party, in blue overalls, sat against one of the walls – behind most of his charges – in whispered conversation with one of them. No one took any notice of the three visitors who stood for a couple of minutes watching while the deeply-absorbed horticulturist, the only really interested man in his class, mixed little phials of earth and chemicals and stirred them with glass rods. Crow beckoned his two companions away into the conservatory. As they went Crow commented, 'You couldn't imagine a much more peaceful scene than that, eh Miss Lewis?'

'They don't seem exactly excited by the subject,' she replied. 'Do you ever have trouble at these classes?'

'Sometimes, yes,' said Crow, 'but rarely at the gardening classes. They seem to appeal more to the restful types. The only others who join them, I mean of the livelier inmates, do so to try and steal tools, either as weapons or for escape. The tools are counted and checked three or four times a day. No, there's not much interest in this class for you. I really brought you up here to meet one of the "B" Wing men who is in charge of this whole gardening and rabbit-breeding unit. You might say, in a way, he's a sort of trusty, although you can't have them in a mental institution in the same way as you do in a prison. But this chap's steady, reliable, never given a spot of trouble in the ten years he's been here, although he doesn't mix with the rest. He stays here, pottering around looking after things – the conservatory heater, the tools, the rabbits and that from dawn to dark every day of the year. But he's sort of shy. Don't worry if he doesn't say anything to you at first. He very rarely says a word to anyone.' They followed Crow through the adjoining doorway – there was no door – and then into the comparative gloom of the rabbit shed. One unshaded electric light bulb hung unlit from a central beam of the roof of white-washed hardboard.

As they entered, past layers of gardening tools stacked just inside the right of the doorway, there was a flicker of russet, and from a table against the near-end of the partition wall, a red squirrel bounced to the earth floor. It stopped for an instant to half turn its head, tiny tufted ears as alert as its bright button-black eyes. Then, with a flick of its curved, bushy tail, it was gone, up and over a row of rabbit hutches, up the wooden plank walls and into the shadows of the beamed roof. At the same moment their attention was attracted by the figure of a man in loose overalls at the far end of the hut, reaching in to one of the rabbit hutches. There was a scratching and a thumping as he pulled from the hutch a huge white and tan rabbit. Methodically he grabbed it by its back paws and holding it with his left hand, at waist height, flicked the edge of his hand with a soft thump against the back of the animal's neck. The body instantly became limp. He lifted it a little higher as he squeezed its stomach to eject the urine. Then he put it among half a dozen others on a small board table in front of him. At that moment he saw for the first time his visitors, who had begun walking towards him. Abruptly he turned his back, reached into a hutch and they heard again the sound of the soft impact that broke another animal's neck, this time held almost furtively, so that the action of killing was screened by his body. He placed the dead rabbit on the table with the rest of them and then slowly turned to face his visitors. He was immensely broad and well over six feet tall. With the dirty opaque window of the north end of the hut behind him, he was half in shadow.

Crow spoke first, with a slightly forced casualness which had not been noticeable in his contacts with other patients. 'Good morning, Michael. It looks as though you have another rabbit stew for us?'

The tall man's huge hands hung limply by his sides. He said nothing. His huge dark eyes, set deep in a face in which all the features seemed to be abnormally enlarged and prominent, moved slowly from Crow, to Dr Bligh, to Miss Lewis and back again. Then he said, 'I was killing them. It's very quick like that. It doesn't hurt them at all.' He turned and picked up one of the bodies from the table and held it out towards the three visitors.

'You see – the neck – just behind the base of the head, here, clean broken.' He seemed displeased at being interrupted and his explanation was given in a dull, detached tone, neither hostile nor defensive. His voice was deep, from the back of his throat, with, in sound, the satisfying quality that velvet has to the touch. Its even tonelessness contrasted with what one would have expected from an individual whose whole body, as well as his face, seemed gnarled, rough-hewn, almost to a degree of caricature. Crow made no reference to the man's remark but stepped back a pace and with his hand on her arm guided her forward. 'I've brought a new member of the medical staff to meet you, Michael. This is Miss Margaret Lewis. She is here to help Dr Robertson and his staff, though she is not a doctor. She is a sort of social adviser, both to the staff and the patients. She is here to help us all.' He paused and before there was time for what he feared would inevitably be an awkward silence he turned to Miss Lewis and added, 'This is Michael Loft. He is one of our more – experienced – patients and we count on him a lot. He looks after everything in this gardening and rabbit-breeding area. In fact he started the rabbit-breeding. A few of the other patients drop in to help him with the tools from time to time. But Michael's the boss around here.'

Miss Lewis made a slight inclination of her head, but Loft was not even looking at her. The slightly patronizing tone of Crow's introduction had provoked no reaction whatever. For one so large and ungainly he had a disconcerting ability to remain more than just still or in repose. His absolute immobility was cataleptic, as though his very presence was isolated in a vacuum across which no contact could be made. Even the movement of an eyelid, the stirring of a hand, the changing of his weight on his feet, might have indicated some kind of thought or reaction. But there was nothing.

Dr Bligh stepped briskly forward and ran a hand over the heaps of pliant fur on the table and he too spoke like Crow, with a slightly forced brightness.

'You've got a good crop here, Michael. What lovely fur. What do you do with the pelts, you don't throw them away do you?'

The monolith became a man again and Loft turned to the table beside him, putting one of his great hands on the rabbits and gently ruffling the fur. His voice had a slight Staffordshire burr, but it was still that of someone whose education had passed considerably beyond secondary school.

'No, I don't throw them away. I fill them with straw and hang them up to dry and sell them. A fellow comes from Berkhampton every couple of months and buys them from Joe Norton. He puts the money in with the rest of the rabbit money, for the hospitality fund. But I don't hang them up in here. They're all nailed to the roof next door. It wouldn't be right to hang them here for the other rabbits to see.'

Crow laughed a little awkwardly. 'D'you think they'd know?'

Loft turned his slow, heavy gaze towards him and his thick-lipped, wide mouth lifted a little sideways in what might have been a half smile or an expression of sly contempt. Neither his eyes nor his voice gave a clue. 'They wouldn't like it,' he said. Then he began, with extraordinary gentleness, as though afraid to hurt them, to put the dead rabbits one by one in a sack. Now the dim light from the conservatory doorway showed more clearly a face grotesque in the over-emphasis of each feature; prominent cheekbones under taut, sallow skin, falling into deep cheek cavities; a massive lantern jaw support-ing a broad fleshy mouth. The skin around the eyes seemed sucked into the darkened sockets and the eyes themselves only held in place by the heavy, unblinking lids. The nose, slightly arched and broad-ended, with thick, back-drawn mobile nos-trils. The impression given by the man's head was that of power in repose. Yet the atrocious ugliness of the whole effect was curiously softened by a sort of brooding, animal compos-ure, part submission, part reverie. Filling the sack with dead rabbits he had become remote again, as though, while still

78

staying where he was, he had abruptly withdrawn his presence. Suddenly, as if from nowhere, there was again that russet flicker, and the squirrel appeared, sitting on one of his shoulders. Loft placed one huge hand to stroke its arched back, without moving his head.

Miss Lewis caught a signalled look between Crow and Bligh, and without another word the three of them turned back into the gardening half of the building. For the first time she looked up at the roof, to see the thirty to forty straw-filled rabbit skins, stretched on nails.

'So that's where he puts them,' she said.

'An extraordinary man,' said Bligh at length, as though the remark were the conclusion of some unexpressed reflection of his own. They walked slowly back towards the main dining-hall where the first midday meal sitting for a few 'A' Wing and a large group of 'B' Wing patients was just being announced by the kitchen bell.

'He's crazy about animals,' said Crow. 'Pets are not allowed here. The only way he could keep something, apart from goldfish or a canary, was by proposing the scheme as a cash-raising project in aid of the canteen and hospitality funds.'

'Then that means he has to destroy his pets all the time,' said Miss Lewis.

'No, not at all,' Crow explained. 'He has two couples which are his own particular property and personal pets. Their offspring are put in with the rest, but his two couples are untouchable, like his squirrel, which he weaned with a dropping tube when it was brought in by someone, a tiny baby. Its mother had been shot. He grooms them all for hours and talks to them more than he does to anyone. The squirrel is probably the favourite. It crawls all over him as if he were a tree or something. I've gone in there sometimes and he's been whispering to it, sitting on the table in front of him just as though it understood every word. But once there's a stranger in the place it never keeps still and he never even looks at it. He calls it just by moving one shoulder – and there it is. Sitting right there. Right out of nowhere, it seems to come.' He shook his head. 'But he's an impossible man to understand, Loft. But then – that's not my job – it's the doctors'. To me, anyway, he just seems shy. People seem to scare him, like we did just now. As far as security's concerned, Slater has no worry about him. It's hard to understand why he's still here.'

'Perhaps he has good reason to be scared of people,' Miss Lewis suggested.

'Why?' said Dr Bligh. 'Because they've shut him up in here?'

'No – maybe because of what he's done to them.'

'It's not that, he's not scared in that way at all,' replied Bligh. 'He's scared simply because he's been kept here far too long and he's lost touch with society. And they've kept him here that long because he's so damned awesome-looking that with the reputation of an ex-criminal lunatic, there's no one in the outside world who could bear to have him around. When the world's decided that a man who looks like that *is* mad, because he *has been* mad, then he's better locked up where the sweet sane folk can't get at him.'

Miss Lewis turned to the young doctor and took his arm. 'Now, now, Dr Bligh,' she reproached, gently, 'a little while ago you were being cynical about the insane, now you're being cynical about the sane. Whose side are *you* on?'

'Just mine,' laughed the doctor. 'I'm a powerful minority of one and nothing I can say will change a thing, nor matter to a soul.'

7

The Diary of Margaret Lewis

EXTRACT 2

The first time I ever saw the survivor was by candlelight, presiding at a sacrificial ceremony, naked except for a crude hide cloak hung back from his shoulders, covered in the entrails and blood of a skinned cat. The last time I had seen him he was standing in the dock at the Central Criminal Court of the Old Bailey, accused of killing my child, among others.

Now, over ten years later, I meet him again, a dead creature still warm in his hands, a small heap of furry bodies in a heap on a table in front of him. The monster is still a dispenser of death, but now he accompanies it with a reputation for loving the little beasts he kills. He would have said he loved Cheryl too, no doubt, if he had been given a chance. I have occasionally in the past wondered how I should feel when I encountered the survivor again. I had little fear that I should falter or be overcome, but there was always a risk that emotion might betray reason. This was not so. I do not think my heart beat one pulse faster, and I felt like an athlete, or an astronaut, or a soldier who has trained so well and for so long for a superhuman task that when the reality comes, he wonders why anyone should think it a feat of strength, or courage or skill. The survivor seems to me to be still a brute of transparent viciousness – even more so than I had expected to find him after so many years. I recognized him at once, through his sullen arrogance and apeish deformities, the marks of malevolence and depravity indelibly chiselled on his face. I do not understand yet what game he is playing with his well-meaning and simple keepers, but I shall find out in my own time and maybe it will serve me for his destruction.

When I set eyes on him, revolted as I was, I did not deliberately calculate how I was going to kill this monster. In fact, at that moment, the precise thought – 'Here is the man I have hunted to kill for ten years' – did not enter my mind. Along with my sense of revulsion at the sight of him, the only other emotion was a marvellous sense of fulfilment, of having arrived somewhere and feeling that for the moment, nothing else mattered. I do not for the present propose to worry over the details of just how I shall deal with him. I am certain that as long as I remain on the alert, events will show me the way. I shall first try and get to know him, win his confidence, discover his weaknesses and his capacity for pain. There is no more need for anxiety, and time is no longer of importance. The rat is in the trap.

On that day in February, fifteen years ago, when I realized Cheryl was on the threshold of becoming a beautiful young woman needing my closer guidance and care, I talked with Alan about my feelings. He agreed with me that I should stop my work and give all my time to our daughter. I was then a regional probationary officer, covering a large area and supervising the work of others. So my work, with no fixed hours, meant that I was often away from home all day and until late in the evening. Cheryl was a day scholar at her school, but except for Saturdays and Sundays I was never able to spend much time with her.

I finished my job on the first of March, five days after Cheryl's twelfth birthday and from then on our life changed marvellously. Each morning I walked to school with her, had lunch ready for her at midday at home and each evening I met her at the school gates. Sometimes after she had done her homework the three of us went out to a cinema or had dinner out. I took her once a week to the local repertory company play, and on Saturdays we went either to the theatre or the music hall in Wolverhampton. Cheryl was not precocious, nor did she seem to have any inclination to isolate herself with her own school friends, who, at that age – twelve to thirteen – were already becoming conscious of their clothes, their looks and their attraction for boys. But I did not smother her with my attentions and presence. She had a group of three or four school friends with whom – typical of their age – she formed a sort of anti-boy alliance and I always left them alone to their whispers and giggles, when they came to tea at home. Sometimes one or two of them would join us for an outing in the car on Sundays.

On Alan's advice, a little before her thirteenth birthday I tried to explain about what are called 'the facts of life' and to calm in advance any shock she might feel at the arrival of puberty, which was imminent. Cheryl laughed with affectionate exasperation, 'Don't be silly, mother, I shan't think I'm bleeding to death or that I've got some disgraceful disease. We all know all about it. I bought my first box of sanitary towels six months ago – I had to.' She told me she had gone shopping with one of her school friends who had called at a chemist's shop to buy her supplies, and Cheryl had pretended that she needed some too because, she told me, 'The other girls make fun of you if you haven't already started when they have.' We laughed when Cheryl teased us, 'You'll be warning me next not to go too near to gooseberry bushes in case I get pregnant!' So that was that.

Somewhere about half way through her thirteenth year she began to accept the brother of one of her girl friends as just tolerable male company and then only when he was with his sister. The boy's name was Bryan Tyler, his sister, Jane. Bryan was a well brought-up lad, a technical school engineering student at the awkward age of sixteen. He was very shy, especially when Cheryl was there, and judging by his stammerings and blushings, was going through the pangs of first love. Cheryl responded in a normal way for most girls of her age; she either ignored him or treated him as an amiable half-wit, in which course she had the ample collaboration of his sister Jane. About a year and a half had passed since I had given up my job and I had grown to know my daughter intimately. Though I never made the mistake of trying to be her 'best friend' and swamping her with adult comradeship, we had a close and affectionate understanding and my earlier alarms about the advent of womanhood were completely set aside. She seemed to have an inherent balance and self-sufficiency which, combined with her complete affection for us, assured me that if she ever made any great mistake in her life through lack of experience or judgement, she would confide in us.

Though she was our only child, we did not see her as a potential saint or sage, and neither of these qualities would have appealed to us in a daughter. Her tempers were fierce and furious, but they generally succumbed rapidly to her feelings of affection or to her sense of the ridiculous. We realized with relief that in character she was all we could wish for, without being exceptional – save in the matter of her looks. Although she never used her beauty to particularize herself, the risk was that others might do so. But she was not in the least vain and quite uninterested in clothes, in the sense of fashion. While her friends could hardly wait, at the weekends, to get out of their atrocious school uniforms and into their stocking tights and mini-skirts or jeans and tee-shirts, pop-idol eyelashes and the rest, Cheryl's favourite garb was a pair of dark corduroy slacks and a roll-neck pullover. A great many tears were shed at one time because we refused to allow her to have her hair cropped like a boy, but she compromised by rolling it up into an untidy chignon or a long pony-tail, held by elastic bands or even a piece of string. In fact her natural beauty, allied to this casual lack of pretension, distinguished her from her fellow puppets, to their disadvantage, though I do not think this was a calculated intention on her part. Her vitality and the intensity and passion she applied to every act and thought made her a natural pole of attraction among her school friends, and Cheryl, although not scholastically the top, was a leader among all those with whom she came in contact.

The three years from her twelfth to her fifteenth birthday were the happiest we had ever lived. Very soon after Bryan Tyler became an accepted companion, with his sister Jane, two other girls introduced their own brothers into the same group of school friends. They all met at the homes of different members twice a week. On Wednesdays, half-holidays, Cheryl was the hostess and three or four girls and two or three boys came for high tea and a pop session with Cheryl's record player. We gave them the front room for these sessions and Alan and I kept to ourselves. Those of the children who wanted to smoke did so. Cheryl tried but didn't like it. Eventually this group took to passing one evening a week, Fridays usually, at a coffee-bar discotheque, only about fifteen minutes' walk from the house. I had no objection to this. Cheryl was always with the boys and girls I knew, and we knew most of their parents too.

In any case, so long as Bryan was there I had nothing to worry about. It was impossible to know how Cheryl really felt about him, she probably did not even know herself, but she had come to accept him as her particular champion among the boys, if ever she needed one. The coffee-bar discotheque, run by a long-haired Italian boy named Tino, was a respectable place, a long way above the pin-table café style. Apparently a few couples danced, Cheryl told me. But for the most part of the time they all sat around listening to music and discussing. Discussing what? Cheryl could never tell me, and when I asked she replied, 'Oh, absolutely everything!' By the end of her fourteenth year she was out with her friends, either at one of their homes, or at Tino's, an average of three evenings a week. She was happy, mentally and physically healthy, and normal. The characteristic which pleased me most was her desire to know and understand about everything with which she came in contact. She read the newspapers in detail, and once, at the time of a pit-disaster, the causes of which at first seemed unclear, she consulted all the documentation in the local lending library on the subject of coal mining and eventually posted off a heavy envelope to the National Coal Board giving her views as to the probable causes. This habit of getting involved with whatever she felt strongly about pleased us a lot and we did all we could to encourage it.

Early in her sixteenth year disturbing things began to happen, though they were apparent trivialities to start with. I noticed Cheryl becoming more and more subdued. The word sulky would even have come to mind if I had not known that such an attitude was quite foreign to her nature. This was the time of the Easter holidays, yet Cheryl spent hours alone in her room. She would start playing a record and then switch off half-way through. She read, but I found half a dozen open books lying around the room as though thrown impatiently aside. She began to do something she had never done before. She could abruptly leave the house without a word to me, slamming the door behind her. When she returned she went straight to her room. She offered no explanation of her absences of an hour or so each time, and I never asked her any questions.

Only when I had fully grasped the nature of this new mood did I reflect on the fact that it had begun three or four weeks earlier and had grown so gradually as not to attract any particular attention at first. Thinking further back I was even more puzzled when I recalled that in the weeks previous to this depression or whatever it was, Cheryl had been at the peak of her form – almost excited, permanently indefatigable. Sometimes, returning from her coffee-bar discotheque sorties in the evening, it had been impossible to get her to bed. She would insist on sitting up with us in the lounge, or if we had gone to bed to read late, she would sit on the bed and hold forth on her theories about whatever was intriguing her at the moment. She was flushed with excitement and one felt that inside she was burning with suppressed energy. It was nothing to alarm us. This was simply Cheryl being herself, though intensely so. On reflection this later moodiness was perhaps a natural reaction of tiredness, Cheryl was growing fast. But such a swing between two extremes in such a short period worried me a little and I asked Alan to have a talk with her and see whether perhaps she should not be sent to one of his colleagues for a proper check-up. He felt it was not necessary. This was just one of those periods of adolescence when a child becomes abnormally sensitive and minor disappointments, a quarrel or a broken friendship, can seem like the end of the world. It might do more harm than good to make too much of it. He put her on a course of vitamins. Then, as suddenly as it had descended, the mood of dejection lifted, and Cheryl was back again to normal. A few days later she was back in her super-buoyant spirits and at moments it seemed as though she saw and felt everything almost double life-size. I was still worried in an indefinable way, though this second wave of exultation – it was nothing less – brought only cheerfulness and affection back into the home. I decided that for a while it would be necessary to accept this alternation of moods, in gradually decreasing degrees, until the old balance was restored. This was simply, as Alan said, a development stage.

One day I was looking through her desk in her bedroom for a small address book I had loaned her when I lifted up a blank and seemingly empty envelope. A half dozen flat, circular pills – pale blue in colour – fell onto the desk. Across its centre each pill had a thin crevice, to break it in half. I shook the envelope to see if there were any more and a small folded piece of paper fell out. On it, in Cheryl's hand, was written in column form the days of the week and against each day, a figure, mostly twos and threes. Against the Friday was a five, the Saturday, three and on Sunday, one. On the previous Sunday she had been to the cinema with us.

At the bottom of the column was written 'Six left, must keep till Friday'. My hands were trembling as I swept the little pills together and put them, with the piece of paper, back in the envelope. It seemed I lived an age of anguish until Alan was back from his visits and I could tell him of my find. 'They are some kind of pep pills, I should say,' he finally commented. 'Judging by the taste and texture, amphymetrine.' We decided to put the envelope and the pills back where I had found them and to tell Cheryl how worried we were about her and ask her to tell us her troubles so that we could help. That evening at the table we told her, as gently as possible, that we were sure something must be troubling her. Would she let us help her by telling us what it was? There was no response, no contact. Cheryl flushed at first, and then vigorously shaking her head, said, 'There's nothing – nothing.' She refused to say any more. Then we told her. She received the news of my find with a flood of tears and inconsolable sobbing. But we had never been a family for recriminations and Cheryl knew she had nothing to fear.

When she had overcome her tears, she told me, 'I took them because the others did. You know how it is, if you don't do the same as the rest, you're an outsider. The others took them because one of the boys dared them to. And when we had, it didn't seem bad at all. They weren't important to us. They didn't seem to do anything very much. There's this man, I don't know his name, but he's a Londoner, he comes to the discotheque and sells them to one of our group and we all pool in together and buy a whole box. Separately they cost sixpence each. All they seem to do, perhaps, is to make our conversations – our discussions – a bit more exciting. And the music sounds better. But you could really hardly notice much difference. I felt in the beginning as though we just *had* to get more excited simply because we knew we had taken a pill or two, while in fact we *always* got terribly excited anyhow – arguing all together. I often felt that we used to get just as excited before the pills came.'

We talked with her late that night. I think the three of us felt relieved that we could get this thing in perspective. It was the first occasion for a long time that we had been able to talk to Cheryl normally without feeling baffled or frustrated by either of her two extreme moods, withdrawal or exhilaration.

It was later that Alan told me he had had the impression of having missed small sums from his surgery cash box for more than the past month. He had been perplexed but decided that he had miscalculated. He was never very good at counting anyway.

When Cheryl had been able to get the pills, she had been using an average of about fifteen a week. The 'let down' when she had not obtained her supply explained her depression and tiredness. Alan and I realized that the situation was bad enough, but not dangerous beyond recall. It could happen to any curious-minded child to experiment when faced by the challenge of conforming with a group of her own age. To us the God-given miracle was that we had found out so soon, and been able to discuss the situation with Cheryl without damage to her confidence and affection. It was an adolescent problem that we had caught in time.

Alan decided not to go to the police because the inevitable inquiries which would follow would have done more harm to Cheryl than otherwise. Instead he called on the Italian discotheque-owner Tino and warned him that the next time he had reason even to suspect that drugs were being peddled on his premises he would call in the police. Tino protested his absolute ignorance and promised that he would see that nothing of the kind could happen again.

We decided to talk to Bryan Tyler, quite casually – without telling him what we had discovered – simply to say that we were a little worried by Cheryl's odd moods and ask him if he could give us any explanation. He said he had no idea. We cut down Cheryl's visits to Tino's to once a week and were relieved to find that in the following weeks there were no especial highs or lows in Cheryl's moods. She had become herself again. The subject of the blue pills was never touched upon. There was no sign of addiction. It seemed as though our lives could be resumed with as much happiness as before – but more vigilance. Alan and I agreed that we had been a little too ambitious for Cheryl. We had misread the signs of her physical and intellectual development, and in the thoughtless pleasure of seeing her grow we had seen and encouraged too much the young woman while neglecting the child who was still there.

There was one noticeable change, and we took it as a good one. The composition of her group of school friends who visited her and had late tea parties at the house once a week changed. After the first party following the pill incident Bryan and his sister Jane came no more. They called once, later, very briefly, explaining that they had both begun attending night classes and it was extremely difficult to find free evenings. Bryan seemed sad and subdued and much more shy than usual and Cheryl ignored him completely. I felt that the poor boy had been frightened by the tactless questioning to which Alan and I had submitted him. Cheryl had acquired a new 'tolerable' boy, who too was always accompanied by his sister.

Within a month of Cheryl's resumption of her former normal spirits, when the danger seemed passed and blue pills like part of a bad dream, her group of friends had changed entirely except for one girl.

Then came the night when Cheryl failed to return home. She had told us that she would be spending the evening at the home of a school friend. We phoned a little before midnight and they told us that Cheryl had not been there at all that evening. We did all the necessary things, phoning around to friends and to Tino's and eventually telling the police and asking the local press to publish a photograph and description of her.

Two days later she was brought home in a police car. They had found her wandering in the early morning in the streets of Birmingham, dazed, only half coherent, penniless. Alan called in a fellow doctor, a close friend, who concluded that she was suffering from shock, perhaps caused by drugs but equally possibly due to some other kind of traumatic experience. She had no injuries, she had not been assaulted, she was still a virgin.

For two days she remained quite calm, exhausted and seemingly lost in a reverie from which nothing we said could arouse her. We avoided questions as much as possible – in any case she would not answer – except the first time, when I asked her where she had been and she replied, 'A long way – further than possible. I saw all the world, where I was.' It was an eerie, nightmarish statement that to me seemed infinitely sinister as well. Yet there was no trace of fear or regret. She spoke distantly, as though half dreaming. The doctor said that physically she was in good health, and apart from her exhaustion she suffered a little from anaemia. We were not to trouble her with questions but to let her return to as normal a life as possible as soon as she regained her ordinary composure.

Alan and I both felt sick with dismay, not simply at not knowing what had happened, but with a dreadful prescience of what could or might happen next. What were we fighting? How could we defend our child without knowing just what we were up against? Our complete ignorance of the enemy – intangible and diabolic, outside our reach because unknown – left us with a sense of helplessness. There was nothing to do but wait, hope and pray perhaps.

Within ten days of Cheryl's return she was up and about the house, subdued, tired, yet once more with occasional flickers of the old fire of enthusiasm, as though the embers were slowly reviving. Again, no word was spoken of her experience. Her doctor, Alan's friend, said he believed she had no recollection of what had happened to her. He advised against consulting a psychiatrist until we saw the stage at which Cheryl's return to normal seemed to stabilize. Within three weeks she seemed to be herself again, at least, a quieter version of her old self. All the same qualities of enthusiasm, interest, warmth of heart were there, but as though they had been scaled down so that they never overflowed with the same abandon as before. There were moments now of abstraction, when Cheryl, without being either depressed or sulky – or even unhappy – seemed lost in daydreams of some world of her own. Anyone who had never known her before would have accepted her as a normal and healthy young girl. Only her occasional bursts of demonstrative affection towards her father and me were perhaps more than customary for the average English child, though they had always been natural for Cheryl.

This time there was no return to Tino's. One or two of her friends called to see her, but on individual visits. In various forms, most no doubt over-dramatized and well embellished, the story of her disappearance and return by the police had circulated in the district and either her school friends themselves or their parents felt that association with Cheryl should be avoided or at least suspended until she showed that she had really returned to her old normality and that the incident was really isolated and exceptional. We were discussing the possibility of her return to school – the idea of psychoanalytical treatment was abandoned – when Cheryl disappeared again.

She left the house this time so quietly that I did not hear her go. It was in the middle of an afternoon. I went up to her room to call her for tea. I found only a sheet of paper on her desk. It read, 'Please don't worry, Mummy and Daddy. I know what I'm doing. I've got to go and keep an appointment. I swore I would, but I'll be back very soon. I love you. Cheryl.' The paper was placed on top of a heavy volume she had taken out of the local lending library a week before and over which she had pored for hours every day. It was entitled *Witchcraft in Mediaeval Britain*.

They brought her back to the local general hospital in an ambulance four days later. She could not walk or speak, although she was fully conscious. She had been bestially raped and ill-treated. All over her body were hundreds of tiny cuts, no more than skin deep, each about three quarters to one inch long. They were not scratches but clean-cut incisions as though made with a razor. We did not know it then, but the survivor (I prefer to use his proper name as little as possible) had already begun the final stages of his work.

You who are reading these words now, police, lawyers, no doubt psychiatrists as well, all of you who may be concerned with the events which will finally bring my story to its conclusion, may wonder why I need to torture myself by writing down these details – I almost added – of what happened so long ago. I despise that qualification of events. 'So long ago—' I have never been able to classify the importance of events in which I was involved by the time elapsed since they occurred, and it is one of the weaknesses of human morality and courage that such a qualification should almost always be introduced to forgive, or to extenuate or soften something which happened in the past. To me, the simple passage of years, time, heals nothing. Those red tracings which enmeshed Cheryl's body like some fine web of gore, are still as real, as agonizing and as wicked as they were ten years ago, as they will be ten years on. I can still see them as I could then. Now, as then, I can see her face, unscarred but as grey and immobile as a mask of clay. Her mouth moved a fraction as she tried to speak and she attempted to draw one bandaged hand from beneath the blankets to touch me and reassure me. That – all that and more – is just a series of words on a page to you who read it now. But I beg you to try – close your eyes for an instant and try – and *see* what I am describing and believe that it happened to the person dearest to you, and then realize that the monster responsible is at your mercy, after years during which you have only lived to make him pay the price. Is there, then, anything remarkable about my resolution and perseverance to inflict death and suffering in return?

I have always felt that until the survivor has paid in pain and extinction for what he did – and I have still only recounted a fraction of it – Cheryl's own suffering will never end. I am sure that from the moment he is no more a survivor I shall never again recall visually – as I do now – Cheryl in all her fear and pain. With his extinction Cheryl's suffering will be replaced forever by the reality of her joy and beauty. The pain and the death of evil will have effaced the pain and the death of innocence. With such conviction, can anyone believe that I am not doing what is right and inevitable?

I have met in Brockley so far only one individual who seems to have, momentarily, the courage to perceive and admit the horror and futility of this place. He is the young doctor Peter Bligh. He spoke yesterday of 'the horror of these people', and 'the unbelievable wretchedness they have sown around them'. Admittedly, once he has spoken he is ashamed at having allowed himself to speak so cynically. But I too feel deeply depressed at the futility of this institution and of the lives of most of those in it – staff as well as patients.

The patients – there are certainly exceptions for whom there may remain hopes of contributing creative joy to life – but most of them, from what I have already learned, have nothing to offer the world and might just as well be out of it. They came from the mould chipped, cracked or deformed and their maker should have broken them on a heap of rejects. They say life is sacred and I believe and feel that to be true. That is why real lives, full, complete lives should be protected against the destructive rottenness of half-lives. Everything – every chance to bloom and survive and propagate – should be given to those capable of complete fulfilment. The others, the pain-givers, the half-lives, should be eliminated and their afflictions prevented from infecting the world. I believe that a few of those here are more than half-lives. They are the victims of society, who have broken down under more than reasonable strain. They are ill and will be restored. Two of this kind I have met already and they have both moved me profoundly. One is Annie McBride, who was the slave-wife of a maniac-sadist, a pervert whose practices in the seduction and murder of small children drove Annie out of her mind. She might have died, like Cheryl did. Or Cheryl might have survived, as Annie did, and would have merited saving, as Annie does. The other is called May Saunders, an orphanage-bred girl like myself, who stole four children, of which two died of neglect. May's only fault was this love and urge to possess and protect a child. Thanks to her orphanage upbringing this suppressed natural instinct had not been fitted properly into her scheme of life. If she had not been afraid of men in her orphanage, then her need to cherish would have first been satisfied by a man, and then by their own children. The confusion of May's mind is already completely untangled and her search for love seems capable of taking a more balanced and social form. Very soon I believe she too will be able to contribute the qualities of motherhood to the world. But will the world let her? I shall do all I can to contribute towards her release, but it will be very difficult. At the time of her committal here, after her trial, the newspapers called her 'The Pavement Monster' because it was on the crowded pavements of city shopping centres that she stole children from their perambulators. There would be strong popular opposition to her release. But I hope that I may live to bring it about. My feelings for these two women, Annie McBride and especially May Saunders, are very important to me. There has always been a risk that in living a life completely dedicated to killing, my love and compassion might dry up and I should cease to be a complete person – just a solitary widow motivated by a secret hate. But all through the professional life which I have been obliged to adopt as my cover, on my way to the survivor, I have had to help patch up broken lives and I have never allowed a moment to elapse without being personally involved in sincere emotions for those who have needed my help – so long as it has never diverted me one step from my path to the survivor.

I have always seen my need to stay a complete person – with a capacity for tenderness, capable of new love and affection – as a duty to Cheryl. When it is all over and we shall be re-united, I want still to be the person who was her mother.

8

Robert Welles's favourite henchman among his fellow 'C' category inmates – to whom he referred aloofly as 'my colleagues' – was a ratty little man, David Evans, former second officer in the Merchant Navy, whose habit of setting fire to his cargoes in mid-ocean had led to the loss of half a dozen lives and two ships before he was detected. His defence was that he had never intended to set his ships on fire. He was trying to smoke out 'niggers' whom he believed had stowed away in order to murder him. Evans was only five foot three inches tall. His first two wives had chosen other partners during his voyages. His only child, a boy of seven, had died of meningitis during one of these episodes. He had three times failed his First Officer's ticket. His persecution mania was not without a certain logic, and could have inspired more sympathy if it had not been expressed in such an incendiary form by such an unsavoury individual. After five years at Brockley he was practically as sane as he ever would be and just as malicious as he had always been. He had a permanent chip on his shoulder; he was viciously racist; he had the instincts of a bully with the nature of a coward, and an overwhelming lack of confidence in himself. This last characteristic was the principle reason for the mutual attachment between him and Robert Welles. Evans needed a 'leader', and Welles needed just such people as Evans to reassure himself that by his class, culture and intellect, he was a superior being. Welles had the ideal character for turning valets into *Gauleiters*. His large bed-sitting room, the best in

'C' Wing, was on a corner of the first floor with a window looking due north, and another west onto the main rear courtyard. Neither of these views was elegant but they were the best available behind the main hall building. The north window looked onto the hen-houses and poultry runs two hundred yards away. To the north east could be seen, at the same distance, the piggery – ten large sties, half of them open, half roofed, surrounded by a low white-washed wall. To the west and almost in the centre of the kitchen gardens was the large ancient barn with the conservatory posed against its southern end; all this was 'the gardening unit' or 'gardening block'.

Beyond this again was a large orchard of pear, apple and cherry trees, separated by a tall privet hedge from the three acres of kitchen gardens. Looking directly north Welles could see, beyond the poultry-runs, four hundred yards of uncropped grass and tall weeds, with a few very old and decrepit apple trees merging into a heavily wooded and overgrown strip a hundred yards deep which ran all along the northern edge of the park. A few yards beyond this, but not visible from the hall, was the fifteen foot, smooth stone wall, the boundary of the north end of the park. It was topped with glass chips. This, running out from each side of the front lodge gates, enclosed the whole of the Brockley Old Hall park. Immediately in front of his west window, Welles looked across the rear courtyard onto the boiler house with its yellow brick chimney and the main kitchens and dining-hall, which were in the centre of what had been the old stableyard. Beyond these was 'A' Wing, the west wing of the main hall, at the rear of which was the redbrick building containing the laundry, carpenter's shop and metal workshop. So for the trouble of walking a few paces, from one window to the other, Welles had a wide picture of the comings and goings in the daily life of SP9. And he made the best of it. Now he lounged on the chintz-cushioned window-seat of the north window, Evans half facing him from the east window seat.

'That's her, alright.' Welles peered across to the window behind Evans as three figures left the main doors of the kitchen and mess-hall block, and began to walk across to the carpentry and metal-work building. The two men on the first floor of 'C' Wing watched in silence as the party disappeared into the carpenter's shop. Welles spoke first. 'I saw her go by yesterday. She looks a bit leathery.'

There was a sneer in Evans's sing-song Welsh-accented reply. 'This story about her old man being a Governor of India or what have you. They all say that when they're half niggers. That skinny face and a tan like that – she's an Anglo-Indian all right. You want to watch it. They're a two-faced bunch of bastards the Anglo-Indians. I had a chief steward once—'

Welles cut him short impatiently. 'All right Dave, drop it this time. Do you want to get out of here or don't you?'

The little man's animal face, dark eyes too close together, mouth thin and weak, twisted into a fawning grin of assent. Welles went on, 'Well, you know there are only two ways out and it would be a pity to have to go over the wall. I saw my father's lawyer yesterday. Things are not going very well about my release. But if I get out, you can count on me to do everything to get you out too. You'll be the first president of Welsh Wales after all, Davy *bach*. So long as you play it right. But Doc Robertson has put in an unfavourable report on my lawyer's special application. Now we shall apply for a special tribunal. This Miss Lewis could be an important witness in my favour – if I get on with her. That's where you come in. I want you to be really nice with her – especially when you talk to her about me. I'd like her to think of you as a real inside tipster for "C" Wing – that way, you can feed her whatever we want. So – be nice, Dave boy. Drop the nigger business and try and talk like an educated man. You don't fail first officer three times without picking up a *bit* of culture, do you?'

An expression of sinister bashfulness flickered across the little man's face and Welles did not wait for any other answer.

'All right then, be sweet. Be the nice, big, bluff sailor-man.' Welles ended his words with a huge roll of belly-laughter.

There was a knock at the door and almost immediately it swung brusquely open. A large red-faced middle-aged man stood on the threshhold with an air of hesitation that seemed to combine caution with good manners. He peered in hesitantly.

'Come in, your majesty,' said Welles, standing up. 'How is your utmost imperial highness today?' The visitor, who had a rather pleasant expression of wide-eyed simplicity and friendliness, half raised his right hand in a gesture of acknowledgement and smiled timidly. 'No titles, *please*,' he said. 'You know that's all over now Mr Welles, but thank you all the same. I'm very well as a matter of fact.' He walked into the room with a certain slow dignity as he spoke. 'I just dropped in to tell you that the new woman, the Indian or whatever she is, is going the rounds again. Maybe she'll come and see us today.' He sat down. 'I was in the gardening place half an hour ago and she came in and said hello. She said the soil here's too acid for tomatoes. She's rather nice.'

'Did she ask you what you were here for?'

Welles was the only individual in SP9 – patient or staff – who could joke with Herbert Strang about the particular weakness for which he had been confined.

Strang had lived for twenty years, from the age of fifteen to thirty-five, secretly convinced that he was the king of the world. The conviction was quite a harmless one, for he never mentioned it to anyone, until he decided at the age of thirty-five that he was being made to wait too long for public acknowledgement and decided to call attention to his rights. In a wild twenty-four hour whirl he appropriated whatever of his 'subject's' property he fancied, mainly clothes and jewellery, set fire to whatever he disapproved of – mostly petrol pumps, newspaper shops and libraries and electrical goods stores, and violently assaulted anyone who opposed him, to cries of 'Le Roy le veult' – mediaeval French for 'It is the king's wish'. He had passed his first three years at Brockley in a state of imperious and frenetic violence, but for the past four years he had lived in a state of docile resignation, still convinced that he *had* been king of the world, but accepting that after having been deposed and exiled by his enemies he was now being trained to rejoin his wife and three children and take his place as a private citizen. He was a printer by trade and up to the time that his impatience for recognition got the better of him, a man of excellent reputation and a likeable character.

'As a matter of fact, my dear old king,' said Robert Welles smoothly, 'we were just saying, Dave and I, that she looks rather a pleasant old girl and may be a very agreeable addition to this place. Did she give any hint of what she is supposed to do here?'

'No, she just said she had joined the staff and was looking

forward to getting to know all the patients.' The door opened again, but this time with no hesitation or formality. The newcomer was Joe Norton, the same thick-set young man they had seen a few minutes earlier escorting Miss Lewis into the carpenter's shop. He was good looking in a rakish, craggy way, with tight curly black hair extending in long, fuzzy sideboards almost covering his ears. He wore a collar and tie, black denim jacket and dark well-pressed trousers. His short, clipped Cockney accent conveyed an impression of cheery good humour.

'Mornin' chums, 'ows tricks?' He swaggered across the room and sat heavily down on the window seat beside Welles. The others murmured uneasy greetings and lapsed into a shifty silence. Welles offered him a cigarette and asked, 'What's new, Joe?' Norton answered with a shrug of his shoulders and silence descended again. David Evans, trying to make his departure seem casual, yawned, rose from his window seat, slapped Joe Norton on one shoulder as he passed. 'Well, I'm off,' he said, and winked at Strang. 'There's a jug of tea ready in the day-room. Come on Herbert, let's go down and get some.'

They left together, clearly with a sense of relief, and their carefully nonchalant departure ended the atmosphere of restraint between the two remaining.

'They're alright,' said Welles, 'they're a hundred per cent. And they know when to go.' He paused. 'What's up?'

'Just wanted to tip you off, Mr Welles. The new woman, Miss Margaret Lewis, she's coming round to visit "C" Wing after lunch this afternoon. She'll be here about two-thirty. Just thought you might like to know.'

'OK.' Welles nodded. 'Anything else?'

The other reflected, eyebrows raised for a moment. 'Nope, not special. Of course you know the old girl's well in everywhere. They all go for 'er in a big way – right from the colonel on down. Doc Robertson too. My little birdie friend tells me she's got contacts in the Ministries as well, direct and good.'

Norton's 'little birdie' was the colonel's secretary, Rosie Fletcher. Joe Norton was the only man who had ever looked at her as though he felt she might be a desirable woman. He was the only man, she felt, who had ever undressed her with a look. Actually at that moment he had been thinking out his bets for

99

the following Saturday's football pools and his eyes, though diverted roughly at the level of her navel, had been focussed on nothing more than the probability of an Everton–West Ham away draw. But that moment, two years ago, had changed Rosie's life and hopes. Rosie was a scraggy blonde, a spinster on the wrong side of thirty-five, who stubbornly tried, and failed, to keep her looks a match for her waning hopes. Ever since that day when she had misread the glazed look in Norton's eyes, she had quadrupled the thickness of the foam-padding in her brassieres and subscribed to a woman's magazine specializing in underwear. A light squeeze on the elbow, a brushing caress on one shoulder, or a tap on the buttock at discreet hip-level, were all the rare considerations she received from Norton. But they were enough to send her, from time to time, into dizzy moments of heart-pounding. Returning each night to the three-roomed flat she shared in the village with her mother, she hurried down the avenue of Brockley Hall and the lane to the village in the hopeful dread that the shadows might include one cast by Joe Norton, who would – who would— There never was such a shadow, but she became more and more enslaved by her meagre ration of furtive and casual touches, which were measured in the time she could keep talking to Joe and hold him in her office. She was not really conscious of giving him information and she had no idea that he regarded it as more than private gossip between them. But it caused him to hang around, and while he did so there was always the chance that she would feel a hand smoothing her bony shoulder, or thick fingers sensuously pinching a little fold of skin at her elbow through her blouse or the back of a hairy hand brushing against her hip.

Joe Norton, as right hand man of administrative superintendent Crow, although he only held the rank of a grade two clerk, had considerable authority in the hospital, as well as complete freedom of movement. Information to Welles was power, and in the first year of Norton's work at the hospital Welles had become aware of the fact that his potential value was to be measured in the combination of his weakness of character, his venality, his access to the sources of authority. Welles had made his advances with suitable discretion and it had not taken long for the weakness of one to recognize and salute like an ally the evil of the other. Now, from time to time, an average of once a month on a Saturday off, Norton would take a drink in a small, inconspicuous pub at Berkhampton, twelve miles from Brockley. There, a shifty little solicitor's clerk, who had no clear idea of what he was doing, would regularly accept a half of bitter from Norton and at the end of some painfully barren exchanges on the beer and the football pools, would pass him a sealed envelope containing sometimes ten, sometimes fifteen pound notes. Thus Norton had become almost dependent on Welles for the little extra reward that sweetened life, just as Rosie had become dependent on Norton. Welles's instinct for all that was weak and venal had been faultless in its perception of Norton and though the full truth about the man would not have surprised him, he might have found it rather disquieting in the circumstances.

Joe Norton's real name was Alfred Pyke. He had begun his adolescent life as a borstal boy, for repeated petty crime and violence. From borstal he had gone to prison, for more subtle forms of larceny – usually achieved through glib talk and a quick eye. While working, in one of his periods of liberty, as a clerk in a Berkhampsted warehouse – a job which he had taken with a view to examining the possibilities for future peculation – he had answered an advertisement for a job as a grade two clerk at SP9. During his six months at the warehouse, mainly due to his need to attract no attention, he had worked hard and well and was thought of as a serious and reliable young man. A genuine recommendation to this effect – plus the fact that there were no other applicants – had got him his job at Brockley. Now, three years later, with his job as canteen manager and his private arrangements from time to time with patients and their visiting relatives, notably Welles, he was doing very nicely, a firm fixture in the routine of the hospital, considered reliable and responsible by the administrative staff because he was always cheerful and ready to take on extra work whenever he was asked. He was not liked or trusted by the medical staff because he was too popular and too familiar with some of the patients. There was a vague feeling among some of the doctors that Norton made friends more easily with the least trustworthy and more incalculable of the 'B' and 'C' Wing patients. Welles himself was certain that Norton was making other side profits by smuggling in forbidden goods but he was never sure what they were. He put the question directly to him once and Norton pretended not to understand. But he gave Welles a clue a few weeks later when he produced a small medicine bottle full of purple heart-shaped pills. He wanted two shillings a pill. Welles, who had never in his life drunk, smoked or drugged, told him, 'Take those out of my room at once. If I ever see you with anything like that again near me – you'll be out of a job.' Norton never offered Welles anything again except the canteen wares that had been ordered and paid for, and his steady flow of hospital gossip, extracts from official correspondence, and more rarely, extracts from medical progress reports on patients, including those on Welles himself. When the two men were alone together their relationship stayed practically on a master and servant level. Most of the other 'C' inmates sensed that some kind of 'arrangement' existed between Welles and Norton and they had learned that when the two were together it was best to leave them alone.

By two-thirty Welles had gathered his closest cronies in his room and a pot of instant coffee was ready for serving in honour of Miss Lewis. In addition to Welles himself, 'Evans the Ship' – one of Welles's sardonic titles for the little Welshman – and 'King' Strang, there were five others. The rest of the twenty-five 'C' Wing patients were dispersed, at work-shop classes and in the gardens. The other five in the room looked no less normal than one might have found gathered at midday in any saloon bar. The oldest among them and the most likely to attract attention, by a certain air of distinction and authority, was Daniel Morley, a forty-nine year old company director who had been sent to Brockley from a London prison where he was serving a twelve year sentence for indecent assaults on children, mostly, but not all, girls. The prison psychiatrist had decided that Morley would benefit more by treatment than by punishment. He was considered at Brockley as the most balanced and reliable of all the patients, one of the fairly simple 'depressives'. He had been a successful company director at the age of forty, living in apparent happiness and affluence with his wife and three children. His assaults on children were carried out with gentleness and discretion, with the result that his activities were not discovered by the police for a long time. When he was first apprehended, his lawyer asked for twenty-two other cases (with which he was not officially charged, but for which he admitted guilt) to be taken into consideration in his sentence. He was heavily fined and put on three years' probation, on condition that he underwent psychiatric outpatient treatment. A year later he was arrested again and fined more heavily on condition that he took his treatment in an approved mental home, which he did for a year. Three years later, with an almost interminable list of complaints against him from all over the country, he was sentenced to twelve years in prison. His family had left him, his company was liquidated by bankruptcy and the only person in the world with any hope or time for him was the prison psychiatrist who had sent him to SP9. He was one of the few patients at Brockley who knew, understood and felt completely the crushing weight of his shame. Though he endured his psychiatric treatment, under the general surveillance of Doctor Robertson, with patient docility and did his best to collaborate, he had no faith in it. Two months earlier, prompted by a newspaper paragraph about a solution proposed by a German, who like him was a compulsive violator of children, he had forwarded through Colonel Barthropp a confidential request to the Ministry for castration. There was still no reply.

Morley's closest associate – friend was hardly the word – was Albert Mikes, also part of the Welles clique, a mild little man with a wispy ginger moustache, a permanently aggrieved expression in his watery blue eyes behind double-thickness, steel-rimmed spectacles. Mikes was thirty-two, once a prosperous garage owner who had made the mistake of marrying an attractive strumpet who taunted him with having made him a cuckold with everyone in sight. Mikes poisoned her with cyanide and might have got away with a reasonable prison sentence if he had not extended his vengeance to his family-in-law, using a shotgun. His father and mother-in-law and another of their daughters, as well as her child of six, who happened to be there, were all blasted to death. His trial ended with his indefinite commital to SP9 on the grounds that he was unfit to stand trial. Claud Simmons, a willowy, fragile youth, a vacuous,

nondescript university failure had finally sought to draw attention to himself by littering public parks and playgrounds with
poisoned sweets and writing anonymous letters to the press
warning of 'mass exterminations by the Avenger'. His warn-
ings had perhaps prevented many more lives being lost, but his
score in deaths was three children and seven dogs.

Roger Thame, son of a prosperous farmer, had ruined his
father as well as a number of neighbours by burning barns and
outhouses, stock sheds and stacks, because he said that one day
he became possessed by the desire for the excitement he had
felt as a little boy when his father burned his stubble and
called it 'setting fire to the fields'. Roger had suffered a kind of
return to childhood and at Brockley was growing up for the
second time.

Noah Sims, a prayerful, devout young Quaker, had been
brought up by his mother, who was widowed at twenty.
Twenty years later she had taken a lover and Sims had found
them together in bed. He had shot them and burned down the
house over their bodies.

These five were, with Evans and the king, the inner circle of
Welles's coterie. The five were distinguished by the fact that
their aberrations had applied to particular circumstances, in
the past, and so far as could be seen in the surroundings of a
special hospital they were about as sane as anyone in the world
outside. The only reason they were still held under their original court committal orders was the doubt whether they would
or would not revert to their original violent or unsocial reactions in other situations, once they were returned to normal
life. This was something which, under the artificial conditions
of an institution, it was always hard to estimate. Misjudgement
would result in the usual press reaction, challenging the policy
of setting dangerous lunatics at large, always a question bad
for the political health of party-appointed Ministers.
Responsibility for the release of such patients was therefore
widely spread, so that if things went wrong afterwards, as they
sometimes did, there could be little blame left for those at the
top. This dispersal of responsibility meant that a wide un-
animity of opinion was needed in favour of release. All these
factors governing the main objective of SP9 – cure and release
– often created a complex of frustration in the staffs which was

echoed in the minds of the more perceptive or informed patients. All around and among them they saw and felt an effort and a will for their cure and release. Yet somewhere higher up in the remoter spheres of the powers governing their lives they felt there were other elements operating by standards which no efforts of their own, no simple human considerations, could affect.

The advent of Miss Lewis with the power of independent recommendation seemed to offer a new hope for individual claims to be heard unobscured by the fixed prejudices and remote provisos of a ministry. It was almost as if they had sensed the terms of the colonel's remark to his executive staff: 'It will rather seem to the patients as though she is more on their side than on ours.' Indeed it did seem so. Since her arrival the grapevine had not missed a whisper of her words or movements and everything seemed to confirm that she represented an unorthodox element, something 'worth a try'. No one was going to be very disappointed if she failed to live up to their meagre hopes. Anyone who had reached a special hospital knew that hopes were just for dreaming.

As they waited in Welles's room, the instant coffee bubbling in an aluminium heater attached to a wall-plug in the corridor – they were forbidden inside the rooms, but could be used from the corridor with an extension – there was little conversation. Against the wall on an elegant side-table was a row of coffee cups bought from Joe Norton's canteen selection. Welles was the only one present who was trying to give the impression that he was not thinking of what he could get out of the new contact. He was trying to explain to Daniel Morley one of his own particular theories, to the effect that in modern times Napoleon Bonaparte would – unjustly – have spent his life locked up in a special hospital.

'And so would Hitler,' said Morley.

'Nonsense,' replied Welles. 'Hitler would have locked the world up in a special hospital. That's what he tried to do anyway. And he was right. Special hospitals should be reserved for the middle-class sane, the balanced bourgeoisie.'

'Well in that case,' countered Morley who sounded bored, 'why did Hitler fail to do it?'

'He was outnumbered by all the raving sane,' said Welles, with a sneer.

'I'll bet you wouldn't say that in front of your psychiatrist.'

Welles smirked in mock modesty, eyelids fluttering. 'I'm not *that* crazy,' he said.

The conversation was interrupted by Joe Norton who peered into the room and announced in a stage whisper, 'She's down in the day-room for the moment. I'll be bringing her in here in five minutes.'

'Let's get on with the coffee,' said Welles, moving across to the side-table. Picking up the aluminium pot he began to pour. 'After all, we didn't send her a gilt-edged invitation, with the exact hour of the reception. She might as well see that we live our own lives here just like they did at the Vice-Regal Lodge.' This last remark was lost on his guests who had long since grown accustomed to his references intended to demonstrate his own superiority of class and education.

They all stood up clumsily when Joe Norton eventually brought Miss Lewis into the room. Normally no one stood up for any of the women at Brockley, but Miss Lewis's well-tailored tweed suits and sober but smart twin sets, her cheerful friendliness combined with her confident air of authority set her far apart from any of the other women staff, or visitors. There was no sense of an institution about her, no grey odour of 'the service'. She was different because she was refreshing and incalculable. As most patients remarked with satisfaction, 'a lady'.

Joe Norton made the introductions in a way which at first startled the gathering, and then gave each member in turn a gratifying inner glow. Norton, whose work of surveillance and transmission of staff orders took him on continual rounds of the hospital, was, by some tacit understanding between the two of them, becoming a regular escort for Miss Lewis and she had briefed him on the kind of introduction she wanted when she met patients for the first time.

'Mr Welles – Mr *Robert* Welles,' said Norton with what he considered a worldly flourish, '– er – a university stoodent. Mr Welles is an expert on special 'ospitals and 'as passed 'is degree in literature 'ere and is now passing another on the Law.' It was not usual to shake hands on meeting patients, but the atmosphere and surroundings on this occasion prompted it. Norton moved on.

'Mr Daniel Morley. Mr Morley's a, er, a business man.'
He reddened slightly as he just managed in time to prevent himself adding – 'detached from Wormwood Scrubs'.

However much some members of the staff, to some extent the colonel and certainly matron, raised their brows at this kind of approach, it was in itself a sort of therapy which worked wonders with most patients, whose pleasure was more than momentary at being thought of as people in their own right, and not simply as 'cases'. Joe Norton excused himself as soon as the introductions were completed. He knew most of the patients disliked and mistrusted him and he felt, indeed appeared, rather incongruous at times in his role of equal and escort to the probably redoubtable Miss Lewis. Welles, as seemed natural, took over the direction of the conversation, handing Miss Lewis her cup of coffee – 'One lump or two, dear lady?' – with the kind of elegant ease which he felt set him above his fellows. He was fairly tall and the confinement and his comparatively easy mode of life, which had been his lot from an age when most young men develop to a mature and active life, had left him paunchy and flabby. His sallow, oval face, with wide prominent eyes, a sensuous, weak mouth and his longish, wavy fair hair, carefully brushed and combed, gave him the air of an Edwardian dandy. This was accentuated by the fact that he wore for the occasion a bottle-green velvet smoking jacket and a ruffled, tieless shirt. Yet despite his suave manners, the accent of polished sweetness, he conveyed to the minds of all those who met him the impression of a restrained capacity for causing pain. However unanalytical one might be, he left an uneasy impression of having been in contact with something malignant.

He began by asking Miss Lewis if it were true that patients to be released to normal life would have to pass a period in criminal probationary hostels.

It was true, said Miss Lewis. Well, did she think it was fair? Was it within the spirit of the Mental Health Act of 1959? There was absolute silence for several moments as the group in the room were introduced for their first time to one of Miss Lewis's lengthy, studied pauses for reflection. It was an embarrassing habit until one became used to it. Eventually she said, 'I don't think it's unfair. The object of special hospitals is

to cure people and get them back to useful life. If this policy is
to be intensified and the discharges from hospitals speeded up –
which is in the interests of the patients – then every available
channel towards rehabilitation must be used.'

There was some affirmative nodding of heads in the group,
which was pressing more closely around her and Welles. It was
true that her answer was given with something of the smooth
speciousness of a Ministerial minute, but it was no more to
Welles's taste for that.

'But is it fair that in the process of speeding up discharges
from special hospitals because they're inadequate in every
sense of the word, we – guilty of nothing more than having
been mentally ill in various ways and for varying periods –
should be tainted by the association with convicted criminals
before we are declared sane and free?'

Now the nods of the listeners were on his side and the close
circle of faces turned to Miss Lewis. She looked round at them,
her eyes slowly travelling the half circle of expectant faces.

There was a more intimate, relaxed note in her voice as she
replied this time and her smile was one of friendly confidence.

'You who are in a high category of understanding and well
advanced in successful therapy,' she began, 'will I hope permit
me to speak especially frankly.' She did not pause for the few
gratified murmurs of assent, but went on, 'I must remind you,
as Mr Welles will confirm, that the Mental Health Act pro-
vides that special hospital patients can only be people who,
apart from being capable of reacting to treatment, have dangerous, violent or criminal propensities. Do you think that,
once cured of these propensities and re-united with the normal
world again, the fact that you have shared open lodgings with
ex-criminals is going to make much difference to people's attitudes to you?' She paused for a second, but no one cared to
reply, and she went on quickly. 'I am sure you will understand
and you won't feel offended when I tell you that the ordinary
convicted ex-criminal, violent or otherwise, will always find it
more easy to be accepted back into normal society than you
will. Crime is something people can understand. Crime is
wicked, but it's not mad. People, simple people outside are
afraid of mental derangement. They know nothing about it.

They are not at all convinced that it's the sort of illness which can be completely cured. They know nothing of modern methods of treatment and they have mostly maintained their old-fashioned prejudices and fears and suspicions. You must understand what you will be up against when you are discharged – terrible prejudices, stupid conceptions, extraordinary ignorances. You will find your readjustment in society much harder than that of an ordinary criminal. It certainly won't be the fact that you've had to associate with ex-criminals that will make it any worse for you.'

This time she had held her audience rapt. This was the kind of frank, even brutal talk which flattered them, because it challenged them to understand and accept it. Its honesty and sincerity invited them to be confidants of the speaker. These were not attitudes they often, if ever, encountered in official contacts. The murmurs of agreement, friendly and quite positive, showed up Welles's argument for what it had really been – a transparent attempt to rake up a cause for the kind of discontent on which his leadership thrived. Welles put on as brave a face as he could, with a supercilious smirk, which was intended as a smile.

'Your views are certainly open to discussion, Miss Lewis.' He spoke with his usual patronizing assurance. 'But you see you are speaking primarily as a *sane* person' – the emphasis on the word was a sneer – 'as well as someone who is already free, and will not have to face the taint of criminal association to become free. It is very easy for you to say that a little criminal association is nothing to what we already have to live down. But you cannot deny it is *something* – as if we don't already face enough problems in resuming a freedom which has never ceased to be our right. Is that criminal association something or is it nothing?'

Miss Lewis was evidently suddenly bored with the subject. She answered, almost offhandedly, 'It is certainly not something worth getting stirred up about.' She had already half-turned to Morley as she spoke, and she added quickly, to him, 'Now, Mr Morley – you're a businessman – tell me, don't you think that with all the manpower we have here we could make some better profits out of our chickens and pigs and other projects?' She had hit by chance, or perhaps with a hint from

Norton, on Morley's favourite theme. This was a subject permanently debated among the patients. Welles was defeated. He had lost the initiative, and what he had wanted most – the chance to impress Miss Lewis in front of his followers.

From patients funds the conversation turned to herself; what was she supposed to do – could she help and would she consider individual personal problems? These were the real questions they had all wanted to put – including Welles himself. Their reactions were the same as those everywhere in the hospital – an eager and sudden awakening of hope – hope for more contact, less evasion from the frustrating impersonal routine of an institution overcrowded and understaffed, like some great grim ship imperceptibly drifting somewhere on a faceless ocean, without the trace of a wake nor any destination on the horizon.

As she left, Welles, as host, showed her to the door and took the occasion he wanted for a few rapidly-whispered words. 'Do you have an office, Miss Lewis, where one can speak to you in private? No – well how can one speak to you on personal subjects?'

'That's a serious problem,' she answered, 'but for the present we can always go for a stroll in the park, or I could call on you in the middle of a morning, if it wouldn't upset your studies too much?'

'Please do, and thanks for coming.'

Norton was waiting for her in the corridor to continue her rounds.

'Knock it orf alright wiv 'is nibs?' he asked.

'Mr Welles is very charming,' said Miss Lewis prosaically.

Later at lunch she related her morning encounter in Welles's room to Dr Robertson. The Doctor relished her account of the argument with Welles, but was mildly alarmed at the frankness with which she had expressed herself.

'How did they take it?' he asked.

'They seemed very sophisticated and balanced about it,' she said.

'And Welles, would it help if you saw my record of his case history?'

'No thank you,' she said firmly. 'I have a strong impression that it would do the contrary. I'd rather not.'

9

Eventually the clamour among the patients to present her with their particular problems of despair or complaint, which they felt were not heard through the normal channels, was such that Colonel Barthropp was obliged to try and find space for an office–sitting room where patients, and perhaps relatives too, could talk to her in private.

The accommodation problem at Brockley had long passed the stage of improvisation. There was not a room, nor the corner of a room, that could really be spared. The removal of the original old stairway, a flamboyant affair splitting two ways above an arch in the centre of the entrance hall had left most of the space which had been turned into administrative offices. At the back of the hall there was still a small single-width, glass-panelled door leading out onto a short pillared balcony from which steps went down to the left and right into what had been the old courtyard–stableyard, now partly filled with the red-brick complex of newer buildings. On the right of this hall door was a narrow stone staircase to the first and second floors and beside it the offices for the accounts staff, secretarial staff and the Administrative Warden Robert Crow. On the left of the door, but about twelve feet from it, was the small cubby-hole serving as office for Crow's secretary. Beyond this was the small office of William Slater, the deputy super-intendent for staff and security. The colonel decided that a space between the rear hall door and Slater's office could just provide the small 'consulting room' she needed. It was simply a question of putting up three thinly-constructed walls.

The authority for a new construction required the approval of no less than three different Ministries, applications and architect's forms in quadruple, plus minutes of explanation. Since all these would go the rounds of the Ministries for initialling and inspection from the aspect of finance, health, security, policy and works experts, the financial approval could take anything up to a year. By an arrangement with the regular building contractor who was shortly due to put in a non-competitive tender for the building of a new brick poultry house and an extension of the pig sties, the creation of Miss Lewis's 'consulting room', twelve feet square, was achieved without authority, without record, officially non-existent. It was finished in forty-eight hours and half encompassed the last big window opening onto the rear of the ground floor central area. Though it was simply just a white, light-filled box of three walls, it was enough. The colonel, not entirely assured that she would appreciate this exceptional effort on her behalf, explained, 'This isn't a personal thing, y'know my dear. It's essential for the hospital and the overworked staff – myself as much as anyone. The patients have taken to you remarkably. As a graded psychiatric social assistant and so on you will take a great amount of excess work off the medical and administrative staff. And now, you see, we've made a niche for you. Although, let me tell you, my dear Memsahib, it's a niche which doesn't really exist in the files of the Ministry. It's a completely non-existent space and it would be best not to talk about the little – er – stratagem by which your – let us call it a consulting room – was created out of thin air. Just consider it's been there for years. When I die, I'll make it official and leave it to the Ministry in my will. That'll baffle them.'

The colonel furnished what she preferred to call her 'consulting box' with a few pieces of obsolete furniture from among the dusty debris stacked in the basement, which in the previous century had been the kitchen area. She tried to make it look not too hygienic and functional, which was not difficult, with the only desk available an old-fashioned, pompous roll-top affair, its yellow varnish scraped and split, smelling of years of institutional indifference. After that there was just room for two armchairs with flattened springs, but they did not look too bad when their lumpy cushions and faded chintz covers had been washed and ironed. Dr Robertson proposed her official hours for receiving should be from nine to eleven each morning, except Saturday and Sunday, and by special appointment, from four to five in the weekday afternoons. Rosie, the colonel's secretary, whose office was across the corridor, would make tea for her.

The creation of the 'consulting box' marked the true installation of Miss Lewis at Brockley. As soon as instructions were received by all wardens on the patients rights of access to her, the floodgates of lamentation opened on the barren little consulting room. Roughly three out of five of the complaints or demands were either groundless or already provided for by some section of the Mental Health Act and therefore unanswerable. Those which were groundless provided the greater problems. For as far as possible the complainants had to be convinced that their claims were without foundation, yet sent away without a sense of lasting grievance. The two valid complaints out of five were mostly trivial, but they meant work.

'Please find out why my wife hasn't been to see me for two months and doesn't answer my letters'; 'I was promised a special tribunal three months ago to hear my claim for release – what's happened to it?'; 'There's a man who sleeps next to me who wakes me up several times every night and spits in my face but the wing warden won't take any action when I complain – can I be moved to another dormitory?'; 'There's a man in my ward who has a bottle of whisky hidden in his mattress and when he gets drunk he's dangerous – please do not identify me with this complaint'; 'Will you write to my wife and tell her I'm going to get out of here and kill her. I dreamed last night I saw her in bed with the lodger'; 'My daughter's only fifteen and I've just had a letter from my wife saying she's pregnant – can she be looked after?' And so on and on. The feeling that such questions could be asked and answered in confidence without perhaps coming up against personal prejudices among the regular ward staff gave the patients the feeling that they mattered; that they were people still wanted in the world and not simply shoved away behind walls and shut up until they got better or withered away. In a way too it gave them a sense of power – someone would listen to them and maybe even take action against those who wouldn't listen to them. The feeling that their lives still really mattered to someone else was a basic incentive to the wish to be cured.

One of the early callers to the consulting room was not even a patient. Mounalal, the Pakistani ward-maid asked for a special afternoon meeting, at tea-time. It seemed as though she hoped her visit would pass unnoticed.

As she sat down facing Miss Lewis, she spoke softly. 'Matron has said that I have to go.' Despite her spare, bony little body, she still showed no trace of her condition. When she was asked what she would do she explained that she had relatives – a whole host of them – living in Nottingham. She would go back there and stay with an aunt and, if it were not too late, have an abortion on the Social Security. Then perhaps matron would give her her job back afterwards. No, she said, she did not want to keep the baby because she didn't really know who the father was. And even then—

It was clear that Mounalal wanted to talk about her pregnancy but did not know how to begin. Miss Lewis had never yet questioned her about it. She had resented the implication that she should become a kind of stool-pigeon for Matron Smith. If a squad of detectives had failed to find out how pregnancies occurred, it was no business of hers to unravel the great Brockley mystery.

Mounalal began by extracting a promise that Miss Lewis would do nothing about what she was told until Mounalal had left, and even then she would never reveal her source. This promise given, she began to talk, though she still needed some prompting. But when the picture of what had happened gradually began to form Miss Lewis realized that this was no simple matter of personal grievance. The gentle persistence with which she drew out the full appalling story – over endless cups of tea and convulsions of tears – extended it to almost two hours.

Mounalal had been a virgin when she first went to work at Brockley and she had never given any thought to the likelihood of changing her state. Most of the women staff slept in the staff quarters, a series of plain brick villas which bordered the half mile of road between the lodge gates and Brockley village. Mounalal had shared a room with two other girls in one of the women's staff villas when she first worked at Brockley. After a few months, another ward-maid, Gladys Davies, a Welsh girl, showed her a sudden friendliness. She invited her to move into one of the six tiny rooms, reserved for ward-maids, in a small penthouse type of building, on the roof towards the rear of the east wing of the main building. It was directly above the section of private rooms reserved for the 'C' class women. Mounalal had accepted because she did not like to seem cool towards the first gesture of friendship she had received at Brockley, and after all it saved her a walk of almost a mile each way, morning and evening. The ward-maid's quarters had been built as a low superstructure – a penthouse in fact, but with no exterior exit onto the roof – late in the nineteenth century, years before the hall's last owner had given it to the government. The lead-covered low roof of this construction had skylights in the ceiling of each room and the central corridor. It was so low that from ground level at close range it was screened by the stone-pillared parapet which ran all around the top of the building. It was only after she had moved in to the room which had fallen vacant in the ward-maid's quarters that Mounalal began to realize there was something unusual about the place. The six small rooms faced each other, three by three across the corridor. At the south end of the corridor on each side were the washing and toilet facilities and a narrow stairway leading down to the corridor of the 'C' women's quarters. There was a good deal of giggling at night from some of the other ward-maids' rooms and Gladys Davies explained, though not very clearly, that this floor was variously known as 'the ward-maids heaven' or 'the sky's-the-limit house'. It was several months more before Mounalal found out why.

She awoke one night just as the clothes were ripped from her bed and a man's body tumbled on top of her. While a woman, unidentifiable at first, held her by the hair and crammed a wet cloth into her mouth, Mounalal was raped by at least three men before she lost consciousness, paralysed by fear and pain. When she recovered, still in the dark, the woman was bathing her head with the damp cloth. Mounalal recognized the voice of Gladys Davies warning her that she would be 'chopped' if she raised an alarm or spoke to anyone about what had happened. She told no one but she felt that every movement, every contact she made, was watched by other nurses or ward-maids. Gladys avoided her, but when she was unable to do so, she refused to speak to her.

There were no keys to the doors of the ward-maids' rooms. For a week of nights Mounalal lay in sleepless dread, prepared, the next time, to scream or die. But she had no chance. They came again two weeks later and she was gagged before she had time to move. This time there was only Gladys and one man, to whom she heard the ward-maid say as she twisted a hand in Mounalal's long hair and held a foul floorcloth against her face, 'Give the little black bitch hell, Joe.' At one moment in the struggle she managed to get her hands on her attacker's head, and felt the bushy sideboards of his crimped curly hair, covering his ears. This time Gladys made no effort to disguise her identity. When the man had crept out into the corridor, Gladys switched on the light and as Mounalal lay sobbing, leaned over and slapped her hard, with a fast series of palm and knuckle blows. 'That's for being a black bitch,' she whispered fiercely. 'That's what one of your own filthy niggers did to me. Good luck to your little black bastard.' A few weeks later the scandal of the unexplained pregnancies of the three women patients – all 'C' class – and of Gladys, broke and the Prison Investigation men arrived. Mounalal alone knew where the pregnancies occurred, but she had no idea how a man or men could possibly get into and out of the ward-maids' quarters without passing through the security doors on the floor below, or through the skylights of the penthouse. She was quite certain that the last man who had raped her was Joe Norton and she fancied that from time to time during the investigation she found him at unexpected moments in her path. Though he never spoke a word, there was something intense – and, to her terrified mind, menacing – about his expression, as though he was trying to convey a warning without openly admitting that he had any reason to do so. Mounalal, with her timid reactions and fragile appearance, had no trouble in convincing the members of the inquiry team that she knew nothing. She had not the appearance of a girl likely to be involved in an unwanted pregnancy and her numb silences and head-shakings were accepted as confirmation of her ignorance of the whole affair.

Miss Lewis sat for a while, silent and aghast, at the end of her story. The Pakistani had no tears left, and no words, and the two of them sat, each with their own thoughts, for several minutes.

'When do you go, Mounalal?' Miss Lewis asked her.

'In a week's time, Memsahib.'

'Very well,' said Miss Lewis. 'Now, this is what I want you to do. Think, think hard of everything that happened, every word you heard, anything at all which could help to give us a clue of who the men were and how they got in to the ward-maids' quarters. There are surely some little details you have forgotten in your story. Now – pull yourself together, dear, don't start crying and go away and *think*. There must be something more you can remember. Even the tiniest details could give us what we want. I'll see you here at the same time tomorrow. Tell matron to let you go – if she asks.'

By the following afternoon Miss Lewis had carried out a detailed examination of the 'C' women's quarters and the ward-maids' penthouse above, to which the only access was by the narrow stairway from the third floor.

The main stairway from the hall entrance, behind the administrative area, led to the first and second floors, at each of which were grilled iron doors, always kept locked, and then directly into the women's wing. The heavy iron-grilled door at the top of the stairs, directly facing the glass enclosed office of the women's duty wardress, was occupied day and night. At the rear of this landing was a glass-panelled steel door looking onto the rear courtyard. This door, always locked and bolted from the inside, and well in view of the duty wardress's office, led onto a metal stairway – in theory a fire escape – which ran down the outside wall of the building to the courtyard, without giving access on the way to any other floor. This stairway was never used in normal circumstances and the keys were kept on the board of the duty wardress's office. Except for these two stairways, with their metalled, bolted and locked doors under the direct eye of the duty wardress, there was no other means of access to the women's quarters. For the most elementary safety reasons there obviously should have been, but that was another matter. All the windows on the women's floor, including those of washrooms, toilets, pantries and the rest, were thirty-five to forty feet from the ground, and well-barred. It was this hermetically sealed aspect of the women's quarters, especially at night, which had influenced the Prison Investigation sleuths to concentrate on outside possibilities for the contacts which procured the pregnancies. There was considerable movement all over and around the main building and gardens and out-buildings during the day. The investigators had become certain that some gap in the day security programme had permitted men and women patients to meet in some obscure corner of one of the buildings – a garden shed, a henhouse, a storeroom of the kitchen block or even the basement of the main block. There were indeed plenty such possibilities and at one time or another over the years they had all been tried, with more or less success. After the first day the detectives were satisfied that the women's quarters, and this meant too the ward-maids' penthouse above, were so impregnable as to merit no more consideration in their inquiries.

The fanlights in the six rooms and the corridor of the penthouse had for a brief while been considered as offering a solution. But their steel frames, with rust blooming through the cracked paintwork, were solidly screwed into the roof structure.

By the time of her next appointment with Mounalal Miss Lewis tended to feel along with the Prison Investigators, that there was no corner of the women's quarters or the penthouse above which could have been used for anything remotely resembling a love-nest. But she knew she was wrong.

Yes, Mounalal said, without enthusiasm, there was one little detail she had remembered. At the time of the second incident, when only Gladys and Norton had visited her – she was quite certain now that it was Norton – she had heard him whisper to the girl, just before she put the light on, 'Tell the boys to get back to the cupboard, I'll be right down.' At the back of her mind at that moment Mounalal had felt a wry sense of relief at knowing that though the others were in the women's quarters somewhere, she was not on their list this time. She had felt that they must be going down to the third floor 'C' women's 'private quarters', the twelve small private rooms of which seven only were occupied now by Matron's seven 'C' sisters. The recollection of the beating she had received from Gladys had obscured the memory of the remark about 'the cupboard'.

'Why did you tell me all this Mounalal?' Miss Lewis asked her. The Pakistani now seemed drained of emotion, composed, and soothed by having at last unburdened herself of the tale of her afflictions.

'You were kind to me, Memsahib, and I thought it might be useful to you to know. Something terrible could happen this way, if it goes on. Only – please – never mention my name. Even in Nottingham I'll still be afraid of him – Norton. He's one of those sort of men, well, he'd find you out anywhere, I feel.'

Miss Lewis left Old Brockley unusually early that evening, leaving her Mini in the parking area. She went on foot because she wanted to think. By the time he reached her cottage she had made her decision. She would keep Mounalal's story to herself. Her own basic justification for this decision was to avoid a security eruption which would disturb the routine and customs of SP9, to which she was now accustomed, and perhaps present her with new problems of access to the survivor. The second was that perhaps the survivor himself was associated with Norton in his sexual forays and this could provide her with a useful situation. In any case she was determined to pursue her own inquiry from the point where the Prison Investigation men had left off. She had two clues they had never found; the name of the man – and the word 'cupboard'.

IO

In the weeks since her first meeting with Michael Loft, she had been to visit the gardening unit half a dozen times – ostensibly to look in on the classes that were being held there and chat with one or two patients who worked, pretty apathetically, at keeping the greenhouse tidy and tending the small cast iron stove for the heating system, which was also used to make tea.

Her acquaintance with Loft made a curious but definite progress. When she walked along the rows of rabbit hutches, trying to be amiable with their occupants – poking dandelion leaves through the wire – Loft at first watched her suspiciously from the end of the hut, and never offered a word. He returned no word of greeting and her few attempts to start conversations about the rabbits or the gardens faded away in mumbled monosyllables until he turned his back and got on with his current occupation – usually repairing the hutches or building new ones.

The day after her last meeting with Mounalal, she surprised him playing with a baby rabbit. He was standing at the far north end of the rabbit barn, his great unwieldy form silhouetted against the grey light filtering through the grime of the windows. At first it was difficult to see what he was doing. He held his hands together, high above his head, then brought them slowly down to his face, whirled them upwards, then down again. It took a few moments for her eyes to become accustomed to the light, before she saw, cupped in his immense hands, a furry bundle of baby rabbit, its ears laid back, eyes round and startled. He was swinging the tiny creature upwards, then bringing it down to rub noses with it, as one might play with a small baby. As he played he talked softly, but the words were a low indistinguishable murmur. She began to edge towards him along the beaten earth floor between the rows of hutches. Now he had turned the baby rabbit on its back in one hand, and with a finger of the other he was stroking its stomach. With a sudden frantic kick the little animal wriggled itself the right way up and Loft almost dropped it. At that moment he saw Miss Lewis. He stood stock still as she hastened her last few steps towards him, as though to assure him that he had not really been spied on. She spoke quickly, with a short nervous laugh. 'Isn't it difficult to kill them when you've made friends with them, like that?' He had stopped, with the baby rabbit in one hand, his other relaxed and massive by his side. His arms too were abnormally long. He shifted his feet uneasily and then a half-smile, the first she had ever really identified in his expression, spread across his face.

'It is a problem that does not arise,' he said, and she noticed for the first time that his heavy lower lip seemed to provoke the trace of a lisp. 'I don't make friends with the ones I have to kill. This one isn't for killing. His name is,' he paused, 'Little, I think. But I'm not sure yet.' She moved beside him and stroked the trembling bundle of fur in the palm of his hand.

'Do you have certain ones you never kill?' she asked.

He explained that he did. There were the two original couples he had bought as pets a long time ago, with his own money. Since pets were not technically allowed he had been obliged to breed for the kitchens and for sale, but he was permitted to keep the two original couples. One of the four was ill, probably dying. This little rabbit he had chosen from the other litters, to take its place.

For once he forgot his reserve, and his usual air of sullen distrust disappeared as he spoke of his rabbits, called his 'four old ones' by name, and showed them one by one to his visitor. The new young rabbit, who might perhaps be named Little, he explained, had been elected to succeed an enormous white buck called 'Him'. He was the one who seemed to be ill and would soon have to be replaced. The four originals – 'Him', 'Her', 'Kick' and 'Nibble' were their names – all seemed to know him and came when he called. Even out of their cages they stayed pressed against his feet, noses twitching. He picked them up by folds of skin along their backs. 'Some people pick them up by the ears,' he said, 'but that's quite wrong. It hurts.'

Then suddenly, while he had seemed quite absorbed in his exposé, and without a word which could have explained his change of mood, he behaved as if she were no longer there and began cleaning the zinc trays placed in the bottom of the cages. She waited several minutes to see if this was perhaps simply a pause in their contact, but he was on his knees, whistling softly between his teeth, completely preoccupied by what he was doing as though all his consciousness of her presence had been suddenly effaced by something beyond his control. Before she left she stood at the south doorway, adjoining the conservatory, watching him. His incredibly ugly face, as he moved among the three-tier rows of cages, wore an expression of tranquil, almost beatific content and absorption. As she stood in the doorway, her eyes were caught by the neat alignment of tools stacked and hung on the wall of the gardening shed, and of the rabbit shed itself. There were two sharp, pointed sickles, a scythe, a little rusty but with a savage sweeping blade; there was a pick-axe, its steel point polished bright by the earth. There were several crow-bars and some sharp metal stakes, a heavy woodsman's axe and two smaller ones for splintering. With an impulsive movement she held out her right arm in front of her as though to study the back of her hand, fingers splayed, extended and tense. For a moment she gazed at her hand, its tendons rigid, outlined as though carved in old ivory, its fine slender fingers tapering to oval nails, long, beautifully-manicured, with a natural varnish.

It was a hand that combined elegance and strength, in perfect harmony. Against the colourless light it was without a tremor, profiled like a claw. She dropped her arm to her side and walked with a light and vigorous step back to the Old Hall.

II

The Diary of Margaret Lewis

EXTRACT 3

It will now be clear to those who read this journal that I knew
the truth of the unexplained pregnancies and, in view of my
hopes and intentions, had good reason to keep it to myself.
Perhaps that decision, by the time this is read, may have had
some grave consequences. Perhaps the activities of Norton will
have been responsible for disastrous events, which I could still
prevent. This is a danger I am leaving to chance and it is not
one, in any case, from which my conscience will suffer. It is far
more important that nothing should snatch my victory away
when it is so close. A redistribution of staff and maybe even of
patients at this moment would be disastrous to me. Norton,
though he would be difficult and dangerous to blackmail, could
be useful, since I have found precisely how he worked. In any
case it is quite clear to me, my instinct confirms it, that the
man is a vicious crook, and a racketeer. He is not the man
for instance, to have the monopoly of canteen sales and I
strongly suspect that the several bottles of liquor which I
know to be hidden in the patients' quarters found their way
in through him – and not for nothing. In the same way I
believe he has actually turned contacts between men and
women patients into a profitable business affair. In case the
system of these contacts has not been discovered by the time

this is read, I am including it here for the record.

The ward-maid Mounalal has told me how she was twice raped while sleeping in the ward-maids' quarters in the penthouse above the west wing. The ward-maid Gladys Davies, since dismissed for a pregnancy which she refused to explain, acted as what could be called mistress of ceremonies, because she was once raped by an Indian and she used Mounalal for her revenge. She helped Norton and other men to rape Mounalal in the ward-maids' quarters at night. I am convinced that no force was needed in the other contacts between men and women patients and staff and my inquiries indicate that the first initiative for these frolics probably came from two or three 'C' class women patients in collaboration with one or two ward-maids, with Joe Norton acting as pimp among the 'C' and perhaps some of the 'B' class men. My own inquiries really began to be successful from the moment that Mounalal told me that during one of the occasions when she was raped in her room, she heard Norton tell Gladys Davies to order some of his male accomplices 'back to the cupboard'. From this clue onwards, it was pretty easy. To begin with I examined the ward-maids' quarters a second time. At one end of the short corridor which separates the six rooms is the stairway going down to the 'C' women's floor. At the other end there is a ceiling-high, double-doored linen cupboard, a pretty solid affair. The first time I looked into this cupboard it signified nothing. It was only when I looked at the whole building from the outside, at the rear, that I realized the cupboard must be the way in. For the end wall of this wing, against which the cupboard is built on the inside, has a wide and thick chimney channel running up the outside of it all the way to the roof. The chimney pillar projects high above the roof. Around it at the top is a steel platform, built to give access to the chimneys from the outside.

The end of the wall of the old east wing of the main building is covered, for the first two storeys, by an extension which contains the 'B' men's quarters. The roof of this extension, against the wall, is flat and has a large skylight. From the level of this roof upwards there are metal rungs fixed in the old chimney outer wall, probably put there during the last century. At about the height of the base of the flat roof – the penthouse fitted flush into the chimney wall – there is a metal plaque about three feet square, not easily noticeable for it was once painted a brick red, and where the paint has peeled it is well rusted. As this plaque is well above the level of the ceiling of the women's quarters it would not seem to give any access to the inside of the main building and in any case all the fireplaces inside the building were bricked up years ago. When I had seen all this I went back to examine the penthouse linen cupboard again. The lowest shelf was about four feet from the floor, and from the floor up to this, the cupboard was packed with clean linen, blankets, eiderdowns and bed covers. When I pulled all this out I found the back of the cupboard lined with several thicknesses of old wall paper, not on a plaster or brick backing, as might have been expected, but on a huge board. When I pulled hard with my finger-tips at one of its rough edges it fell easily into the cupboard, completely unattached to the wall. Peering forward into the empty chimney I could see the cracks of light on the three unhinged sides of the metal plaque, slightly lower and to one side, on the opposite wall of the chimney. On the inner wall, mounting inside the chimney from below and going upwards to where I could see the light above through the chimney pots, was another series of iron rungs. No particular acrobatic feat would be required, even in the dark, to swing the metal chimney plaque open from the outside, reach inside the chimney and climb across to the rungs leading up to the cupboard opening. Either a ward-maid or one of the women patients must have found the false cupboard-back and realized its possibilities. Norton, whose duties took him everywhere and who must have found an instinctive ally in the Welsh ward-maid, was the obvious channel for communicating the invitations which must have followed this precious discovery. There was no reason why an understanding should not have been reached between the ward-maids and the 'C' women on the floor below to share the 'facilities' thus made available. If the survivor should be one of those included in the penthouse orgies it would certainly be a useful possibility in the context of my intentions for him. He is one of the 'B' patients living in the flat-roofed building which gives access through the skylight to the rungs on the outside of the chimney. If he is friendly with Norton, then he is probably one of the party; I wonder what the drop is from the steel chimney plaque down to the bottom of the inside of the chimney – four floors down to the bricked-up basement – and how long a man with a broken back or a cracked skull would take to die down there? Perhaps I am being unduly optimistic. Time will tell.

I seem to have begun at last to make a breakthrough in my contacts with the survivor, but the effort is greater and much more painful than anything I have had to do for many years. My wretched imagination inflicts on my mind a whole series of images and associations which sicken me and make even more difficult the humiliating pantomime of interest and friendliness which I am obliged to display. Those bulbous hands fondling a rabbit as they once did Cheryl; the semi-idiot, incoherent murmurs of – I suppose – affection with which he bewilders his rabbits, probably in the same style with which he once expressed desire and satisfaction; that monolithic mask hiding God knows what perverted and diabolic atrocity behind its expression of false beatitude – all his pretensions to unworldliness with which he once enticed children away to steal their minds. All these realities and associations flood my thoughts the moment I find myself in his presence, trying to draw him out with fatuous conversation about his wretched little beasts. Yet if I am to do my best, something better than just butchery, I must know more about him and his present thoughts and reactions; I must get behind the ridiculous façade which the staff at Brockley – I presume even the psychiatrists – take for reality. Because a patient is willing to settle for rabbits and become docile and apparently trustworthy within the limits of the hospital, then due to pressure of under-staffing, he is abandoned to his own resources and will one day, doubtless with a clear record, be transferred to a non-security hospital or released. That is to say, he *would* be if I were not here.

My first real contact with him, in which he acknowledged my existence and appeared to return my interest, so revolted me and tried my powers of restraint that for a few moments I almost gave way to the temptation to eliminate him on the spot. As ever, I had Alan's thirty-eight automatic in the bottom of my bag, but even apart from that, rarely can anyone contemplating murder have had such a splendid opportunity as I did at that moment. The man was on his knees – his head partly in an open rabbit hutch. I stood half a dozen paces away, within arm's reach of a magnificent array of tools for dispatching someone. My hands are long, slender and very

126

feminine and my small-boned wrists appear fragile, but I estimated at that moment I would have had no difficulty in swinging the sharp point of a pick-axe between his shoulder blades
– or the shiny-bladed axe into his skull, though I was more
tempted by the long curve of the great scythe sweeping across
his skinny throat. At least I know that if I should be compelled
to abandon my hopes for a more just retribution, the circumstances for a rapid and effective settlement are always handy. I
found too a satisfaction in not killing him when the opportunity presented itself so perfectly. It was as though in my
mind I had all the pleasure of killing him, yet kept him to kill
him again some other time.

He now accepts me more than he does anyone else in SP9,
although he does not always speak to me. When he does eventually recognize my presence he looks at me only very briefly,
but enough to give that curious lift to one corner of his mouth
which passes for a smile. Then he goes on with what he is
doing. But I feel that a strange sense of communication exists
between us. I can sense that when I am there he is quite relaxed and feels some sort of satisfaction at my presence. I
cannot explain why I feel this is so, because there is nothing
positive I can identify in his attitude. I just know that he wel-
comes me and feels glad I am there, as though he feels I am
more part of his world than anyone else. On occasions I have
stayed for as long as twenty minutes just watching him work,
and his occasional glance in my direction seems to include me
in the general picture he expects of his surroundings. Even the
squirrel, of which he is intensely jealous, although no one else
has ever tried to be friendly with it, has several times run up
my arm and stayed still an instant on my shoulder. I take it a
few peanuts each time and I suppose it considers this a feast. It
is a fascinating little animal with a distinct character and although I have never been particularly interested in animals I
am very fond of Squirrel. As with his pet rabbits, the survivor
avoids all anthropoid names. The squirrel's name is just
Squirrel.

The most puzzling element of the situation is the absence of
any sign that the doctors and psychiatrists realize the association between the survivor's terrible past and his present-day
preoccupations. His criminal activities were based on an obsession with animals and the fascination of his drug-induced mys-

ticism for young people, who then became involved in a kind of black worship of animals, and the deliberate abasement of human characteristics. I wonder how long it is since anyone here consulted his record and drew some conclusions based on his past activity and his present state of mind. Fortunately it does not matter because wherever his present activities might seem to be leading him, I shall be there first.

After Cheryl had been taken to hospital unconscious, raped and covered with razor-scars, Alan and I were told that she had been found by a gamekeeper, in a wood near Shrewsbury, thirty miles from home. She was lying on a heap of old sacking and some dirty blankets. Gypsies who had been seen in the area a few days before were questioned by the police, but they had had nothing to do with Cheryl's absence. For the first ten days in hospital she was hardly able to speak clearly although she seemed to see and feel our distress. She cried with us and tried to give us every possible sign of affection of which she was capable. But after a month in hospital it was impossible to make her talk about her experience or anything to do with it. Neither to Alan nor me, or to any of her doctors, would she make any reply to any questions. At first she tried to assure us feebly that 'it was nothing to worry about'. But after a little while the only reply to questions was to turn her head away and remain silent until something else – not a question – was said. Then she would talk, a little weakly indeed, but with no trace of fear or shock. Except for her physical condition and her refusal to discuss what had happened, her experience had left no perceptible mark on her mind. The razor cuts – there were four hundred and thirty-nine of them altogether – covered her whole body, ending at her wrists, ankles, and the base of her throat and neck. Each cut was no more than three-quarters to one inch long, barely passing through the outer skin in depth. They had been made with extreme care. Those on the body ran parallel to it, except above her breasts, where they began to splay out in a perfectly uniform pattern towards her shoulders and then carried on down along her arms. Those on her arms and legs followed the lines of the limbs. The whole design of the cuts, there is no other word for it, followed harmoniously the line of her body. They healed very quickly and left, to begin with, very fine red weals, like tiny pieces of thread. If they gave her pain she never showed it, though each day they were all washed with alcohol.

Once when the doctors were examining the scars and speculating on their origin, as Cheryl arched her naked body to look down on the bizarre symmetry that clothed her like a fine body-stocking, I thought for a moment I caught in her lowered gaze a flash of something like pride.

She caught my eyes and quickly turned her head, but I could see a glow spreading across her face, of pride or embarrassment, I could not guess.

Cheryl was allowed to leave the hospital after a little more than a month, but on the doctor's advice we put her in a private convalescent home where her return to normal living could be carried out with unbroken care and observation. Until now the doctors had forbidden the police to question her and it was decided that she should first be examined by a psychiatrist. He was completely baffled by her reaction. He gave the opinion that she had probably been under hypnosis or the effect of a hypnotic drug and he believed that she was still basically under the effect of some sort of hypnosis. He could not identify in what way her mind was still 'possessed' by her experience, but he was greatly struck by the wave of resentment and inflexible resistance which flooded through her the moment a question was asked about her injuries or anything to do with her experience. It was not that she became frightened or in any way dismayed. Her resentment was protective, as though to try and shield her experience from outside. Eventually he gave up hope of making contact with her because, knowing his ultimate interest, she refused to speak to him at all, even when he talked of subjects remote from herself or her condition. He eventually allowed the police to speak to her. I was surprised that the detective and plain clothes sergeant who called to see her were not from the locality but from Scotland Yard. They spent a whole afternoon alone with Cheryl while I waited in the matron's room. They made no comment when they left but simply said they would return the next day.

Then they spent three more hours with her and when they left, the inspector, Denis Marshal, told me, 'There is nothing to be done. She won't discuss anything at all with us. We have tried to talk about music, dancing, the cinema – anything that might interest her. She simply refuses to speak.' Before they went back to London they had a long talk with Alan. There was no objection to him telling me what they said – they had simply preferred to leave it to him to tell me whatever he thought fit.

Their primary interest, they said, had been in trying to trace a man called Michael Loft. All that was known about him was that he was the founder and leader of a mystic-intellectual sect of animists, who used drugs, mainly hallucinatory, and recruited young people, boys and girls, all over the country. Loft was known to have started the first group of the sect in a flat in Bloomsbury. Since then the sect, name unknown, though sometimes called The Beasts, had expanded to form small groups in half a dozen large provincial cities. Yet not one of the groups, including the London one, stayed long enough in any one place for the police to catch up with them.

Their rites were unknown, but combined with drug-taking, appeared to be extremely dangerous as well as barbarous. As a result of them a girl of eighteen and a boy of seventeen were in mental homes. The girl had been found in an empty flat in North London, which members of the sect had broken into and used for their meetings during one weekend. She was apparently incapable of speech, beyond indecipherable miauling sounds, and she clawed furiously at anyone who approached her. The boy had been found in similar circumstances, but in an empty house in Birmingham. He had become quite mad – scrambling on all fours. He would only sleep on the floor and seemed to have adopted some of the characteristics of a dog. A few suspected members of the sect – the police for want of a better name called it 'the Loft sect' – had been traced and questioned. Neither threats nor promises could persuade them to speak a word. Two youths who had been suspected of attending a sect meeting had been found in possession of drugs and sent to reform schools. They appeared perfectly normal, but even under the conditions of continual surveillance, it had never been possible to extract a word from them about Loft and his sect. Loft's name had only become known after the most persistent police inquiries which, it was noted, had led not to the usual working-class industrial or commercial centres with which juvenile delinquency was in those days more associated, but to middle-class university areas such as Oxford, Bristol, Leicester, Manchester, Exeter and York, as well as London. In these cities police had traced nearly a dozen youngsters who were said to have met Loft, casually, in coffee bars and discotheques and whom he had invited to attend sessions of the sect. For various reasons these young people had failed to attend and had later found the addresses they were given locked up or abandoned. Except for the boy and girl who had become insane, no one was found who was positively known to have attended one of the sect's seances. All accounts of them were second- and third-hand, but even allowing for some exaggeration in the re-telling of the story, they seemed to have been sinister and horrifying events.

Beyond his description, nothing was known of Loft. His background and origins as well as his precise movements were quite untraceable, despite the fact that he must have looked fairly unforgettable even among a large crowd of people. He was six foot three inches tall, his features and limbs were grossly enlarged, and by all accounts, his eyes were unforgettable and terrifying. There were only intermittent traces of him, in areas well separated, and neither the times nor the places gave any pattern of movement which could help the police. The only common clue was that middle-class youngsters were recruited in school, college or university surroundings where there was already a market for drugs, even of the most elementary kinds, and once an individual had attended a sect gathering – never twice in the same place – there was no hope of obtaining any information from him or her. According to the few who had seen Loft, and fortunately for them, failed to attend the seance to which they were invited, his age was difficult to determine. Guesses ranged between twenty-five and thirty-five. Those who met him agreed that he had a great charm, and yet, in conjunction with his impressive physique and eerie face, a power of command which seemed hypnotic. One might almost have said, summing up the various reports on him, that his repulsion was compelling. The police had told Alan that they considered it far from certain that the harm he had done already was limited to the two children rendered insane, for they believed that one of the inducements offered to those invited to join his sect was a generous amount of free drugs, starting with amphetamines and going on through marijuana to LSD and other harder drugs. The Scotland Yard men made it clear to Alan that Loft, for the potential of harm he could do to young people and the discipline and secrecy he seemed able to impose on his followers, made him one of the most dangerous criminal eccentrics at large. They were mystified that a man with such distinctive physical characteristics should be able to move about the country from clubs to bars and cafés while leaving so little trace. The police were quite certain that Cheryl had been one of his victims. Her case was a model of the two others which had ended with the irreparable mental breakdown of the boy and girl. Cheryl, they said, was lucky to have suffered little more than a scarred body. The girl who had lost her mind had also been sexually assaulted long before her final absence and she too had been mutilated, though in a different fashion to Cheryl. The outer corners of her eyes had been slit quite deeply, as far as her temples, as had the tip of her nose, all the way down to the top of her upper lip. The mutilation of the boy had consisted simply of the amputation of the fleshy end of his nose up as far as the cartilege and bone.

After three weeks of convalescence Cheryl seemed sufficiently recovered to return home. We had already planned a month's holiday – it was now the beginning of July – in the fishing cove of Tredegan in South Cornwall where we had taken two furnished rooms in a small cottage only a few hundred yards from the sea. 'How lovely – there'll be lots of gulls,' was all she had said when we told her. Just as, after her first disappearance, she had become a slightly paler version of her old self in terms of character, so she was even more so now. All the same qualities could still be perceived, but this time so subdued that I often felt my heart was breaking. This was still Cheryl, but it was as if her image, her spirit, her mind, were all diffused and came to us dulled and ill-defined, filtered of life and vitality by some invisible screen.

She was affectionate, she appeared sometimes moved by our suffering and tried to console us, but without great conviction and never with any promise for the future.

We did not feel that she was more than very superficially touched by our sadness. The only remark she ever made, just before going on holiday, about her experience, was 'What happened was inevitable – nobody's fault. It's nothing to worry about.' Alan and I tried to extract some ray of hope in analysing these words, but they gave us the most meagre consolation. We became resigned to the fact that this time there was a definite, perhaps permanent, reserve between Cheryl and us. She was evidently happier alone, spending hours sitting listening to her discs or reading.

As we had promised the inspector to advise him of any development and of our movements, Alan telephoned Scotland Yard to give our holiday address. The inspector warned him that Cheryl should be watched closely, should never carry any money, should not be allowed out alone, or even out of our sight, and we should take precautions to make sure that she could not leave the house during the night.

'Do you really think she is likely to disappear again?' Alan asked him.

He replied, 'If her conduct follows the pattern of those others who have come under his control, she will try and disappear again. Take every precaution you can against this, because if she does, it may be the last time you will see her.'

How long was this life of hide and seek and suspense to go on? Alan asked.

'It will all be over when we have found Loft,' said the detective, 'but until then your daughter's life is in danger.'

We only learned later that plain clothes men from Scotland Yard watched the village bordering our holiday cove to keep an eye on strangers in the area, as well as our own movements.

For a while the holiday brought back to us an echo of better days. Cheryl seemed quite happy to be with us, perfectly absorbed by the simple occupation of a country seaside holiday, swimming with an underwater mask, sunbathing on the secluded beaches, picnicking and walking along the gorse and heather-topped cliffs, or fishing for mackerel from a rowing boat. Halfway through the holiday we were all at last beginning to relax a little. One evening we spent drinking draught cider in a small pub a mile down the cove. Cheryl drank lemonade and cider and not very much of it, but walking home in the moonlight she lost all her reserve and chased around us, laughing and dancing like the warm, wild creature she used to be. She was in one of those tempestuous, ecstatic moods in which I had always loved her best. She went chasing up and down the steep banks of the lane pretending to be a bird and making owl cries, swooping down and swinging her arms around us.

There were fractional instants that evening when we were living only the present, and the pain of the past and the fear of the future were in suspense. One especially hot day when we had picnicked on the cliff tops – Cheryl preferred them to the beach because she could spend hours on the extreme edge watching the gulls – we had lain dozing in the long grass when Alan suddenly sat up and said, 'Where's Cheryl?' We thought she had been sitting beside us. With a rapidity which revealed to each of us how constantly our fears lay almost on the surface of our minds, we were up and running along the cliff-edge path, Alan in one direction, I in the other. Erosion and collapse had created small shallow valleys along the cliff tops and on the brink of one of these, only a few score yards from where we had been lying, I saw Cheryl. She seemed to be waltzing among the tufts of gorse and heather – arms outstretched, head back. She would stand poised for moments on tip-toe with her fingers fluttering like the wing-edge feathers of a gull as it hangs suspended on the wind. Then, knees bent, she would mime the downwards swoop, the turn with the tilt of the wings, the climb back to the wind-held balance – on tip-toes again.

She was not at all abashed when she saw me sitting watching her, and called out laughing, 'I'm a gull,' and I answered, 'You're the most beautiful gull of them all, darling.'

'Yes, I am,' she said. 'I think I've got exactly the motions. I've decided I'd rather be a gull than an owl. Gulls are the real dancers of the air.'

We were sunbathing on the beach two days later – we had all become beautifully bronzed – when almost identical thoughts came to Alan and me, a moment after Cheryl had been pirouetting in front of us, showing off a new bikini, a minute cotton affair, bought in the village store. As she darted away towards the sea, Alan turned to me and said, 'The scars will never go.'

'No,' I said. 'I can see that.'

'Do you realize what they look like?' he asked.

'Yes – I see now,' I replied. We had both suddenly understood the same thing. The scars had not bronzed at all. Instead they had gone even whiter with the sun, and against the deep golden-copper of the rest of her skin they shone like fine gossamer threads. Their perfect symmetry with her body could have made them the symbols of a bird's plumage.

'He's trying to make her a bird,' Alan said. I nodded. He went on, 'Is there any other mutilation he can do or might do, in that case?' He paused to think and then answered himself. 'I don't think so, thank God. It seems effective enough as it is. Of course you realized what he did to the other two, the boy and the girl? He'd given the girl cat's eyes and nose and he tried to give the boy the snub nose of a dog.'

I nodded again. We had both thought of this long since but because we could not see what the intention with Cheryl had been, and because we were too sickened and afraid to speculate about it, we had each been reluctant to admit our identical thoughts. Now, while Cheryl's underwater breathing tube bobbed and spouted along a reef of rocks off the beach, we found we had regained enough courage to speak about the threat to her for the first time since the holiday had begun. We came to one important conclusion. The idea of becoming a bird was evidently firmly fixed in Cheryl's mind. Yet she spoke about it, she played openly at being a bird without restraint or reserve, which she would not have done if she had associated the idea with anything that had happened during her disappearance. Therefore this obsession had been planted in her subconscious mind and she had no conscious recollection of it. This seemed to confirm the verdict of the psychoanalyst at the nursing home, that she was still basically under the influence of some aspect of hypnosis. If the suggestion of becoming a bird was still prompting her subconsciously, what other promptings – or *instructions* – might there still be effectively planted in her mind to be acted upon sooner or later? This was a terrible thought, for we felt it touched on the real state of affairs. Loft had not finished with her. Even here on this sunlit beach and placid sea his evil mind was exercising its power and there was no way of fighting it. It seemed that our best hope would be to keep Cheryl under our control long enough for whatever obsession he had planted in her to weaken and wear away or until he himself was captured. After two weeks of sun and close, relaxed companionship we had been stupid enough to think that Cheryl was safe and that the end of our suffering was in sight. We had slackened our vigilance and looked for danger from the outside, while it lay among us, implanted in Cheryl's mind. But we felt, or at least we comforted ourselves with the idea, that Cheryl herself had not really changed, had not ceased to feel for us as always; the real Cheryl was still there, only obscured for us by a transient obsession. All we needed to win her back was time. From then on, without her noticing, we redoubled our efforts to protect her from further flight. Yet after our previous suffering, that month in Cornwall was as perfect an experience as we could have wished, and filled with far more happiness than we had ever expected to know again. It was the last happiness of our lives, for all of us.

On our return home Cheryl lapsed into her previous moody reserve. The vicarious pleasure of flight and freedom which she had felt watching the gulls from the cliff tops of Cornwall had fulfilled something of her obsession. A grimy industrial area of Staffordshire and the confinement of its dreary streets must have seemed to her doubly oppressive, especially as in spite of all our care she began to realize that she was never to be left alone for a moment, except in her own room.

We called in her doctor and asked him to invent some quite technical pretext to justify her continual surveillance. He told her that she still showed traces of shock from her injuries and that this could cause an attack of dizziness in which she might require immediate help. Consequently she was never to go out or move around the house alone. I believe she accepted this, although it did nothing to restore her spirits.

Inspector Marshal from Scotland Yard called again and confirmed his previous warning. Two more children, a girl of fifteen in the north and a boy of sixteen in London had been found in empty apartments suffering from shock and apparently inexplicable mutilations. The girl's head was shaved, and her ears, fingers and toes had all been amputated. This had occurred in her third flight from home. Her virginity had been surgically terminated apparently without severe suffering or violence, on her second disappearance from home. She was now completely out of her mind. The boy's nose had been cut off in the same way as with the first boy, but in addition the corners of his upper lip had been sliced off. When he was found he was still under the effects of a heavy dose of LSD and had never recovered. The Inspector added that he probably never would. There was to us a terribly sinister implication in the news that the girl had been raped, even though only surgically, on her second disappearance, and had still disappeared again for her final mutilation. So – there *was* a third time. Rape did not terminate the obligation to answer the call.

12

The flood of applicants for interviews with Miss Lewis in the 'consulting box' diminished considerably after the first few busy weeks of its institution. The baseless complaints or claims were fairly soon exhausted and her visitors were reduced to those with genuine problems or simply those who found comfort in exercising a right to be received in privacy at their own requests, to talk about no matter what. They were a time-wasting group, but they needed the same assurances as any others. One of the most likeable among them, and with the most extraordinary problems, was Tom Lacey, a former theological student at a Jesuit college, committed to Brockley on a magistrate's order without having been the subject of any criminal proceedings. He was a cultured, naturally gentle boy of twenty-three. He had been strictly brought up by a widowed mother, an ardent Catholic, whose life's ambition had been to see her son an ordained priest of the Roman Church. One day he had taken his small sports car, an axe and a sledgehammer, on a tour of more than twenty churches and one northern cathedral, where he had battered the altar crosses to splintered wood or shapeless coils of metal. On the following day, with the police of half a dozen counties chasing him, his dementia had turned against any object or combination of objects which formed a cross – window frames, builder's scaffolding, objects in shop windows – he could see blasphemous crosses everywhere. He had finally been caught climbing a telegraph pole along a country road with the object of smashing the crossbars carrying the lines. For almost all of his first year at Brockley it had been necessary to keep him under forced restraint, for even the sight of the crosspanels of an ordinary wooden door was enough to stir him into a frenzy against what he considered to be a diabolic plot by the profane to destroy the meaning of the true cross by blasphemous and frivolous imitations. For three years now he had been sufficiently in control of himself to close his eyes or turn away whenever he perceived the form of a cross in some mundane object or design. He recognized now the illogicality of his reasoning and the illusion of a profane world plot had long since been rejected by his mind, replaced only occasionally by a sense of physical nausea and sometimes vomiting whenever he perceived too distinctly the profaned form of a cross. He had just become a 'C' class patient and the psychiatrists considered him one of their classic cases of mental re-establishment. But he was one of the two out of five of all the patients who never received visits from friends or family. His mother had never allowed him any friends and had kept him a stranger to his few relatives. Now, to atone for his 'fall' and her own disappointment, she was taking her novitiate in an Irish convent where she would soon become a nun. She sent him little sacred postcards in colour – without crosses – on occasional saints' days and signed them only with her novitiate's name. He was one of the very few 'C' class patients who never attended mixed social evenings and mixed classes at Brockley. Suggestions by his psychiatrist that he should at least attend the monthly staff-patient dances had disturbed him so much that the subject had been put aside for a while longer.

His first two visits to her consulting room perplexed Miss Lewis. When he said that he required her advice on whether to take up gardening or poultry raising, he did not give the impression of being really interested in either occupation. It was the same when he asked her advice on what to read in the Brockley library and explained that he had read all the volumes of Dickens and needed something lighter than Shakespeare. His problem, when it finally emerged through a discussion of romantic literature, was simply that he was worried about sex. In his outside life it was not a subject that had ever interested him. It had been a kind of biological formula of which he had been aware, but without it seeming to have any personal application to him.

The 'sex' of which he had heard from his fellow patients at SP9 was either beyond his comprehension or seemed too revolting to be related to human activity. He had never discussed sex with his psychiatrist. He said that since he knew nothing about it nor had any thoughts on it, he could hardly discuss it. In any case, he refused to do so. But now, he confessed to Miss Lewis, he was worried.

In the last few months he had found himself 'looking' at some of the women patients – one in particular – as they had moved about the grounds. The critical stage of this situation had been reached, in his view, a few days earlier when he had seen a group of women patients crossing the rear courtyard, between the kitchen and the hall doors. The wind had been blowing hard and he had perceived the shapes of the thighs and the breasts of one of the girls in a way that he had never done before. But to him the most alarming part of this experience – and it was the first time it had ever happened – was to find that he continued deliberately, with the aid of the wind, to calculate the position and forms of the thighs, buttocks and breasts, in fact, divining the bodies beneath.

'You mean undressing her with your eyes?' said Miss Lewis casually. The youth gave her a swift, shocked glance and waited a few moments without replying. Then he went on to tell how he was revolted and disgusted with himself at the discovery of these vicious and surely abnormal tendencies. He was afraid to speak about it to his psychiatrist, and if he had already been allowed to resume direct association with the Church, he would have been even more ashamed to speak of it to a priest. He had prayed fervently for guidance, but he admitted he needed a direct human reassurance. Was he showing the tendencies of a sex maniac, and should he appeal to Dr Robertson for help? His sincerity was appealing, touching. He had forced his 'confession' out by an agonizing effort that left his usually pale face even more ashen than usual. His large dark eyes under level but thick brows carried the appeal of a prisoner awaiting sentence.

'Why ever did you come to me about this?' she asked, and though something inside her made her want to laugh or cry or both together, she tried to keep her smile casual. 'If you would be ashamed to admit this to a man – why not more so to a woman?' And she added with a wry laugh, 'I *am* a woman you know, even though not a very young one.' He tried bravely to return a weak and quavering smile, but she saw in his eyes the beginning of a great relief.

'Yes, but – you see—'

She interrupted, 'What you are trying to tell me, Tom, is that I'm a middle-aged woman and not a pretty girl, so it doesn't matter—'

'No, it's not just like that.' He stopped, exasperated. 'I'm sorry. I didn't mean it like that. The only men I've talked to most of my life have been either doctors or teachers of some kind, or priests, and so I've always been more or less intimidated by them. I didn't think of you as either a man or a woman or a teacher or a doctor, but a person – with a kind of neutral understanding capable of helping without simply judging.'

'Thank you, Tom.' Her voice sounded matter-of-fact, but it was not easy. 'I can tell you right away,' she went on, 'that you are one hundred per cent normal. Not a sex- or any other kind of maniac. This is not a matter for a doctor, or an analyst, or a social worker like myself – but just for a man. I'll make an appointment for you with Dr Robertson, a quite private, confidential, man-to-man appointment, and he'll tell you that you are quite, quite normal. In case he doesn't have time to tell you more, I'll tell you for him – you're a decent young chap, Tom, with a good and decent life ahead of you. Don't worry any more. Now, off you go and don't hide your eyes. There's no wind about today.'

As he closed the door she could not help thinking of May Saunders, 'the pavement monster', the abductor of children who needed love – and a lover. They were both orphans of the facts of life. Full of love and yet not knowing what it was.

13

Since the installation of her consulting room it had not occurred to her that Robert Welles would still be expecting her to call on him in his room for the private talk he had requested. Yet Welles's name remained absent from the daily lists of applications for private interviews, until the morning she found a neatly folded note on her desk, placed there doubtless by Joe Norton.

'Dear Lady,' it read, 'Having heard that your consulting room has become the mecca of the disconsolate, I have refrained from adding my voice to the clamour. But I should be most happy if you would care to take coffee with me in my room at two to two-fifteen this afternoon and spare me just fifteen minutes of your time. With my respectful salutations, I remain, Dear Lady, yours sincerely, Robert Welles.'

It was just the sort of precious-pretentious note she would have expected from Welles. But she decided there was no great advantage in insisting on his following the 'normal channels'. She did not share his own impression that he was in any way a 'senior' or privileged patient, but neither did she feel like taking issue with him on a trivial point of procedure.

He was alone, waiting for her, the coffee pot heating on a small occasional table beside the electric plug in the corridor, when she knocked on the door. He advanced to greet her, hand extended with an affectation suitable only for a mental home or a dilettante's salon. There was something about every exaggerated gesture or phrase of Robert Welles that left a suspicion

that he had his tongue in his cheek and was impudently playing a part to which his special situation as a mental patient
entitled him. He conducted Miss Lewis to his largest chintz
armchair, placed her coffee on a low table beside her, lit her
cigarette and sat down on a window seat.

He gave the physical impression of an elegant slug that had
been slightly dried out and cleaned up. He opened the conversation on a note of apology.

'I don't want you to think that I have any special right to
the privilege of receiving you in my room rather than taking
my turn with the rest in your consulting room. The box is
obviously a splendid idea, and I believe very much appreciated by those who do not have the chance to possess private rooms. But there seems to be one snag. Everyone knows
who goes to see you. Some get jealous because they believe
others are trying to obtain favours or privileges which will perhaps stop them from getting their share, or will favour some for
release at the expense of others. The big gossip of every day is –
who went to see Miss Lewis today and what for? Well, I
didn't want to get mixed up in that and frankly I don't think it
should be necessary for us who have our own rooms. There are
two of my friends, with their own rooms, who have asked me
to say they would very much like to talk to you too, but alone,
in their rooms.'

Miss Lewis replied briskly. Her attitude seemed to imply
that she was not keen to be trapped into social chit-chat with
Welles.

'Alright, if you wish. I do not wish to embarrass anyone.
Now, what can I do to help you, for instance?'

'My problem is just the same as anyone else's,' said Welles.
'I want to get out, and I believe I am fit to be let out. Any
abnormality I may have now is due to the fact that I have
been closeted in here, cut off from the world during ten of the
most formative years of a young man's life. I came here when I
was eighteen. Now I am twenty-eight. Not once during my
detention have I ever been guilty of violence or any abnormal
act. In that time I have taken a degree in classical literature
with honours and shortly I shall pass my law degree. That's all
very fine but I haven't a clue as to how to live in the world.
Yet Dr Robertson opposes my release, despite the fact that

my father is prepared to engage all the fully-qualified male nursing assistance imposed on me by the authorities twenty-four hours a day, as well as to pay for intensive analytical treatment – or whatever is deemed necessary – in my own home, at no cost to the taxpayer.' He was breathing rather heavily and he paused, studying the tips of his well-manicured fingers. 'I had thought I was entitled to request a hearing by a special tribunal. Now my lawyer is told that the court order under which I was committed here has a judge's restriction on discharge, which means that the most a special tribunal could do for me would be to transfer me to an institution of a lower security category – some other fantastically overcrowded bedlam where I should no doubt share a ward with seventy-five drooling epileptics.' He was silent, looking out of the window, conscious that he had begun to be drawn into the sort of tirade which he had sworn to himself to avoid. When he resumed he spoke in a lower, more controlled tone. 'If I am kept here another ten years and then released, I shall be quite useless, quite incapable of living in the world, nostalgic no doubt for the protection of my little padded cell. I shall have a string of degrees; I shall be erudite – and incapable. A model of institutional neurosis.'

He stopped and then asked suddenly, 'Do you know my record? Do you know why I am here?' She shook her head. 'I killed three or four young men – so I am told. I have no recollection of what happened. I didn't even know them. Their names, their identities were entirely strange to me when they were read out to me by the police. Ten years have passed and now even my analyst doesn't know what to talk to me about. I have no problems, no complexes – yes, I have one. If I am mad, then the rest of the world ought to be locked up in one huge padded cell, a super-cell and I ought to be their chief medical superintendent. And what's more, I know of a good half dozen of my friends here – "C" Wing men – whom I would pick as my assistants.'

Miss Lewis sat and watched him, fascinated. He was gradually ceasing to be aware of the reasons for her presence – of her presence itself. The pupils of his large watery eyes seemed to be growing darker and larger, while seeing less. His former suave pretence of balance and control was ebbing away as he went on, 'Who is sane? What is sanity? And who is really qualified to answer those questions? The sane, of course! But not anyone with creative imagination – not people who've reached out and touched their dreams – not those who've pulled the chain on the world and flushed all its stinking excreta out of their lives – not those who've seen enough truth to strangle all the lies and the furtive, menial liars propping up the world's shabby Moloch – so that they can lick out the gold-tinted shit it farts out at them—'

His words seemed to shock him back to a sense of her presence and his own desertion from his stock role of cultured gentility. With the rapidity and masterful control of a first-rate character actor, the expression of malevolence and revulsion that had begun to distort his flabby face disappeared and his features fell back into their well-bred folds of condescending urbanity. 'Ah!' he said, almost whimsically, 'now I see, my dear lady – I have shocked you. Do, please, forgive me for allowing myself to become carried away. Now you see perhaps what I mean when I say that in ten years – ten? – five more likely, I shall be a raving institutional neurotic, if not worse.'

There was a moment's pause before she asked in her usual matter-of-fact non-committal tone, 'What can I do for you, Mr Welles? You've told me yourself of Dr Robertson's decision – the uselessness of a special tribunal for you. What do you think I can do? I'm only a PSA, which as you surely know means no more than a psychiatric social assistant. *I* can't release you!'

He leaned forward, hands on his knees, an expression of painful concern spreading awkwardly across features long-since formed by insolence and scorn. 'Do please, first of all, before another word, say you forgive me for my quite disgusting language, my dear Miss Lewis.'

'Nonsense, young man,' she gave him a tight-lipped smile, 'you're forgiven if you think it's necessary, but after all, I meet a lot of exasperated people in my job. They're the ones I'm supposed to help most. But tell me now, seriously, what do you think I can do for you?'

The oil and sugar were back in his voice now. 'I understand, Miss Lewis, that you have friends of considerable influence at much higher than institutional level. Of course, I'm not asking you to go beyond your authority or competence. But, in view of what I have told you about my father's willingness and ability to assure my restraint and treatment according to official specifications and at his own cost, I thought that perhaps you could call my case to the attention of someone who might have it properly looked into.'

'I could not possibly do that without speaking first to Dr Robertson. In any case I shall be obliged to tell him of this request. Nor can I go against any advice he may give me.'

Welles's narrow, rounded shoulders sagged and his flabby chin sank on his chest. This time he was not acting. His pudgy fingers twisted invisible threads on his knees.

'Miss Lewis, my father is very, very rich. His gratitude to anyone who could help having me transferred to private care would be – well – more than you can imagine.' He was watching her closely. What he saw did not dismay him, but neither did it encourage him to go any further. To his kind of mind a seed had been sown. In time it would probably take root. It was enough for the present. Indeed there was nothing either way in Miss Lewis's reaction to show that he was right or wrong.

She stood up, a formal, dry smile on her face. 'Very well, then it is agreed Mr Welles. I will have a few words with Dr Robertson. Now, who are your other friends who want to see me?' He preceded her to the door, now all graciousness, the pure Welles-image-of-Welles again. 'Ah, yes, dear lady, of course. How kind of you. They are – in fact I took the liberty of suggesting that they should wait for you in their rooms. They are Mr Morley – the ex-business man, you know, in room seventeen, and Mr Herbert Strang, the dear old ex-king, room nine – both really nice people.'

He waved her on down the corridor with the cordial flourish of a good host bidding god-speed to an honoured guest.

146

14

Herbert Strang, a plump, balding, roseate complexioned man of forty-five, though a printer by trade, had believed for twenty years that he was king of the world, and the world was trying to keep the secret from him. He was gentle and timid, and yet perhaps due to his years of secret conviction he carried his shoulders as though he was constantly afraid that an ermine bordered cloak of state might slip from them if he was not careful. He carried the air of greatness-assuming-modesty, presumably another heritage of his now shattered illusion.

His simple and modestly-furnished room was just large enough for a wash-basin, a small plain table, a steel-framed bed, a creaky chair and a tired-looking, splintered cane arm-chair. There was a large tall-boy in the hall beside his door, padlocked. The room's decoration consisted of one large photograph of Mrs Strang and the three young Strangs.

Herbert Strang sat on the edge of his bed while the cane armchair swayed and creaked alarmingly even beneath Miss Lewis's fragile form.

'Now Mr Strang, what is your problem?' she began brightly.

The ex-king of the world polished his shiny forehead with a large checked handkerchief and puffed with embarrassment through pursed lips. He found it very hard to break into the subject. Finally he said, in a voice flat and toneless with despair, 'I don't want to go home. I want to stay here.' Miss Lewis knew that Strang had been recommended for return home, for outpatient treatment if it was felt necessary. He was due to leave Brockley within six months. He had long since renounced his belief that he was the king of the world. He was now prepared to accept, without any collateral arrangement, that he had been deposed by the world's states as a result of the new popular democratic trends, and he had declared that he was quite happy to go back to being a printer.

'Tell me,' Miss Lewis replied gently, 'whatever has made you change your mind?'

He looked at her under lowered brows, suspiciously, pulling gently at his lower lip like a sulky child.

'Is it true that you were brought up in India?' he asked. Yes, she told him, it was. 'Well,' said the ex-king, 'in that case I'll tell you, because in that case you're probably not a royalist nor one of Them.' There was a distinct capital letter to the emphatic accent he put on the word 'Them'. He went on. 'I had practically no followers in India, with the result that They didn't bother much about me, either. You see, I do not want to say what I am going to tell you, either to a Royalist or to one of Them. Though most of the people who run this place, and even some of those who pretend to be patients, belong to Them, there are one or two secret Royalists among the medical staff. You will realize why I needed someone impartial like you to tell what I have to tell you. It is this – I don't want to be sent home because I'm afraid of being assassinated.'

'Assassinated?'

He nodded solemnly. 'Yes, I'm afraid so. You see, when I was overthrown by Them and put in here, naturally a huge, even vast, section of the Royalist population stayed loyal, secretly. They have kept their faith and their hope. When I go out into the world again they will undoubtedly make a move to restore me, and of course,' he said this shaking his head sadly, 'they will fail. However, in the turmoil and uncertainty of the moment, *They* will be obliged to kill me to put an end to the Royalist plot. They're quite ruthless, of course, and They've always been after me, though in the earlier years, They were afraid to make a move. Now, if I were to tell this to a doctor here, who is a Royalist, he would of course say, "Don't worry, Your Majesty, we have everything under control, we'll protect you" – and so on. If I were to tell it to a doctor who is one of Them – well you can imagine – danger of a Royalist plot? They would massacre thousands of Royalists, my wife and family, take them by surprise. You, I can trust. You could put in a report saying that I've got hallucinations or something – that I've gone mad, I mean *really* mad, this time. Then they won't let me go. They'll keep me here. There'll be no Royalist plot, my wife and family will be safe and nothing will happen— Don't you think that would be best?' His wide, round eyes looked at her with appealing candour.

She looked at him gravely, nodding her head slowly as though weighing his argument. Then, 'Yes,' she said reflectively, 'yes, I suppose I could. But you know a report like that would have much more weight – much more – if it came from a doctor. Now I know for certain that Dr Robertson is a purely scientific man. He hates politics. He is devoted simply to the welfare of his patients and all those who may be in here – for whatever reasons. I give you my solemn word he's not one of Them, nor a Royalist. Now if you were to tell him about this – this new situation – in absolute confidence of course – only he and I will know – I'm positive he'll arrange for you to stay. Really. On my honour.'

The king sat pensively twisting his handkerchief for a few moments. Then he looked up at her. A slow and very sweet smile spread across his oval pink face.

'I believe you,' he said, 'I trust you. I'll tell the whole terrible story to Dr Robertson, if you could please ask him to see me. In confidence, of course. Top secret, of course.' The king gave a great sigh of relief and wiped his brow with his handkerchief, and then went on, more calmly, 'You've saved thousands of lives Miss Lewis, mine as well. You've no idea how much I want to stay just an ordinary person, I always did, in fact but – well – the Royalists and They wouldn't let me.'

'How did you find out you were king if the whole world wanted to keep it a secret?'

He gave her a sly smile and his artless eyes twinkled. 'It was easy. Right from the time I was a boy at school. Things kept happening, sometimes good, sometimes bad. When they were good things, like finding a shilling, or passing an exam, or winning the school hundred yards and later on getting a good job, meeting my marvellous wife who is a male-breeder – imagine,

149

three fine boys, princes – well, all that kind of thing was arranged for me by the Secret Court because I was King and there were certain priorities that just had to exist and I had to be helped a little, they had to make it seem like an accident, or chance, because they didn't want me to know.'

'Why?'

'Well, because I wasn't ready for the job. I had to be taught humility. I had to be taught how to lose sometimes. When things went wrong, it was on purpose too. All planned to harden me up, train me in initiative, courage, persistence, philosophy – all part of a king's training. But it had to be done without my getting a swelled head and thinking I could do what I liked.'

He fell silent, shaking his head gently with tolerant regret. 'They were very stupid. It became as plain as daylight to me what was happening. The pattern of good and bad, success and failure, happiness and disappointment, all calculated, balanced, worked out, you know. All those ups and downs. Marvellous training, of course. By the time I was fifteen I was quite certain I was King of the World. Though, mind you, I never let on that I knew. Never. I played the game with the Secret Court, and the Secret Police and my Secret Ministers, all the time. Just simple Herbert Strang – that was me.' She stood up to leave, and he shook her hand, clasped tightly in both of his. 'Thanks – thanks for all our lives,' he whispered fiercely.

She opened the door. 'I'm so glad to have been able to help. Don't worry any more. Everything will be looked after, in strictest confidence, of course—' She paused.

'It's alright,' whispered the ex-king of the world, 'you can call me Mister Strang.'

Why there should have been a small lump in her throat as she walked on down the corridor to room seventeen, she couldn't quite tell.

The room occupied by Daniel Morley, the chronic ravisher of children, earlier introduced to Miss Lewis by Welles as 'a business man', resembled a monk's cell. It contained a small table, a chair, a bed and a tall varnished pine locker. The white walls were bare except for a heavy, black wooden cross over the bed. The only book to be seen, on the bedside table, was a cheap edition of the Bible given to all patients. There were no family photographs, no effort at relieving the forlorn austerity of the minimum of government-issue furnishing. Even the flimsy piece of threadbare red matting which was supposed to serve as a bedside carpet had been rolled up and put on top of the locker. The wood floor was scrubbed and smelled of disinfectant. It was the room of someone who wanted a room to hate.

At forty-nine Daniel Morley looked nearer to sixty. His iron-grey hair was clipped short in a graceless crew-cut which hardened his once florid, well-filled features into a prison-mask of drab impassiveness. It was possible to identify the traces of a certain refinement and presence in the bearing of his broad, strongly-built figure, but the current identity of the man was fixed in the grey reserve of his pale eyes. They were enfolded, above and below, in creased pouches of skin, so dark that it almost looked bruised. Their expression was that of a man utterly defeated by himself and the world, with not the faintest flicker of a riposte. Looking into them one knew that not in the remotest refuge of his mind was there left a trace of pride or hope. His voice was firm and deep and his accent was that of a private school education. As he sat on the edge of his bed – Miss Lewis poised uncomfortably on the one small wooden chair – he wasted no time on preliminaries. In a crisp, detached voice he told her his dismal history of child molestation through each descending phase of his moral and material demolition, down to the twelve-year prison term which he was at present serving.

He had been sent to Brockley for a more specialized treatment than could be given him in Wormwood Scrubs prison where he was technically serving his sentence. He explained, in his empty-sounding voice: 'Except for my particular aberration, I have no criminal tendencies. I am not violent or unmanageable, I have no wish to escape, but I *do* want to be cured. Consequently, from a security point of view there was no objection to my being placed here, and in the "C" Wing, where the security is, to say the least of it, pretty poor.' He was silent as he placed the tips of his fingers precisely together, his elbows on his knees and his narrowed gaze directed just above the level of Miss Lewis's head.

'With my remission for good behaviour, conduct or whatever they call it I shall be freed from here and discharged from Wormwood Scrubs in only three more years and shall not be entitled to close confinement and intensive treatment as an internal patient again until I have sexually assaulted another child. This will occur very shortly after my release, and it may even occur several times before I am once more arrested and sentenced again, to begin the round of quite ineffective cures to which I give, as always, my fullest co-operation. And so it goes on – and will go on – unless one of two alternatives is to be accepted.

'I must make it clear that I have never once hurt a child, and if, during my activities, a child becomes frightened, I leave it at once. But the fact remains that – beyond and despite all reason, all my upbringing, education and all I have lost – I am a compulsive sexual offender against children. There is no humiliation, no degradation, no odium which I have not suffered as the price of my obsession. It is quite impossible for me to suffer any more than I have done, nor to fall any lower. And yet – as the situation is at present – I shall undoubtedly continue.

'Now I spoke of two alternatives. The first and easiest of these is castration. I am quite convinced that as far as I am concerned anyway, it would bring about the character change which would give me the chance to live a reasonably useful life, and, intellectually speaking, one satisfying enough to be worth living. Two months or so ago I forwarded through Dr Robertson and the chief superintendent, Colonel Barthropp, a request to the Ministry for castration, laying out in full the arguments I have just given to you. Neither the colonel nor the doctor was very hopeful of an affirmative reply. I have recently asked my analyst if there has been a reply and he simply shakes his head vaguely. There is always some reason why the colonel is not able to see me. I feel sure there is a reply – one way or the other. This waiting is – forgive me if I seem to use a rather worn and melodramatic expression, Miss Lewis – this waiting is quite literally hell. Because the answer, one way or another, will leave me between two pretty frightful alternatives, castration – or suicide. Yes, suicide is the only other alternative. Yet, you know, for all the little I have left in the world, I don't want to die. I can still see, hear, smell, touch, deliberate, react, and socially I would like to go on doing so. But not at the price I have been paying and will have to go on paying if nothing can be done to change me. Could you please exert all the influence and authority you have to try and have me informed about my request?'

He sat upright and let his hands drop in a gesture of weary submission by his sides. 'There, that's all I wanted to ask you.' His exposé had been so simplified, so logical and unhesitating that there had never occurred a moment when Miss Lewis's intervention would not have seemed superfluous. Now, at the end of it, as they sat facing one another, there still seemed nothing for her to say. Morley was leaning forward now, arms folded, gazing at the floor. He seemed not to expect any word from her, but as she stood up to leave he looked up at her with his beaten, uncurious eyes. 'Do you despise me, Miss Lewis?'

She studied his face for a moment, but before she had time to answer, he thumped the palm of one hand against his knee, exclaiming, 'Hell, what a stupid question! Of course you don't. What I should have said was – do you pity me very much, Miss Lewis? Do you?'

'I am really sorry for you Mr Morley, and I will do all I can to help you,' she said. When she closed the door behind him, he was lying on his bed, arms by his side, staring at the ceiling.

15

She was on her way to the colonel's office when, crossing by the main kitchen-mess-hall block she met Joe Norton, who greeted her with his usual sprightly *bonhomie*. On an impulse she stopped him, and quite aware that she might be letting her sense of hierarchy slip, she asked, 'Do you have one moment to spare Mr Norton? I would appreciate your opinion on one or two small points.' He answered with some obscure cockney gallantry and accompanied her to her consulting room.

When they were seated in the 'box', she told him, 'You can help me because you have less formal relations with some of the patients than any of the medical staff, which means that perhaps they remain more natural with you than with us.' She seemed ill at ease as she gave her somewhat unorthodox explanation, sincere though it was. Norton lit a cigarette and nodded non-committally.

'I want you to tell me what you think of one or two patients, in confidence of course, and I mean, what *you* think, not what you think the doctors or anyone else thinks or ought to think – just *your* opinion of them as people, *and* as patients.'

Norton grinned and blew a cloud of smoke across the desk. He seemed not displeased by this sign of confidence. 'Shoot,' he said.

'First of all, I'm interested in this man Michael Loft,' she began. 'Is he a friend of yours?' Her voice, always thin and crisp, was calm, almost casual. Norton's reaction was spontaneous without even an instant for reflexion. 'That nut?' he

said. 'Never got a word out of 'im. Not even when we're coun-
tin' rabbit skins. 'Ee's a regular crackpot, that feller. Don't like
no one. Talks to 'is ruddy rabbits and squirrel all day.' He
went on, quite misinterpreting the object of her question. 'No,
miss, yer don't need to 'ave no fear of 'im. I know 'ee looks like
a monster and 'ee scares the daylights out of most people
around 'ere, but 'ee's as 'armless as 'is rabbits. It beats me why
they keep 'im 'ere. You visit 'im quite a bit I see, eh? Well
that's your job, I suppose. But you don't need to be scared.
'Ee'll never lay a 'and on yer, Miss Lewis.'

'Good.' She seemed relieved as she went on: 'Now, what
about Mr Welles? How do you find him?' Norton's reaction
was as though all his mental responses had suddenly been
shifted into a lower gear and his bright sparkle was replaced by
a wary and calculated absence of reaction. He flicked the ash
from his cigarette and studied the spiral of smoke from its end.
'Welles?' he said reflectively, 'Mr Welles? A very eddicated
gentleman that one.' He paused and repeated, 'Very 'eddicated.' It seemed as though Norton had no more to say as he
gazed purposefully at his cigarette.

'Dangerous?' she asked.

Norton cheered up instantly. The question indicated to him
that the whole conversation and Miss Lewis's interest had no
other object than her own safety. He laughed out loud this
time. 'Dangerous? Mr Welles?' He sounded almost boisterous. 'When I said gentleman, I meant gentleman. There's another of 'em ought to be allowed to go. But for a better reason.'
He tapped his forehead significantly. 'That Mr Welles is more
than just sane. 'Ee's a brain, that's wot 'ee is.'

She said, 'You visit him a good deal, don't you?'

There was the faintest trace of a defensive tone in his reply,
although her question had been spoken with no trace of critical
implication. 'Well, I suppose I do,' he said. 'There's nothin'
wrong with that, you can be sure. There's two reasons why I
see Mr Welles quite a bit. First, 'ee's the canteen's best cus-
tomer. I get up to ten or even twenty quid a month special
orders from 'im, all paid for on the nail every month by 'is
dad. Five quid's worth of French liver paste – foy grass they
call it – last month alone. Then I like to listen to 'im talk about
the law – specially the criminal lunatic law of 1959 or some-

155

thin' like that. It's a real treat to listen to Mr Welles spoutin' about the rights of the nuts. I'll tell yer Miss Lewis, 'ee knows a sight more of what 'ee's talkin' about than some others what I could mention workin' in the same front 'all area – my respects of course – your goodself excepted.'

'Yes, I know what he thinks about sane people,' she said. 'You obviously agree with him.'

Norton shifted awkwardly in his chair, and stabbing his cigarette in her desk ashtray looked up and gave her a heavy wink. 'Well, if I 'ad a mind like 'is, you wouldn't keep me in this place long.'

She stood up, abruptly. 'Thank you, Mr Norton, for your opinions. They'll be a great help to me in evaluating these patients. And now I must go and see the colonel. Oh, by the way,' she added as though by a sudden afterthought, just as they were separating at the door, 'I hear that poor little Indian ward-maid Mounalal has been sent away pregnant. You haven't had any news of her since, have you?'

Norton stopped for an instant as though he had been slapped in the face, but recovered himself practically instantly. The sharp note of his answer showed how clearly she had caught him off his guard. 'That little black – er – kid? Why should I 'ear from 'er? I never spoke two words to 'er in me life.'

As Miss Lewis turned and walked towards the colonel's office across the corridor, he stood in the doorway staring after her. The expression of astonishment on his face was not without a growing look of shifty unease as though he was still only half-consciously perturbed by the coincidence that two of the three people mentioned by Miss Lewis, Mounalal and Welles, were, or had been, associated with the more dangerous of his nefarious activities.

16

Colonel Barthropp was always glad to see Miss Lewis. Even in their briefest daily moments of contact she brought him a whiff of nostalgia, carrying a thread of better days into the sad and sullen air of SP9. In addition he was genuinely grateful for the way she had integrated into the life and functions of SP9. She had managed to make herself necessary without treading on anyone else's ground. She was a universal prop, on the fringe of almost every function of the hospital, willing, available, helpful and cheerful just wherever or whenever she was wanted. But the colonel was still the only person at Brockley who dared to call her by her first name.

'Hello Margaret, my dear, come in, come in,' he boomed, pushing aside the heap of papers on his desk. 'What can I do for you?'

She sat down. 'I'm worried about the patient called Morley, the one who wrote a letter asking to be castrated. Because he cannot get a reply, he asked me if I could try and find out if there is one and whether he could be told as soon as possible. He's not in a very good way. Mentally, I mean.'

The colonel flicked through a card-index case on his desk. He frowned. 'Mm, yes. Actually Dr Brandt is his visiting psycho-analyst. In fact we have had a reply from the Ministry. I passed the letter on to Dr Robertson about ten days ago. It's really for him to decide how to handle the matter from now on. In consultation with Dr Brandt, I suppose.'

'The reply – was it favourable?'

The colonel looked at her solemnly for a moment over the top of his spectacles and brushed a corner of his moustache upwards with the back of his left hand. They both knew that she was technically exceeding her official authority, but they knew equally well that for her almost freelance functions to be effective they needed flexible limits.

'Favourable?' said the colonel. 'In either sense that is hardly the word. Talk to Dr Robertson about it. But I'll tell you what the Ministry *said*.' He pulled a dossier from a filing cabinet beside him and read out slowly, 'It is not the practice in any institution or criminal detention establishment to permit the exercise of any form of mutilation not justified by medical or surgical considerations.' The colonel looked up. 'They mean no,' he said. 'Why do you ask Margaret?' At that moment his desk interphone buzzed and he clicked the switch to reply.

'Any idea where Miss Lewis is?' The voice was Dr Robertson's. 'Oh, it's not in the least urgent,' he added when he learned she was in the colonel's office. 'Just whenever she cares to drop in.'

'She'll be coming up right away,' replied the colonel. Switching off his interphone he told her, 'You might as well see Robertson now since he wants to see you anyway. But, tell me, about this patient Morley, was that all he wanted to speak to you about?'

'Not exactly. He wanted to explain that if the Ministry reply refuses castration he intends to kill himself. In the meantime, as he says, the waiting for one or other of those decisions is pretty hellish.'

'Naturally,' said the colonel. 'You tell all that to Robertson and let him decide.'

Dr Robertson greeted her cheerily in his cramped consulting room – though it was quite a bit larger than hers. 'The colonel says you have things to tell me? Well you start first,' he said, 'I've got nothing more than a social anecdote to tell you.'

She told him of her meeting with Morley and his state of despair driving him to thoughts of suicide.

'We're not going to tell him of the Ministry reply for a while yet,' he told her. 'First we are going to try and condition him

158

as much as possible for a negative reply. But in the meantime I'll assure him that I'm making serious and angry efforts to get a speedy reply. That should calm him for a while. But as a matter of fact I have some statistics from Germany and Denmark – I think it is – showing that even castration is no positive cure for what troubles him. At least two per cent of those treated by castration revert to their former behaviour; the real figure of those not detected as recividists is probably much higher. We shall tell Morley about the decision when we believe that further psychiatric treatment has made him able to accept it without violent reaction. Only then shall I be able to tell him that I have applied for permission to try a new hormone treatment, which has so far shown remarkable results, in tests, with no reversion or side effects. That should be good news to him. But he'll have to wait to accept the bad news first.'

She told him of Welles's appeal to her to try and intervene for private treatment in his own home under approved care and conditions. The doctor's face hardened and he shook his head at the first mention of Welles.

'Welles is today a severe psychopathic personality, with a brilliant analytical mind. Consequently he is one of the most dangerous patients we have – in a certain sense. He is certainly the most difficult to treat. As he has realized himself, institutionalizing him is only going to aggravate his case. Yet, how can we treat him outside any institution? Apart from the court order on his preventive detention, he's far too potentially dangerous.' The doctor grinned and said dryly, 'If my conscience had a price – and who's hasn't? – I still could not calculate how many noughts it would run to before I would let Robert Welles out into the world.' He shook his head slowly, 'Aye – the poor man's in a trap. The longer he stays here – to my mind – the less chance there'll ever be for him to be released.'

The doctor brightened when she told him about the assassination fears of the ex-king Strang and his reasons for them. 'You see, my dear, *that's* where you're a life saver for us. He would never have told that story to any of us – and he might have been discharged with disastrous results. I'll see him and tell him how non-political I am and promise to keep him quite a good while longer. The poor man's a delusional schizophrenic – not lost to life yet and with plenty of hope for him.'

He paused and looked up at her, friendly, relaxed. 'Well, you seem to be moving around very effectively, my dear. Your presence and your activity, even among patients you have not been able to help directly, are having a good effect – I mean an active therapeutic effect. You're doing more than you probably realize, just by being yourself. Are there any other patients in whom you've found a particular interest?'

She shook her head thoughtfully and then looked up – her brown eyes wide and candid. 'No,' she said, 'no, I don't think so.' Then hesitantly, as an afterthought of little importance, added, 'Well, there is perhaps one who interests me a little. His name is Loft. He looks after the gardening block and the rabbits. Is he one of those due for release? He seems to live only for his animals.'

'He'll never see the outside world again,' said the doctor, 'but as long as we leave him alone to go on doing what he's doing, he's quite harmless. He might even be quite harmless outside in the world again – if the world would have him. I don't know. He's a very remarkable case. I'll send his medical dossier round to you, if you're interested. If you can make a breakthrough there, you'll be doing what more than ten years of psychotherapy have failed to do. Does he react to you?'

'He's beginning to, I think,' she replied.

'Well, keep at him,' said the doctor. 'It could be that you might rekindle some spark of contact in him which would give us another chance. I say it *could* be advisedly, because I myself, as well as others even more qualified, gave up hope of any progress with him quite a few years ago. Anyway his case history might help you.'

She thanked him and was just preparing to leave when he stopped her with an exclamation of impatience. 'Idiot that I am, I had forgotten the real reason for which I wanted to see you. Sit down, my dear.'

He became absorbed in wiping his thick, double-focus lens spectacles and while he held them in his hands his eyes lost their most notable characteristic. Their quality of penetrating personal contact disappeared and the man's own mind became veiled by a vague wall-eyed gaze. He took an unusually long time polishing his lenses – with a small square of buckskin – and began to talk before he had finished. His voice sounded nervous. 'I – er – met a mutual friend at a dinner party last night. A retired hospital matron – charming old lady – you must have known her as Matron Marion Blake when she was at the George's Cross General Hospital in London. I expect you remember her?'

If Miss Lewis's expression had changed, the doctor would not have perceived it for he was still polishing away at his spectacles. He continued to do so, as he went on, 'Miss Blake – she is the aunt of a doctor friend of mine who lives not far away – was talking about India and so I said that we had a psychiatric social assistant who was brought up in India, and mentioned your name.' There was another pause and the unfocussed gaze was directed with a certain bland-benignity towards the motionless figure of Miss Lewis. 'She remembered you at once, most kindly, as a promising young probationer nurse, hard-working and ambitious apparently – who had been brought up in the Indian Railways Orphanage and later adopted by a senior official of the Indian Civil Service.'

Now his spectacles were back in place, adjusted comfortably, and the keen eyes came back to life to seek a response in the impassive gaze of the woman before him. Her mouth shaped an acknowledgement with a fleeting, humourless smile. 'Yes, of course I remember Matron Blake. She was a great inspiration to me.'

Something like a breath of relief, to be sensed rather than heard or seen, moved the doctor and his words came hurriedly as though to break a tension none but he had felt. 'She said how much she had regretted your sudden departure, to marry some young doctor apparently. And then she lost trace of you. She asked, of course, to be remembered to you.'

'Thank you, doctor. But why are you telling me this? Does it matter that—'

'Good heavens,' Robertson replied, 'I am just telling you, as I said, a social anecdote and passing on a friendly word. I do hope I have not upset you by mentioning the orphanage thing. You didn't conceal it from anyone. No one ever asked you. If your Indian Civil Service parents were adopted ones – well, that's no one's business but yours. If you were once married to a doctor, well that's your business too.' He waited in silence but she said nothing. As if to excuse himself further, he went on, 'I did wonder whether I should mention to you my meeting with Matron Blake, whether it might embarrass you too much. And then I thought I would feel rather deceitful in not telling you that I knew about the orphanage and your marriage. I preferred to tell you and to assure you that having been brought up in an orphanage and having been married changes you in no way as far as I'm concerned – and is the business of no one at all in this institution. Those facts, which I came across by pure accident, belong to you and no one else. I have no reason to mention them to a soul. You are a tremendous person, with a magnificent record of service, and that's all that matters to us here.'

He leaned back in his chair and began polishing his glasses again. 'So, I do hope you will understand. I really felt it would be more honest to mention those facts I stumbled across and to add, of course, that I don't think one whit the less of you for being orphanage-bred. Quite the contrary.' He put his glasses back on again and ended with an expression of relief and a note of friendly finality in his voice. 'Well, now, shall we not talk any more about the subject? Just best regards from Matron Blake, and that's all.'

She sat rigid and mute. He mistook her silence for gratitude. Her thin lips were so tight that the fine creases of her age showed no longer as the soft traces of humour and understanding around the edges of her mouth. They had become fine crevices of fear and defiance. The knuckles of her right hand grasping the end of her chair arm were white with the force of her grip. She closed her eyes for a moment.

'Are you alright, Miss Lewis? I'm so sorry if I upset you.'

The doctor pushed back his chair in alarm and was beginning to move around his desk when she opened her eyes and gestured with her hand to stop him. She shook her head. 'No, please, Doctor. I'm terribly sorry. Do sit down. I'm perfectly well.'

He moved back hesitantly to his chair. It was the first time he had ever perceived the assured composure of her features touched by any expression of weakness. But it was a transformation hardly to be counted in seconds. When she spoke again her voice had regained its habitual note of precision and assurance.

'There are some things one likes to forget. I had thought the Railways Orphanage was quite effaced from my life.' She paused and the doctor nodded. 'So it is. You were more than correct to mention your accidental knowledge of this part of my life, you were very considerate. It was unpleasant for you, and I truly appreciate it.' Her eyes smiled up at him. 'Now we can forget it together.' She picked up her large practical handbag, almost dispatch-case size, by its long shoulder strap and turned towards the door. 'I've quite a round of people to chat to this afternoon and it's already late. I really must move along.' She spoke with a business-like detachment and the doctor acknowledged her words with a friendly nod. As though the door she closed quietly behind her framed still some kind of image that puzzled him, the doctor sat motionless for some moments, staring at the place where he had last seen her.

Margaret Lewis walked casually down the first-floor stairs to her consulting room in the front hall. She smiled a warm greeting to one of the nurses and two of the women patients she was escorting to their third-floor quarters, and called cheerily, 'Hello Jane, hello Rose – had a nice walk? It's a bit chilly isn't it?' The three of them, the nurse and the patients, smiled back in reply. It was a brief contact without significance. Yet the two patients, both middle-aged, greying women, went on up the stairs with lingering smiles, as though the trivial encounter had left echoes of comfort in the spaces of their minds. The briefest meeting with 'the Lewis lady', as some of the patients called her, almost always had that effect.

She passed on into her consulting room and looked at her watch. There were still ten minutes to go before the first three patients on her afternoon visiting list would be due. She lit a cigarette and sat at her desk unmoving, expressionless, one slender hand stretched on the writing-pad in front of her. The focus of her eyes was fixed on some point of thought, far beyond the curling cigarette smoke and the white walls. She felt as though something had cracked in her mind. As though some high, undeviating wall she had built to lead her on a determined course had suddenly begun to sway and crumble –

threatened to end and leave her suspended in no known place. She had lost count of her steps and what came next. Her face was ashen grey.

Suddenly, swinging her satchel sharply onto her shoulder, she left the room.

There was no class in the gardening block that afternoon. As she approached she saw from the outside two patients in their blue working dungarees sitting smoking in the greenhouse. Her approach to the doorway linking the conservatory and the two halves of the barn was soundless. The early winter afternoon was overcast and to the left, from the doorway, the long rabbit barn was gloomy with soft, ill-defined shadows. She halted in the opening, a hand's length from the regular stack of gardening tools. Just inside, and not more than four or five feet from the doorway Michael Loft was kneeling on the ground, head bent over the cloudy white profile of a huge buck rabbit. The animal, docile and content, was squatting at his knees while he brushed its thick coat with long gentle strokes, slow and sensual, beginning from the narrow crest of its head between the flattened ears, down into the curve at the back of its neck and along the humped back to its tail. He was making sibilant murmuring sounds as he passed the short, stiff-bristled brush – it looked like a clothes brush – sometimes along its back, sometimes along its flanks, and once, almost with the tender precision of a sculptor, along the whiskers on each side of its plump cheeks. He was completely absorbed by his grave and loving grooming of the acquiescent animal.

Miss Lewis stood in the doorway with the muscled stillness of a cat, watching and listening for the moment when the reaction of its prey is bound to be too late to parry or evade the quick stroke of death. To her right were the garden tools. But neither the scythe she had once favoured, nor the pick, nor the axe, were nearest to her right hand. Instead, almost on its own, on the outer range of tools was a square-cut metal bar, about an inch thick, pointed at the base, hammered flat at the top, used by the gardeners to mark out new lines for flower-beds, paths or fences. It reached to her waist, conveniently hand-high, a rusty but formidable weapon.

With a minimum of movement she took it in her right hand and as she stepped well forward with her left foot, she swung the bar, as one might draw a sword from its sheath, in a quick upward curve that brought it around and then downwards with all the impetus of its weight towards the bared neck of the man kneeling almost at her feet. As the bar commenced its deadly downward swing – with the interminable perception of critical instants – she observed the shadowed bulge of the seventh vertebra and she knew that between it and the base of his skull the metal she wielded would break his neck even more swiftly than the edge of his hand would break the neck of one of his rabbits. The full arc of the swinging bar was almost completed when Loft, in a single movement jerked up his head and began to pull himself back from his knees to stand upright. Instead of thrashing across his neck, the bar grazed the top of his forehead just below the hairline and with a soft thud glanced downwards, scraped over his heavy, bulging brows to bounce bluntly on the high ridge of his nose. The weight of the bar and the unexpected impetus it had gained beyond its point of aim wrested it from her grip and in passing, its pointed end tore open the throat of the white rabbit.

The shock of the blow had rocked the man back on his haunches and now, stunned by pain and shock, he crouched, head down between his knees, his hands clasping his forehead.

With hardly an instant's pause she stepped forward and picked up the heavy end of the bar from where it had fallen beside him. Her eyes saw nothing but his immense ragged mop of dark hair straggling out around the great bowed head, still immobile, and submissive like an ox waiting for the pole-axe.

She swung the bar again to shoulder height, then gasped as the movement sent a pain like the rasping of a dull-edged knife searing through her sprained right wrist. This time the bar fell with a dull rumble, harmlessly to one side.

Loft raised his head for a moment, took his hands from his brows and tried vainly to wipe aside with his knuckles the veils of blood coursing down over his eyes.

In an instant Margaret Lewis was on her knees, the hand that had held the iron bar now fumbling painfully in her satchel. Then frantically she scattered on the floor the objects in her bag which seemed to screen the one she sought most. Her cigarette case, her lighter, bundles of keys, purse, notebooks, pen, vanity case, all came tumbling out before the snub-nosed steely-blue automatic for which she waited. In the same instant in which she snatched it up she checked with her thumb that the safety-catch was off, and then lifted it to the horrifying mask of crumpled skin and oozing blood, a foot away from her face. She had already tensed herself for the blast that would this time tear through his battered forehead, when some kind of brutal logic bid her stop.

Why kill him now when he was hardly capable of knowing or fearing what was happening? Why grant this misery the mercy of instant oblivion? Why not keep the memory of this hideous moment in which to luxuriate while she waited for another chance, when she could tell him first that he was face to face with Cheryl's mother?

Quickly she dropped the automatic, and among the heap of belongings poured from her bag she found instead just what she needed – a large, clean, folded pocket handkerchief.

She partly unfolded it and began to raise it to his forehead, then paused halfway through her gesture. It would be quite useless. The top of his forehead had been scalped. From the hairline down almost to the level of the ridges of his thick brows, his forehead was peeled raw and a lap of skin, crumpled, still too impacted to bleed freely, hung down almost across his eyes. Only from the high arch of his nose, sheared to the bone, blood was just beginning to flow profusely. She tried to place the folded handkerchief to staunch the flow, but with a sharp gesture he brushed her hand aside. He picked up the dying rabbit and held it to his cheek. His blood mingled with the smeared mess of scarlet from the gash in its throat. The animal gave a few convulsive kicks and then lay limp.

The blood had now begun to drip from the huge hooked end of his nose, and the drops were fast becoming a stream. He took the handkerchief from her and held it to the bridge of his nose. The pink raw strip of his forehead was now beginning to flush red as the blood pulsed once more through the crushed flesh.

Perhaps all this had lasted a score of seconds. Loft looked down again at the still form of his rabbit, as though to try and grasp what had all happened so suddenly.

Now he looked at Margaret Lewis for the first time in all the eternal seconds of their encounter. She caught in his blood-dimmed eyes a glimpse of the terror that his stumbling, pain-broken words conveyed.

'Miss Lewis, I didn't mean to frighten you – I wasn't going to hurt you. I didn't even know you were there. Please, please don't tell them I frightened you. Maybe I moved too suddenly. But I was only going to stand up – that's all.' He was silent a moment as he tried to wipe the blood from his eyes, from his mouth.

'If I frightened you – of course you were right to defend yourself. I know I'm ugly. Fearfully ugly. The doctors say I'm going to die of it one day. I frighten people just because they look at me. You were right, Miss Lewis – to be frightened. But please don't tell *them*.'

Unconsciously one of his great hands was fondling the still form of the rabbit at his knees, while the other, with her handkerchief, saturated with blood, tried to stem the stream dropping like a shredded scarlet cloth across his whole face. The desperate supplication of his voice was echoed in the half-blinded eyes with almost animal appeal as for a moment they searched her face for a response. She said nothing. Her gaze fell to her hands in her lap. They were splashed with blood. She said, 'Michael Loft, of course I'm sure this was a – well – a terrible misunderstanding. Yes, I was afraid – by the way you moved. I was trying to defend myself. But I believe you. I made a terrible mistake. Please forgive me. I'm desperately sorry. Come with me now to the infirmary and I will tell them that,' she looked rapidly around the shed, 'that one of your rabbits escaped and in chasing it you fell into the pile of garden tools. Will that do?'

He pressed a blue-dungareed forearm against the crimson flood of his forehead and eyes, and winced as a fold of skin stuck for an instant to the hard dry tissue. 'Yes,' he said, 'that will do. Bless you, Miss Lewis. It needs a saint to forgive an ugly man. Ugliness is the most unforgivable sin. Pretty wickedness can always be excused. Only ugliness is entirely wicked.' He looked down again at the still form of the dead rabbit at his knees. 'That was old Him, I mean Him was his name. He was the first of them all. He was due to die very soon. He was ill but I consoled him a bit. He practically loved me. But he died because I frightened you.' His deep rich voice faltered and with a kind of agonizing clumsiness he leaned forward, his gory forehead on his folded arms, across his knees. 'Because I frightened you – I killed him,' he seemed to murmur to himself, 'but for Christ's sake don't tell them it was like that.' And then he fainted. As he rolled slowly over on to his side, one huge arm almost covered the splayed form of the dead rabbit – as though to gather it in a crude embrace.

She threw her littered belongings back into her satchel and hurried away to fetch help.

17

The Diary of Margaret Lewis

EXTRACT 4

When the story of Margaret Lewis at Brockley is done it is possible that even by then no one will have realized that the 'accident' suffered by Michael Loft was in fact my first clumsy attempt to murder him. It was even more than just clumsy. It was ill-judged, mis-timed, misplaced – everything about it from beginning to end was wrong. My aim with the iron bar was misdirected because he moved a fraction of a second too soon, and he thought I had hit him in self-defence because his sudden movement had frightened me. That would have been my explanation anyway, if he had not agreed to a very much better one. Because he felt that my apparent reaction of fear might be considered justified by the hospital authorities, and he would lose the liberty of his gardening block and the company of his animals, we invented the lie of the 'accident'. This suited me perfectly because it meant no change in routine or circumstance and gave me another chance to kill him without panic and haste, with proper planning and forethought.

I must explain to you, my unknown readers and judges, how I came to try and kill the survivor on a moment's unbalanced impulse, without a practical idea in my head.

Suddenly that afternoon Dr Robertson had revealed to me, I believe with the kindliest intentions, that he had accidentally learned of my upbringing at The Railways, and of my marriage while a probationer nurse, as he put it, 'to some young doctor'. This information came at a dinner party given by a doctor friend of Dr Robertson, attended by Marion Blake who about twenty-eight years before had been my first hospital matron in London. The old lady, she must be getting on for eighty now, had remembered me when my name came up in a conversation about India. So far as Dr Robertson informed me, she had only revealed my orphanage origins and my marriage to an unidentified doctor. She appeared to know nothing to associate me with Cheryl Hayes or the Loft case.

But while Dr Robertson was telling me the story I felt as though my life and all it stood for were falling apart. For one instant I felt exactly as though I had been stunned, knocked into space with nothing left to cling to. Even though I realized by the time I had returned to my office that he knew nothing that mattered except that I had concealed my real origins and upbringing. I did not wait long enough to think things out. I felt trapped. How much more would the old matron remember the next time, or even at any moment now? How much might Robertson casually learn if he started asking questions about me elsewhere, just because his curiosity had been aroused? In Loft's records file no doubt the name Hayes must be repeated quite frequently – Dr Alan Hayes – Mrs Margaret Hayes – Cheryl Hayes.

In my mind I saw time closing in on me: official reaction, Dr Robertson's reaction – for the man is far from being a fool – at the association of the names of Loft and Hayes. All my years, sustained by love and hate and patience, could be wasted by one more dinner-table conversation and the muddled memory of some doctor's old aunt. Or even by a telephone call by Robertson to the Ministry to make a general check on my antecedents. I panicked then at the thought that there was no more time left to plan, to luxuriate in the means and measures of destruction I could choose. There was only – just – perhaps, the time to kill before the be-all and end-all of my life might be snatched from me. When I walked over to the work-shed in the gardens to confront the survivor, I still had no idea how I was going to destroy him. I was simply resigned to the fact that all the finer degrees of the process I had hoped to be able to plan would have to be abandoned in favour of what would be a simple execution without delay. For an execution, an elimination – no I prefer the word extermination because it has verminous assumptions – I knew that only the simplest tools were needed and that these were at hand for me. I don't know why, but I did not think of my automatic in my satchel at all, perhaps because in all my fantasies on the death of the survivor it has never figured. If necessary I felt prepared, without any subterfuge, to make a frontal attack on him with whatever blunt and beastly instrument was at hand. He would surely never have acted fast enough to have repulsed it because he would never have felt in any danger from me. I hoped at least to be able to use the scythe, a hammer or an axe. As it was, circumstances gave me the illusion of complete surprise – the dim light, his preoccupation with his blessed rabbit, an iron bar as well placed to my hand as the hilt of a sword. I knew it had to be like that. It was heavy, that bar, and as I brought it up to shoulder height I had to bend my knees to reach the top of the curve. Then to give it all the weight and momentum possible I stood straight, and reinforced my shoulder and my arm by bending from the waist. The combined strength and weight of my body, which is little, and of my timing, which is much greater, went into that blow. For one instant as the bar was at the peak of its curve my weight, my balance, my hopes, my hate, my years of loneliness, were all behind it. It weighed a lifetime. Rightly placed it would have shattered the neck of an ox. I saw, in the detached and detailed way one can look at a cloud or a mountain or a distant horizon, the exact form of the vertebrae above which I was going to smash in the back of his curved neck. The long straggling hairs at the back of his head, irregular and animal, I noted with revulsion. I even noticed in that dim light that he had what looked like a round brown birthmark on the side of the bony nodule in the middle of his neck. That would crush too. For more than one, more than many instants I perceived all the details of the place where the iron bar was going to exterminate the survivor and re-unite me with Cheryl. Then he lifted his head, and his body, at the same time and it seemed to me as if the iron bar sheered off the front of his face. For a moment too I felt as though my wrist was broken and even to write these words now gives me great pain – a double pain. One of a wrench that almost broke it, another for the failure of which I am reminded by every stab of twisted tendons. Even when I had missed, but at least stunned and mutilated him, I need not have failed.

My resolution was as fierce as ever and I realized instantly that kneeling bleeding at my feet, stunned, he was in fact giving me the chance to retrieve the bar and, piece by piece, blow by blow, mash his body – especially his face – beyond recognition. That is what I was about to do when my sprained wrist gave way. It seemed as though I would be reduced after all to putting a bullet in him while he was still too stupefied to realize that this was payment from the mother of Cheryl. And then I suddenly understood that I need not go on at all. Here was a sort of bonus for my vengeance, in the form of Michael Loft, gruesomely mutilated, his flesh and bone ground through by the extension of my own force through an iron bar. This was a rewarding little extra, like a satisfying rehearsal after which he could be repaired and made fit for the real death I wanted for him – if I could keep my head the next time.

That is why I changed my automatic for a clean handkerchief.

I have been absent on leave for two days now, theoretically 'upset' by having witnessed the 'unfortunate accident' to Loft which needed twenty-one stitches in his forehead and eight more along the bridge of his nose.

For the past forty-eight hours I have not been able to forget the shock of flesh and bone being crushed by my own hand, shooting like an electric current from the slashing end of that bar into my hand, my body, my mind. Whatever happens now – however I do it in the end – I shall treasure the memory of that horrific, magnificent moment. The dull but vibrant thud of the metal as it hit his head and seared his scalp will be a comfort and strength to me when suddenly in the night I feel the faint, softly insistent fingers of weakness and pity plucking at the strings of my heart. They are too taut for that kind of music now.

What I must do at present is to put down in words – it is so much more effective than just thinking, because thoughts go on and on so quickly, but words on paper stay there and you can go back and measure and reflect on them and adjust them and adopt them finally so that you have a kind of written charter of belief and intention – to go back to the beginning of this dis-ordered sentence, I am trying to put down in black and white my feelings and the conclusions which must be drawn from them. They are:

(1) Brute violence must be well planned in the future and with pre-vision to protect it if necessary from interference or failure by the immediate use of my automatic.

(2) In any event my determination to kill or bring about the death of the survivor, in the most unpleasant circumstances possible, remains unchanged, for the reasons already described. There is no place in the world for the two of us.

(3) To avoid having to employ means of elementary violence, including shooting, I must get to know more about him, his conditions of life and his habits. I expect he will feel under an obligation to me because I stuck to the lie on which we had agreed about his 'accident'. His own version supported it per-fectly of course. The damage he suffered was not beyond what one might expect for a man of his height and weight stumbling head first amid a pile of gardening tools. It was certainly more credible than the idea that someone of his height could be hit across the head with an iron bar by someone of my size.

(4) With Matron Blake's recollections of me awakened, time is no longer on my side. I must never lose a chance nor miss an idea for a solution.

(5) I must for you, my future judges, complete as soon as pos-sible my story of Cheryl so that you can never underestimate the force of my motivation, nor imagine that anything that has happened can have weakened my purpose, or the love, and the hate, that keep me fighting towards it.

Cheryl, after our wonderful Cornish holiday, accepted with increasing difficulty the restraint which, on the advice of the police and with the help of her doctor, we imposed on her. The Scotland Yard inspector, Marshal, was quite categoric – as long as the man Loft remained at large, Cheryl's life was in danger. One more escape would probably be her last.

To resume: there were now four young people, two boys and two girls, mutilated and irretrievably out of their minds as a result of their experiences with Loft and his beastly sect.

So long as Loft was at large there was no question of Cheryl being allowed to return to school, or of her living even a fairly normal life at home, since all her movement must be controlled and watched.

Six weeks after our return home Cheryl escaped again, this time during the night. Her room was on the first floor, on the rear side of the bathroom, which separated it from our own room, at the front of the house. The windows of her room looking out to the side and back of the house were the old-fashioned sash-cord style, many times painted over and rather warped. It usually took two people to open and close them – and always with an unmistakable creaking and thumping which could be heard all over the first floor. We always helped Cheryl close them at night. The head of the stairs was opposite the door of our room. The front and back doors of the house were always locked at night as were the doors of all the downstairs rooms. Alan kept the keys in our room. So we had no fear of Cheryl getting away while we slept. I realized later that in fact our day security, for all our vigilance, was not really water-tight and that if she had seriously planned a day escape she could have succeeded. But, because we were always on the alert and continually checking her whereabouts, a day escape would never have given her more than a few minutes advance on our calling the police.

On that night we all went to bed rather early, about half-past nine. It was ten o'clock when Cheryl, in her quilted blue dressing-gown came in and kissed us goodnight. She was calm and poised, as she always was now, but gentle and sweet – perhaps a little absent. After she left us we heard her go to the toilet, which was next to her room at the end of the corridor, right at the back of our quite typical suburban semi-detached villa. We heard her leave the toilet, the sound of her own bedroom door opening and shutting. The next morning we found that Cheryl had realized and taken the one still possible way out. She had gone through the small, square, hinged window of the toilet, by two bedsheets tied together and attached to the water-pipes. This little window was so high and small and obscure that we had never thought of it. It was at least six feet above floor level, but much less above the level of the toilet. She had reached it by standing on her small bedside table placed on the wooden lid of the water-closet. Presuming she had gone before daylight, she could have had up to seven or eight hours start before her absence was noticed.

Alan phoned the local police and, as arranged, they called Scotland Yard. The police inquiries, the interrogations, the searches – all the hopeless inevitable routine that was gone through is not relevant to my story any more than it is necessary to describe our feelings as day after day the police reports were negative. We had felt ever since the end of our holiday that we had already half lost Cheryl and I am not at all sure that in our own private thoughts we had ever believed that Loft would be caught before the Cheryl that was left would be gone again – this time for good.

The police spent hours in Cheryl's room examining and fingerprinting everything, but after four days the inspector told me they had found no fingerprints beyond our own and Cheryl's and no correspondence or notes by Cheryl which might give them a clue to any contact she had outside our knowledge. A week after her disappearance I began tidying up her room. The police had left it in what was doubtless to them some kind of order but to me seemed an untidy mess. I spent the whole day putting things back in their place because all kinds of little items, letters, postcards, clothing, books, souvenirs, all touched memories of other times and tempted me to sit down and day-dream, through my tears, about the past.

I was surprised to find, in a huge oddments box which she kept under the end of her bed, the heavy library volume on witchcraft which she had once read so avidly. I sat for a while idly turning the pages, wondering what it was about the book which had so attracted Cheryl's attention. It was just what its title implied, a serious, well-documented historical record of the old medieval practices of witchcraft, with no sensational or romantic views on the subject. I was just about to close it and put it aside when I noticed on the inside of the hard cover at the back Cheryl's handwriting in faint pencil. The writing was certainly hers although it was not the usual poised and well-rounded lettering. This was slanted and tight as though written in a tremendous hurry, as though it might be an idea she wanted to write down before it slipped from her mind. She had written, 'Stupid to drag yourself over the ground tied to the earth and the shadows of the trees and the hills living in the bottoms of chasms seeing no further than the next ridge of concrete row of chimney pots clouds untouchable – be a bird – I must be a bird – I am a bird – I will be a bird – my wings are growing.' This unpunctuated, garbled string of words looked as they read – as if they had been written in some kind of frenzy of disordered thought, like a prayer or a challenge. A few inches below was written in the same feverish hand one other line. It read, 'The Disco Swing Club 27 Ballard Street NW 7.'

Cheryl had taken this book from the lending library ten days before her second disappearance – the one from which she returned mutilated. So it had still been in her room when she returned from her convalescence and spent a week at home before going on her Cornish holiday. It had been there for the six weeks since our return from Cornwall. So these scribbled words and the address could have been written by Cheryl as long as four months ago – or only a matter of a few days. In my view they were probably written in the week she spent at home, between her convalescence and the Cornish holiday, because the bird fixation was already then deeply planted in her mind. But the date was unimportant for the moment. It was the address that mattered. Within a few minutes I was phoning Inspector Marshal. The words written by Cheryl, he said, were a final and absolute confirmation that she was involved with the Loft sect. The address would be checked immediately. It was certainly that of a discotheque in North London and its written association with Cheryl's thoughts on her bird identity might be the first positive clue to a contact between her and Loft or some of his followers. The Inspector said he would let me know immediately the results of an investigation into the Disco Swing Club. There was no telephone call the next day. By the following day the suspense was too much and I called the inspector again. The club was being watched, he said. It was a local rallying point of a band of average pop-minded youths and girls but there was nothing positive against it in police records.

It had been subjected to the usual police checks in the past without the discovery of any notably illegal activities. There had been fights, some members were strongly suspected of pot-smoking, and more than a year previously a case of distribu-

176

tion of 'purple heart' pills had been traced to the premises. There was nothing more we could do, he said, but wait and watch.

When we talked it over that evening Alan and I did not agree with him. Here, for the first time in all this appalling engagement with evil, we had a positive clue, a *place*, which in Cheryl's mind, by some unknown contact, had been associated with the intangible horror trying to destroy her. However innocent the Disco Swing Club itself might be, it was the first point we had ever found on the trail that linked Cheryl to Loft. However remote from North London might be the present address and activities of Loft and Cheryl, this club was the end of a thread leading eventually to them and we agreed that we must inevitably try and follow its course – whatever Scotland Yard was doing.

I left for London the next day and booked into a small hotel near Tavistock Square where we had stayed before on family visits. The very evening of my arrival I set off for the Disco Swing Club in North London. I was dressed – I suppose 'disguised' would be the word, though I am not trying to dramatize my role – in an old three-quarter length camel hair carcoat. I had had it several years and it was scruffy and badly worn and seemed to me – for want of an old duffle coat – to be sufficiently ambiguous to be acceptable in the sort of atmosphere I expected. Under the coat I wore a short, tight, blue-jean skirt which I had bought that afternoon at the Camden Town end of the Edgware Road. Above the skirt I wore a thigh-length Indian-print chemise which I had bought in a shop which sold incense and statues of Gandhi and imitation ivory carvings, just near the British Museum. My hair in those days was still a tawny copper with natural waves and I had never cut it short. But for this exploit I had pulled it tightly back from my forehead beneath a band of Indian cotton print, leaving a small fringe in the front. This was, at the time, my idea of a suggestion of the hippy-Bohemian image. Under my car-coat and over my chemise I wore a long chain necklace with an oval pendant, zinc, probably made in Birmingham and imitating a splatter of vaguely Oriental designs. I wore blue fish-net stockings and low-heeled blue-black shoes with false buckles representing I forget what – but some other time and some other culture. I was, I hoped, the perfectly confused image of Western-Oriental non-conformist culture which passed for originality and the spirit of revolt against a bourgeois appearance.

The main problem I anticipated would be my age. Though I could hardly pass for less than thirty, and even then only in a dim disco-light, I was still attractive, even striking looking. But I was obviously beyond the age group of the average hippy or pop-fan. I counted on my small, trim figure and my long, wavy, copper hair falling to a little below my shoulders to reduce the appearance of my years. I put on a trace of cyclamen-coloured lipstick, a little dark-brown eye-liner, and a very fine layer of pale foundation cream.

The Disco Swing Club was hard to find. Ballard Street was a side street of small shops, groceries, hardware, a laundry and dry cleaner, electrical accessories, all of them shabby and run down with paint-chipped fronts and dirty windows. There were some little side alleys marked with the chalk squares of hopscotch games of the children. There were a couple of grimy-looking public houses, with the bitter odours of damp beer cellars belching through their pavement cellar-traps. Ballard Street was what would be described locally as an artery of the main circus area of this far from glittering North London suburb, the Totten Green Circus. It was presided over by an ancient red-brick citadel of the North London Metropolitan railway, flanked on one side by a Quik-Snak coffee bar and on the other by a café-pin-table bar called the Gilt Chip. The circus seemed to be the general evening rendezvous of the pop types, the fringe hippies and their girl friends and their would-be girl friends. Ballard Street led off the circus on the other side from the Underground. On first appearances it had not the air of the kind of place which gives one a boisterous welcome. In addition it made quite a secret of the whereabouts of its number 27 because no one had bothered for years to repaint or re-establish its faded and broken numbers.

Number twenty-seven eventually turned out to be a newsagent-tobacconist-sweetshop with a sideline in what I believe are called 'girlie' magazines. Outside the shop there was no sign of the club. Eventually, convinced by counting, and the elimination of all the adjacent shops, I entered the corner shop which had to be number twenty-seven and asked the man behind the counter for the Disco Swing Club. Without looking up from his newspaper he jerked a thumb to a corner of the shop where – above a shabby, dim stairway going down to the basement – hung a signboard lit by the intermittent flashes of a single light bulb, announcing 'The One and Only Disco Swing Club. Members Only.'

The time was ten-thirty of the evening of my first day in London. The stairway down to the club, uncarpeted, sinister and tortuous was lined with pop-posters. The club-room at the bottom was simply a garishly painted stone walled cellar, the ceiling partly screened by rattan which also framed a soft-drinks bar in the far corner of the room. There were benches around the walls, a few small tables on one side and tall stools at the bar where a hi-fi set produced a fairly moderate racket of the usual sounds. The centre of the floor was surfaced with some sort of thick green glass lit from below by multiple differ-ent coloured lights. The whole effect, with the stab and the wail of the music, was pretty nightmarish, to me anyway. The young man behind the bar, long-haired in a flower-chemise, asked me if I was a member and when I said no, added rapidly, 'Fifty pence please,' and handed me, without any other formality, a small folded membership card. There were two or three couples going through various forms of agitation in the centre of the glass floor, three or four young men and a girl at the bar and a few others seated around the cellar walls. In that dim light I aroused no one's curiosity, sitting on a bar stool, smoking and sipping some kind of cola drink. I smoked very rarely, though in the right atmosphere and at the right moment, when I needed to concentrate my thoughts, I found it useful and not unpleasant. It served me now, both to think and adopt some pretence of detachment and at least I could inhale and exhale in a manner consistent with my general ap-pearance.

Eventually it was the young man behind the bar who took pity on me and opened a politely uninterested conversation which gave me a chance of making myself known, since I knew that whatever I said to him would rapidly become part of the club's general knowledge. I told him that I was a writer and had been asked by an American magazine to research the English section of a world-wide review they were preparing on all aspects of 'youth protest'. My job, I explained, was to get to know, not simply to interview, but really become acquainted with that part of the English youth belonging to the 'revolutionary' protest groups. I made it clear that I was very much in sympathy with them and that this was a great opportunity – since I was so 'elderly' – for putting across an objective and understanding interpretation of what preoccupied the young English boys and girls. The young man behind the bar – his name was Maxie – held a few whispered conversations with some of the other club members in the hour that followed the revelation of my identity. I could see that I was considered an interesting and perhaps useful character by most of the young people and a suspicious and dangerous one by some. An hour later I was sitting with half a dozen boys and girls explaining what I was looking for in the way of background opinion and information. The first cautious and challenging edge of their questioning was wearing off, I felt, with a rather touching rapidity, showing me how much these boys and girls wanted to talk. They wanted someone to listen to them, not necessarily to argue and discuss but just to *hear* what they had to say about who they were and the reasons for it all. My position about this feeling was easy because not only had I nothing against them, but I was *for* them, because they were all the kind of children who could at any moment fall – or have fallen – into the same trap as my own child. These were not the seducers of Cheryl. These were children of the same kind, who in their search for some kind of new understanding could easily be tempted into desperate and wild situations in which they would be easy victims of the same sort of evil. Though they all spoke to me at first with an undertone of defence and suspicion, I suppose the fact that they understood or felt subconsciously the fact that I loved them and feared for them established an easy-going contact quite quickly. After an hour or so of talk with more than half a dozen of the more persistent or curious, who gathered around me at a table in the corner, I felt sure that I was making some good friends. We had talked of drugs, of police persecution and its apparent reasons and of all the growing multiplicity of blind routine obligations which had become necessary for the most simple form of living. With most of what they had to say I was already in great sympathy, if not in one hundred per cent agreement.

Cheryl and her friends, and my observations of them all over the past two years or so, had conditioned me to the thinking of these young people, which was basically anti-authority, opposed to the kind of inflexible administrative autocracy which blocked all hopes of humanist reasoning and channelled the young into the production lines of a consumer society. I knew it all. Although my basic Scottish-Kashmiri origins had given me a strong sense of established convention, a tendency towards rigid moral judgements, my convent up-bringing – the objective side of my experience – had made me a rebel and a sympathizer with rebels.

The first time in my life that I really began to understand this contradiction in my character – the conflict of instinctive tradition with objective flexibility – was curiously enough in the Disco Swing Club of Ballard Street NW7. It was there that all my earlier attempts to understand, and communicate that understanding to Cheryl, expanded to a mass of young people who until then I had generally regarded, without any serious thought, as the immature froth of irresponsible current youth. That first night in the Disco Swing Club was incredibly revealing, and most of that revelation made me ashamed of my ignorance.

It was three o'clock in the morning when I left and I had made at least two good friends who asked me to meet them the following night at ten o'clock. They made no promises and they gave no information, but they accepted without hesitation my false context of 'writer' and I could tell that they were really prepared to help me to obtain the explanations and background I said I needed. One of these two boys was known to me as Johnnie, and the other as Bill.

I had given the address and telephone number of my hotel in Tavistock Square and my name. They could call up and check at any time on my existence and identity. During the difficult hours of conversation with these two boys and the others at the Disco Swing I was questioned a good deal – as an international journalist – as to why I had gone to a little club of no importance and not very many members rather than beginning my inquiries in the mecca of clubs in Soho and the south west of London, or the Cromwell Road, or Chelsea? From their point of view this was a suspicious point. I replied that the pop and disco clubs of central, west and south London – Soho and Chelsea especially – had no national characteristics. They were not particularly English, they belonged to the international hippy gangs and I might just as well be in San Francisco as Charlotte Street or the King's Road or Kabul. But a little known club in the north of London had the attribute for me of being really national and this was what my assignment was about.

The two boys, Johnnie and Bill, wild enough looking in the style of the day, were intelligent and basically good characters. During the long night of talking they had become fascinated by my ignorance of 'the scene' and honestly dedicated to teaching me what it was all about, in a defensive sense. They also had a kind of protective attitude towards me and I knew I could trust them. The others in the club, girls as well as boys, had drifted in and out of the conversation, but none of them seemed to care to come across to my side with the clear kind of explanations which would take me right across to their side, as did Johnnie and Bill. Johnnie was the less prepossessing of the two, and on first acquaintance the one with whom it seemed impossible to carry on any balanced conversation. His hair had grown into a great hideous puff-ball and he looked like a blond golliwog. He had never shaved in his life and the lower part of his face and upper lip was framed in an uneven haze of fine, blond, curly beard. His face was long and mournful, pimpled and greasy. He was above average height, but stooped, and incredibly thin. He wore a dirty, embroidered bush jacket, black corduroy jeans and leather sandals without socks. Around his neck hung a steel and nickel chain with large links, carrying a white metal insignia of the Peace Corps. Bill was less intelligent but a less discouraging spectacle. His hair was washed and combed and hung in ringlets only halfway down to his shoulders. He had a light two-day stubble of beard, wore a blouse-type blue-jean jacket over a fairly clean roll-necked pullover. His denim trousers were tucked in to Mexican style boots. He had a clean-cut look and might have been handsome but for a weak chin and an underslung jaw. Johnnie was twenty-two and had finished an upholsterer's apprenticeship, and when he cared to work, perhaps a week or two a month, could earn up to twenty-five pounds a week. Bill – I never knew their surnames – was twenty years of age, a technical college 'drop-out' who could all the same earn up to thirty pounds a week as a bricklayer's-mate apprentice. They had both left home some years before and lived sometimes in cheap lodgings, sometimes in squatters' colonies in empty houses. They had gone through the process of taking various kinds of stimulants and occasionally smoked pot and took part in hippy festivals, peace marches and transcendental meditation congresses. They spoke and thought of girls as their equal companions, and sex as a sort of 'fun game' without any emotional strings or obligations, unless 'the bird forgot to take her pill'. I began to realize, as the hours of talk went by, that all their unexceptional qualities and often aggressive attitudes concealed a mass of complexes which stemmed from characteristics which were instinctively 'good' but which had never found the right environment or sympathy for proper expression. They were bitter too, like most, because so far as they could see the world's main concern – or rather the main concern of the world's establishments – was whose bomb would blow everything up first. Those who should have been their betters, and were certainly their elders, had nothing more to show or offer than a divided world in which moral standards were the enemy of 'success'. It paid to be brisk, swift, sharp, cunning and as idle as possible so far as real work was concerned. Out of their disillusion was being formed a deep hostility to the established world and its procedures. In their hearts they felt that this too was leading them nowhere, and yet they had given up positive thought and action. What was valuable to me was that they were at least intrigued that an adult from outside their world was really trying to understand their point of view, and even seemed sympathetic to them and their anti-philosophy. For this they were willing to be completely at my service to explore 'the scene'. They would be my guides and sponsors for wherever I wanted to go, whatever I wanted to see or know. The fact that Johnnie and Bill had attended hippy and pop gatherings and similar functions in many parts of the country satisfied me that they were 'hard core' members of the 'underground' and that eventually I should be able to test them for knowledge of Loft and his sect. I had made no mention of the subject and I believed that was best until I had gained a more solid foothold in their confidence and their world. The mention of Loft might scare them away from me.

The following afternoon Johnnie telephoned me at my hotel. He seemed relieved to find that I had really answered to the name and at the address I had given. He said that he and Bill had seen and heard enough of the Disco Swing Club and wondered if I would like to visit, with them, two or three other discotheque type clubs and perhaps a 'pad' where a number of their hippy acquaintances lived communally. I asked no questions but said I would be glad to go wherever they thought might be interesting and relevant to my research. In fact I felt that I really had made a good start along the trail I was seeking. Johnnie gave me a rendezvous for ten o'clock that evening at the entrance to Paddington Underground Station. I telephoned Alan to tell him what I was doing and then set off to kill time by wandering around London. For a while I stood on a pavement in Piccadilly Circus and watched the mass of international hippy types squatting, lying or loafing behind the steel railings of the Eros island in the centre. Their only interest for me was the thought that perhaps in their midst there might be just one who had met Cheryl, or Loft – perhaps just one who could give me the clue which would lead me in time to save Cheryl's life and mind. I crossed over and sat down among them wondering how one could start talking and asking questions, just suddenly like that, in the middle of Piccadilly. Anyway I did. But the first two I spoke to were German, the next Danish and the English pair I finally found moved away without a word. I eventually had a chat with two girls, but they hadn't come up from South Wales to talk to an odd looking woman of uncertain age in Piccadilly and we didn't get very far. It was the same in Trafalgar Square. I made no contact worth encouraging. I was the wrong age and I didn't look the right type. Perhaps I looked more like a policewoman in disguise. But as I moved hopelessly and uselessly among the crowds I felt a gnawing anguish at the thought of how precious every minute of the hour and the day had now become. If

Cheryl were still alive, she would certainly be on a course towards her death. And yet here I was playing a game of being interested in the forlorn and woolly philosophies of lost children, of arguing with them, listening patiently to them while every moment a tortured part of my mind was saying – 'Where is she now – is there still time – oh God, give me the time to reach her first.' Yet I realized that the time I needed would have to be enough to win the absolute confidence of my two friends Johnnie and Bill. If I was patient long enough and our trust developed even more, perhaps I could even tell them the truth and ask for their direct participation in the search for Cheryl.

It was to be three o'clock the next morning, after smoking my first marijuana cigarette and feeling slightly light-headed and a little sick, that I decided to do just that.

We had met as agreed at Paddington and began our round in a coffee bar near the middle of the Edgware Road. From there we went to a discotheque in the other direction, somewhere towards Notting Hill Gate, and then to another near Shepherd's Bush. At all of these places I was obliged to plunge into conversations which were provoked for me by Johnnie and Bill with young people of all degrees of 'way-outness'. Not very many of them stayed interested for very long and some simply got up and walked away without a word immediately I was introduced as a journalist. A few were prepared to try and explain their beliefs or hopes or disillusions or whatever it was that motivated them – I found it more and more difficult to follow. From time to time I threw out vague hints about curious sects and magical ceremonies but there was no reaction except uninterested ignorance. The only words I really wanted to say were 'Has anyone heard of Michael Loft and does anyone know where to find him?' But it wasn't the time yet. From the discotheque near Shepherd's Bush Johnnie suggested that we should go to a private 'pad', the two upper floors of a house which had become a squat for any friends of the young man who was the 'proprietor'. His father was a wealthy property owner and the son had walked out of university, left home and gone to squat in one of his father's unlet and half-furnished apartments. His father did not care to have him evicted, and now he lived there, in six rooms on two floors,

packed with his homeless hippy acquaintances. The house was
somewhere near Earls Court. From the outside it appeared to
be a respectable residence in a quiet and pleasant square. The
apartment that had become a communal pad was on the last
two of the five storeys. The squalor and the overheated atmosphere, smelling of a combination of dustbins, stale cooking,
drains and unwashed bodies made me feel sick for the first few
minutes. After the immediate contrast with fresh air was no
longer noticeable I forgot about it in my stupefaction at the
spectacle of each room through which we passed. In some only
candles burned and one sensed rather than distinguished the
sprawled mass of bodies covering the floor. One of the largest
rooms, on the lower of the two floors, was lit by what seemed
to be a revolving glass bowl with dozens of different coloured
facets. The turning bowl sprayed the darkness of the room with
shooting stars of multi-coloured lights and left one feeling dizzy
and in danger of losing one's balance. In a corner of this room
sat a long-haired youth, stripped to the waist, cross-legged on a
small stool. His arms were extended above his head, fingers
,stretched. His eyes seemed closed. Every few seconds, his torso,
shining with sweat, would give a convulsive twitch as though
an unseen force had thumped him across his shoulders.
Johnnie told me this was the room kept for those on an LSD
trip. In another corner crouched a group of about half a
dozen, kneeling or sitting on their haunches on the floor, in a
tight circle, head to head. They were all shrouded in blankets
or voluminous clothing and it was not possible to distinguish
either their number or the sex of any of them. They were
chanting in a slow, rhythmless monotone the word 'Om'.
Somewhere amid the whirling constellation of coloured lights
someone was plucking – aimlessly – at a guitar and the discor-
dant notes seemed to harmonize wierdly with this visionary
scene. In the main room, which was the principal centre of
activity, an electric light bulb shone from the end of an un-
adorned cord in the centre of the ceiling. In a small kitchen
next door – filled with dirty crockery and overflowing dustbins,
stale refuse and unwashed crockery, some boys and girls were
making coffee, swilling the dregs from already dirty cups
directly into the refuse on the floor. They were smoking and
arguing noisily. In another large room, furnished only with a

sideboard and a small kitchen table and layers of dirty mattresses, were about ten youths and girls stretched out on the floor or on the mattresses smoking and listening to music, faint and indefinable, coming from three loudspeakers attached to an electric record player. Two of the couples lay lightly clasped in each others arms and seemed to be engaging drowsily in sexual intercourse. Black sprawling letters a foot high painted on one wall of the room proclaimed 'Fuck war and screw your neighbour!' Spaces in between the lettering had been filled in with scribbling large and small and in all colours consisting mostly of the best known four-letter words.

After Johnnie and Bill had talked in whispers for several minutes to the group in the adjoining kitchen I was invited into the large room and introduced to a group of boys and girls lounging on a mattress in one corner. They had evidently accepted to see if they could put up with talking to me for a while and the atmosphere was far from welcoming. I was given a small stained cup of black coffee, without sugar, and invited to sit on the corner of a mattress and explain what I was 'after'. The reception was sullen rather than openly hostile, though the questions I went through and the discussions that followed showed an aggressiveness to which I responded with very little heart.

After perhaps an hour, in which I seemed to make no headway, I felt obliged to accept a challenge to smoke a 'joint', a loosely rolled rice-paper tube of marijuana, with the paper tied in a sort of butterfly knot at one end. The argument was that if I were really a journalist worth any consideration, and had never smoked pot, then it was an experience and I should be glad to try it in the interests of my research. They showed me how to smoke it – holding the tube between my third and fourth finger, and drawing in the smoke by cupping the hand and holding one end, the first finger and thumb, to my mouth. This meant drawing the smoke directly, in long gusts, into the lungs. It may have lightened my head a little, but my main reaction was feeling sick and dizzy. Whether it was the result of this experience or entirely due to my increasing exasperation, I do not know. But when my 'joint' was finished I decided that the time had come to give up all pretence and tell the terribly urgent truth, in the hope that I might find at least one or two who would listen and be able to help me. The opening of my 'confession' was difficult to make and met such a hostile reception that I had to beg to be allowed to continue to explain why life and death were involved. At the first mention of Loft's name I realized that these young people, hippies or whatever they might be, looked with the same mixture of fear and contempt on Loft and his followers as people of my generation did on hippies, perhaps even more so. Most of them had heard of Loft and his sect and they all considered him dangerous or crazy or disgusting – nothing at all to do with them. When I managed eventually to put across the fact that I was trying to trace my own fifteen-year-old daughter who had already been mutilated and fallen under Loft's power, the mood changed to one of genuine sympathy and horror and other young people from all over the apartment tried to join our group and listen to my story which I was able to tell in almost dead silence. But an important, and angry, part of their reaction was that I should have been so ill-informed as to have begun my search for Loft and his followers among the pop-hippy groups. That I could ever have associated them with what one of them called 'a mystic fascist group' outraged them. Whatever else they might be, they said, they were not sadists and perverts yet. Though none of them at first could think of a clue which could help to guide me to Loft, they all had second- or third-hand ideas about him and his sect – someone who told someone who told someone they knew. These remote associations were debated in fierce little discussions which spread rapidly through both floors of the 'pad' and even those who had no ideas or hopes to offer came to the big room with the electric light to look at me and often mumble selfconsciously some phrase which was meant to convey sympathetic understanding. Finally, out of one of the earnest discussions which had developed away from the rest, in the kitchen, one of the boys with the nearest idea to a hopeful clue was brought to me by Johnnie. This youth had last heard of Loft only a week before from a friend of his who had quit the hippy scene to join the beast-sect after having attended one of their forty-eight hour seminars in the Midlands. A week ago this friend had told my informant that Loft was coming back to town 'for a big do', which was expected to last a long time – perhaps a couple of weeks. He had spoken of it as a sort of congress of the countrywide members of the beast-sect which was to be the first of its kind. His friend, he said, had not made up his mind yet whether to go or not. Did he know where to find the friend? Yes, he said, he thought he did. Could he find him *now* – could he try and discover the whereabouts of the Loft gathering? The young man – he was a Canadian – became evasive as Johnnie, Bill and I and a handful of others, who had become my champions, urged him with increasing desperation to try and think of something to do to help immediately. He admitted that he was scared, first of all of the police – and how did he know, he asked, that I was not really working for them? He was scared secondly of the members of the Loft sect. He despised them, yet such was their reputation – vaguely mystic but certainly terrifying – that he like many other hippy types was physically afraid of becoming involved in their affairs. He eventually agreed to accompany Bill and Johnnie and three or four others who had been really shaken by my story to see his friend on the pretext that they were interested in taking part in the latest Loft congress. But his condition was that I should be sent home at once and if an address was obtained it should be communicated to me by someone entirely unconnected with this night's proceedings. He was still far from assured about the reason for my interest in Loft. In case I were a police spy, he said, he wanted a guarantee from Johnnie and Bill and the others that any information reaching me about Loft would be passed on by an untraceable source. This was promised. I knew anyway that I could count on Johnnie and Bill to do anything possible to get the information and pass it on in the way promised. I was told to go back to my hotel and await instructions which would be given the next day by telephone. I gave Johnnie and Bill ten pounds each – with difficulty, because they did not like to feel they were being paid – so that shortage of cash, for taxis or anything, would not delay their inquiries.

It was daylight when I got back. I had walked a long way before finding a taxi. But I was hardly able to sleep more than two or three hours and by eleven o'clock that morning I was down in the hall waiting for a phone call. It came – from Johnnie – at three in the afternoon. He sounded tense and strange and hurried.

'Listen, Mum,' he said, 'go to the corner of Cambridge Terrace and the Edgware Road, the south west corner where there are three telephone boxes. Wait by the middle box. There'll be a chap to see you at seven o'clock this evening. I don't know what he'll tell you. I don't know a thing. Never did. If you're not alone, or if anyone's watching you, well this chap won't turn up and that'll be that. Don't contact us at the club again. We don't know you and they won't let you in. Bill and me, we've done all we can and that's the real truth. 'Bye, Mum – good luck.' He hung up.

I was there at twenty minutes to seven. Several people used the call boxes and left without so much as a glance at me. At ten past seven the three boxes were empty. Two minutes later a tall, well-dressed youth, his hair neatly trimmed, his suit formal, entered the middle phone box. But he kept his foot in the door and while pretending to phone he whispered to me, 'Walk down the south side of Cambridge Terrace. Keep walking until you are spoken to and don't look in the direction of this telephone box.'

I had never seen him before and he was far from my idea of the kind of individual I had expected. I had walked two hundred yards along Cambridge Terrace and there was still no one near me. I began to fear that whatever the scheme had been, it had gone wrong and I was alone and clueless again, back where I started. A moment later, from behind a hedge screening the forecourt of one of the blocks of houses along the terrace, a man stepped in front of me. He turned abruptly to face me and asked me the time. But as he did so he was scanning the pavement across the road and in the direction from which I had come. He said quickly, while I was still trying to pull up the sleeve of my coat to look at my watch 'Get a pencil and a bit of paper and write down this address – quick.' Even before I had written it all down he was across the road and heading up a side street towards Paddington Station. The address he had given me was number fourteen, High Drive Park, West Ealing.

It was a good thirty minutes by taxi, far out in the western suburbs. High Drive Park was a wide, quiet avenue of Victorian mansions, each with double gates at the entrance to a short drive. Many of the houses were screened from the road by trees, chestnut, small fir trees, rhododendron hedges, holly bushes and the like. This had once been a fashionable suburban residential area. Now the newer, more popular suburbs of Greater London had flooded around it and the elegant 'carriage' atmosphere was enveloped by an air of shabby desolation. The road was poorly lit and the numbers were hard to find because many of them were metal figures which had long been painted over the same colour as the gates. Most of the houses, judging by the columns of bells and cards which could be seen at the tops of the front-door steps, had been converted to flats. They all had basements, then two floors with bay windows on each side, then a third floor with smaller windows and finally the dormer windows of the servants' quarters. Number fourteen was like all the rest but appeared to be completely abandoned. All the windows were dark and the double gates were closed with padlocks and rusty chains. The front garden, so far as I could tell, seemed wildly overgrown and the little circle of lawn in front of the pillared porch was waist high in weeds and grass. While I was trying to distinguish details of the lawn and the short drive which encircled it – passing in front of the porch – something caught my eye. I thought at first it might be the reflection of a street light in the wet grass, or a glow-worm. Then I realized that I was looking, through a gap in the grass, at the top of a basement window, just visible at ground level through the railing which closed the area below one of the ground floor front rooms. By manoeuvring and peering closely through the street railings, I could see a fine long streak of light where the blinds or curtain failed to cover the window-top. There was definitely a faint light in the basement. I tried the ground floor flat of the house next door, with the excuse that I had called to see a friend who had lived at number fourteen – and it appeared to be closed up. Did anyone still live there? The woman who answered the ground floor bell at number sixteen seemed surprised at my question. 'No one's lived there or been near the place for the past five years so far as I know,' she said. 'The owners shut it up over a court action about someone's will or something like that. The whole place is overgrown, a jungle for all the cats of the district, it's a damn nuisance. Sorry you've come all this way for nothing. Goodnight, dear!'

By walking to one end of the road I discovered that the backs of the even-numbered houses opened onto a narrow alley, on one side of which were the back gardens of the houses and on the other a line of rusty cast iron railings, broken and awry, separating it from a line of trees and some playing fields. The heavy iron back-garden gate of number fourteen hung lopsidedly on broken hinges and would be hard to push open without the clanking of rusty iron. The garden was a wilderness, almost completely hiding the back of the house.

It took me a good twenty minutes to find a telephone box, ten more minutes to get put through by Scotland Yard switchboard direct to the home of Inspector Marshal. As soon as he had listened to the basic elements of my story, where I was, and how I had been tipped of the address, he told me to wait on the pavement in the drive on the opposite side to number fourteen. On no account to do anything which might alarm whoever might be inside. He would arrive with police assistance as fast as possible. As soon as I had described the house and the result of my inquiries next door he seemed to be in a great hurry to end our conversation. I think he was afraid that I might panic and try and force an entry on my own.

The police arrived within twenty minutes – three radio patrol cars, two large, black, closed vans and an ambulance. There were no sirens, no noise. Inspector Marshal got out of the first patrol car and asked me the way to the back of the house. Uniformed and plain clothes police were getting out of the other cars and the two vans. I explained the way to the back and the Inspector sent a strong group of plain clothes and uniformed men in that direction, telling them that when they were inside the back garden to blow their whistles and charge into the house by windows and doors. He told me, 'We'll go in at the front as soon as we get their signal, Mrs Hayes, and you can follow us. Watch out for people climbing out of the windows or hiding in the shrubbery in the garden.' Then, with the rest of the plain clothes and uniformed men, he waited under the shadows of the trees of number sixteen. When we heard the whistle from behind the house the police moved along the pavement and opened the padlocks of number fourteen almost noiselessly and then charged across the tangled patch of lawn and up the front steps. After a few moments of manipulation with a bunch of skeleton keys the double front door swung open onto a darkened hall. We could hear the police from the back of the house forcing the doors and the sounds of breaking glass. There was still no light to be seen in the house and still no reaction to the noisy trampling and banging of the police squads. The hall smelled strongly of sandalwood incense. Handtorches showed a large stone stairway with a heavy balustrade mounting from the right of the hall. Under the stairs at the end of a corridor leading from the hall was a glass-enclosed stairway going down to the basement. Across the hall from the front door was a high, panelled double doorway – to the left, the doors of two more rooms, one on the front of the house, the other at the side. The double doors in the centre of the main hall evidently opened onto a large room running the whole width of the house and looking out onto the back garden. As police rushed up the stairs and along the corridor to the basement stairs the Inspector tried the knobs of the double hall doors and finding them locked burst them open with a heavy kick at the lock. The bolts at the tops and the bottoms of the doors were ripped from their fittings in the door frames with a splintering of wood and cracking of plaster. It was distinctly a crash entry as the police wrenched both doors fully open, yet the first reaction from inside the huge room was no more than a few muffled cries of alarmed questioning. For how long the police stood as though stunned on the threshold while their handlamps swept to and fro the length of the room I do not know, but their sudden arrest and silence was a curious climax to the battering onslaught in which they had been engaged seconds before. The reason was the horrific detail which every beam of torchlight picked out in the huge, dimly-lit room. It was so theatrically gruesome at first sight that one's mind was hardly able to accept it as reality. I think that was the reaction of the police as well. For just as long as the people in that room remained immobile and silent, their conscious minds struggling with their drugged stupefaction to understand and react to this wild intrusion, so the police too stood fixed in the doorway as if not believing what they saw.

The end of the room, to the right of the entrance, was entirely filled across its width by a platform about four feet high and perhaps ten feet deep. At the back of the platform, against the wall, stood a long low table on which a score of candles of varying heights and thicknesses were burning. Above the table, fixed to the wall, was a T-shaped structure of heavy beams.

Hung by the wrists from the top extremities of this construction was the naked body of a woman, young or old, it was not possible to say for her whole body seemed as though clothed in a tattered mantle of blood. From between her legs, at the level of her genitals, projected the large head of a dead bird.

The wall around the wooden structure to which she was tied was splashed with blood, most of it dark and dried, but some, especially around the woman's body, still shining a dark red in the light of the candles. Hanging from the wall too were a dozen or more animal skins, not dried or tanned, but fresh and stained with torn and ragged edges casting monstrous shadows in the flickering lights of the candles and the sweeping beams of the handlamps.

At the moment the doors had been turned back by the police, a man, naked except for a long, narrow, skin cloak, its ends attached around his neck, had been kneeling on the platform in front of the candle-lit table. In his arms, outstretched towards the figure on the wall, he had been holding up the limp body of an animal about the size of a cat. It had been savagely mutilated and its entrails hung down to his chest, dripping red. When he turned towards the doors, a few moments after the shattering entry of the police, I could see that his face too was bathed in fresh blood. When he stood to face the intruders, the handlamps showed that apart from the hide and hair cloak hanging from his neck, thrown back across his shoulders, he wore only one other garment, if such it could be called – the head of a ram, black, with wide, symmetrically curved horns, hanging from a cord around his waist and just covering his sex. His thighs and his stomach were bloodstained. The whole place reeked, suffocating with raw flesh and blood, incense, stale alcohol, marijuana and unclean bodies.

In the very few seconds between the time the gigantic man on the platform turned to face the police and the outbreak of panic and turmoil on the floor of the room it was not possible to absorb the details of the rest of the scene. But I could see that the whole platform itself was covered with crouching, or sitting, or recumbent bodies, all naked except for crude skin scarves, head-dresses or skimpy cloaks. My impression was that of the fifteen to twenty crammed on the platform around the 'altar', at least seven or eight were sleeping, drugged or unconscious after some kind of mutilation. The others, blood-stained though they were, seemed comparatively alert, for they reacted no less forcibly than their leader.

Down on the floor of the hall there was no light, but a shadowy sea of bodies, mostly dressed in ordinary hippy style, sleeping, making love, smoking, drinking and a few strumming guitars as though for themselves alone to hear. Out of a total of some twenty-five, I saw not more than three quite naked, two girls and a man.

The smell of alcohol, it was found later, came from stacks of gallon jars of crude red wine, empty or overturned at the back of the room. In the flash before chaos I heard vague music, with drums predominating. It was coming through a door across the room, which led to a huge Victorian-style glass conservatory overlooking the back garden, its glass panes glued over with either black paper or felt.

The signal for absolute pandemonium came when the leader – I took him to be Loft, in all his panoply of the Chief Beast – with a cry, hoarse and deep with anger, leaped from the platform into the mass of bodies below. He was followed, though less resolutely, by some of the others on the platform. He turned and made for one of the windows, shielded with black cloth and giving onto the back garden, just to one side of the conservatory. He ripped the cloth aside and to a shattering explosion of glass, leaped through the window. The police at the door had plunged into the mêlée of recumbent bodies on the floor to try and catch up with him. But well before they were halfway across the floor they were as though trying to cross quicksands, stalled in a morass of clutching hands and clinging arms pulling them down.

From all parts of the house now came the sounds of scuffling, of banging doors and the thudding chase of footsteps, shouts and screams and the hysterical imprecations of drug-crazed boys and girls. You could hear them above the tumult, their long breathless monologues rising higher and higher in pitch until they sounded like animals, as they cursed, pleaded, threatened, begged. They were the terrifying sounds of people who had lost touch with reality, who were living nightmares in which their fears and their pleas were as unreal as their threats and their curses. All this you could hear in the mounting pitch of voices. The flashing of electric torches, the crashing of glass, the streaks of yellow candle-light leaking into the corridors where shadowy forms lunged and fled and sobbed gave all the effect of a frantic saturnalia. It was impossible to imagine how it could end.

I had been swept from the hall doors into a corner of the main room by the onrush of the police and the counter stampede of the panicking crowd. I stayed there for a while rigid with shock and disbelief. This was more, much more, than we had ever imagined. Was the girl or woman on the semi-crucifix on the wall Cheryl? It is hard to believe, but the initial shock at the sight of that room was such that it never occurred to me even to wonder where Cheryl could be among that mob. I suppose for a while my mind refused to associate anything that could have happened to Cheryl with such a sight as this.

Within a few minutes the police had installed powerful arc lights and in between the deeper shadows they cast, their contrasting pools of white picked out the faces of the beast-followers in horrible detail.

The candles were rapidly overturned and extinguished and the bright spotlights no longer left any doubts as to the details of the hellish tapestry surging along the corridors and through the rooms of the house. The haggard faces of the young devotees lost the suggestion of pagan mysticism with which candle-light might have endowed them and became simply the faces of dirty, unkempt, demented adolescents awakening from one nightmare to another.

The police had to beat a way through the main room to allow the ambulance men, a nurse and doctors to reach the recumbent group remaining on the platform. One policeman dashed from the room to vomit from the front door steps a moment later. A good many of the house occupants, who had largely outnumbered the first group of police, had swept out of the rooms, down the stairs and out of the front door into the garden which was filled with the sounds of bodies crashing through the shrubbery and the shrill screaming of some of the youngsters whose drugged minds were doubly shocked by the violent intervention of the police.

I counted seven stretchers carried from the main room and though as each one passed with its sheet-covered form, I longed to step forward and see if Cheryl was there, my body refused to move. The doctor in charge of the ambulances – there were now several as well as more police cars – stood a few feet from me. The inspector met him and I think said something like, 'What's the score, doctor?' The doctor, now looking almost as gory as the original occupants of the house, replied, 'Two dead for certain and four or five more very bad, and God knows how many others too crazy to leave with your people for the moment. You'd better let us have them first, or I can't guarantee they'll ever be normal again.' This was the moment when I found myself capable of moving again, and I stepped forward – to ask I suppose for Cheryl – but passed out.

18

Tom Lacey, the ex-Jesuit student whose fear of sex-obsession had led him to seek guidance from Miss Lewis, walked alone in Brockley Park.

He was trying to repeat in detail to himself the interview he had just had with Dr Robertson. The doctor had, as Miss Lewis had promised, talked to him on a man to man and not on a doctor to patient basis. Some of the rather basic truths pronounced by the doctor had shocked the young man at first, but in the context of the doctor's later explanations he had begun to perceive a world, and ways of living and thinking, from which he had been completely isolated by his theological studies and his mental breakdown.

'How old are you?' the doctor had asked. When he had replied, 'Twenty-three,' Robertson had smiled a little wryly. 'When I was sixteen,' the doctor said, 'I could spot the suspender belt buttons under any woman's dress at fifty yards and I can tell you there weren't many brassières thick enough to hide the outline of rosy nipples from me. I used to play a game with some of my school friends seeing who could count – on oath of course – having detected the greatest number of nipples during one day. Mind you, we'd none of us ever seen a naked living breast, and if we had we'd have turned and run for help. We were just entering the curiosity-fantasy stage. We were on the threshold of becoming men. We were about fifteen and you're twenty-three. The realization of the sex-drive, or the libido as they call it to-day – you can call it old-fashioned desire or what you like – is probably more shocking and painful to you than it was to us, because you are already a man and capable and in need of being one. Your fantasies are an expression of a physical need that has become painfully pressing.'

Then there had been a rather complicated explanation of the mental, physical, social and intellectual functions of the sex-drive and the doctor's insistence that sex was not impure but an essential part of complete human love. The day would soon come, he said, when Tom Lacey would be free to live a full life in which wind-blown skirts would be something to be associated and rationalized with the woman he loved. A good deal of it remained obscure for the young man. Some of it seemed shocking, but most of it went deep into his mind to be stored as raw material for long reflection in the days to come. Above all, he told himself, he felt quite free from what had seemed, in the context of Brockley Hall, the signs of impending doom within himself. He was *not* a sex-maniac.

It was as he was reaching this conclusion that he saw Miss Lewis. She gave him a friendly wave as she passed along the front of the main building. Then, as he turned and began to walk towards her, she paused and waited for him. 'Well?' She smiled at him with cheerful confidence that his meeting with Robertson had given him the assurances he needed. It had. But now, because of what seemed to him its intimate revelations, he felt afraid to talk to the one person he had once thought of as 'neutral' and sympathetic.

'Well,' he stammered, 'yes, it was – well – it helped a lot. He's a very nice man Dr Robertson.' And he looked quickly away.

She tried to speak with a lightly bantering note. 'And so, you're quite normal after all?'

'Yes,' he said, but there was a trace of sullenness in the rest of his reply. 'But it appears that I shall not be able to take my normality to any natural conclusion so long as I'm shut up in a madhouse. I shall have to be satisfied with the wind and fantasy, I suppose. And when am I going to get out?' He paused abruptly as though ashamed at having aimed some of his anger at the person he had first turned to for help. When he spoke again it was as someone hoping to be forgiven and offering something intimate and secret in advance. But he still looked sheepishly down at his feet. 'The doctor said I should learn to rationalize fantasy with a woman I shall love. I suppose that's really the true sign of love. I feel it is. If I'm right, then I'm already in love.' He looked up at her, half-afraid of her reaction to his hesitant words.

'In love?'

'Yes. She's called May. May Saunders, the baby-stealer.' Now his confession poured out, pleading for understanding for something he could no longer keep to himself. The doctor's words, he said, had confirmed what he had felt about himself already. He was normal. He wanted to give love. He wanted to receive it. His need, he said, had fixed itself on the girl called May – the first one whose wind-blown skirt had shamed him. Day by day, night after night, he said there seemed to be less and less women in the world and more and more of May. And now it seemed to him that the whole world was May – and without her to fulfil himself he felt he would die. He talked with all the sincerity and hopelessness of a youth in love. He had made great progress, she thought.

'Have you spoken to the girl?'

Yes, he said, he had spoken to her. No more than just a hello – how are you – nice day – on quite a dozen occasions and each time he had felt his heart pounding and his breath catching. And each time she seemed to be feeling something too until finally there was something passing between them more than words or just looks. He was sure, sure, that she felt the same way for him. But would they ever be able to tell one another? Sometimes, he said, when he saw her approaching with a working party of women inmates he felt so weak that he was afraid he wouldn't have the strength to meet her eyes with his. And fantasy was over. It was her eyes, her mouth, he wanted to look at now, not the shape of her legs beneath her wind-blown skirt.

As they had begun to talk they had started strolling to and fro across the tall grass just behind the far end of the parking area. Miss Lewis listened without comment for she feared that one word at the wrong moment could bruise this magic intimacy.

When he seemed to have finished they both remained silent,

Tom still a little afraid of her reaction, she, thankful for the simplicity of it and her sense of having received a gift. There was no comment she felt she could make without puncturing the moment with anti-climax. Finally it was Tom who spoke again, despondently.

'I suppose it sounds stupid. Well, impossible anyway. I'm sorry. But you see I felt so terribly full of it all. I *had* to tell you.'

She smiled at him. 'I'm glad you've found out, Tom. I've nothing more to say. It's none of it stupid, none of it impossible, even if . . .' She stopped. Tom might be out, free in six months. May, probably not for years. 'You're half-way free of SP9 already.' She touched his hand and squeezed it quickly. 'Now, I must be off,' she added, her usual well-controlled self once more, 'Mister Loft is back at work with his rabbits again and I want to go and say hello.' She gave a dry little laugh. 'I haven't seen him since he nearly killed himself chasing one of his favourite rabbits and killing the poor beast instead.' She turned and walked towards the kitchen gardens and the gardening sheds.

19

After the 'accident' Loft had spent ten days in the infirmary and another week convalescing during which he had fed and cleaned his animals twice a day but spent the rest of the time in the 'B' Wing day-room. She had only seen him once, in the company of others, to exchange a few polite words. This was the first time she was likely to meet him alone since the iron-bar incident, but she walked into the garden unit and through it to the rabbit section with a purposeful, swinging pace. Loft was standing at a work-bench sawing a piece of wood and he neither saw nor heard her enter. For a full two minutes she stood in the doorway, watching his huge stooped form swaying to the movement of his arm. Beside her were ranged the same tools she had seen before; the scythe hooked by one of its handles to a nail; the pick, the axe, the heavy spiked iron bars, the sledge-hammer, the long, shiny-spiked garden forks, rakes, shovels, the whole armoury of mayhem from which she had once chosen her weapon, and missed. This time her gaze swept past them all and she stood silent, as though hoping to break her presence gently to the man absorbed in his noisy work. Finally his saw cut through, a piece of wood fell, and as he bent to pick it up he saw her and turned with a slight start. Now she was walking quickly towards him with a reassuring smile.

'Good morning, Mr Loft. I'm so glad to see you back again, among your animals. How are you? How is your nose healing?' He put the piece of wood on his work-table and touched a wide band of sticking plaster stretching from the bridge of his nose to the top of his forehead.

'Yes, Miss Lewis,' he said, his deep voice halting and timid, 'I'm quite well. Thank you. It was nothing, really. Just a bit of skin off, that's all.'

'Well, I'm so glad,' she said, almost with a note of indifference. 'But is there anything I can *do* for you? Is there anything you may need that I could perhaps ask the superintendent about for you?'

He looked down at her silently, yet there was something awesome in his eyes which would have seemed more appropriate in the eyes of someone looking up. His hands which were holding the piece of wood were clasped waist-high in front of him. Suddenly with a quick flicker of russet, like an autumn leaf in a gust of wind, the squirrel ran along the bench and sprang onto his shoulder, where it perched, its tense little body ready for its next spring. Its black eyes seemed to sparkle with some indecipherable query. Without turning his head Loft took it gently from his shoulder and dropped it gently to the floor. He watched it scurry away and then stay fixed, clinging flattened to one of the walls before merging with the shadows of the rafters. Only then, with a visible effort of concentration, did he bring himself to speak again. 'Would you like a cup of my tea, Miss Lewis?' he asked her. He pointed to a soiled and dented enamel teapot and two enamel mugs on the workbench.

'Yes I would, thank you,' she said. 'You make it yourself – here?'

'Yes,' he replied, 'they give me a ration of tea and milk and sugar from the kitchen, for me and the two men who work in the conservatory, and I make it on the stove. It's going even in summer. Just with logs and bits of wood.' He poured her out a mug of the rusty coloured liquid, pushed over a milk bottle and a carton of lump sugar. 'Help yourself, miss.'

She thanked him and was grateful for the preoccupation she could show with pouring out the milk, putting the bottle down again, selecting two lumps of sugar and seeing them ripple into the thick brown liquid.

'Here,' he said, and pushed across a battered little nickel teaspoon. She stirred and even the hard tinkle of the spoon against the side of the mug was a welcome break to the silence.

Loft spoke again. 'I want to tell you how grateful I am to—'

She cut him short with a brusque gesture and then her words came, rapid, firm and with no emotion. 'Mr Loft, there is one great favour you can do me. Please don't think I am being rude. But do understand that you have nothing to thank me for. If you were about to mention the incident of your – your – unfortunate little accident, then please don't. *Please do not*' – she emphasized each word slowly – 'ever mention again what happened or what you thought happened – or what anyone else thinks happened. The greatest favour you can do me is to join me in forgetting all about it – forever. Can you do that?'

He reflected a moment then nodded once. 'Yes, Miss Lewis.'

'Good,' she said. 'Now tell me the news of all your little animals. Are they alright? Did they miss you too much?'

He made no reply. He opened the door of one of the wire hutches and pulled out by the scruff of its neck a magnificent doe rabbit, mottled black and tan with a few speckles of white. For a moment before he handed it to her he cradled it in his arms and bent his ungainly head over the animal in a gesture of protection and affection, that became like a ceremony with each successive rabbit he showed her. It was as though, having picked them out of their hutches, it hurt him to let them go. To each one he gave a name. The older and larger of the does, he said, was the one called Her. 'It's a real name,' he explained, 'just like the one that used to be called Him – well – you know.' The new baby rabbit elected to survival, successor to Him, was definitely to be called She, not Little. By the time he had shown them, including the latest brood of baby rabbits not destined for domesticity, Miss Lewis had completely forgotten the names, so solemnly announced by Loft.

In a mood of expansiveness, like nothing she had ever seen of him before, he showed her the squirrel's tricks. He held one arm out straight in front of him and made a clicking noise with his tongue, and no matter where the squirrel might be, in the shed or scampering in the bushes outside, he would come leaping like a little russet flame flickering upright on the man's forearm. His tiny snub nose turned inquiringly towards Loft's face, black-button eyes seeming to look at nothing in particular yet to see everything at once. Loft fed him small crusts of old toast, clicked some more, and the agile spurt of flame was extinguished up among the shadows of the roof beams.

'You know,' he said, 'Miss Lewis, I think a squirrel is one of the perfections of living creation. You cannot look into a squirrel's eyes and read what it thinks – you have to watch its whole body; its tail which can twitch and flicker while the rest stays as motionless as a stone; its minute front paws are a perfect thought ... It has the actions of a bird, without cruelty or aggression or even time to show fear. It is the perfect little living machine, a piece of unperverted wildness and wilderness. It is an example of complete beauty – of movement – of thought – of colour – of gentleness. Untameable, incorruptible.' He was silent a moment and then added, more softly, 'There are no human squirrels.'

She felt expected to say something to end the silence that followed. 'What do you mean – no human squirrels? Are other animals humans?'

Now the sly, slow lifting of the corners of his wide mouth, and a slight narrowing of his great bulbous eyelids seemed to signify that he might be indulging in his manner of a rare smile. He turned his head away and looking out of the grimy cob-webbed window replied, 'No, Miss Lewis no animals are human, but all humans are animals of some kind or other. Or birds. At least they would be if they were pure, if they weren't corrupted by the things that have converted them to human form and wickedness. Only animals are pure. Every human, at least, well, just the better ones, is an animal trying to be itself again.' He spoke with a strange gentleness. There was a purring tone, like a caress, in his voice and she thought to herself that it was compelling, even beautiful.

'You,' she said, 'are you an animal?'

'I am all animals,' he said, 'but shut away in this dreadful place I am partly a squirrel. My soul lives in Squirrel. His life is my life. Clumsy and horrible though I am, when I see him move, then I live. It is a remote and trivial compensation for what I should really be, but it keeps me alive. My rabbits are comforting, but dreary, pitiful, poor things beside Squirrel. I know in my own heart I am as rapid, as tense, as sprung with life as he is. I know that, liberated, I could vibrate with life; that no movement, sound, colour, or odour could escape my senses; that I could be all of life – all of sensuous, intelligent life, living to the limit with the wonderful senses of an animal, free of all the thick, clouding, doubting, treacherous intelligence of the human. Man is nothing but the purest distillation of nature's perversion and agony – nature's most terrible mutation.'

The words were spoken with a sort of poetic balance, a rhythm calm and reasoned, hiding for a moment the fact that they flowed from a mind that was mad. Base and crazy as might be their sentiments, she felt they had an unexpected power and compulsion, coming from the huge, unkempt, malformed creature who had spoken. He had made his statement with his soft, smooth, purred delivery, and the last phrase carried no more emphasis than the first. Nor, as he spoke, did his physical aspect change. The sly, slow trace of what passed for his smile had lingered faintly on, but he had spoken with the relaxation of a man dreaming and drawing his words at random from some distant space in his mind. Partly in wonder and partly to pick up the thread of his thought, Miss Lewis repeated his final words.

'Nature's most terrible mutation?' She reflected a moment. 'That seems to me, Mr Loft, a harsh judgement of a very wide subject. It needs a lot of thought and discussion. I don't think I could perhaps follow you that far. But tell me, if all humans are really animals, perverted – as I understand you to believe – to human form, does each human being retain something of his or her animal charactertistic?'

'Of course,' he replied.

'Tell me then,' she went on, 'what sort of animal am I?' He turned more directly to her and without expression scanned her face.

'Do you feel any kind of kinship with any beast?'

'No, I don't believe so. I feel essentially human. I have compassion and love, which I certainly cannot identify at once with any animal.'

'Compassion and love, as you call them, are the destructive streaks of human character. They are anti-nature. One day, misused, misdirected, misunderstood, because they have no place in true existence, they will destroy nature and mankind too.'

'But you, Mr Loft, as you fondle your little animals and talk to them, are you not showing them love and compassion?'

Only a slight movement of his head and an interplay between the fingers of both hands showed how pertinent was this question. Then, 'I am not showing compassion, nor love,' he said. 'I am simply expressing my own affinity with them, my own desire to be like them, to *be* them, to belong to their kind.'

Because there seemed no immediate reply to this she waited a moment before her next question. 'If I feel no particular affinity to any sort of non-human creature, can *you* tell me what sort of animal you really think I am?'

He leaned back on the side of the work-bench, his great angular hands, as much bone as muscle, hanging limply, and turned his head slowly to gaze at her. He was more relaxed, more in possession of himself than she had ever seen him. He was more than confident. In a quiet way he was almost dominant. There seemed an eternal pause while his dark, lustreless eyes scanned her face, then looked down at his feet, back again to her, then again to the ground, then slowly around the shed as though detailing each object in it.

'I see you as something of infinite resourcefulness and cunning. Sharp, swift, secret, incapable of deviation.'

She waited. But he was dreaming again. 'A cat,' she ventured, 'or something like that?'

Once more he brought his gaze slowly to bear on her face. 'No, Miss Lewis, there is nothing feline about you at all. Nothing canine either, nor bovine, nor serpentine, nor equine, nor all the rest. None of that. To me, at any rate, you are a little bird of prey. Keen, pure, swift – as I said, incapable of deviation, resourceful and cunning. There is something too keen about you to be earthbound.'

'A bird . . .' she repeated.

'Yes, a bird,' he said, now with the torpor gone from his voice. 'A bird with tight, close-knit, firm-flecked feathers like the flight of arrows.'

They both fell silent and still. After a few moments Loft

picked up a small board, fixed it in the wooden vice of his table and began to saw slowly through it. She stood in front of him, her leather satchel hanging loosely on its long shoulder strap, her arms down by her sides, hands slightly clenched, her head bent in thought. But it was clear that as far as Loft was concerned the conversation was ended and whatever he had been for a few moments he had reverted to the identity of the morose, solitary guardian of rabbit hutches and gardening tools in a special hospital for the criminally insane.

20

The Diary of Margaret Lewis

EXTRACT 5

After the police raid on the congress of the beast sect I regained consciousness in a police car in the convoy of ambulances and police vans going to hospital. I was sufficiently shocked to be kept under sedation in a bed in a general ward for that night and most of the following day. It was late in the afternoon when Inspector Marshal came to see me with a plain clothes police officer who was to take a preliminary statement from me. He was not prepared to tell me very much. He could only say that among the seriously ill and injured was Cheryl. He refused to answer when I asked who was the woman who had been crucified at the 'altar', and, concealing the truth, simply told me that no one was dead, but a dozen youths and girls in all were in serious danger, physically and mentally. A number of others, after preliminary treatment in hospital, were being detained for compulsory committal to institutions where they could be looked after and nursed back to health. He said, 'As soon as we have precise news of your daughter's condition we will call you.' The leader of the sect, the man we had seen conducting the ritual sacrifice – it was a cat – at the 'altar' had indeed been Loft, but he and about a dozen others who had been there that night had escaped.

Two days later, after Alan had come down to London and joined me at the hotel, we were called to the hospital. A nurse told us, 'We think it best that you should see your daughter now; she is very ill.'

The creature we saw hardly resembled Cheryl. She was under sedation, completely bandaged from head to feet and undergoing continual blood transfusion. All we could perceive of her were her eyes through small slits in the bandages. They were not closed. She had no eyelids. 'It' was Cheryl, whom we were seeing for the last time. Two days later she died. The cause of death was loss of blood and shock, but Alan told me later, much later, that he had seen the medical report. There was not an inch of skin left on her body. She had been carved and scalped to the bone in many places and crude attempts had been made to graft bird skins on to parts of her body. She had been identified by the police only by her fingerprints, for the insides of her hands and fingers and the soles of her feet were the only parts of her body untouched by the atrocious 'ceremony' to which she had been submitted. It was still little comfort, though I admit it was some consolation, to learn that during all the time she had been in the hands of the Loft sect she had been kept on hallucinatory drugs which attenuated the physical and mental suffering by cloaking it with powerful illusory convictions. Maybe Cheryl really believed she was be:ng transformed into a bird, for that was the crazy intention of Loft and his 'apostles'. The total price of that ghastly night was eventually the death of three young girls, Cheryl among them, and of two youths, one of them only fifteen years old; and six other boys and girls were seriously mentally deranged and in need of long-term care. How many others who were to suffer in various forms for the rest of their lives was not calculable at once, but it was probably more than a score.

Loft and six of his chief 'apostles' were caught by the police a few weeks later at a similar assembly of the sect, and all of them were eventually found 'unfit to plead' by the courts. Loft was the only one charged with murder – the murder of Cheryl – although there were eighteen other charges against him for assault and illegal possession and use of drugs.

I went once to court during the magistrate's preliminary hearings, before the committal to the Assizes, because although it had not by then become clear that he would never pay the penalty, I was already in the state of mind in which the only overwhelming and passionate desire of my life was to see him suffer and to know that he was in custody and was certainly going to suffer. Even then he had begun to show the signs of gigantism, the overgrowth of bones caused by a disease known as acromegaly, and his huge head, with his heavy-lidded eyes, his prominent jaw and his giant hands gave his presence in the dock, even between two policemen, an element of terrifying evil. My very first impression, the one that has stayed with me throughout these long years, was of something remote, indescribable, not associated with a human presence at all. Although in the accused's box he seemed dazed and confounded, sometimes even cowed, he was so gigantic and ill-formed that he seemed enveloped in an aura of what I can only call other-world beastliness. Quite regardless of what he had done to Cheryl and others and my consequent objective feelings about him, I found that I did not react to him quite as I would have done to a human being in the same circumstances. Yet, by all outward characteristics, he was clearly human. His disease had not yet progressed, as it has since, to kyphosis and curvature of the spine and he stood tall and upright. The veiled expression of the great eyes conveyed nevertheless an impression of sullen defeat emphasized by the way he hung his head and appeared neither to see or hear what went on around him. It never occurred to me at that time, when the death penalty still existed, that the day would ever come when I should feel called upon to settle the score with this sub-human thing. But when the conviction did come to me, a few months later, I still never really thought in terms of killing a human being – only of the anticipation of submitting this creature to the maximum of fear and pain of which it might be capable before eliminating it and effacing the evil which had taken away my daughter.

What do I feel now?

As I write this and recall that last extraordinary conversation in the gardening shed in which he spoke to me as I believe he has never spoken to anyone in all his years of detention, I know that I am dealing with a madman, imbued with evil, whose lucidity and logical adaptation of his fantasy to his own reasoning makes him as dangerous as ever he was.

I felt my face flush when he said that he himself was 'all animals' – not just one simple animal, as he classifies all other individuals, myself included. He said, 'I am all animals,' and so reveals his belief of himself as the Great Beast to be still a reality in his mind. More than ten years here have done nothing except to teach him how to resist the detection and confuse the diagnosis of doctors and psychiatrists. Underneath his aspect of sullen indifference and childish preoccupation with his little animals, there is nothing changed. He is still the same bloody beast wearing a ram's head that I once saw standing like a nightmare monster in front of the flayed body of my daughter. Now, because I once missed my aim in trying to kill him, this wretched creature trusts me more than anyone else in the world – enough to tell me that I too, like my daughter, whose life he took for just that same reason, am really a bird transformed into a human! If I needed any more fuel for my resolution to destroy Loft he has given it to me himself. But I need no more. I exult at the realization that before he dies this idiot animal is delivering to me alone something like trust and faith. These can now be added to the weapons with which I can possibly hurt him most before he dies.

I still have not found a way to kill him. Maybe after all I shall have to use Alan's automatic. I know I am strong enough to pull the trigger because I have practised it many times. Its magazine is always charged. But this is still a solution I shall try to avoid as long as time permits. To have to shoot him would seem very like complete failure.

Since I finished writing the above I have received from Doctor Robertson a whole file of the medical and psychiatric past of Loft. None of it softens me. It only brings me to the conclusion that, however sad may have been his childhood, or unfortunate his adolescence, he is the source of some unadulterated evil, born of itself, acting consciously and in no way an attenuating circumstance. I have reflected many hours on my contact with him in the past months and on the medical report and I refuse to believe that Loft is anything but an embodiment of evil. I cannot afford to believe otherwise, now.

EXTRACT FROM CHIEF MEDICAL SUPERINTENDENT'S REPORT SP9

Michael Grangeford Loft

The patient was born of working class parents, brought up by his stepfather after his natural father had abandoned his mother before marriage. Mother was a hotel servant, stepfather a waiter and later a lorry driver and garage mechanic. Michael was despised by his stepfather and feared and misunderstood by his mother. She had never wanted him and even after her marriage to his stepfather, tried to have him adopted. He was a studious and exceptionally bright boy, and from local council school obtained a scholarship to a good grammar school on the Welsh borders of Herefordshire. His stepfather tried to oppose his continued education at grammar school and wanted him to go to work at once as a farm labourer. The educational authorities were forced to intervene to permit the boy to continue his education. His grammar school career, as a boarder, was scholastically successful. His home life remained tragically unhappy. Sources for this are his headmaster and other masters. At the age of eighteen he passed brilliantly his Higher Matriculation in art, literature and history, and won a scholarship to a Midlands university. After he had been at university a year his stepfather was sentenced to prison for life for the murder of his mother. Michael Loft quit university to take up an eighteen month art scholarship with residential studies in Paris and Vienna. From the time he left to take up this scholarship he never saw or communicated with any of his relatives or former acquaintances. He had never been popular at school and had no friends. He was always introspective and appeared completely detached from people and his surrounding circumstances, but never gave any impression of suffering from his loneliness. In fact many of those who knew him in his school and university days say that his apparent introspection and inability to relate with people and circumstances was due to an innate arrogance and sense of special superiority. It is true that his school work always showed a degree of confidence and assurance which was considered remarkable by his teachers. He was always highly sensible to being punished or even to finding himself in close competition with his classmates in his work. A few of his former schoolmates say that his attitude was simply due to shyness. There is no trace of anyone who was ever close enough to him for this difference of opinion to be decisively settled

After his eighteen month scholarship courses in Paris and Vienna he was offered a junior art teaching post in a provincial grammar school in the north of England. He never replied to the offer and it is difficult to trace his activities from this time, when he would have been nearly twenty years old, up to the time of his arrest when he was about twenty-seven. As far as the police have been able to discover, through those who had remained in contact with him after his art studies in Paris and Vienna, he stayed on in Austria until about the age of twenty-three. He took occasional jobs but at other times completely disappeared from the circles of his acquaintances who were mostly artists and students. He became a member of some fairly scatter-brained semi-intellectual groups in Munich and Bonn, as well as in Vienna, and he spent some time in Berlin.

During his time in Germany he is known to have become interested in 'black magic' and was a member of a small inoffensive sect which promoted the intellectual revival of an obscure animist cult. This was based on the theory that human beings were simply perverted mutations of animals and that true life fulfilment lay in the re-acquisition of the animal sensibilities of each individual and the elimination of human characteristics – considered to be 'deviations' created by evil forces. Twice during this period, according to the German and Austrian police, he was involved in minor drug offences, the possession of minute quantities of marijuana and heroin. There was no reason to believe that he was seriously addicted. It was not until Loft was back in England, at about the age of twenty-five, that the police had their first intimation of him as the founder and leader of an animist-mystical sect of young people who referred to themselves as 'The Beasts'. Police records at first simply noted the fact that this group had been found to associate with suspected drug users and should be checked on from time to time. It later became clear, when incidents of mutilation and mental derangement were discovered in association with Loft, that he was preaching the active achievement of 'pure' animal characteristics. This, according to his theory, involved the gradual elimination of human behaviour and values, particularly the fantasy side of human sexual behaviour, 'romantic' desire, eroticism, etc. This was achieved by the forced sexual satiation of the novitiates, followed by the 'purification' of desire and the association of the personality and character with the bird or beast from which each individual was supposed to be a deviation. Once the 'suggestion' created under the influence of hypnotic practices and hallucinatory drugs had been accepted, there followed the imitative mutilation of the subject. This generally took place during 'congresses' of those of the Loft followers who were felt to be ripe for physical initiation. It seems that by this time the capacity for independent reasoning or the exercise of free will had been completely eliminated in the chosen subjects.

By the time Loft was arrested, a total of four girl and three boy members of his sect had died as a result of mutilation during rites, eleven others were mutilated in varying degrees and including these a total of eighteen were suffering severe mental disturbances, and would probably suffer in some degree for the rest of their lives. Police believe that a number of other unexplained cases of mutilation and mental derangement of young people were certainly associated with the beast sect, but they have been unable to find the evidence to prove it in a court of law.

One of the common characteristics of those who have attended a beast sect reunion is an unshakeable refusal to talk about it. Loft does not seem to have any of the characteristics of a regular 'hippy' or conventional 'fringe' type of character but at the time of his arrest he was a regular user of marijuana and hallucinogenic drugs, though he does not appear to have been addicted to any others. There is no doubt that the drugs sales rings encouraged the sect, and shielded it as much as possible from police curiosity because it was a good market.

The police remarked that although Loft had avoided discovery and arrest for certainly over a year, he seemed indifferent to his arrest once it had been carried out. He remained apathetic, non-violent and quite uncooperative. He answered a great deal of his interrogations in German and seemed at times to believe sincerely that he was still in Germany and in some undefined situation. He insisted on the repetition of two German phrases; 'Selbst-identifizierung mit Tierpersönlichkeit' (self-identification with animal personality) and 'tierische Eigentum-lichkeit des Ich' (the animal quality of the ego). These phrases and others similar, in German, also occurred frequently in his interviews with prison psychiatrists. After his first year in Special Hospital Nine it was felt that the only effective occupational therapy which could be assigned to Loft without danger would be work in the gardens. He showed himself willing and apt and even talented in managing kitchen garden routines and this has again provoked a resurgence of his animistic tendencies. He has become quite well known, not only in the hospital, but in the region, for the extraordinary delicacy and skill with which he can mend broken wings, or even legs, of birds of all sizes. He shows an exceptional sympathy and patience with small animals. He has treated some of the cats and dogs of the outside staff with a skill which has amazed local veterinary surgeons. Eventually he was allowed to look after the special hospital rabbit breeding. The selection and abstraction of rabbits for the kitchens or for sale is carried out by him. Though the fact is not officially recognized, he is allowed to keep certain rabbits to which he has become particularly attached. He is also strongly attached to a squirrel which was brought to him when it was only about two days old and which he succeeded in rearing by hand. This kind of association with his past tendencies has been strongly opposed by some visiting psychiatrists. In view of the fact that no psychiatric treatment and no amount of questioning or discussion has ever produced the slightest disclosure from Loft about his previous activities or his animist theories and practises, it has been felt by the medical direction of SP9 that Loft's authorized association with domestic animals, under regular control, carries no risk and might well provoke a breakthrough in communication with him.

(NOTE: In the two years since the above was written, such has not proved to be the case. Signed Medical Superintendent.)

(NOTE: In the three years since the above note there has been no change. The association with domestic animals seems to be neither deleterious nor of any particular assistance to the treatment. Signed Chief Medical Superintendent.)

(NOTE: The differential diagnosis at ten years after the patient's confinement to SP9 has remained and remains unaltered from the original diagnosis by Home Office psychiatrists, which resulted in the verdict 'unfit to plead' – either schizophrenic or a severe psychopathic personality. Signed I. Robertson, Chief Medical Superintendent.)

This was the substance of the main general medical report on Loft in the dossier sent to me by Dr Robertson. The other parts of the report, which I have not included here, are more technical and record personality and results of regular tests on memory, insight, judgement, general information, attention and concentration, orientation and obsessive phenomena. I have retained as relevant to these notes the fact that the psychiatrists consider his ideas to be delusional rather than obsessional; that he refused to consider himself as mentally ill and considered at all times – and still does – even ten years after the beginning of his treatment – that all his actions were justified by his beliefs, yet showing a perfect knowledge of and distinction between right and wrong. He refused nevertheless to consider the assessment of his behaviour in ethical terms. His intelligence tests showed him to have an IQ considerably above the normal, on the Mill Hill scale 120 and on the Mathicis 110. On entry he was found to be suffering – as I had thought – from acute acromegaly, the enlarging of the bones, which in his case appeared to have commenced probably before epiphysical closure, that is to say before the bones had actually stopped growing, perhaps at seventeen or at the latest, nineteen years of age. Five years after his admission to SP9 there was a medical note to say that this was developing into kyphosis, a curvature of the spine, which today accounts for his slouched appearance, despite his great height.

The characteristics of acromegaly are all there, the increased size of hands, feet, supraorbital ridges (such as brows and cheekbones), and lower jaw. The skin thickens and coarsens and subcutaneous tissues have increased in depth; the nose and ears, particularly the tips, are conspicuously thick. Loft once said to me that a doctor had told him he would die of his 'ugliness', but in fact it is not likely to be the direct cause of death, only of a slowed mental activity, and perhaps an increased degree of irritability, which could be dangerous in an already unstable subject. There has never been any change made by successive psychologists and medical officers in the first differential diagnosis: 'Either schizophrenic or severe psychopathic personality.' But several specialists agreed earlier, at the time of his trial, that he could have suffered a severe schizophrenic illness at about the age of twenty-three, which would be during his period in Bonn, Munich, Vienna and Berlin. This was the time when very little was known of his activities beyond what the report on him described as his association with 'scatter-brained, semi-intellectual groups'. There would appear to be a period of almost five years when such a serious and remarkable illness could have overtaken him without any record of the event, for in fact virtually nothing is known of his early life on the Continent.

I have spent many hours considering this report on Loft and I have never wavered in my intention concerning him. He is not an object to be pitied. The fact that science can classify, label and detail the origins of what is in the final assessment simply evil does not soften nor deter me from the object of the last ten years of my life – to be revenged on the survivor. The satisfying elation I felt at hacking into his flesh and bone and my decision to wait for the final round change nothing. There will be better ways. Only, thanks to Matron Blake, there may be less time to devise them.

21

Weeks had passed since the 'accident' to Michael Loft. No more than a red wavering scar from the top of his forehead almost to the tip of his nose was left to recall it. For it was no more a subject of conversation or even passing mention, particularly in the presence of Miss Lewis, whose chill expression at the mention of the incident had rapidly put an end to its discussion.

But she had made a show of continuing a sympathetic interest in Loft and although she had many cases of far greater urgency to attend to, she kept up her regular visits to the man in the rabbit shed. These brought her an increasing conviction that his habits seemed to offer no suggestion to the solution she sought, so long as head-on elementary violence remained out of the question. From seven-thirty in the morning, when he took his breakfast in the dining-hall, to dinner time at midday, and then to high-tea time in the evening, he remained in or around his rabbit and gardening shed. He had no friends and no other preoccupations or interests than his animals, and his collection and distribution of the gardening tools. Yet each day's delay might bring nearer some new recollection of old Matron Blake, which, recounted to Doctor Robertson, could be fatal to the solution Miss Lewis was seeking.

Despite Loft's evident deep respect for her and his gratitude at the secret they shared of the truth of his 'accident', he never spoke freely again of his theories and sometimes even failed to acknowledge her presence in his shed. Yet she felt that what might have seemed to an ordinary observer as complete indifference concealed in fact a quickening of secret welcome. Sometimes she felt that in his silent indifference, absorbed in the relaxed pursuit of his work and companionship with his animals, he communicated a sense of comfort and response in the indefinable manner of a wild creature. In her silent presence, she sensed that he was not on the alert nor the defensive. It was as though he considered her no more an intruder but as a confidant in his secret, introspective world.

Sometimes a sense of being pleased, almost proud at the undemonstrative acceptance of her as the sole ally of his solitude was followed by an instant sense of shock and recall that this was the enemy, that this confidence must be converted to one of her weapons for his destruction. Her mastery of him should be no more than another seal on his death warrant. Then she would realize that she was not solely the victim of emotions unstrung by the humility of this gross creature, but also of the violence she had done him. Sometimes she feared that the fact of having crushed his flesh and drawn his blood and then to have forgiven *him* for it, the fact that she had ever pitied him even for an instant, might have dulled a minute fraction of the sharp edge of her hatred. This realization would haunt her, and she would return at night to her cottage to exorcise it by writing through the night of the horrors suffered by Cheryl, of her love for her two lost ones, and – almost as though it were a prayer – of the loathing she must keep fresh for the man who had survived.

Among all this, at every moment of rest or silence in her day's occupations she searched the limits of her imagination for the idea she needed for his elimination. Torture, long drawn pain, some blinding agony dragging its way to death were all part of the haunting dreams of suffering which sustained her. Despite this, her long night sessions of remembrance and desolation still strengthened her against the elementary solution of a bullet. It would be just like letting him go and simply shutting a door behind him for ever. Then she would think of Cheryl and her mind would say: 'It must be more than that.' The gun would remain the ultimate emergency solution. If her identity should be discovered she might still have time to walk over to the gardening shed and put six bullets into that knobbly trusting face or that mountainous rounded back. But she never ceased to pray for the time, courage and luck to find something more beastly.

The end of the year had brought some moments of unusual tension to SP9, as though the vigour of summer in its effects on the patients was giving a late last fling to all their subjugated obsessions and secret torments before, like the year itself, they settled into the grey despondency of winter.

There was one week when drug-incensed male patients in 'B' and 'C' Wings provoked the turmoil of what a true Bedlam must have resembled. It was thought to have been on a visiting day that a whole load of minor drugs, mostly amphetamines – known as 'sweets', 'blues' and 'black bombers', had somehow found their way into SP9 and been almost indiscriminately distributed. The effects varied from harmless euphoria to aggressive defiance of authority, and in any event an intensification of each mania and delusion. On one day alone eighteen of the close observation cells of the male blocks were occupied and the general hysteria had spread even to some inmates who had taken no drugs at all. There were two cases of LSD – lysergic acid – hysteria and for a whole morning through the corridor of 'C' block there had drifted the sweet herbal perfume of what was clearly the cruder quality of 'hash'. It was occasionally sold at other times in the hospital's underground 'market' for anything between twenty-five up to fifty pence a 'joint', depending on supply and demand, and was normally smoked in brief euphoric sessions in one of the outbuildings. But this rash – it might almost have been called an orgy – of drug taking seemed to have been organized on a massive scale and most of the partakers abandoned normal precautions. Body searches and examination of lockers, bedding and wardrobes produced a score of pills, a few butt-ends of 'hash' and even a few minuscule white micro-dots, the most dangerous commercialized version of LSD. This was considered by the staff as the most hazardous drug in indiscriminate use in a criminal asylum, since its effect was always to intensify the state of mind of the individual who took it. LSD was used for treatment for certain cases in SP9, but in doses measured in millionths of a gram and under very close medical surveillance. But compared to this the micro-dots were as hammer blows to a wisp of down.

The miracle of that week was that the violence it engendered resulted in no more than a few bruises, a great deal of hysteria and some panic among the staff. It was usually visiting days which provided a steady traffic of the more elementary kind of drugs, and alcohol, directed almost invariably to the more advanced of the patients who were less well supervised and could even take visits strolling in the grounds with their wives and families. Drugs, money and alcohol were often passed from mouth to mouth when patients and relatives kissed. Sometimes the patient who was allowed to serve tea to visitors and the patients they were visiting would consent – for a small tip – to pour a tiny flask of spirits into the tea or to accept a few 'purple hearts' or 'black bombers' to be passed on later to the patient for whom they were destined. All these and other tricks, even though well known, were difficult to control and absolutely impossible to eliminate entirely. They followed strictly the pattern of the average criminal prison with the difference that the inmates of SP9 had far more money available than a criminal prisoner, and a security surveillance far less severe.

Miss Lewis, as one of the very few, with Superintendent Slater, who had any great experience of penal institutions, was appalled by the apparent ease with which contraband of all kinds – even pornographic books from Denmark – found their way into SP9. But she felt, in her own particular circumstances, that it would be unwise to make enemies among the staff by commenting on the situation. She realized well enough that any major drive to tighten up security might deprive her of the one individual she thought of as her own secret weapon in some possible future contingency related to the survivor – Joe Norton.

She was in no doubt that he was the key to most things which occurred out of line in SP9 – he and his allies of the night-time sorties up the chimney to the ward-maids' penthouse quarters.

It was Norton who, with his usual shifty *bonhomie*, delivered a message to her one morning at the end of what had become known to the staff as 'The Great Pill Week'. Even the most amiable of his smiles could never conceal, to Miss Lewis's mind, the strong taint of a leer and it was with this twisted simulation of graciousness that he called on her one morning with a message from Robert Welles.

'Mr Welles would be most 'appy if you would take coffee with 'im this mornin', Miss. 'Ee ses it's very important an' 'ee'll be waitin' from eleven-thirty on.' She said briefly that she would be there. Norton left her with a wink which might have meant anything.

Neither Welles nor any of his close cronies had been involved in the previous week's drug incidents. Welles never took anything stronger than coffee and China tea posted regularly from Fortnum's. Since her first meeting alone with him she had taken coffee with him on many occasions. Each time she managed to avoid the kind of profound discussion on the respective merits of the sane and the insane in which he had once tried to involve her. She found him interesting and even amusing, provided one could laugh openly at the stinging irony of some of his witticisms. This morning she was surprised to find him, again, quite alone. Coffee was prepared for two. There seemed no note of challenge nor the usual note of cynical mockery in his still youthful voice as he greeted her. His politeness seemed to border on real humility and instead of the usual vindictive sparkle, his light brown eyes seemed subdued, even sad. He served the coffee, lit her cigarette for her, and after a few moments of silence began to talk nervously, unsure of himself, unlike Robert Welles too.

'You must wonder why, once again, I have asked to see you quite alone,' he began. 'Well, I've been thinking more than usual lately about, well – about the seriousness of my situation. I believe I am quite sane in all the most serious connotations of the word.' He looked at her with a wry grimace that might have been intended as a smile. 'Yes, I know. They all tell you that. But if no one else in this place cares to believe it, I think you at least will give me a fair hearing. At least this time. Because I promise to behave. There's a special reason, a very special reason why this time I want you to believe that I am quite sane.' He paused. 'Are you with me, Miss Lewis? May I go on?'

She nodded and said nothing. Once a question like that

from Robert Welles would have been ironic or sarcastic. Now there was no bantering note in his voice. The ponderous mockery of his usual conversations had never carried any deep convictions and sometimes she had wondered whether he had not been mocking himself as much as anyone else. But not this time.

'Let me repeat, though in a rather different, a more reasoned way, what I said to you at our first private meeting. This time, I assure you, it will not deteriorate into the appalling and vulgar tirade it did then. I am fully in control of myself.' He breathed deeply, almost a sigh.

'Ten years ago I was found guilty, while in a mental state which relieved me of responsibility, of murder – of several murders. I never had any recollection of such events and I never have had since. For ten years I have not done or said anything which would not seem normal, if done or said by any normal man. I have carried on my studies and passed my university examinations brilliantly, as you certainly know. Yes, I know I have been a difficult and mainly unpleasant person, but these are no more than the ordinary characteristics of a great many sane and intelligent people. There are plenty of people, sane, living free, normal lives, who are eccentric in some way or another, arrogant, impatient, unpleasant, malicious, vain – and with other characteristics similar to mine as well – who are never considered insane. I feel that my naturally rather intolerant nature, with all that it has implied over the years, has probably been considered, unjustly, as part of my derangement, whatever that may be. But is this fair? I was a vigorous young man with a full appetite and capacity for life when I came in here. In a few more years I shall be a middle-aged stranger to the world; well-read, well-educated, completely unsuitable to be thrust out into life, and incapable of carrying on any useful function. I am rotting, putrefying alive in this institution where no one gives me any hope and where my only pastime is using my education, my bitter wit and my father's money to humiliate, bully, intimidate and irritate the people around me. To impress the patients and depress the staff. Do you think I have given you a fair and objective summary of myself and my circumstances, Miss Lewis?'

'I think perhaps you are on the harsh side,' she said, 'but on

224

the whole, apart from whatever medical reservations there might be and of which I am unaware, it is a pretty fair summary of what seems to be your situation.'

He smiled for the first time. 'You really *do* talk like a lawyer, Miss Lewis. What caution! What reservations! However in view of what I have just said, and even considering your reply, why cannot I be given the chance of appearing before a visiting mental health tribunal? Why do no recommendations for considering my provisional discharge ever go forward? Why, in other words, so far as I see it, have I made no progress in ten years towards being considered more responsible? Why, after ten years of impeccable behaviour am I still confined as a criminal lunatic?' He added, quickly and for the first time with some note of sharpness in his voice, 'And will *you*, with your influence and your responsibility, do something to help me? I am trying to show you that I am sane. What I want to know is, will you do something about it?'

She tried to speak as gently and in as friendly a way as possible without showing the exasperation and frustration she felt. 'Mr Welles – I cannot interfere with the treatment or the judgement of your own psychiatrist. As I have already told you I have only the training of a psychiatric social assistant and no more. Your own doctor alone can assess the risks or advantages of releasing you.'

He interrupted. 'But I have not had a single black-out in ten years. The last one was my first and only one. I've matured physically and mentally since then. I was a retarded adolescent in those days, going through all kinds of bewildering physical and intellectual changes. This place has done for me what I was sent here for – I am balanced and stabilized. All I ask is a chance to continue the same treatment, if I have to, in the same conditions of control and restraint, in my own home, under the care of my parents.' He paused, hesitantly as though uncertain to say what was in his mind, and then, rather more softly, went on, 'There would be practically no limit to my father's gratitude to anyone who could arrange for me to be moved to home care, as I think I mentioned to you before. Now, could anyone have spoken to you more sanely, more clearly, than I am doing to you this morning?'

She let pass the possible double implication of his final

words, and in one of her long, disconcerting pauses seemed to be impassively taking stock of all the objects in the room. These included Robert Welles himself. There were beads of perspiration along the top of his prominent forehead, just below the thinning hairline. His full red lips were indrawn, tense, and he sat forward on the edge of his chair watching her face as one might an oracle, about to pronounce the words that could save or condemn. Her reply seemed again weighted with all the reserve and patience she could summon.

'I can tell the chief medical superintendent and your own visiting psychiatrist of this conversation, and of the conclusions about it – on which I agree with you. What you have said has this time been balanced, objective, at least mostly, and normal. You have spoken in a perfectly sane and logical manner. Yes, I am quite prepared to say that.'

As she spoke she wondered why the drops of perspiration stood out on his forehead. Was it the effort of his restraint? Was this well-balanced presentation of himself frustrating the malicious and venomous character of the man to a point of perspiration?

'Is that *all* you can do for me – dear lady?' Those last two words and the tone in which they were spoken implied a spark of the old – and maybe the real – Robert Welles, and the mockery they seemed to convey brought back the old note of challenge to his voice.

He went on, 'I had hoped by talking simply and sincerely to you that I could have enlisted your more positive help in higher spheres. I had hoped that you might have understood that my life is at a critical point. From now I either rot forever or I can go on a little longer, providing I really have something to hope for, some promise on which I can count. All life consists of having something to look forward to. Take that away, and you might as well be dead. Don't you agree, Miss Lewis?' How well she knew the answer! She gave a noncommittal shrug and Welles went on. 'I know your duty and your authority have limitations somewhere. But you are a rather special person. I feel that you have deep understanding and great strength and compassion and it is to those qualities that I am trying to appeal. I had hoped that the way in which I spoke to you would have made you feel justified in doing something more than – well – giving a sort of pat on the back for me to my visiting psychiatrist. That won't get me very far, in fact it might do the very opposite of what I hope for. Can you not send a minute of your own to the Ministry, can you not have me examined by a revision tribunal – can you not in fact step over the hierarchy of psychiatrists and superintendents and act on your own convictions at a higher level?'

'No, Mr Welles, I cannot,' she said. 'I'm sorry but I can only go as far as I have indicated. You have overestimated my authority.' She pulled her shoulder bag into place and stood up.

Welles stood up too. Now the blandness and humility had gone from his expression. She could never have believed that in so short a time the controlled tension of his features could have changed so greatly. A pink flush was spreading across his face. The indrawn, tense mouth resumed its full, aggressive, cherubic form. The air of judicious sobriety and balanced calm was fast fading. But he was still under control, still clearly exercising a restraint that was almost breaking. His voice now conveyed a mixture of cold anger and bitterness, but there was still a note of pleading too.

'Miss Lewis, you don't know, you cannot have understood how much I counted on this morning. It is not just a phrase when I say that my life is at a critical point between rot and hope. I know you have influence, maybe not authority, but influence, to change the beastly, inhuman indifference there is to my case.' He collapsed in his chair and put his hands to his forehead. 'Oh, God, if only I hadn't been rich and favoured and spoiled here, and hated too! I would probably have been out by now. But no, I've got to pay for being Mister bloody Welles!'

She stood and looked down on him. Was this yet another Welles act? Was this a new angle to the old Welles posture? Or was it perhaps the real Welles, beaten and at bay?

'I'm sorry, Mr Welles,' she said gently, 'it's not my fault if you and others have exaggerated my standing here. I can do no more for you than I have told you. But I promise that I will do that to the very best of my capability.' He was silent for a moment. She wondered if he were trying to weep and instantly reproached herself for a harsh and cynical reaction.

Welles looked up. 'Alright,' he said, 'I'm beaten. There's no hope for me the decent way. It looks as though you are leaving me to make my own solution.'

He stood up and held out his hand. His voice was cold and the old note of mockery was back. 'Thank you for calling, Miss Lewis, I hope you will remember this morning for a long time. The day will come when it will have a meaning for you.' She took his limp, plump hand as he swung open the door and she was out in the corridor almost before she had time to realize it.

Back in her cubby-hole office she wondered what he had meant – 'The day will come when it will have a meaning for you.' Was this a personal threat to her? Was it a suicide threat? Welles was not a suicidal subject. She made a note on her programme pad to talk to Dr Robertson about her meeting with Welles. She admitted to herself that – acting or not, honest or devious – he had impressed her.

Even more, he had for the first time aroused her sympathy and interest. She decided she had neglected him. It was his own fault because he was usually so insolent. He was quite right about himself. He was paying for being rich and privileged and bloody. But it was partly her fault too. Perhaps one day she really would be able to help him.

She turned a little wearily to her next problem, a letter from a 'B' Wing male patient beginning, 'No one has been to see me for two years and I can get no reply to my letters—' My God, she wondered, do I really have the right to worry about myself and my problem? It was a doubt that she quashed even faster than it had passed through her mind. Anyone who knew her, who had seen the usually wise and gentle face of 'Miss Lewis' in that instant would have been shocked.

22

It was a winter's day, tired, sad and damp. The great trees of the park, the oaks and the elms, the beeches and the chestnuts, that had seemed so permanently stately and assured even at the end of a long summer now seemed to hold their bare limbs with tired disdain, dripping away an icy drizzle. The humid mist of the closing dusk of late afternoon framed the old hall in a way that well became its role of SP9 – a shabby demoted dwelling place of resentment and despair.

It was a little before the hour of high tea, which some called supper. Nearly all the outside workers from the gardening block, the carpenter's shop, the laundry, the poultry pens and the rest of the detached buildings had drifted back to their day-rooms to await the tea call. It was not a moment when anyone would pay much attention – even if they heard it – to a few brief and anguished cries from the piggeries. It is true the noise was heard by one or two male orderlies escorting their charges back to the main building. But in a special hospital no one goes investigating cries which do not seem to be in their own immediate department. Particularly at tea time. The cries from the piggeries were brief, and after all, part of the general sound pattern which eventually ceases to be a special signal to the mind. It was only after tea time that the absence of a member of the men's 'C' Wing, Morley, and his close friend Albert Mikes, a simple-minded and harmless basic depressive, were noted as missing. Briefly there was a move to sound the siren for an escape until one of the orderlies remembered the noise that had come from the piggeries.

In the corner of one of the sties their torches showed Mikes sitting dazed and disconsolate amid the soiled straw, still holding in his lap a long, bloodstained kitchen knife. Just inside the closed portion of the sty, which contained no pigs, a man's body lay spreadeagled in the straw. His trousers were pulled down around his ankles and between his open legs there gaped all the red remains of what had been a rough and ready castration. He was already dead, of shock and loss of blood. Daniel Morley, the chronic ravisher of children, had given up waiting for a reply from the Ministry for his request for castration. At the cost of his life, he had persuaded a simple-minded fellow patient to carry it out for him. Now his problem was solved more surely than he had ever hoped.

The knife was rinsed and swiftly returned to its place in the kitchen, from which its disappearance had never been officially reported. 'B' Wing Warden Burke and his staff were relieved that their awkward problem concerning the knife had finally been solved. The manner of its solution was certainly embarrassing and provoked a severe reprimand from the colonel, which was soon forgotten. Jim Blake, the cook, was glad to get his knife back. It was one of his favourites.

Perhaps the only individual in all SP9 who was much shaken by Morley's terrible death was the chief medical superintendent, Dr Robertson. He told Miss Lewis, 'After the Ministry's negative reply on castration, which was to be expected, I received authority only this morning to begin a treatment of Morley which would probably have cured him within a year. It was by the insertion of hormone oestrogen pellets. I was going to tell him about it tomorrow.'

23

For several weeks now, at the instigation of Miss Lewis, May Saunders – 'the pavement monster' who had snatched children from their perambulators – had been given the full 'C' Wing privileges to which until then her medical reports had not entitled her, simply because her consultant psychiatrist had not updated them in reference to hospital facilities. Now she was attending the few mixed classes which were held, social competence, dramatic art, folk dancing, rural studies and cookery. Tom Lacey, the former Jesuit seminarist, whose mania against the sign of the cross had brought him to SP9 and whose fear of his own sexual arousal had made him the confidant of Miss Lewis, had also become a member of all these classes just before May joined them. This was no coincidence. Their names had mysteriously appeared on the class lists and Lacey's fear of participating in mixed classes was quickly dissipated. In fact he had already been twice suspended from folk dancing classes for holding May's unreluctant hand after the music had stopped instead of returning immediately to the supervision of the men's side of the room. This was perhaps not too significant, for it often happened. The lingering touches of hands was one of the risky and thrilling excesses for which even the most stable of patients would take the chance of punishment or reproof.

May Saunders was not the most striking of several good-looking women patients of SP9, but despite her terrible record – of fear and simplicity – there was a fresh fragility about her, a demure but warm femininity which qualified her as one of the most attractive. Perhaps that was why, at the very beginning, the wind in her clothes had made her more attractive to Tom Lacey than any of the others. In any case her unexpected adhesion to the mixed classes had worked, with all the smooth magic Miss Lewis had foreseen.

May Saunders' and Tom Lacey's love was not the usual institution infatuation, nourished on rare glimpses over long periods of separated fantasies. As long as glances could be exchanged during escorted walks in the grounds, or on the occasional organized outings in the summer, infatuations would always exist. But they were the stuff of dreams and they never became really personal, for their objects could rapidly change according to the convenience of circumstances. This was not the case with Tom and May.

In the narrow intimacy of her consultation room Miss Lewis was able to talk to them separately, to listen to the confidences of each of them without telling either that she knew of the other's feelings. While hoping she would fail, she tested them by pretending to discourage them both.

When Tom Lacey had been the first to speak to her openly of his discovery that he was in love, he had come a long way from the day when he had been frightened of himself reacting to the sight of a windblown skirt. He had changed in other ways too. Dr Robertson had told Miss Lewis that Tom Lacey was passing rapidly beyond the need for SP9. 'We'll have him out and under ordinary day clinic supervision by the spring,' he said.

Lacey now spoke freely of the mania which had obsessed him, analysed and almost ridiculed it, even though it still remained an identifiable shadow over his conscious mind.

'You know that I'm actually in four or five of the mixed classes now?'

'Yes, of course. You have been for quite a while.'

'Well, I wanted to tell you. May is a member of the same classes too. She's been, I suppose you would call it, promoted. You remember what I told you about her?' He looked at Miss Lewis out of the corners of his eyes, nervously measuring her reaction. There seemed to be none.

'Yes. Yes, go on Tom, I'm listening.'

'Well – there's something more about her. More than just – her shape and all that. I think she's very beautiful. But I don't know how to make any more progress.' He was still short of what he wanted to say but Miss Lewis was unmerciful.

'What do you mean – beautiful? There are lots of things very beautiful in all sorts of ways. Explain yourself. What are you trying to tell me?'

'Well, I mean – she makes me feel as though I could do practically anything for her, or with her. I could be terribly strong. I could reason things out and not be stupid and, well – what I am, I suppose – crazy or unbalanced.'

'It's a curious sort of reasoning, Tom. I don't really see why a girl, or the sight of a girl, could make all that difference. Why couldn't you feel strong and decent without her?'

He sounded puzzled and disappointed. 'I don't know. But that's the way it is.'

'Have you talked to her? Have you told her you're in love with her? Has she told you something special?'

'No. I've still hardly spoken to her. We've touched with our hands in the dancing class of course. We've looked at each other a lot. We do that every time we have a chance. I can tell she feels the same way about me.'

'How can you when you don't even know what you mean when you say you're in love? Has she told you?'

'No.'

'Well, listen Tom. All this that you've been telling me is about being in love. But you've still got to discover just precisely what it means, what it signifies to you – that it could and should imply for your future, for you both. It's no good talking a lot of vague nonsense to me. I can't help you with that. What are you going to *do* about it, what do you *want* to do about it? Think of all the implications – if you are sure this thing is real and true. Then come back and talk to me about it, in confidence of course.' She wanted him to see, to discover for himself that inside these walls there was no room and no future for what he felt, so that when the time came he would find the solution she intended to offer as less desperate, less frightening perhaps.

He was very grateful and went away promising to analyse all the logical implications of the bewildering, satisfying and

233

yet frustrating emotions he felt.

May had never been especially unhappy in SP9, nor conscious of any sense of confinement, let alone something as severe as detention. Between her convent orphanage and SP9 the odds were largely in favour of the special hospital, except that she had never been able to understand why there were no babies there. For she loved tiny children more than anything in the world. The very sight of one had always given her an irresistible yearning to take it up in her arms and enfold it in the overwhelming wave of comfort and protection she felt flooding through her whole body.

On four occasions when she had found small babies left alone in their perambulators on the pavements outside shopping centres, this compulsive reaction had eclipsed all her conscious sense of restraint, so that each time, in trance-like moves, swift and alert none the less, she had suddenly found herself hurrying away through the crowds with a baby in her arms.

Twice she had hidden them in abandoned buildings – carefully tucked away under old timber and rubble while she went out to beg or steal food for them. Each time, when she was caught, and the frightening, hostile people who represented authority had forced her to reveal her hiding place, the infants were sleeping and May was only wrenched from the claws and fists of mobs of screaming furies by the police. On the two other occasions, her weakness had ended in physical pursuit which had stamped her mind with nightmarish memories of turmoil and hate that sometimes shocked her awake with her own screams in the night.

All this was the limit of her sense of guilt and the boundary of her capacity for crime. Yet the headlines had indelibly stamped her with the easy catchwords of 'pavement monster', and it was this more than any judge or psychiatrist which had set an indeterminate seal on her days as a criminal lunatic.

All this, in long awkward exchanges, sometimes deadlocked in interminable silences, Margaret Lewis had been able to extract gradually from May's harrowed memory and shocked emotions. It was only then, when she was sure that May had exposed her whole experience of these elementary instincts and their occasional disastrous overflow, that she had ventured on

234

her first hesitant probe to what might become match-making.

Once May had been moved into an individual room of the women's 'C' Wing, Miss Lewis had, for the first time, tried to sound her on her understanding of the wider world.

'Do you wish there were babies here for you to look after?'

'Yes I do, miss.'

'Would you like to have a baby of your very own?'

'Well, yes, of course, miss.'

'Do you know where babies come from? I mean do you know how they are born?'

A long silence.

'Babies come from men and women who like each other, who love each other. Did you know that?'

A shorter pause. Then a hesitant, 'Yes, miss. I knew all about that a long time ago.'

'Sometimes, May, do you like looking at men?'

It was only a whisper this time. 'Well, maybe – yes – but – well only sometimes, miss.'

'Well, now that you go to classes with them you'll probably see one you like. There's nothing wrong in that. You can smile and say hello to him and chat with him, if you like. But come and tell me about it. I promise not to tell anyone. I'll help you, Do you understand?'

'Yes, miss. Thank you.'

That had been the very beginning of Margaret Lewis's presumptuous match-making. It was the one preoccupation in SP9 which gave her the greatest unqualified pleasure and made her heart beat a little faster. Not only was it creative and constructive action, but to her own mind it was a reassuring confirmation that she really was proceeding along her way towards the burning of her boats.

The next time the subject of Tom and May was discussed was during a visit to her office by the young man in question. He carried a brown paper parcel. It contained a box of canteen chocolates, expensive by SP9 standards, seventy-five pence for a one pound box. Presents were permitted, as well as censored correspondence between male and female patients, so long as they were both 'C' class. But Lacey had come to ask Miss Lewis for the favour, on this first and special occasion, that she should present the box to May on his behalf, with a brief note.

'Why don't you want this to go through the normal channels, Tom?' she asked.

He shifted uneasily. 'They might not explain to her properly
who it was from, or they might do it clumsily and frighten her.
Or they might tease her about it and frighten her, so that she
wouldn't look at me any more. I felt that if you explained to
her exactly who it was from and that there was nothing wrong
about it, she might take it the right way.'

'The right way? What do you mean?'

'Well, I mean, I want her to know that I like her and would
like to be her friend, and for her to like me, that's all.
Sometimes in these classes the men frighten the girls – some of
the girls seem to like it, judging by the way they speak to them
when the nurses aren't near. Not all the girls are frightened.
Some are worse than the men. What I mean is, I don't want it
to seem like any of that to May. I just want her to like me and
to know that if I'm saying it through you – then it's alright.'

The note accompanying the chocolates read, 'Hello May. I
hope you like these. From Tom. PS See you at the next class.
Tom.'

'Alright, Tom. I'll give her the box and your little letter. But
I think you may be wasting your time and your money. I
doubt if she's interested in men. Do you think she'll remember
your name?'

'Oh yes, I do. I'm sure.'

She sent for May two days later and gave her the box and
the note. She told her, 'You can say, if anyone asks, that I
handed them to you. But read the note now.'

The girl read the note slowly, a nervous frown darkening her
pale, clear forehead. She kept her eyes on the note for quite a
while after she had obviously finished reading it, as a pink
flush rose from her neck to her cheeks. She dared not look up
at Miss Lewis, and she stared at the note, as a refuge for her
embarrassment. She would have gone on, no doubt, staring
indefinitely, but Margaret Lewis broke the spell.

'He gave them to me to give to you, so it's quite alright
May. You remember this young fellow called Tom, don't
you?'

'Yes, miss.'

'Is he nice? Do you like him?'

236

'I think I do, miss. I'm always – well – he keeps getting into my mind all the time. Even when I'm thinking of something else.'

'Well, he seems to like you. He told me he thought you were the prettiest girl in all the classes. And the nicest.' May crumpled the note lightly in her hand and clasped the box of chocolates close to her breast, but said nothing, staring at the floor. 'I think he is a very nice young man, really,' said Miss Lewis. 'I'm glad you like him too. It *was* nice of him to send you the chocolates, wasn't it?'

'Yes, miss.'

'Alright, May – off you go. Don't eat all the chocolates at once. When you see Tom Lacey again, say thank you to him, will you?'

'Yes, I will, miss. Thank you, miss.' She sidled through the doorway, her face glowing and the knuckles of the hand that held the note clenched tight and white. Miss Lewis lit a cigarette and watched the smoke of her first long draught billow above her desk with an air of satisfaction. What she thought of as her 'parallel purpose' seemed well launched on its way.

24

It was near noon when the siren sounded from its late Victorian bell-tower on top of the kitchen block. It was rather a stupid arrangement because it could mean anything from a fire to a patient's escape, and in the intervening stage, before the word could be passed around, it simply created a general panic without guidance. According to the degree of one's sanity and responsibility, or lack of sanity and fear of responsibility, one reacted in different ways. These different reactions and their differing degrees contributed to a general tension and confusion.

The nurses in 'A' Wing rapidly locked all doors while the 'A' Wing patients began crying, whimpering or howling in their respective fashions. In 'B' Wing there was a gathering of tension, though the doors were locked a little less hastily, mainly because at least half a dozen of the keys were being carried by patients, though there was a good deal of panicky scurrying to and fro by the staff to find the patients and get them back to their quarters for a detailed check. The check-up in 'C' Wing was much calmer and the patients usually returned to their quarters by themselves and waited quietly. This time there was no smell of smoke, no cry of fire. What was it?

The siren had been sounded on this particular day only after a long and secret panic among the staff.

Around eleven o'clock in the morning a male nurse of the men's 'C' Wing had noticed a certain quietness in the area of

Robert Welles's room. Until then there had been no serious check. This was normal. Like all individual rooms, that of Welles had two doors, the obligatory spy-hole being in the middle of the inner door. Welles had always kept it blocked by a strip of surgical tape and for years no one had bothered to try and look in on him. Every morning his own personal servant and henchman, 'Evans-the-Ship', the little Welsh ex-officer of the Merchant Navy, had brought him his breakfast and made his tea for him, with his personal electric kettle plugged into the power point in the corridor. In the mornings no one had the time – and it was not felt to be really necessary – to check the 'C' Wing patients, certainly not to the degree of a fixed roll-call. Eventually the 'C' Wing duty orderly, intrigued by the silence and lack of activity around Welles's room, began to investigate. There was no sign of Evans, no sign of the usual morning-coffee visitors, and the electric point in the corridor, to which usually either his percolator or kettle stayed permanently linked, remained barren. There was no reply to a discreet tap on the door. When it was eventually opened, there was Welles's elegant bed-sitting room suite quite empty. The large divan-bed was made up, the table cleared and bare, and the air of abandon accentuated by the drawn chintz curtains. The unbelievable implications of this discovery had taken a good quarter of an hour of checking and counter-checking to reach a degree of real alarm. But even then the evident conclusion was so hard to accept that the sounding of the siren had been delayed another fifteen minutes.

The idea that Mister Welles, the man of words, the intellectual, effete and verbose, could have actually descended to such a banal action as escape took a long time to sink into the bewildered collective mind of SP9. For before accepting that possibility they had asked themselves, 'Where would you look for a man like Welles if you did not really believe he had escaped?' He would hardly be the type to hide out in the piggeries, or the rafters of the gardening shed, or the outside toilets. He would never have climbed up through the hatches into the lofts. It was hard to imagine him crouching under the fruit bushes, barren as they were, nor yet under the Chapel altar. Yet in the despairing hope that Welles was only trying a teasing escapade as a new fashion of mocking his warders, all these and more solutions were explored in vain. The only other alternative, that he had gone over the wall, was the very last to be accepted, since it as well seemed so out of character for a man whose madness was his pride.

Yet the appalling reality had reluctantly to become accepted – Robert Welles, the 'padded-cell lawyer', had actually behaved with the simple sanity he despised, and escaped over the wall. By the time the siren had wailed out its vague alert it was clear that Evans-the-Ship had gone as well. The ally, acolyte, henchman and valet had shared a room with four other 'C' Wing inmates, none of whom remembered having seen him since tea-time at six-thirty the day before. A suitcase of personal belongings, normally kept under his bed, was gone too. No one remembered having seen Robert Welles after six-thirty the previous evening, so they had surely gone together, some time after dusk. So the siren's wail was a little late. By the time everyone had been informed of what it was all about, the real panic was over. Welles and Evans were away, and far away, one a paranoic psychotic, the other a bewildered schizophrenic at the very least. It made some fine headlines in the press next day, for they were not the sort of escapes it would be advisable to keep secret. Their departure had left not a trace in SP9, not a shred of cloth on a piece of bent barbed wire on the whole perimeter of the Brockley Hall estate. No ladder displaced nor missing. Nothing disturbed anywhere. But it gave SP9 a lot to talk about.

A week later, leaving her cottage in the morning, Miss Lewis was surprised to find there was some mail in her cottage letter-box. Usually no correspondence of any kind was delivered there. All her mail, private or official, went straight to SP9. This time she picked up the envelope lying inside the door as though afraid of it. When she opened it she glanced first at the signature. It read, 'Yours in freedom and pity, Robert Welles.' The postmark was 'Nice. Alpes Maritimes. France.' The letter read:

Dear Miss Lewis,
Neither of us realized what a great service you did me the other day when you refused to intervene with the au-

thorities on my behalf. Had you given me the slightest sign of sympathetic encouragement or understanding I should still today be a privileged inmate of Brockley Old Hall, living on in the treacherous and futile hope of being given some serious medical and human consideration. I must confess I was in deadly earnest when I spoke to you. I did truly intend to do everything that will, power, good faith and honesty could achieve to prove that I was trustworthy and sane enough – in the medical if not in the intellectual sense – to be released into the proper care and attention of my father. I don't know why I suddenly became weak enough to believe it possible to deal honestly with any institutional authority. It must have been a bout of mental fatigue. Also perhaps the fact that I recognized in you something of myself, the same sort of capacity for unshakeable resolution and steely persistence, which made me feel that if by chance you *did* take up my cause, it would be won. Quite apart from that, I rather like you too. Well, there it is, thanks to my god the devil, and to you, I failed and was obliged to take this tiresome and rather humiliating alternative, which I had long held in reserve, well before my last appeal to you. I brought little Evans out with me, theoretically travelling as my secretary-servant, because I am much too far out of date with the customs of daily life to be able to be accepted without arousing suspicion. If and when he gets tiresome my father will arrange to have him dumped elsewhere. I must say I am getting the hang of life in the outside world very rapidly, and I find it in many ways most agreeable. I am already confirmed in my opinion that most people outside mental homes are simple fools, working together, elementary and harmless, in some sort of unspoken truce called 'social ethics', mainly because they are afraid of one another. They are certainly of no danger to anyone like myself.

In the coming years, in a South American state where superior wealth and intellect are both appreciated, in that order, I shall be able to prove that even though intolerant, arrogant and hasty-tempered, I am quite as fit and certainly more worthy to live in the free world as any of the simple plodding morons I find around me on the Promenade des Anglais.

I am writing to you because, first of all, I want to show you what – in your terms – a great mistake you made in not acceding to my request for help. You were about the only person at Brockley whose respect and confidence would have been worth having and I suppose now I want to make you sorry that your error of judgement caused you to miss a chance of doing something useful. As the years pass I shall write to you regularly, by a devious route, so that you will be able to see how well I have been able to manage in your famous 'sane' world. Sanity certainly does not begin in Brockley Hall because escape was pathetically easy and would probably be just as easy for anyone without a penny. With the funds available to me from the outside I was able to be driven away, Evans and I, and our two suitcases, in the canteen van, which wasn't even checked at the main lodge gates. The infamous scoundrel who was well-paid to take us out is a fellow called Norton. He has long been receiving a fat weekly envelope from my outside representatives, and will, I hope, eventually be detected, if he has not already scurried away to blow his pay-off. You may of course give him away if your conscience so dictates, but really I do not think you should get involved, even on the basis of this letter, because if he is still there he probably has an alibi and will deny everything anyway, and he could be a nasty enemy to have even for someone with a record as unimpeachable as yours. He is a born jail-bird and will inevitably find his way back to his natural surroundings without your help.

The sun is shining on a blue and sparkling sea and although the cretinous Frogs around me try my patience somewhat with their garlic and ignorance of any known language, the situation is on the whole sublime and I find it delicious at last to be treated with the complete subservience I deserve.

By the way, it may be of some interest or even value to you to know that at the request of Dr Robertson, Superintendent Barthropp has written off to the Home

Office or some Ministry, asking for your security clearance. Apparently there was not one in your records received at SP9. I wonder what is worrying Dr Robertson? Is it just a bureaucratic formality or is there something sniffy about you after all? What a fantastic joke if it turns out that the valiant much-decorated heroine of confined spaces turns out to have been some kind of naughty girl! Please forgive me, I'm only feeling rather whimsical, but it did occur to me that this little tip might interest you. I got it from Norton who reads all the files and all the correspondence his bony girl-friend Rosie Fletcher leaves lying around in her office. I may tell you that there is no fiddle or skulduggery that goes on in Brockley which Mister Norton does not mastermind in exchange for a good cut. But don't take him on. He is very sharp.

Yours in freedom and pity,
Robert Welles

She had read the letter for the first time standing in her front doorway. Then she went into her little living-room and read it again, sitting down. The news about Norton was no surprise. It was true that he had his own closed van for canteen supplies and the lodge gatekeeper never checked the regularly known vehicles. But the information of Dr Robertson's request for a security check chilled her. There had been no such things as security checks when she first joined the service. This was a custom which had grown up in later years, and even then no one had ever bothered to check her original personal records and create a 'security clearance' for someone as well known and trusted as the famous Margaret Lewis. It was just possible that even a security check-up would never go further back than the original engagement ten years ago of Margaret Lewis as a Court Probation Officer. It should never need to go as far back as Mrs Margaret Hayes and the Loft case. But there was a terrible risk that it might. Was this move of Dr Robertson's simply based on the incident of Matron Marion Blake's revelation that Miss Lewis had once been married to a doctor, and had lied about her origins and upbringing? Or was it a simple bureaucratic formality? Whatever the answer might be, this move could provoke the end of the known Margaret Lewis, the end of her story, the end of her mission, if she did not hurry up. It was now the eve of the Christmas holidays and there might be some delay in tracing back ten or so years and coming across the clue which could link Margaret Lewis with the mother of one of the victims of the Loft case. It depended on how long ago Robertson had asked for the security check.

She carefully folded Welles's letter away in her desk, unthinkingly patted the side of her shoulder-bag where a small but heavy object nestled among the personal effects, and set off for another day at SP9 with a certain sense of relief that events were now being precipitated. She had been right in her instinct about Norton and she still felt right to reserve her knowledge of his activities, not simply to avoid stirring up the authorities, but possibly as a weapon she might need more than ever.

25

For the next twenty-four hours there was never an instant when the problem and its urgency was out of her mind. In fact there were two problems. For weeks now she had been brooding on the final solution to the problem – which she had created herself – of May Saunders and Tom Lacey. After she was gone, after her 'crime', there would be no one to follow through their story and to help it on its way to a happy and valid ending, which it deserved and of which she felt certain it was capable. Since she was going to become a criminal and her professional life would collapse and she would have no demands on the future, she felt free to profit by taking at least one bold, unorthodox and officially unpardonable initiative. She was burning all her boats – so why not light one little ember more that would at least leave no bitter ashes?

Lacey was due for outpatient treatment in the spring. May Saunders, certainly no more unbalanced than many childless but maternally-obsessed women, would probably never be allowed out as long as there existed a Sunday press to howl its pious, circulation-building protest. For these two Margaret saw a solution, but not yet the precise means to reach it. If May became pregnant by Tom, and he demanded to marry her, they would by law certainly be allowed to marry and most probably continue treatment as outpatients, if necessary, living together in a hostel or even in a normal non-criminal psychiatric hospital, where they could still be happy and fulfilled.

For problem one, the death of Loft, the end of the survivor, the situation had become even more simplified. Under the threat of the search for her security clearance, which would be no clearance at all, she must resign herself to a simple and rapid operation requiring no complicated planning or special circumstances. Obviously this must be immediately after the Christmas holiday. How could she manage to organize May's pregnancy before that?

It was after those twenty-four hours of intense reflection that she felt it would be possible. The solutions to both problems lay with the proper use of Joe Norton. He was like a weapon which had suddenly been provided by a divine hand, she thought to herself ironically.

On a late afternoon three days before Christmas she found Norton in his canteen store and asked him to call in to her room the moment he was free. Five minutes later she was face to face with him across her desk. He was – as ever – confidently at ease. Margaret Lewis intended to lose no time in putting him where she wanted him and her first words held more truth than ever she herself knew.

'Norton, you are a criminal.'

For a fraction of a second he must have thought it was a joke. The cold detachment of her features instantly told him that it was not so. Then he almost choked on his cigarette, grasped the arms of his chair and leaned nearer to her, across the desk. He gaped and his cigarette butt stuck in the corner of his mouth.

She gave him a few moments for this point-blank broadside to take effect. Then she went on curtly, 'Now, listen to me, Mr Norton. What I am going to say to you may give you your only chance to stay out of trouble, if you have any sense. I can help you by keeping quiet. But I want help in return. Don't let us waste time arguing about the facts of your criminal record, known or unknown. I have them written down in a safe place from where they will go straight to the police if you fail to accept the offer I am going to make to you. Do we understand each other so far?'

Norton blinked and nodded very slightly. He crushed his cigarette in the ashtray and waited.

She went on: 'I have a letter from Mr Welles relating

how you helped him and Evans to escape, the money you re-ceived for your help on this occasion and on others previously. Mr Welles lists the other activities by which you have been lining your pockets for quite a long time – drink and drugs and so on.' She felt quite safe in generalizing beyond the facts she really knew. It would cover every piece of villainy for which Norton was responsible, and the more he thought she knew the better her hold on him.

Norton sat back in his chair now, his puffy face drained of its usual rubicund flush, his eyes wide and shocked and his mouth still agape.

She paused before launching her secondary broadside. 'In addition, Mr Norton, I have a written declaration by the former ward-maid Mounalal concerning your activities in the ward-maids' penthouse. I have no doubt the police could obtain more from the Welsh girl named Gladys, if necessary. So rape and violence among other things, will be listed in your record, if you don't do as I say.' She looked him in the eye for a moment until he dropped his gaze and gave a couple of feeble nods. He was evidently considerably shocked, his de-fences, even his will to defend himself, shattered.

'Now,' she went on, quite sure of herself, 'this is what you have to do. You will be at the Christmas Eve staff–patient supper and dance I suppose – on Saturday night?' Norton nodded again. 'After the supper and when the dance has got properly under way, you will take two patients, one by one, from the gymnasium where the dance is held and put them in the back of your catering van. Then you will drive them to my cottage and leave them there. I'll give you a spare key to the front door. Then you will come back to the dance and carry on as though everything is normal. Do you understand as far as that?' Another nod, rather sharper and more composed this time.

'The second service I require from you, before the end of next week – and I mean Friday at the latest – I want twelve LSD micro-dots. Twelve only. You will get them from your usual source.' The last phrase was a colourful touch of bluff. 'Is that understood?' Once more there was nothing else for him to do but nod. 'When do you think you can get them?'

Norton measured his reply. He knew it would commit him

entirely to her. Yet, otherwise – there was nothing she didn't know apparently. So went his thoughts. Now he spoke for the first time. A voice subdued, for Norton, yet still anxious to be reassuring. 'You can 'ave 'em on Tuesday, miss, that's the day after Boxing Day.'

'Very well. I'll take that as a firm promise. See that it's kept.'

Relief was beginning to bring back the colour to his face. His stunned-ox expression had faded and he reminded her of a deflated balloon which was gradually being blown up again.

'Yes, miss. It's a deal, a promise. No trouble at all.'

'Wait a minute, Norton. That's not quite all. I want the birth certificates of May Saunders, "C" class patient, and Tom Lacey, also "C" class, on my desk here by tomorrow evening at the latest. In a sealed envelope addressed as "Personal" to me. Just slip them out of the records file in the registry – while you seem to be looking for something else. Work it out for yourself anyway. That should be no problem to a man of your extensive ingenuity.'

The irony was lost on him. It was the easiest condition of all to fulfil. He just smiled, quite widely this time, and said, 'Okedokey, Miss Lewis.'

'Good. That is all I am asking of you. The escape should be just as easy. Everything's very relaxed on a dance night. Then as soon as you have given me the micro-dots – and don't think you can fool me with just any little white pills – you must give your notice to the chief superintendent. Invent any excuse you like but get out of Brockley Old Hall, and for your own good stay as far away as possible from it forever. I will say nothing to anyone about you, so long as you carry out what I have just described to you and then clear off. Is everything understood?'

Norton frowned and gained a little time by shaking a fresh cigarette out of his packet. He knew he was beaten. SP9 had been a good, cushy beat, easy money and, he had thought, no risks. But obviously the game was up. He was lucky to be able to get away without a word said nor another mark on his long, dark record. He nodded again. Miss Lewis felt that it might be advisable to obtain a more concrete acknowledgement than a silent nod before she let him go.

She said more slowly, 'I want to be sure that you understand and accept what I've said Mr Norton. You realize that what I know about you, plus whatever would undoubtedly be discovered if the police made inquiries, plus your record – because I'm sure you have one – would put you away for five or ten years if I were to say the word. So I want these two services and your departure for keeping my mouth shut. Have you really got that clear in your head?'

Norton's self-possession was returning now. He swallowed noisily and half-grinned foolishly. 'Yes, Miss Lewis. I've got it all now. It's a bit of a surprise, see? Sort of knocks yer out, all that, all of a sudden. Like they says in the papers, I'm not givin' yer no comment. But it's a fair deal. Who are the two patients I've got to get out?'

He looked relieved when she told him. 'Thank 'eavens, it's a nice quiet pair not likely to get excited nor nuthin'. It's a piece of cake Miss Lewis. The deal's on, as I said. Just one thing. When I've put them in the cottage, do I lock the front door and 'ow do I give yer the key?'

She thought for a moment, then, 'Yes, that's it. You lock the front door. When you come back here to the parking area you'll find my Mini unlocked. Put the key on the floor, just below the steering wheel. Come back into the dance and carry on normally and don't speak to me at all during the rest of the evening.'

Confidence was fast flowing back as the realization of the situation sank into Norton's devious mind. He was safe after all, and, who could tell – the role of accomplice to this influential old dame, whatever she was up to, might help him unload some of the responsibility for other things onto her, if he were ever cornered later. An accomplice in villainy of the great Miss Lewis! This was something. He smiled, leaned forward and patted her hand lying on the desk.

'So you're doing a good turn to them two. Sweet on each other, eh? And you and me's the father and mother Christmas for 'em, eh, Miss Lewis?' He laughed at his own wit, stood up and stubbed out his cigarette as he turned to go. 'Happy Christmas to all of us, eh, Miss Lewis. See you Saturday night.' He winked and went. As she sat rigid at her desk, the expression on her face might well have removed the stupid smile from Norton's. He might have wondered whether a deal was really a deal – and in whose favour.

The solution of the LSD micro-dots for the survivor was a tremendous relief. It was a beautiful solution. She wondered why she had never thought of something like it before. Vengeance, like everything else, should march with the times. An LSD overdose was simple, needed no long planning or special circumstances, and its power of mental, and eventually physical, suffering could be guaranteed to surpass any ordinary, brutal measures of painful extermination which she could devise.

One micro-dot would have almost disastrous results in a schizophrenic or psychotic patient, or even a normal but unstable and depressive character. She had decided to drop all twelve micro-dots into the tea permanently brewing on the wood-stove in the survivor's rabbit shed. Twelve should provide a 'trip' from which there would be no return, certainly no mental return to anywhere outside a strait-jacket or a close supervision cell for life – and more probably, no physical return anyway. If he did not kill himself in the frenzy of whatever LSD provoked him to do, he would die most likely of a cerebral stroke.

The unexpected sequel – her own complete dissociation from the event – left her with a problem she had never anticipated; what to do with herself afterwards? She had always taken it for granted that she would be a convicted murderess sentenced either to a similar institute for the criminally insane, or a life sentence in prison. It had certainly never occurred to her that she might never be associated with whatever happened to Loft, for the idea of personal execution had always been an accepted essential of her plans. Now – unless she deliberately proclaimed her responsibility, she would continue to be the admired and respected Margaret Lewis – with no particular purpose to carry her through the rest of her life. Suicide? Well, perhaps, but it might seem an admission of shame or guilt. For the present she decided to put that problem aside. She would decide on her own future when the LSD had done what it should do to Loft – separated him forever from his little animals, ripped apart the sullen pretensions of a master-beast – taken him to live or die in an infinite hallucogenic hell of unspeakable horror.

26

Half an hour after Norton had left her, Miss Lewis sent for Tom Lacey, to explain to him the escape plan. The morning after the escape, as carried out by Norton, she would take them from her cottage in her car to Birmingham. They would need to leave very early, firstly to avoid being seen and secondly because there would be a lot to do.

She explained, 'I will put you on a train going north, to Scotland probably, where you can find lodgings and jobs and live as a normal couple. You will then both establish the fact that you can live normal lives in an ordinary community and be accepted by everyone.

'You will both have your birth certificates with you, and as soon as you have both lived in the same parish for three weeks, you must get married at the local registry office. This marriage will be your strongest defence against being separated again. The next strongest will begin from the moment that May becomes pregnant. As soon as she is so, and you are married, write to Dr Robertson and enclose the letter which I will give you for him. It's possible that I shall still be available – somewhere – to intervene personally on your behalf, but for the moment I don't know where I shall be a few weeks from now. Still, Dr Robertson will certainly know if I am – available. Even though you may have to spend some time more in a hostel or simply a home for psychiatric treatment – don't be scared. You will have won. You'll be out of here and you'll be together. You will have a child, and each other, and you – as you once said to me, Tom – you will be terribly strong, able to do anything for May.'

In answer to Lacey's question on how they would live until they found work, she told him, 'I will give you £500 of my own money when I put you on the train. Also a letter saying that I have given it to you as a present. You should have enough to live on for several months if you are careful.'

At first he had seemed too stunned by the prospect of this precipitate freedom with May to be able to grasp all that it meant. But he was an exceptionally intelligent young man and once he had come to accept this rather awesome plan as a practical reality he grasped the implications and the details with an assurance and confidence which comforted Margaret Lewis. He said thank you innumerable times and apologized because the words were inadequate to express his feelings for what she was doing for them. It was decided that he should tell May himself, and only at the moment when at the dance Norton took her out of an exit door leading from the gymnasium toilets to the parking area. It was likely to be something of a shock to May, but they felt that with Tom's arm around her, and Tom's voice reassuring her, she would carry through the plan without panic. The two of them would have to wait for Miss Lewis in the cottage until the end of the dance because, like the rest of the senior staff, she would have to stay until it finished, at eleven o'clock.

27

The Christmas Eve supper dance was one of the biggest nights of the year in SP9. Usually there were modest dances and tea parties about once a month. Twice a year the theatre club put on a variety show or a musical comedy or a play. But none of these events enjoyed the special atmosphere of the Christmas Eve party where the seasonal feeling penetrated the chill prophylactic anatomy of SP9, permitting a flexibility in regulations which was as much favoured by the staff as by the inmates. The event took place in the theatre-gymnasium, a fairly new structure behind the two-storey-high men's 'C' Wing, the extreme rear east wing of the main building, on the same side as the chapel.

The patients had their own small dance orchestra – drums, saxophone, clarinet, guitars and bass, with a grand piano – and this shared the playing at the dance with some powerful hi-fi equipment, because the band too wanted its share of the dancing and the social contact.

All the 'C' grade men and women were present. Even Mrs Ford, the poison-pen banker's wife, put in an appearance, wearing her real cultured pearls and accepting only to dance with senior members of the staff. About half the 'B' grade men were there and a handful of 'B' women who on such occasions usually enjoyed themselves the most and were apt to become a little giddy with excitement at times. So there was a rough total of thirty male and eighteen female patients. The staff present totalled twenty-five men and sixteen women.

Half of them were officially on duty and the others were there mostly because they felt they had a moral duty to perform, to help keep their charges happy, to say words and make gestures which in their way were minute contributions to the halting steps of crippled minds limping forward along the path to the light and sanity of the world outside. All the patients, without exception, had to be watched, discreetly, for over-excitement, which if not stopped or controlled in time could develop into a massive hysteria ending with everyone being led back to their quarters and the staff left with a gloomy sense of their own failure.

This evening was a success from the social and medical point of view and there was no more than the usual stretching of taboos which ordained that men and women, except during dancing, should sit or stand along separate sides of the hall or serve themselves at the standing buffet. There was some mixing at the buffet, and after each dance – hand-holding which lingered on longer than the music. Flirtation and teasing were permissible at such times, so long as the staff in charge felt that the collective spirit of the evening was remaining relaxed, uncharged with any potential tension. The only unpleasant element, practically at the end of the evening, was Joe Norton, who had evidently been sampling a hidden bottle, probably in the back of his catering van in the parking area. He began to be noticeably elated, without being a nuisance – in fact he was rather amusing – about an hour before the official end of the evening. His elaborate courtesies to his women partners, his sweeping bows, his caricatures of elegant ballroom dancing and his wild elaborations of 'pop' gyrations, were all good fun and helped brighten the evening, which was more than could be said for the dutiful small-talk and mild, half-hearted horse-play with which most of the staff covered their boredom or anxiety.

But with success, and the nips at the bottle going to his head, Norton was tending to go a little too far. Finally, at the end of a tango, he held his partner – it was Annie McBride, one of the least stable of the 'C' grade women – in a practically horizontal clasp and pressed a long and evidently much unwanted kiss on her lips. The release of her mouth from his embrace let out a high-pressured scream which for a moment cloaked the whole gathering in chilled silence. Fortunately Annie, wiping the back of her hand across her mouth, returned quickly and calmly to the buffet. Superintendent Slater took his boisterous assistant aside and told him to clear off home with no more nonsense. Norton, a little unsteady on his feet, turned to wave and shout 'Happy Christmas to all' as he left. Not all the women, patients as well as staff, were pleased to see him go, particularly Rosie, the colonel's angular secretary. She had attended the dance for no other reason than the hope of a happy ending in Norton's van on the way home.

Half an hour later, after everyone had been escorted back, in relaxed and cheerful groups to their quarters, and all necessary doors locked, Miss Lewis was standing beside her Mini in the parking area, talking to Dr Bligh. With a great surge of relief she had found her cottage door key on the floor of the car, as planned. She noticed, without mentioning it, that Norton's cream-coloured canteen van was still in the car park, and in the back of her mind wondered vaguely where he could have gone to at this hour if he had not gone home or to the village. He lived in a male staff quarters house in the row of staff houses, a half a mile along the road to the village from the SP9 gates. Perhaps he was waiting to take home some of his fellow staff members, though by now almost everyone had dispersed and the building was completely silent and almost without lights.

The doctor said goodnight and a Happy Christmas and was moving towards his car when a man's scream, hoarse but muffled, came from the far side – the chapel side – of the main building. It was a strange scream, broken by fractions of silence, and each renewed cry shorter and more muffled, as though someone was being beaten and at the same time dragged away into the distance. Then – silence.

'Wherever could that have come from, doctor?' she called through the darkness to Bligh.

'It sounded like the "B" Wing first floor dormitory on the other side of the building,' replied the doctor. 'I'll just go round and have a look.'

Though there was nothing she could do, and it was hardly even her immediate concern, Margaret Lewis followed him down the path to the front drive and around to the side of the east wing. The lights were on in the first floor dormitory and a male nurse was peering through the bars of an open window.

'What was all that?' he called down to the doctor.

'Wasn't it from your ward?' asked Dr Bligh.

'No, it was all quiet here. It seemed to come from behind the building, and then I thought it sounded from downstairs, the "B" Wing day room, underneath.'

But the 'B' Wing day room's windows were dark and silent.

'There's no one in the security cells next to you is there?' called Dr Bligh.

'No one, doctor. It's all quiet there. It was just that one long, broken sort of scream, nothing else.'

They met two other male nurses going around the building on their way back to the car park and they too reported no traceable incident, nothing but the scream in the night, and now complete calm everywhere.

By the time she had driven back to her cottage Margaret Lewis had stopped thinking about it. So had Dr Bligh. He was in bed and already asleep.

Lacey and May were sitting on the settee holding hands and waiting for her. May had evidently been crying, but it was Lacey who was holding the handkerchief. Their relief, when she arrived, though without words, was clearly overwhelming, but their tension and fear did not disperse all at once. She sent May into the spare room to make up the bed – the sheets and blankets were ready – and she made them both cups of hot chocolate, served with cake. When she announced casually that May would sleep in the spare room and Tom with blankets on the sitting-room settee the last traces of tension and doubt disappeared. She had never intended to embarrass them by seeming to push them into bed together at hardly a moment's notice, and she realized it was something she should have allowed tactfully to be understood much sooner. Now she just said cheerfully, 'The thing for both of you is to get a good rest. We shall be up and away tomorrow almost before daylight to find a train going far north as soon as possible. They didn't miss you tonight at the hospital and now I don't think they will before midday tomorrow. It's Christmas Day, there's no work to be done and half the staff are having two days off.

But all the same you must be well on your way before midday, before an escape alarm has been raised.'

Before they separated Tom and May kissed goodnight. It was a light, hesitant brushing of the lips, but Margaret Lewis noticed how May's hand moved to Tom's shoulder and gripped and twisted the cloth of his jacket, pulling him closer. She was glad. She felt – this may be one target, at least, that I haven't missed.

28

The morning after was busy and successful. Tom and May had accepted the unimaginable truth of their freedom and union and they were light-hearted and cheerful as they selected and tried on the clothes Miss Lewis had bought for them – which mostly fitted. Their goodbyes from the train which would take them on the rambling Christmas Day journey from Birmingham to Edinburgh were a mixture of laughter and tears. They seemed to treasure their birth certificates as much as the envelope of fifty £10 notes.

At SP9, Christmas Day was doubly calm, for it was a Sunday. The staff Christmas Dinner was at twelve-thirty and Miss Lewis arrived only a few minutes before. She joined the rest of the staff for drinks in the main staff lounge, a dismal, badly furnished cavern, which wore its allotment of much-used Christmas decorations with a dreary gloom that no Empire Sherry nor even hot buttered rum punch could dispel. Miss Lewis seemed even more cheerful than usual, even elated, as she sipped her rum punch and chatted among the staff.

Norton's van was still in the car park and she mentioned it to Deputy Superintendent Crow over their drinks. Perhaps he had left eventually last night and would be in for drinks in a moment, they thought. Had Crow heard the scream, Margaret Lewis asked him. Yes, he had, but nowhere, in none of the male quarters, could anyone be found who could explain its origin. It must have been someone in his sleep, perhaps one of the 'C' men, in a single room having a nightmare. But was it reasonable to suppose that any of them, even if they had left the dance early, would be that deeply asleep so soon after the party?

'In any case,' said Crow, 'Christmas or Sundays, but always Sundays, Norton comes to my office around five o'clock in the afternoon to discuss orders and work for Monday. He should do so today, even though it is Boxing Day tomorrow. If he doesn't come today, then he's probably gone off somewhere to finish his binge and hasn't come around yet.'

Miss Lewis spent the afternoon sitting chatting to the 'B' women and then the 'B' men in their respective day-rooms. Sometimes chatting was a fair enough word, but sometimes it meant listening to a long, incoherent string of non-words and pretending one understood them. Sometimes it meant constructing a long monologue of banalities amid silence and unreflecting eyes dreaming indecipherable thoughts.

The SP9 siren put an end to this ordeal of doubtful value. As the diminished forces of the staff scurried around to lock doors, put everyone in their place and prepare for the unexpected, Miss Lewis called in to the main administration office to learn that the disappearance of Tom Lacey and May was being signalled – at last. The combination of the dance and Christmas Day had been enough to allow the disappearance of the two 'C' class patients to pass unnoticed for almost twenty-four hours. This would certainly not have been the case if 'A' or 'B' class patients had been involved. Even normal staff insufficiency, outside holiday periods, meant that 'C' class patients virtually benefited from what was the equivalent of an honour system most of the time. Welles's disappearance, still unexplained, had done nothing to change this.

Now, there was nothing more for Margaret Lewis to do in all the bustling to and fro, the questioning, the searches for traces of the departures which, on the evidence, were gradually being associated. She told Security Superintendent Slater that though she had interviewed both of them in recent weeks, neither had shown any indication of discontent, rather the contrary for Lacey at least. He was looking forward to his release in the spring. Nor did she know that they knew or had any particular interest in each other. They had never spoken to her about it. In fact as the inquiries went on, Tom and May were only gradually being associated and it was not until the following day that the police were told that the two escapes might have some connection.

Miss Lewis, her mind at ease, in fact singing a little soundless song to herself, returned to her office to prepare a late pot of tea, and to think, and smoke. After all, she thought, an eight to nine hour train journey was an invaluable advance on an escape alert. There was still no news of Norton. It worried her because such an abnormal incident could presage some kind of hitch in the programme she had laid down for him. So far it had been almost too good to be true. Was the main objective threatened? Had Norton changed his mind and run out on her? Could he be so stupid?

She sat alone, gazing through the smoke spirals of cigarettes, lighting one from another, as her mind, like some silent, invisible mechanism, added, subtracted, computed all the elements involved in Norton's disappearance.

It was at the end of the third cigarette and cup of tea that the facts inevitably merged and led by a single thread to an acceptable solution. The Norton disappearance and the unidentified scream had to be considered as part of the same circumstances. In that case, she felt, she had not far to look.

The duty nurse at the iron-grilled door at the entrance to the women's quarters was glad to see her and it was inevitable that she had to stay and chat and speculate for a few moments on May's disappearance. It was a strain on the impatience that was growing as fast as the ingenious and gruesome theory she had evolved, dreaming over tea and cigarettes in her office. Eventually she was able to move on casually, with the remark that she had neglected to thank two of the 'C' women patients for Christmas cards - painted by themselves - which she had found on her desk.

There were twelve private rooms, some little more than cubicles, in the 'C' quarters, and she might well be in any one of them for a while, if anyone should wonder where she was.

But instead she took the narrow staircase leading from the corridor up to the ward-maids' six-roomed penthouse on the fourth floor. The three who were not on holiday for Christmas were all on ward duty. The rooms and the small corridor were empty. The double-doored cupboard at the north end of the corridor was never locked. Methodically Margaret Lewis piled

the mattresses, blankets and linen from the bottom of the cupboard, up to the first shelf, four feet above the floor, in the
corridor behind her. There was nothing about the back wall,
with its faded and torn Victorian papering, layers and layers
deep, to indicate that this was a wooden panel opening onto a
chimney passage. But, as before, at one extreme edge she
managed to get a finger-tip hold, and pulled. The panel,
which was not hinged, but simply fitted loosely against a metal
frame around the opening inside the chimney, fell easily in-
wards. It was a full three feet high and a similar length. She
took from her shoulder bag the pocket torch she always carried
for use on the path between the house and the car park. On
her knees inside the cupboard, she leaned inside the chimney
and shone the beam of torchlight upwards to where, about
fifteen to twenty feet above, could be seen the narrowing of the
passage at the chimney pots. The blackened metal rungs which
passed inside the chimney, beside the cupboard opening, went
on all the way up at spaces about eighteen inches apart. She
turned the beam downwards. The rung exactly beside the base
of the opening into the cupboard hung vertically downwards.
Only one end of it was still attached to its plaster casing in the
brick wall. But now it was bent and powdered with a rusted
film of freshly crumbled plaster. The rung below was broken in
the same way. The rung below that and the others above were
all intact. It looked as though the two rungs which had given
way had done so through considerable pressure. They had
been already much weakened by the iron ends rusting inside
their plaster holdings. If someone had hung onto these rungs
while pushing hard on the cupboard opening blocked by a four
foot high stack of bedding and linen – it was reasonable that
the rungs would have broken or come out of their sockets. This
was surely what had happened. Norton, in his drunken inspiration for finishing his night in the bed or beds of the ward-
maids, would have bounced his way helplessly down this black
funnel for four floors – a distance of quite fifty feet. It would be
a miracle if he still lived.

On her way down to the basement, she called in on Deputy
Superintendent Crow. He gave a shrug and a look of per-
plexity when she asked if any of the male staff sharing Norton's
quarters had seen him since the previous night.

'No one has heard or seen a trace of him since then,' he said. 'Technically speaking he's missed no duty and he's quite entitled to his hangover. Let's wait until tomorrow and see.'

The key to the basement, because its most important content was bulk food stores, hung on the huge key-board beside the main kitchen door. There was no one there to question her need for it when she took it.

The basement had originally been a network of corridors, kitchens, pantries, larders, wine cellar and general store-rooms. Now it contained unusable and obsolete institutional furniture which no one was authorized to dispose of or cared to try and use, obsolete kitchen equipment, planks, boards, beams and bales of wood and all the rest of the sort of junk that accumulates through years of building alterations until someone has the courage to throw it away. The store-rooms contained sacks of dried vegetables and other bulk kitchen supplies. The central heating pipes passed along all the corridors and the place was chill but dry.

She found her way easily to the extreme north-east corner of the complex, a large cavernous room with a floor of worn flagstones, formerly the hall's main kitchen. In the northern wall the curved pattern of whitewashed bricks showed clearly where the long, high opening of the vast kitchen range and boiler had once been set. This was the wall that blocked off the bottom of the east wing chimney system.

Margaret Lewis stood for some minutes, one ear against the wall, listening. For perhaps ten minutes more she moved slowly along the wall and then began again, this time on all fours, her head against the wall almost at floor level. Then she heard it – a shuffling, a brittle rustle, then a soft scraping, followed a few minutes later by a sound that resembled a deep croaking.

It was, she imagined, the sound a man might make in half consciousness while trying to shout for help. For at least ten more minutes there came no sound. Then once again, more clearly, the distant scraping, the scratching against the wall, followed by a hoarse croak, choking away into something like a moan of pain or despair, or both.

From where he is, she thought, he may just be able to see the tiny specks of light through the chimney pots. If he had the strength he could probably climb back up the rungs – if they go all the way down to where he is. But the sounds she heard were so low down that it was obvious he was lying on the ground.

She lit a cigarette and in the light of the single, dust-coated bulb that barely illuminated the grimy vault, she walked slowly up and down, along the wall, thinking.

To save Norton, if he were not already mortally injured, would mean explaining how and why she had been able to find him and why she had kept her information from Mounalal to herself. It would bring the prison security men back into SP9 with a vengeance, to turn the place upside down and reorganize things in a way that would put her plans beyond a reasonable chance of success. Plans? She asked herself wryly – well, without LSD micro-dots, she had none now. Perhaps, if she had all the time she wanted, in the future she might be able to steal some from the dangerous drugs cupboard where confiscated drugs were kept provisionally, and where in fact the liquid supply of lysergic acid diethylamide for treatment was kept. But all that would mean time and planning, waiting, perhaps indefinitely, for the right chance. Now she had no time. Enough, just enough perhaps, to shoot and kill a man in the next day or so. Nothing, not even another man's life, must obstruct or endanger that objective, now shrunk to the size of a paltry bullet and a death without the long anticipation of fear and pain – unless some last minute circumstances of chance and fantasy played into her hands.

In any case, the absence of Norton from this world could do nothing but good – or rather his continued presence would do nothing but harm. He was the source of all corruption and mischief in this place, and he would spread it wherever he went, all his life, if he lived any longer. Even if one could ignore all the other harm he had spread in SP9, the escape of Welles alone could make him indirectly responsible for the loss of other lives elsewhere. Nevertheless it was not a case of punishing him. Complete obliteration was the solution to Norton's way of life. And by an incident in that way of life he had obliterated himself. This cold logic, untouched by a grain of sentiment, compassion or charity, was her own self-justification for leaving Norton alone to die, for putting him from her mind entirely. He would die, immured and unlamented. Immured already – he was as good as dead.

Her pace of pensive reflection changed to her habitual sprightly and decisive step as she switched off the lights, leaving successive corridors of darkness behind her on her way towards the ground floor. One instinctive gesture she made was perhaps born of the cautious double-thinking which the last ten years of her life had taught her. She stubbed the end of her cigarette against a corridor wall and put the butt in her shoulder bag. Five minutes later the cigarette end was in her office ashtray, and Margaret Lewis behind her desk. The basement key was back on the key-board of the still empty kitchen. She opened a folder marked 'Relatives' Correspondence' and was instantly absorbed in the work for which her capacity for compassion and patience had long since made her an adept.

29

By midday on Monday morning all SP9, staff and patients, was completely absorbed by the mystery of Norton's disappearance. His catering van in the parking area had begun to take on the awesome quality of an adjunct to a story that was perhaps fatal. Everyone wanted a peep at 'Norton's van'.

The disappearance of Tom and May coinciding with that of Norton made no sense at all to anyone, especially as Norton's van was still there. The local police accepted the information with dispassionate formality and Superintendent Slater organized the methodical questioning of all staff and patients about the last known movements of the three missing people. It was curious and difficult to have to try to associate the disappearance of two patients with one staff member. There had never been an escape like it before.

The following day was the end of the official Christmas holiday. Somewhere in the Ministry's circuit of In and Out trays, the reference files and cards, the security clearance of Margaret Lewis would be moving once more along the system towards an inevitable conclusion. Perhaps this was even the day when it was due at its destination.

As she sat and thought about it in her office over her morning cup of tea, she began to feel the weight of tension was too much to bear. Failure would be too much to bear as well. Was time and familiarity with Loft in all his mundane surroundings and tasks going to erode her resolution until she had the excuse that circumstances had made even his elementary elimination impossible? Was she going to pretend to herself, just when the last stretches of the chase lay open before her, that *this* Loft, the Loft of maudlin transports over a squirrel and some rabbits, was not really the man she was hunting?

She half-closed her eyes and lifted her head as though looking at something high on the wall opposite to her. It was the memory of a flayed body, arms outstretched, head pendant, its long dark hair clotted in cords of dried blood. Was this not what it was all about – the reason she was here?

She stubbed out her cigarette and pulled her shoulder bag up from the floor beside her onto the table. She had to fumble right down into the bottom of the bag to find the automatic. She replaced it in the outer pocket, closed by the clip-button flap. She passed no one on the way to the gardening-unit. She walked without her usual swinging step, nor were her eyes searching and alert for a greeting with whoever might be in range.

Loft was alone in the barn, making a frame for a rabbit hutch door on the long, heavy oak table. As soon as she arrived Squirrel came down, with his jerky, cautious crawl, from the shadows of the roof and sat on the table watching her. Loft mumbled a good morning and watched her as he worked, slyly, out of the corners of his eyes.

She stood silent for almost five minutes. This sort of mute communion between them had gradually grown into a habit they both understood. But when she spoke it was not with the casual, slightly conciliatory tone she normally used to him.

'Mr Loft, I want to have a talk, a few words with you.'

He looked up and she saw, as soon as his eyes met hers, that he recognized instantly the difference in the mood of this encounter to all those of the past. He put down the metal plane he had been holding and took a couple of hesitant paces towards her.

'Yes, Miss Lewis, what is it?'

She unclipped the outer flap of her shoulder bag with her right hand and looked down at the work-table as she spoke.

'Mr Loft' – she had never called him Michael, like the rest of the staff – 'this is our last meeting.' She paused, but he said nothing. She went on, 'This is the end of a journey for me,' she looked up at him, 'and for you too.'

The tension of her voice, the stiffness of her body, to some degree had changed her identity in those instants. So it had happened with Loft too. In a fraction of time, unperceived, it seemed that he stooped less, his shoulders had lifted, his pendant lower lip seemed strung a trace more firmly. The wide-ranging gaze of his protuberant eyes, which usually contributed to the impression he gave of remoteness and simplicity, was gone. The heavy, bulbous eyelids were lowered an immeasurable fraction, which gave to the expression of his eyes an unaccustomed degree of calculating intelligence. The purring lisp of his voice was there as ever, but he spoke more surely, a trace faster, as though his mind had been stirred to wider wakefulness.

'I know, Mrs Hayes. I understand very well. This time you are not going to look for a handkerchief in your bag. You will look for your little gun. That is so, is it not?'

She put one hand on the table edge and her breathing almost failed her, so that her words were a harsh whisper.

'Mrs Hayes, did you say – *Mrs Hayes?*'

He looked at her steadily for a few seconds and then turned to face the table. From beneath its top, halfway along, hung a deep tool-drawer, which he opened. He fumbled inside for a moment and then flipped onto the table beside her a thin, postcard-sized, transparent card-case. It contained a coloured photograph of Margaret with, beside her and almost as tall, Cheryl, smiling cheekily as she leaned against her mother, one arm flung casually against her shoulder. It had been taken during that last Cornish holiday, when Cheryl's scars had turned silken pale, and she had been obsessed with being a gull. Margaret Lewis had always carried it in a tight ticket-pocket in the inside of her shoulder-bag. It was the last photograph taken of Cheryl, so like her mother she could have been her younger sister.

Margaret looked up from the photograph. Her face was not shaped to bear easily any emotions but those associated with warmth, affection and humour. The expression of horror it bore now resembled an acutely painful distortion.

Loft spoke casually, with an easy indifference. 'When you spilled out your bag on the floor, looking for your handkerchief after I was injured, this is one of the things you didn't put back. When I returned from the infirmary I found it in the wood-shavings under the table as I was sweeping up.'

She picked up the photograph and gazed at it in silence. Her hand trembled slightly. Loft waited, watching her with an air of detachment, as though she were an object a long way off. Then he went on. 'It's curious. I had sensed even then that there was something special about you. I felt that you represented a point that somehow completed a full circle in my life – or would some day complete a full circle in it. This photograph told me that I was right. I had not realized precisely what I was trying to identify in you, and then this photograph of the two of you – no, it would be truer to say the *one* of you, for you are one and the same person – this photograph showed me quite clearly the identical bird-spirit which I had recognized in Cheryl, and which inspired me to purge her of the evil of being human, and liberate her soul and body for birdsong and winged flight.'

He paused and the sound of his breathing betrayed the dry indifference of his expression.

'Cheryl was my highest achievement – at least, the bird-creature I was creating would have been, if that pack of blundering running-dogs of human pestilence – those police – had not come charging into our sacred ceremony. Cheryl's transmutation would then have been complete, perfect. The world would have been enriched by the most beautiful thing ever created, a creature of which the putrefaction of mankind could never even have conceived.'

Margaret Lewis was watching him now. For the first time since she had met him she saw and felt, like a pressure hammering in her throat and forcing its way up into her mind, the stupendous scale of the insane evil emanating from him, moving through his whole massive body, livening with taut consciousness the usually trance-like torpidity of his massive face. This was a demonic insanity she had never dreamed of nor yet found, in SP9 or anywhere else. Yet there was only a small quaver in her voice as she replied. 'Why was your so-called transmutation simply a process for creating nothing but blood, pain and destruction – foulness and vice?'

'Oh *that*—' He shrugged. 'That was the pus of the abscess which is the state of being human. You see Miss Lewis, Mrs

Hayes – it had to be lanced, scraped free from poison, cauterized without scruple, cleansed, purified. Do you think it was a simple process to carry out effectively with those moronic mongrels of the police sniffing and baying at our heels day and night?' He swept one arm in front of him with a scything gesture of impatience and his mouth twisted into a sneer. 'And they not even knowing what it was all about; not knowing what they were really involved in, programmed like robots, programmed like the so-called doctors and psychiatrists here whose job is to police the limits of the mind – censure and reissue to society those whose awareness has been numbed by psychological incantations! And to keep under suppression and hack away at the minds of those too strong to submit.'

He paused to stare at her drawn face, as fixed as a mask, stamped in a mould of stupefaction and despair. Then he continued. 'We, who are called mad and classified under names like psychotic, or manic schizophrenic – and all the rest of the tags invented by science and society – we defend our faith. Some try violence. Others seem to submit so that they can slip back into the ranks of society's toy soldiers. And yet others' – suddenly his face was transformed by that half-smile lifting one side of his mouth, his eyes moving in a clumsy roll – 'others, Mrs Hayes, do it by living behind a silent screen of submissive simplicity and non-being. Harmless, passive, gentle, impossible to fit back into the rigid ranks of society because, like rag dolls, we do not react. We do not resist. We receive no message.' The half-smile revived, spread. 'We are poor things, sometimes even rather likeable. You may have noticed?'

Margaret Lewis could think of nothing to say. She stayed paralysed, possessed by a shock so far beyond her belief that she was incapable of further physical reaction.

Loft stepped up to her and with his eyes on hers, gently lifted the unclipped flap of her shoulder-bag. She knew she could do nothing to stop him. He found the automatic at once and threw it contemptuously on the work-table beside her.

'You came to shoot me,' he said. 'I've never understood why you didn't do it the first time. Or were you *really* afraid when I moved suddenly? And was the iron bar quicker than fumbling in your bag for your gun? But when you had hit me with the bar – for whatever reason – why didn't you finish me off? I've often wondered, but I've never understood.' He seemed to wait some moments for her answer. She made no sound, no move.

He went on. 'This time, the moment I saw your face I knew you had come to carry out your execution. But you won't do it, Miss Lewis – nor you, Mrs Hayes. You won't ever do it because even though I've disarmed myself completely, you still don't know what to believe. You don't believe I'm capable of rational thinking, in any case. You have pitied me for too long. Don't imagine I have not felt it. Of course I have. And anyone who pities his enemy is already on the way to changing sides. Pity is a fractional gap in the defences that lets in the seed of frailty, of defeat. I for instance am really poor Michael Loft, the awkward, submissive, acromegalic monster, programmed too, like an automaton, to look after rabbits and my squirrel and count gardening tools, in and out, in and out. Ten long years away from the crazy individual, supposedly stupefied by drugs, who happened to take your daughter away from you. One of my followers found her in some high-school disco club and persuaded her to come to one of my meetings. Her mind became mine the first minute I saw her. She was destined for glory the moment the blood had dried. Now, go on Lewis, or Hayes, shoot me.'

He picked up the gun and held it out, butt towards her. She stayed motionless, her hands by her sides, her eyes on his face, as though she were seeing something beyond belief, beyond even vision. He lifted the flap of her bag and dropped the weapon inside.

With a softness that intensified both his lisp and the velvet smoothness of his voice, he said, 'You see – you cannot do it.'

He turned away and moved to the far end of the table, leaning on it with both arms folded, his eyes now on hers as though they were piercing her mind for his words to enter.

'You were sent to me by the mystery that rules all things – to complete that circle about which I spoke a few minutes ago. *You* are Cheryl. No matter that there may be grey streaks in your hair, your skin wrinkled and the fire in your eyes burning low; that you are creased and used and blurred at the edges. You are the mother-soul of Cheryl and you are here so that together we can complete the living proof of how perfect can

270

be beauty once stripped of the perversions of human trappings.'

His whole face was becoming radiant, as though it were the focus of an invisible beam of exaltation.

'Do you not realize how magically we have been brought together to complete that work I began,' he went on. There were convulsive snatches of excitement in his voice as the words erupted in a way that no one in SP9 would ever have associated with Loft, the sullen hermit of the rabbit barn.

'Tomorrow evening at half past six, when supper is over and everyone is cramming around the day-room television, I will go to your car. I will bring a dark blanket and cover myself in the back. We will go away together and I will teach you in secret the wonders of being what you truly are. You remember I told you once? You are a little bird of prey, keen, pure, swift, sharp, secret. It is true that when I said that, I knew already that you were the mother-soul that is Cheryl. But even before that, I knew, I knew. I had known from the first day you came in here that you were meant for my kingdom, just as I knew that Cheryl's soul was mine the first time I looked into her eyes. Now, you were sent to me for this, this completion of the circle. And I shall, after all, make you perfect.'

It seemed to her as though his eyes, which had never quit hers for an instant, at that moment filled the whole range of her vision. From above, below, each side, they enveloped her in webs of infinite softness, then folds of irresistible strength.

And then she was looking at Loft again, the Loft of every dull, dreary, routine working day. He was leaning close above the work-table, head and shoulders bent low over his work of planing a narrow length of white pine, just as he had been doing when she first entered the barn – just as though everything that had passed since then was simply a nightmare that had slipped by in a micro-second of waking thought. But it was not so. She still held in her hand the photograph taken on the Cornish cliffs.

Loft paused in the long firm strokes of his plane to sweep away a pile of shavings. He held his piece of wood to eye level for a moment and then turned to pick out a fresh piece from behind him. He turned it in his hands, examining each edge for knots, and began again the long sweeping strokes. There was no sign of presence in his face, no trace of thought, no flicker even of life. She glanced around the barn swiftly as though seeking some sign of recognition. But the wooden partition walls, the square, heat-blasted, cast-iron stove, topped by its black kitchen kettle, the tangles of gardening tools, the rows of ugly, asymmetric rabbit hutches, the heavy roof beams and the ragged, meaningless shadows they all cast, suddenly conveyed a terrifying sense of massive indifference. She felt there was nothing between her and absolute evil.

She hurried away through the conservatory and across the kitchen garden with short quick steps, head down, like someone trying to restrain an overwhelming desire to break into a run.

In the short, narrow corridor to her office she met Dr Robertson. He seemed preoccupied but cheerful and barely glanced at her as he wished her good morning. Then, as if vaguely uncertain of what he really wanted to say, his head bent in thought as though trying to remember, he said quickly, 'Ah, yes. Margaret, could you manage to spare me a few moments tomorrow morning in my office? It's not – well – no, it's not exactly vitally important, I don't want you to think that at all. But still – would ten-thirty be alright?'

'Quite, doctor. Ten-thirty tomorrow morning.' Her voice was flat and subdued, and she wondered why he had needed to reassure her – so hesitantly – that the appointment was not 'vitally important'. She passed quickly on, a little coldly, it seemed to the doctor, into her office.

Five minutes later she walked out again and drove from the car park to her cottage in the village.

30

The Diary of Margaret Lewis

EXTRACT 6

It seems only polite to those who have read so far to give this diary an ending as well as to put on record the state of mind in which I am finishing my mission at SP9. As well, I need perhaps to excuse myself by explaining a certain dishonesty in some of the recent pages, calculated not so much as to try and deceive a reader as to deceive myself.

It is almost morning and the late winter dawn is a grudging grey creeping up the sky. I have passed a night during which these pages have remained blank, but during which I have found the resolution and strength I needed to face this day and to leave a few words to show that I am not weak and I shall not betray Cheryl.

This time there will be no long grisly threats, or posturing, or squalid stirrings of past memories. Just a few words so that you who have read so far may say: 'So that is how it was – that is how it ended.'

Yesterday I went to the rabbit barn to shoot Loft. In my heart I was not at all sure that I was right, but the increasing risk of discovery and the compulsion of that fixation which has motivated me for so long seemed to leave me no choice. But I failed to shoot him. He had recognized me, quite a time ago, by a photograph of myself with Cheryl which I dropped in his rabbit barn. He taunted me with having pitied him and lost my will to kill him. He was right – then. For a long time I have only been able to keep up my brave, aggressive façade as a merciless avenger of Cheryl by committing myself to paper, by rereading it whenever I needed to refresh my own arguments and courage. For I began to have doubts about the identity of Loft almost from the first time I met him here. Was this Loft at SP9 the same as the one of ten years ago and did I have the right to make him suffer for what he had done under the impulse of another mind, a different identity? These doubts, conflicting with my original obsessive conviction that fear and pain were the only payment for fear and pain, began a confusion in my mind, which, being basically forbearing and compassionate, sapped away at my resolution, tortured my conscience both for Cheryl and Loft, and I think I was being driven insane. Yesterday, partly due to his mental affliction, one of the effects of which is an overwhelming degree of paranoia, and partly due to the force of his undiluted evil, which the science of mental therapy will never recognize, Loft was so sure of himself and of my past signs of pity that he invited me to shoot him. He said that he knew I could not because I had lost the will to do so. Then, and this was where classifiable insanity overflowed into unallayed evil, he identified me with Cheryl and invited me to run away with him and become the subject for completion of his deadly experiment on Cheryl. I believe I almost succumbed to his extraordinary hypnotic qualities. A child would certainly have done so, and probably most adults too. I survived to pass this night by exorcizing his evil with wordless prayer, made up of visual memories, vivid, intimate, brutal, along with every tortured word and revered thought I could hammer into my mind from the past. The conclusion of those thoughts and visions and the sum of those memories, along with the staggering realization of Loft's consciousness and lucidity, amount to this: I have no doubt any more. From the very beginning, I was right. Fear and pain is the price of fear and pain and I am not fighting to revenge an act of insanity. I am fighting to kill evil.

That is all. May those who read this diary think what they will. But of one thing they may be sure. They will be able to say: 'She wrote that on the day she killed Loft.'

31

Even when Christmas is an affair of dutiful jollity, as much in a special hospital as in many less likely places, there's a letdown afterwards in that gloomy timeless hollow week between a dead festival and the birth of a new perspective of an immaculate year. On this morning the rain was half-frozen to hail and those dead, dark leaves of autumn that never go away until spring were limply roused by a turbulent, purposeless wind that merely varied the fleeting grey tones of a mournful sky. Miss Lewis seemed no more than a fraction of the routine herd, assembling for one more unextraordinary day as she walked from the car park to her office, her face expressionless, her pace without spring, shoulders even a little hunched.

She began by trying to decide which letters she should write to families or relatives on behalf of patients who either could not or would not write. Although she invented wildly her phrases of emotional balm, this routine of trying to explain things she usually understood only too well herself, in terms too simple to be adequate, to people she did not know and who in any case would never reply, needed the sort of convinced optimism which was not mobilized in full this morning.

Rosie Fletcher was no help, when she brought her a cup of tea and began to talk in funereal tones of Joe Norton.

'Today they're having their biggest search yet,' she said mournfully. 'The whole of the county police, some even on horseback. And dogs. Like a fox-hunt almost. And for a man! Anyway, they're afraid he might have gone off from the dance walking to the village across country, and got lost and hurt himself and be lying helpless in some ditch somewhere—' She started crying with a lack of charm consistent with everything else about her. 'He's probably dead,' she sobbed. 'He was so tender, too, when he touched me – such a man!' She believed all that she implied. In the few days that had passed, the fulfilment she had only dreamed of was already growing towards nostalgic reality. Rosie was lucky but she didn't know it. She had a developing romance for life, unending and faithful. Finally, dabbing her reddened eyes, she gave way to three patients, two of them ready to dictate their own letters. 'Dear Mum and Dad and sister Rachel I'm fine and hopes this finds you like me. Dear Mum and Dad and sister Rachel love and kisses until we meet again. Your loving son and Rachel's brother Sam.' The wording was always sacred. No error of grammar or syntax was allowed to be changed. In some way those who dictated them almost seemed to see that their short-comings as literary efforts conveyed better than any erudition all the intolerable longings they yearned to express.

The third visitor was a white-haired old dame with the chubby, querulous face of a child on a secret errand. She brought a present, a very stale, slightly squashed chocolate, rolled up in a piece of sticky newspaper. Miss Lewis gave a delighted smile as she popped it into her mouth, dulling the taste by the thought that she had, after all, eaten worse things for lesser causes than the pleasure she saw light up in the old eyes watching her.

It was perhaps the incident of the chocolate that finally awoke her awareness of the day, of herself, of everything around her going on its plodding routine path, while for her, she suddenly felt, everything was 'the last' – the last time that – was a sort of secret ceremony awaiting her in every doorway, in every corner, at every step, in every encounter.

When, at ten-thirty to the second, she tapped smartly on the door of Dr Robertson's first floor surgery next to the infirmary, she had regained her air of sprightly good humour, and her face had refound the mobility that conveyed its lively consciousness of everything around her. Dr Robertson was behind his desk sipping a cup of coffee. His face brightened as she entered and he put down his cup and hastily rose to place the chair for her before his desk. It was an unnecessary and not very usual consideration.

He pushed his cigarette case and lighter over to her as he finished his coffee and then pulled a fresh looking file from a large envelope at the top of the pile of his In tray. He glanced idly down the long grey foolscap pages before he looked up at her. She sensed that he was relaxed and there was something like relief in his voice as he spoke.

'I feel I should tell you, Miss Lewis—' He stopped, shrugged his shoulders and looked up with a hesitant smile. 'Isn't it about time I could call you Margaret without seeming unduly familiar? My name is Ian.' She laughed. This was a companion incident to the crushed chocolate, she felt. Only the undefinable unexpected can distinguish one day from another. The destiny of this one was clearly special.

'I'm listening, Ian,' she said. 'Please go on with what you have to tell me.'

'I was about to tell you, Margaret, that I felt it only right for you to know that sometime towards the end of the year I sent to the Ministry for your security clearance. I found, by chance, that one was not enclosed with the copies of your record when you first came here. It's a pure formality anyway. Bureaucratic nonsense. There are no defence secrets at SP9. But I still thought it right that your file should be complete.'

He tapped the folder on his desk. 'It came through only yesterday. Obviously one had never been made before. Of course, it contains nothing which is not to your complete credit. Very flatteringly so. But there is one thing that worries me, well, more than a little. The record mentions that your late husband was a Dr Alan Hayes. That is something I did not know.'

She returned his look of slightly severe unease with an expression of placid assurance.

'I don't understand, Ian, why that should worry you? I have always worked under my maiden name. I have been a widow for – well – for a long time and the name of Hayes has never had anything to do with my job.'

Robertson stroked his chin slowly and frowned down at his desk, embarrassed. He looked up at her as he began to speak. His voice was formal.

'The files I loaned you on Michael Loft were not absolutely complete. For your information I only extracted the parts relevant to the general circumstances of Loft's life and his mental history. Evidently there was a mass of other documentation with which I had not felt it necessary to burden you – among it evidence given in court at the trial. Some of it contained extracts of evidence by Dr Alan Hayes, the father of the girl for whose death Loft was tried.' He paused and his eyes met hers. 'Was Cheryl Hayes your daughter?'

There was a long silence and she looked away. Then, her eyes on his again, she nodded.

Robertson showed no reaction. Both elbows on his desk, hands clasped before him, he began to talk almost to himself, while his eyes wandered vaguely across the jumble of papers and objects in front of him.

'I suppose, Margaret, ten years can do a lot. But *that*—' He remained silent for a moment. 'It could be that you obtained your posting here for the reasons you gave. It could be that you did not know Loft was here. It could be that his accident in the rabbit barn, to which you were the only witness, happened just as he said. It could be that, like the law, you have acquitted him of responsibility. It could be that you have the strength of mind, the moral grace of a saint. All these "could be's" – please don't let them offend you. They do not indicate any pejorative doubts in my mind. I personally reject the implication of them all, out of hand. Except of course the last one. I have never doubted your strength of mind nor your moral grace.'

His placid, toneless exposition took on a slightly pleading note as he continued. 'But people at the Ministry – like any good bureaucrats – can never accept probabilities as facts or even likelihoods. Whoever compiled your security clearance went back as far as your admission to the service as a full-time staff member, at the time you trained and worked under your maiden name, although you were noted in the records as being the widow of a Dr Alan Hayes, deceased. There was nothing in those records associating you or your life history with the Loft case. Though in the Loft dossier there is the name Hayes, there was no apparent reason for the Ministry researcher to refer to the Loft case when preparing a file on Lewis—

Hayes. Consequently this association has not been made by the Ministry. The Ministry actually does not know that the mother of a brutally assaulted and murdered child is one of the officials involved with his detention and has daily unsupervised access to him. This is fantastic! How long do you think you would be allowed to stay here if they knew?'

She opened her hands in a vague non-committal gesture while she kept her gaze on the desk before her.

Now the doctor, like someone going through a painful but thoroughly considered indictment, leaned low across his desk, and from behind their thick lenses his eyes were full of patient but more urgent pleading.

'In spite of all I have said, Margaret, in spite of all I believe of you, your evident well-meaning interest in Loft, the fact that he has accepted you and you are the first person in ten years to have made a real breakthrough to his mind,' – he paused and concluded with a slow but gentle emphasis – 'I cannot allow you to stay here any longer. The real reason will remain a confidence between us. Neither the colonel nor the Ministry need know why you left SP9.'

She looked at him in silence, her face expressionless. Her eyes roved slowly and calmly across his face, onto the folder before him, to her hands, then gazed, vaguely unfocussed, before her, before finally turning again to his eyes. When she spoke, her voice was calm and reasoned.

'Yes,' she said, 'of course you are right. Technically, and for anyone in a position of responsibility, the situation would seem to be unacceptable. How do you – well – get rid of me?' There might have been just a trace of irony in those last words.

The doctor frowned. 'I'm sorry Margaret. You admit that I'm doing what I must do. That word "rid" was a bit unkind. I'd like us very much, very much indeed, to stay friends. Nothing can, nor ever will, spoil my affection and admiration for you.'

He fell silent, thinking. Then, 'Like this,' he said, with a note of relief after a few moments thought. 'You will write me a letter requesting immediate relief from your duties and a posting to another position, preferably a return to the criminal side of your qualifications. Your reasons will be personal, positive and final, not so much as a matter of physical health as psychological. You find you can no longer support the strain of working with mental derangement and you fear that it could lead to a complete breakdown. This is not a sign of any special weakness. It is the case with many people. I will attach a minute very strongly supporting your letter and at the same time, for health reasons, I will give you indefinite leave pending your new posting. You will be able to continue your work in the service in which you have already made such a brilliant mark. How does that seem to you?'

She sat reflecting, casually, unmoved, as though she were weighing up the merits of some kind of sales talk. Finally she opened both hands in a gesture of resigned acceptance.

'Alright, Ian,' she said, 'I think you have been very fair and decent, as well as understanding. And I would so hate to shock the poor dear colonel. As you say, we'll do it like that. But do please get me posted away as fast as possible. I need the challenge of a job, quickly. A tough job.'

She stood up and hitched her bag on her shoulder. Though he tried to maintain a suitable semblance of shocked regret, Dr Robertson's face concealed badly his true sense of relief that the moments he had feared might have provoked a dramatic and hysterical scene had passed in a remarkably smooth and amiable confrontation. Miss Lewis walked to the door, opened it a little and turned to say goodbye.

On an impulse, perhaps made bold by the calm sense of understanding that seemed to rule the moment, he asked her quietly: 'Margaret, just one thing I'd like to ask you, if you'll allow me?' She waited, hand on the door. 'Did you know that Michael Loft was a patient in SP9 when you applied for a post here?' She looked at him with a mild expression of surprise, and the corners of her eyes creased faintly into what could have been the beginning of a smile. But neither that nor the flat indifference of her voice carried the slightest clue to any kind of emotion. 'Of course I did,' she said, and softly closed the door behind her.

Dr Robertson depressed a switch on the grey plastic intercom unit on his desk and the sharp voice of William Slater, deputy superintendent in charge of staff and security, replied. Dr Robertson spoke with a note of crisp urgency.

'Mr Slater, do you ever have any trouble with Loft?'

'Trouble? What kind of trouble Doctor?' Slater sounded surprised.

'I mean does he obey unusual orders without question – is he ever argumentative with orderlies or nurses?'

'Never.' Slater's reply sounded mystified. 'Never, Doctor. You know very well he's as timid as one of his rabbits.'

'Of course. That's what I thought,' replied the doctor. 'I just wanted to be absolutely sure, as of this moment. But still, this is something I want you to supervise personally. Now listen. I want him locked in a security cell – no – wait. No. This is it. Take one of your toughest and most reliable male nurses at once and go and tell Loft that I find, on checking my files for the end of the year, that he had not had his regulation quarterly check-up since August, and it must be done for the final year's report. As there's no one else available I will personally do it some time today. Got that? Right. Then take him with you to the infirmary. Have the duty nurse put him to bed and his midday meal served there. On no account say anything to disturb or alarm him in the slightest. Just tell him he is waiting for me in the infirmary and he will return to his usual quarters this evening and resume normal routine tomorrow morning. Then leave your tough male nurse on duty in the infirmary, give him infirmary overalls, with orders that no one is to approach or speak to Loft until further orders, and those orders must come from me. What I am telling you now is absolutely confidential and extremely important, as well as for immediate action no matter what else you may be doing. This comes first. And hurry up.'

In the hour that remained before lunch Margaret Lewis resumed the study of her outstanding mail and complaints file and completed the letters and minutes on those problems to which she felt she had found her own particular solutions. Once Dr Robertson himself called in to consult her and looked with satisfaction at the neat array of freshly classified files spread across her desk. 'You'll never get all that done today,' he said. 'When you come to deliver me your letter tomorrow, explain what's left over to Rosie and she'll see that someone gets it done.' He hesitated a moment and then put one hand on her shoulder and squeezed it gently. 'I'm so sorry, Margaret,' he said. Then he left without another glance at her.

She called in to 'B' Wing day room to consult with two patients and pass a few moments of light small-talk with others who were as glad as ever to see her. She even extended her brief circuit to 'C' Wing for a few words with 'King' Strang for whom she had a particular affection. A few more 'last times' she thought to herself. It seemed strange to move through the rambling complexity of stairs and corridors without Norton at her heels offering his sometimes drastic and usually cynically humorous advice in his sharp, back-alley accent. In a way she missed him. Yet in doing so her mind had no thought of the great bricked-up chimney below stairs, nor of the long dark shaft that led down to it from the roof-top. It was as though a small compartment of her consciousness had snapped shut on a certain sequence of events, and now, for her, Norton had vanished without incident or trace.

There was not much of a staff gathering at lunch-time. People drifted in intermittently, ate with morose indifference, and left at once, murmuring excuses about things to be done. The grey day rattling the ill-fitting windows in irritable gusts took the place of conversation. In any case the Saunders–Lacey escapes had exhausted speculation, while the Norton disappearance had now spread in everyone's mind a sense of unease and ill-omen which made it a subject preferably to be avoided.

Margaret took her cup of tasteless coffee from the staff-room urn to her office, to share the silent communion of spiralling cigarette smoke.

She stayed there, browsing among her case histories, her odd scribblings of noted telephone conversations, which she had ranged in the small, red, handsewn, leather stationery and pen-holder which had always faced her on whatever desk she had used over the past ten years. It was part of a desk-set Cheryl had given her, the Christmas before death. After three cigarettes, four short letters and a good deal of pointless fiddling among her files she looked at her watch. It was just two-thirty, always a period of low-ebb in the general activity of SP9, maybe a reflection all the way down the line of the colonel's nap, which he called 'thinking things over' on the leather settee in his office.

As though the hour was one she had appointed for precise action, Margaret Lewis put on her camel-hair overcoat with turned-up cuffs – a little long for her arms – swung her bag on her shoulder and walked out to the parking area.

From the back seat of her car she pulled out a large square shopping-bag, hand embroidered in wool. It seemed heavy. For a moment longer she sat in her car, while she fumbled in her shoulder-bag. She found her automatic – as usual underneath everything else – and dropped it into her wide right-hand coat pocket. Then, her heavy shopping-bag in her left hand, she passed straight from the parking area, on the side away from the manor, along a narrow path through a tall privet hedge. She was out of her Mini and out of sight of the manor in a delay of not more than five to six seconds. The path led in a wide contour from the parking area, past the L shape of the rear of the west wing, on past the laundry and carpentry shops, into the orchard and then sharply to the right through a small trimmed hedge towards the gardening unit – the great divided barn with the conservatory sloping against its southern end. It was an unusual approach that led her practically to the centre of the kitchen gardens, not visible from any point in the main building or the buildings in the rear courtyard.

She entered the gardening unit through the main conservatory door and passed straight to the common opening to the divided halves of the barn. From the conservatory opening the entry to the right led to the rabbit-barn, to the left, to the half of the barn used partly as a potting shed and partly as a horticultural teaching centre, with its stacks of benches piled up against the common board-wall with the rabbit barn.

The conservatory and the horticultural centre were empty, but a solitary inmate was wheeling away a barrow-load of gardening tools through the far north door of the rabbit-barn.

She called to him hurriedly. 'Where is Mr Loft?' He was a friendly, quite stable 'B' class patient she knew well, George Rossel, a keen gardener. He put down the barrow to answer. 'Hello, Miss Lewis. Loft you want? Dr Robertson sent for him this morning. Mr Slater came with a male nurse and fetched him and said he'd be away in the infirmary for a check-up until tonight. I was just bringing the morning tools back so they put me in charge till tomorrow. Is there anything I can do for you?'

For a moment she stood, halted in astonished dismay. 'There's nothing wrong with him, is there?' she asked. Rossel hastened to reassure her sudden note of anxiety. 'Oh dear no, Miss Lewis. It was apparently just Dr Robertson who forgot to give him his last check-up and this morning suddenly decided it had to be at once – today. Slater said he'd be back home here tomorrow.'

She looked quickly around her as though unable to believe what she had heard. Her mouth was a taut line of fury. In one quick glance around the whole barn she noted that Squirrel was sitting motionless in his huge cage screwed onto the wooden partition wall just above the near end of the long oak work-table. Further in to the rabbit side of the barn, on her right, against the partition wall with the conservatory, was the square wood-stove, crowned as usual by the battered old black kettle. She noticed that Squirrel's cage was padlocked, just as Loft usually left it at night.

She moved along to the stove and put her hand on the top. It was barely hot. 'It's a pity to let the stove go out. Squirrel and all the rabbits will catch cold,' she said lightly. But she was talking to herself. Rossel had left with his barrow of tools.

She turned and placed her heavy shopping bag as far as she could under the work-table. It was not noticeable in the deep shadow. Then she turned to the stove. With the square metal top lifted by the hooked poker, she filled it to the top from the long neat row of stubby logs ranged along the wall on each side of it. She had seen this stove on a frosty day only two weeks before filled to the top, with the lid below the kettle glowing red.

She looked at her watch. It showed a quarter to three. She rattled out the ashes from the bottom of the stove and fully opened the air-grille. There was just room inside the top for one more small log pressed hard down. The flames of the new wood were already beginning a dull roar under the full pressure of the draught.

The tubular chimney, a rakish affair partly sustained by strands of rusty wire nailed at the top of the wall and disappearing through a protective, asbestos-padded zinc panel in the roof, was beginning to crackle as the fresh bursts of heat surged upwards.

She left the building by the same way she had entered and returned through the privet hedge to her car, moving quickly. Once again she was not in view of any part of the front or west side of the main manor building for more than a few seconds. In the car she lit a cigarette and inhaled deeply. The rain had not returned since mid-morning, but the tearing wind still swept high and low in angry squalls. Even her Mini shuddered in sympathy with the slow gestures of the black muscled limbs of the tall elms along the avenue. She looked at her watch. It was three o'clock.

This time, after leaving her car, she took once more the back route to the gardening unit. There was no one there. The old cast-iron stove was now in full blast and through a few cracks in the lower joints of the chimney tube the flicker of flames and sparks passed upwards with a roar, sucked into the surges of the wind. Within minutes now the top would begin to glow red. Hurriedly she pulled out the shopping-bag from beneath the work-table and took from it a full yellow plastic petrol can, with a black plastic screw top. She twisted the top as tight as it would go, took the kettle from the stove top and replaced it by the two-gallon can.

Now her movements became even more hurried, almost feverish. She took the same route back towards the car park to begin with, but instead of continuing along the path behind the hedge outside the rear west wing, she took a smaller path leading along the inner wall of the wing. Halfway along, facing into the courtyard, was a door, theoretically an emergency exit, but left unlocked all day as a short-cut from the main kitchens to the infirmary on the first floor. The door opened directly into the ground floor 'B' dormitory wash-house and toilets. From there a narrow staircase led to the first floor infirmary ward wash-house and toilets, from which a door opened directly into the twenty-five-bed infirmary ward.

She met no one on the stairs going up, and there was hardly a flicker of interest as she opened the wash-house door to the infirmary ward. Without seeming to notice any of its occupants particularly she walked rapidly through it towards the central door leading into the corridor, which ran the width of the front of the building from wing to wing. But in her quick glance as she passed she saw Michael Loft – in his off-white cotton issue pyjamas, lying back, hands behind his head, staring at the ceiling. He gave a start of surprise as he saw her go quickly by.

The ward orderly was sitting at a table in the far front corner of the room, talking to another male nurse in white cotton overalls. The second of the two jerked to his feet and started a hesitant step towards her as she opened the washroom door, then seeing who it was, smiled, nodded and said casually, 'Oh, it's you, Miss Lewis. Sorry, I wasn't sure for a moment.' She gave a curt little smile as she went on to the main door without a pause.

In the corners of the room, on the same side as the main central door, were two other doors. One led directly to Dr Robertson's office and private surgery, the other, at the front corner of the room, to the main surgery and laboratory. These two rooms faced each other across the corridor outside and each had a second door opening directly onto the corridor. Once in the corridor Margaret Lewis ignored these two doors. She took the door after that of Dr Robertson's surgery – where his secretary Leslie Maine, in an office of her own, looked after the registry. She half-opened the door, said a cheerful hello to the girl and asked, 'Is the doctor in his office?'

'No, Miss Lewis. He left a few moments ago with the architect to inspect "C" Wing, and then he's going to see the colonel. Is it urgent?'

'No, thanks, I'll call back later. It's not important at all.' Margaret spoke casually but closed the door almost before she had finished.

From the corridor she entered Dr Robertson's surgery by the adjoining door. The lights were on. She closed the door, crossed the room and opened the doctor's private door to the infirmary ward just enough to put a foot and shoulder through it. Turning her head towards the doctor's desk, hidden by the door, she said clearly, 'Yes, Dr Robertson, at once. Loft is here now, as you know. I'll bring him in.' Then she turned and leaning into the room, called, 'Mr Loft, Dr Robertson is ready for you now.' The special male nurse who was slowly walking down between the rows of beds looked as though he might intervene as Loft leaped from his bed. But, still blocking the half-open door, she told him, 'Dr Robertson would like you to keep a close watch on this door and make absolutely sure that no one passes through it except on his own personal instruction. Do you understand?' She held herself slightly aside as Loft passed through into the surgery.

'Okay,' said the tough-looking nurse, 'I'll stay right here, miss. Don't worry. If you need me – just call.'

'Thanks,' she whispered hurriedly and closed the door.

Loft was standing in his flabby flannel pyjamas, looking bewildered, as she turned to him.

'Come with me, quickly, Mr Loft. It's very, very urgent.' Her voice, low and hurried, conveyed a sense of urgency, but Loft seemed slow to react.

She took his arm and then almost had to push him through the door into the corridor, down the narrow main stairs to the first floor, through the back door and down the curved flight of stone steps leading from it. Now they were in the rear court-yard, between the inside walls of the west wing and the cluster of buildings in the centre – staff and patients' dining halls, main kitchens and boiler house.

'Quickly, I think Squirrel is in great danger. The building is on fire and the cage is locked—' She spoke between her teeth with frantic urgency tugging at the long, loose jacket of Loft's pyjamas.

But her words seemed slow to take on any meaning for him and for a few moments he stood quite still, bewildered. Then, still dragging his huge, bare feet, he moved reluctantly after her as she tugged desperately at the folds of his jacket.

Over towards the gardens, still just shielded by a corner of the laundry, there was a flickering glow. Loft broke into a hesitant trot.

'But Miss Lewis – I don't understand— he began. At that moment they turned the corner. A single spiral of flame was just licking its way through the roof of the rabbit barn, along-side the tall, thin tube of the chimney. Through the glass of the conservatory flames could already be seen stabbing through the partition wall. The inside of the barn just beyond the common doorway linking its two halves with the conservatory was well alight and the flames, spun by the wind, were already spiralling up into a fountain of sparks and murky, flame-slashed smoke. Loft started into a stumbling run. When they reached the inside of the long greenhouse, opposite the opening to the two halves of the barn, he stopped suddenly. Then he turned and faced Margaret Lewis, his arms by his sides, but slightly raised as in despair, his fingers splayed. His whole face was wide with a frantic alarm, 'But my god, Miss Lewis,' he croaked harshly. 'I've left the key of the cage in my overalls.'

She looked back coldly into his eyes and took her right hand from her coat pocket. Leaning forward slightly she shot him in the left knee at a range of not more than a few inches.

The crack of the shot was hardly distinguishable amid the crackling of the burning wood and the growing roar of the flames. It was evident that the explosion of the plastic can on the red hot stove had sprayed the whole junction area of the gardening unit, from the tar-sprayed roofing to the heavy pine-planked floors, with liquid flame.

Loft had no idea what had happened to him. His expression of consternation changed to a look of almost childish bewilderment as slowly the smashed tendons of his knee twisted and ripped so that he turned a half-circle to his left as he fell with a loud moan that could have combined the emotions of pain, astonishment and frustration.

Instantly Margaret Lewis was on her knees beside him, almost shouting, with fierce urgency.

'Mr Loft, get up, get up. Squirrel is in there. You can surely wrench the cage off the wall and bring it outside.'

Somehow, using her straight slender body almost as a crutch for his left shoulder, Loft heaved himself to his feet. His left leg could support him – vertically. But to move forward there was no tension and to stop himself from falling he was forced to put his whole weight on the fragile shoulder propping him up under his left arm, while his left leg swung loose, from the knee down a sodden scarlet cloth. Thus he made one hop and a step. Now one more hop and one more step. Leaning forward with an agonizing effort his left hand reached and grasped the edge of the partition wall of the two halves of the barn. The lintel above was already in flames. Barely five feet away to his left was Squirrel's cage on a burning wall, and just below it, the near end of the already smouldering work-table.

He stood there for a moment, head down, breathing heavily, all his weight on his right leg and his left arm, posed against the doorway. This time she shot him from behind, at the level of his right kneecap. After an instant of indecisive swaying he collapsed, with a shout she could just hear, on both knees and then fell forward towards the work-table. Its edge along the partition wall, which was itself a mass of flame, was just blossoming with its first splintered petals of flame. Soon the whole massive table and the floor beneath it would be alight.

Margaret Lewis stood, seemingly indifferent to the smoke or flames, in the burning doorway and watched. Reaching up to the thick table edge, Loft achieved what she had thought impossible. He pulled himself bodily onto the table, waist high. His two legs, from the knees down, swung and twisted incongruously, like the limbs of a stringless puppet. For a moment, half-lying across the table, hands gripping its flaming far-edge, he rested. Then with a supreme effort, leaning on one elbow, he lifted his other arm, fingers outstretched, towards the cage. Just as his fingertips touched the base of the huge cumbersome structure – in which there was no more to be seen the familiar quick flicker of life – the work-table, after swaying perilously for a moment, overbalanced onto its side, throwing Loft backwards to lie spreadeagled, with its massive weight across his waist. The fall had doubled back his broken legs from the knees.

Her face felt as though it would crack with the heat. The pungent tar-smoke burned her eyes and seared through her lungs as she slapped out a spray of flame flung across the front of her coat by a shower of burning roofing.

Then, as she had done once before in this same place, but at that time in pity and horror, she knelt beside Loft. His hands clawed feebly and in vain at the table-edge across his body. His mouth jerked and fluttered in twisted grimaces, but whether he was shouting, screaming, or merely trying to breathe, it was impossible to tell.

His eyes found hers and stayed fixed, wide, perhaps pleading, perhaps trying to convey one last effort at a beast-king's bidding. It was enough for Margaret Lewis that he was seeing her, seeing her eyes meeting his, feeling her mind watching his own as the course of inevitability enveloped it, seeing her hand raising her gun, to point it at his long white throat, with its prominent Adam's apple jerking spasmodically with the agonies of his body. She pulled the trigger and a spot of red quivered in the soft, shocked flesh of the hollow beside his trachea. A bubble of blood expanded and burst. She fired again and had barely the time to see one of those bulbous staring eyes sink slowly in a little oval pool of blood, before she was jerked by the head and her whole body was being dragged along an avenue of fire that ended in darkness and the lashing gusts of wind-whipped smoke.

The last corner of the rabbit-barn to be spared the fire was the far doorway at the northern end, giving directly onto the kitchen gardens. An orderly had raced in from there and dragged her out – by her flaming hair.

When they had finished rolling her blazing body in garden sacking, she lay like a smouldering cinder, her face a raw scarlet under the patchy film of smoke and ash.

Dr Robertson was kneeling beside her when she reopened the scorched lids of her eyes. Her narrowed, blood-shot gaze stayed fixed on him as he lowered his face to hers.

'Margaret—' he said. He leaned yet closer as the raw scar that was her mouth quivered to open slightly and move tremulously.

'It – was – perfect,' she whispered.

32

The Diary of Margaret Lewis

FINAL ENTRY

Since this diary will be my only testament, to be read and judged in some distant future by people who are perhaps not yet even born, I feel that I might as well finish it.

When I began I thought it would be of service to lawyers and judges and mental specialists of various kinds all involved with the decision of obtaining and administering justice to a murderess. Even in the earlier part of my trial for the murder of Michael Loft I was under the impression that the court must know already the whole background of my story from my diary. It was only, gradually, as some of my replies to the judge and to the lawyers seemed meaningless to them, that I began to realize that none of them had read my diary. Whether all those pages of self-incrimination, as well as self justification – for a crime as well premeditated as could be imagined – would have been of any 'use' to me at my trial I do not know, since I was quite indifferent either to the verdict or the penalty. But the diary was unknown – unheard of! As the trial proceeded I realized that the whole structure of my defence was based on presumptions and conceptions quite unknown to me and mostly quite untrue. In fact my diary had been snatched away from the rest of my possessions in my cottage in Brockley, immediately after the death of Loft, by Dr Robertson who rapidly realized its implications, and thinking that he was rendering me a service, kept it and said nothing about it to anyone. It was his evidence at the trial on which my lawyer, appointed by the court, based his defence. And it was all this that left me comparatively 'free' – what a travesty of the word! – sentenced to five years' suspended imprisonment for involuntary homicide.

I must have made a pathetic figure in the prisoner's box, flanked by two policemen – more than half blind behind my huge dark glasses, my mouth strained and twisted with newly patched skin and taut tendons, so that I could barely speak above a whisper, and then only in great pain. I tried to hide my hands, not out of vanity, but because I was afraid that the sight of them, withered and fixed and trembling like pale pink claws, was too disgusting and anyway might have been considered by some in the court as a deliberate attempt to win more sympathy by the maximum exploitation of my wretchedness. A great deal of my hair never grew again, and most of the rest fell out, so I was obliged to wear a wide-brimmed hat – plain dark blue straw. I often felt the irony of the fact that to the jury and the rest of the court seeing me for the first time – in this trial which basically grew from the practice of witchcraft – I myself looked more like a witch than anything else. It's true that I have always deplored, as well as pitied, ugliness, and without employing a great degree of coquetry I have in the past always tried to be agreeable to look at, pleasant if not pretty, though I was that too, once upon a time.

Now this end to my diary, this final accountancy to reach the total of what may be my sins and errors as well as my sorrows, resolves itself really into a last letter to you, my dear, very dear Ian. Keep this diary, all of it, and pass it on one day to whomsoever you may wish so that the lessons of love and sorrow, good and evil which it contains, though they may change a little with the values that change with time, may be of use to someone, someday.

I do not know whether you were right or wrong to have kept the diary, in silence. I only know that you did it for what seemed to you the best reasons. Being the man you are, it must have taken a terrible degree of willpower and courage, and because you meant it well, I bless and thank you with all my heart. You have taken into your mind far more than you bargained for, and knowing your love for truth and order, you have loaded your conscience with a burden which I hope your ingenuity will enable you to unload without too much harm to yourself. However, now that you have left government service and are in private practice I do not see that they can do very much to you. You know how Welles escaped, you know the mystery of the pregnancies; you know how Norton died and where his body lies. I do not believe that the revelation of these things now can do anyone any good, nor the maintenance of their secret do any harm. Your love and compassion for your fellow beings always was and remains your great strength and so long as you allow this to guide you, you have nothing to fear, not even from your conscience. But there is still one problem that I have to leave you. Among the letters I received at the end of my trial, forwarded to me by a newspaperman, was one from Mrs May Lacey – *née* Saunders, as they say. It is among my papers with the rest of the diary in my large adjustable suitcase. May's baby is due in about a month from now. You have their address on the letter. Please try and do something to regularize their situation as far as the Ministry is concerned. They are happy and they are going to call their baby – if it is a girl – Margaret.

Now the last things I have to say to you are about myself. I hope you will try and understand and be as generous as possible in your judgement of me.

Your evidence at the trial, to the effect that I had told you in confidence that Loft's earlier injuries, with the iron bar, were in fact caused by having to defend myself against him and that I begged you to accept the 'accident' explanation to allow me to continue my own form of casual therapy with him, cost you your job and your pension. But it cleared me completely of premeditated murder, explained why subsequently I carried a gun and made me out to be a kind of saintly figure trying to devote love and care to the incredible beast who had butchered my own daughter. No wonder the judge and jury were prepared to believe that I shot Loft in a panic when he lost control of himself at the death of his squirrel – burned alive before his own eyes. There were some moments of that trial when I felt not like a prisoner on trial for murder but more like some martyred heroine attending her own santification ceremony. If I had not been more than three-quarters blind and the equivalent of half dumb – if pain counts – as well as aware of the fantastic and convincing way in which you perjured yourself with practically every word you uttered, I should have tried to intervene – and probably been certified insane anyway.

But if I could have intervened, if I could have shouted, 'Stop this nonsensical fable – *this* is what I meant to do and *did*, thank God,' I would have told them.

I avenged my child and in just the kind of circumstances I had dreamed of for ten years of murderous premeditation, by a death of which I saw and savoured the intimacy, the helpless, conscious sinking into pain and fear and then oblivion. It was an oblivion for evil, not the liberation of a soul. It was not murder, it was deletion. Your own understanding, Ian – fortunately only at the last moment – your realization that with your final association of the names Hayes and Loft, I was likely to take immediate and mortal action, very nearly saved Loft's life. From that moment on it was like a game of hide and seek and kill. But I would like you to know that your perception, your action, your effort to prevent what you thought of as a disaster only confirmed for me the admiration and respect – and what better word to combine those two than the word love? – which I had felt for you for a long time. As I manoeuvred to outwit you, and I had a good deal of luck, my heart was heavy because I was fighting you too and I knew that if I won – as I did – you would suffer too. Please forgive me.

The last moments in that shed were to me sublime. As Loft lay with his shattered legs bent under him and I knelt beside him there were two moments more perfect in their context than anything I had ever hoped to achieve – and I would have told this to the jury too – the first was as he lay, pinned under the table trying to shout – perhaps even shouting, I don't know because there was too much noise – and then as he saw my automatic pointing at him and my eyes fixing his. That was the moment of fear, but fear not yet entirely beyond hope. Then the bullet I shot through his throat did not kill him nor render him unconscious. It did something better. It added certainly to fear (that was the second great moment). As he looked into my eyes then – and I can assure you no two pairs of eyes ever looked closer nor with deeper understanding – *then* he knew, he knew all – who I was he had already known, but *then* he knew *why* I had been there, *why* I had caught up with him. He knew – and this is what I had wanted so much – that his past had condemned him to death and the master of that death was Cheryl's mother. It was when I read that in his eyes that I pulled the trigger for the last time and it was simply luck that the bullet went into one eye and I still had time to watch it drown in the little oval pool of blood brimming to his brow.

Is it really necessary to write all this down? Yes, Ian, I'm sorry but it is. It is as if I am putting forever my signature to that act; it is a consummation of all I wrote and felt in the earlier pages of this diary. It is an assurance to myself – as well as to anyone else who cares – that blind and dumb and tattered and ragged and useless as I am to look at, my real self, the same one as ever – inside – is blazing white with pride. There is not so much as a molecule of regret.

This is not your way, I know, Ian, but it's mine, and it's done.

It was kind of you to offer to come down this weekend all the way to Cornwall, to pass a few hours with this battered old wreck you tried to save. You will be wondering, as you read, why the landlord told you when you arrived, 'She's gone out, but she left this for you.' And he will have handed you this last chapter of the diary, my goodbye to you Ian.

. It was only about half a mile from this village inn where Cheryl, Alan and I spent our last holiday together – the time Cheryl, with the silver scars shining on her sun-tanned skin, danced on the high cliff-tops chanting, 'I'm a gull, I'm a gull.' Remember? It's in the diary.

Well, that's where I am going now – hobbling, alone—

But when I get there I shall spread the wings of a little bird of prey, keen, swift and pure again.

I shall never be a survivor.